SHIVER

SHIVER

Allie Reynolds

G. P. PUTNAM'S SONS
New York

PUTNAM
— EST. 1838 —

G. P. PUTNAM'S SONS
Publishers Since 1838
An imprint of Penguin Random House LLC
penguinrandomhouse.com

Library of Congress Cataloging-in-Publication Data

Names: Reynolds, Allie, author.
Title: Shiver / Allie Reynolds.
Description: New York : G. P. Putnam's Sons, [2020] |
Identifiers: LCCN 2020022012 (print) | LCCN 2020022013 (ebook) |
ISBN 9780593187838 (hardcover) | ISBN 9780593187852 (ebook)
Subjects: GSAFD: Suspense fiction.
Classification: LCC PR6118.E96528 S55 2020 (print) |
LCC PR6118.E96528 (ebook) | DDC 823/.92—dc23
LC record available at https://lccn.loc.gov/2020022012
LC ebook record available at https://lccn.loc.gov/2020022013

Printed in the United States of America
1   3   5   7   9   10   8   6   4   2

Book design by Ashley Tucker

For my mum and dad. Mountain people.

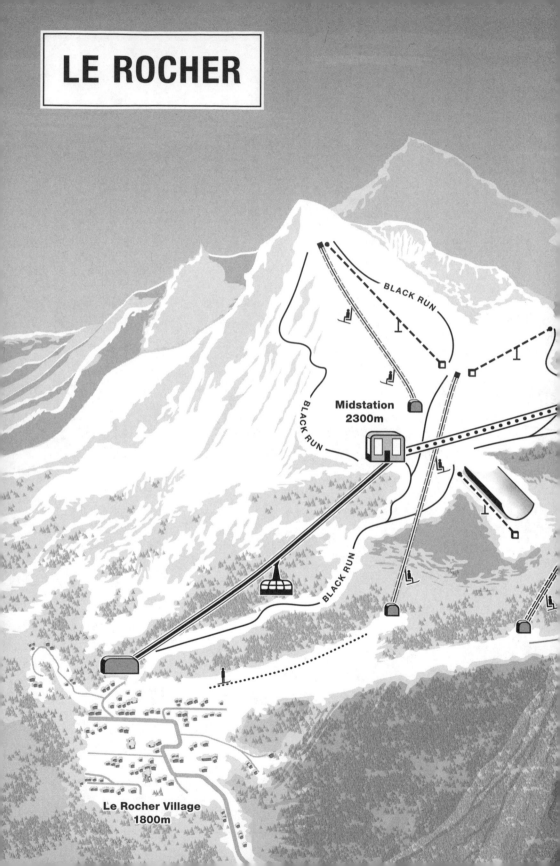

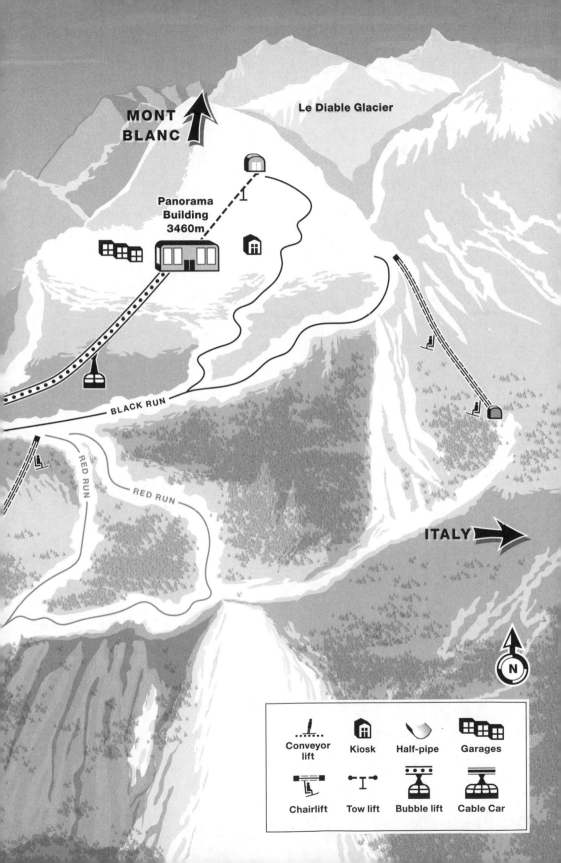

SHIVER

PROLOGUE

It's that time of year again. The time the glacier gives up bodies.

The immense mass of ice up there is a frozen river that flows too slowly for the eye to see. Recent victims brush shoulders with older ones in its glassy depths. Some emerge at the top, others at the snout, and there's no way of knowing who will come out next.

It can take years for them to reappear. Decades even. A glacier in neighboring Italy made the news recently when it produced the mummified corpses of First World War soldiers, complete with helmets and rifles.

Still, what goes in must eventually come out, so I've been checking the local news every morning.

There's one particular body that I'm waiting for.

CHAPTER 1

"Hello?" My shout echoes around the concrete cavern.

The familiar red-and-white cable car sits in the bay, but there's nobody in the operator booth. The sun has disappeared behind the Alps, the sky is pink, yet there isn't a single light on in the building. Where is everyone?

An icy wind blasts my cheeks. I huddle deeper into my jacket. It's the off-season, and the resort doesn't open for another month, so I didn't expect the other ski lifts to be running, but I thought this one would be. How else are we going to get up to the glacier? Have I got the wrong day?

I dump my snowboard bag on the platform and pull out my phone to check the email again. *Know it's been a while but are you up for a reunion weekend? Panorama building, glacier du Diable, Le Rocher. Meet at the cable car, 5 pm Friday 7th November. C. x*

C for Curtis. If anyone else had invited me here, I'd have deleted it without replying.

"Yo, Milla!"

And here's Brent, loping up the steps toward me. Two years younger than me, he must be thirty-one now, and he still has his boyish charm—the floppy dark hair, the dimples—though he looks worn and tired.

He lifts me off the ground in a bear hug. I hug him tightly back. All those cold nights I spent in his bed. I feel bad for not getting in contact with him. But after what happened . . . Anyway, he didn't contact me either.

Over his shoulder, sharp peaks loom, in shadow against the darkening sky. Do I really want to do this? It's not too late. I could make excuses, jump back in my car, and drive home to Sheffield.

A throat clears behind us. We pull apart to see Curtis's tall, blond form.

Somehow I expected Curtis to look the same as the last time I saw him. Collapsed with grief. A broken man. But of course he doesn't. He's had ten years to get over it. Or tuck it all away inside him.

Curtis's hug is brief. "Good to see you, Milla."

"You, too." I always struggled to look him in the eye because he was so damned good-looking—still is—but I find it even harder now.

Curtis and Brent grip hands, Curtis's skin pale against Brent's. They've brought their snowboards; no surprises there. We could hardly go up the mountain without them. Like me, they wear jeans, but I'm amused to see shirt collars below their snowboard jackets.

"Hope I wasn't expected to dress up," I say.

Curtis looks me up and down. "You'll do."

I swallow. His eyes are as blue as ever, but they remind me of someone I don't want to think of. There's none of the warmth I used to feel from him either. For him I dragged myself back to the place I swore I'd never return. I'm already regretting it.

"Who else is coming?" Brent says.

Why's he looking at me?

"No idea," I say.

Curtis laughs. "Don't you know?"

Footsteps. Here comes Heather. And who's that? *Dale?* No way— are they still together?

Dale's previously wild hair is stylishly cut, his piercings removed. His trendy skate shoes don't even look skated in. I guess he's been Heathered. At least she let him bring his snowboard.

Heather's wearing a dress—a sparkly black one—with tights and knee-high boots. Must be bloody freezing, even with the Puffa jacket over it. A whiff of hairspray from her long, dark locks as she hugs me.

"Great to see you, Milla." She must have had a few drinks before she got here, because she almost sounds like she means it. Her boots have a three-inch heel, bringing her to an inch taller than me, which is probably why she's wearing them.

She flashes a ring.

"You guys got married?" I say. "Congratulations."

"Three years now." Her Geordie accent is thicker than ever.

Brent and Curtis slap Dale's back.

"Took your time askin', hey, bro?" Brent says. His London accent seems stronger, too.

"Actually, I asked him," Heather snaps.

The door of the cable car grinds open. A lift attendant shuffles up behind us, black resort cap pulled low. He checks off our names on a clipboard and gestures for us to enter.

The others file past.

"Is that everyone?" I say, playing for time.

The liftie seems to think so. There's something familiar about him.

Everyone else is aboard now. Reluctantly, I join them.

"Who else would there be anyway?" Curtis says.

"True," I say. There were a few others who came and went, but of our original gang, we're the only five left.

Or rather, the only ones still standing.

A flood of guilt hits me. *She will never walk again.*

The liftie shuts the door. I strain to see his face, but before I can get a better look, he heads off along the platform and disappears into his booth.

The cable car lurches into motion. Like me, the others stare through the Plexiglas, spellbound, as we fly over the tops of fir trees, chasing the fading light up the mountain. It's weird to see dirt and grass below. It was always snow. I look for marmots, but they're probably hibernating. We pass over a cliff and the tiny village of Le Rocher disappears from view.

Suspended in the air like this, with the scenery slipping past the window, I get the strangest feeling. Instead of rising up the mountain, it's like we're traveling back in time. And I don't know if I'm ready to face the past.

Too late. The cable car is swinging into the midstation already. We step out, dragging our bags. It's colder here, and it'll be colder still where we're going. A French flag flaps in the breeze. The plateau is deserted. Halfway up, the browns and greens turn to white: the snow line.

"I thought the snow would be right down to the valley by now," Brent says.

Curtis nods. "That's climate change for you."

This is the heart of the ski area in winter, with chairlifts and tows going off in all directions, but the bubble lift is the only one running today.

The half-pipe used to be right there next to that little shack. The long U-shaped channel is just a muddy ditch right now, but in my mind's eye I can see the pristine white walls. Best half-pipe in Europe at the time, and it's what brought us all here that winter.

God, the memories. I've got goose bumps. I can picture our younger selves jostling and laughing. The five of us.

Plus the two who are missing.

A freezing gust swirls my hair around my face. I zip my snowboard jacket up to my chin and hurry after the others.

The bubble lift will take us to nearly 3,500 meters. The Diable glacier is one of the highest ski areas in France. The glossy orange cabins hang from the cable like Christmas baubles. Curtis enters the nearest open cabin.

Heather tugs on Dale's hand. "Let's get our own."

"No, come on," Dale says. "We'll all fit."

Curtis gestures. "Loads of room."

Heather looks dubious and I see her point. These little cabins fit six in theory, but with all our bags it'll be a squeeze. It doesn't help that she's brought a bloody suitcase.

Brent folds his tall frame to enter. "You can sit on my knee, Mills. Give us your snowboard bag."

"Dale can sit on your knee," I say. "I'm sitting here."

Heather ends up on Dale's knee, beside Curtis, with me and Brent opposite, bags jammed in around us. Dale looks so strange without his dreads. With his Nordic coloring, he used to remind me of a Viking. Now he looks more like a game show host.

We speed across the plateau. Such emptiness below. I forgot how huge this area is. Walkers hike here in summer and trails zigzag up. It must be beautiful—a mass of Alpine flowers—but all there is to see today is straggly brown grass and rocky scree. No sign of life, not even a bird. The land looks barren.

Dead.

No. Sleeping. Waiting.

Like something else up there. I swallow and force the thought aside.

Curtis's knee bumps mine as we rattle past a pylon. He seems unusually quiet, but I can understand that. If this is hard for me, it must be a hundred times worse for him.

The invitation made no mention of it but it's obvious why we're here. In the news the day before his email arrived:

BRITISH SNOWBOARDER MISSING TEN YEARS DECLARED DEAD IN ABSENTIA AFTER LEGAL BATTLE

The others can't have been any keener to come than I was, but how could we refuse? It's natural that he'd want to commemorate it.

There's snow beneath us now, glowing lilac in the twilight. Far above are the towering cliffs that give Le Rocher its name. The Panorama building perches on top, a squat, dark shape hunkered down against the elements.

"So how did you manage this, Mills?" Brent says.

"Manage what?" I say.

"VIP access to the glacier. Private cable car ride and all that. Pretty swish."

I stare at him. "What do you mean?"

"This is the shut-down period. Can't be cheap."

"Why do you think *I* organized it? Curtis did."

Curtis gives me a funny look. "Sorry?"

What are they playing at? We pull out our phones. The last time I brought my phone up here, I smashed the screen on my first run, leaving a nasty phone-shaped bruise on my hip. After that, I didn't bother taking it up with me.

I show them the email I received and Brent shows me his. His invitation is the same as mine, except it's from *M* and there's a PS: **Lost my phone. Email me.**

"Here you go." Curtis flashes his—identical to Brent's.

I never could read Curtis. Is this his idea of a joke?

The cabin rattles as we pass another pylon and my ears pop. This is where it starts to get steep. We've begun the long, long climb up to the glacier.

I turn to Dale and Heather. "What did your invite say?"

Dale hesitates.

"Yeah, same as yours," Heather says.

"From M or C?" Brent says.

"Um, M." Heather glances at me.

Why do I get the feeling she's lying? "Can I see it?"

"Sorry," Heather says. "I deleted it. But it was just like theirs."

CHAPTER 2

I don't know what I expect at the top. Music? Candles? Waiters with trays of champagne?

There's none of that. The platform is dimly lit and deserted, the operator booth empty. We drag our bags out. A siren wails and the bubble lift cranks to a halt. They must be operating it from the bottom, saving staff costs, having seen our arrival on the overhead security camera. But after the confusion over who invited us, it's a bit freaky, and from Heather's furrowed brow, she clearly thinks so, too.

Brent looks my way. "Leave our stuff here for now?"

"Don't ask me," I say.

He sets his bags down. I hesitate and dump mine, too. It's not as though there's anyone here to steal them.

The steps are gridded metal to accommodate snow-covered boots. By the time I reach the top, I'm panting. The air's thin up here. I push through the double doors into the Panorama building and breathe in stale woodsmoke. For a moment I have to close my eyes. Because that, more than anything, was the smell of my winters.

Curtis hits a switch and the wooden-paneled corridor lights up. A constant procession of skiers and snowboarders clump through here normally, past the ski lockers and out the main entrance onto the glacier, but it's eerily silent tonight.

Curtis cups his hands around his mouth. "Anyone there?"

Brent's looking at me again; Dale, too. My thoughts turn back to the invitations. Could one of them have organized this? No, I can't see it. As Brent pointed out, this is the shut-down period. A weekend up here must cost thousands at this time of year. Thanks to my online stalking, I know Curtis is doing well for himself. It has to be him. But why the mystery? And are the others in on it or do they genuinely believe I invited them?

"There's got to be someone here," Curtis says. "Let's look around."

We all rush off in different directions, kids let loose in a theme park. It's a maze, this place. The only building for miles around, the multi-purpose, sprawling structure houses the Mountain Rescue, control room, and everything else visitors and staff might need up here. I know the restaurant and toilets, but that's it. Oh yeah, and I once stayed the night in one of its tiny dorm rooms—France's highest youth hostel.

I race down corridors, pressing light switches as I go. There are lots of closed doors. Some open; others don't. This one opens. God, this could be the very dorm I slept in. The damp and musty smell triggers a memory. Brent beneath me on the mattress, his large hands gripping my hips. I stare at the narrow single bunk, then step out, shutting the door firmly behind me.

The next door down is a laundry cupboard—rough white towels and well-worn sheets stacked on pine shelves, the reek of cheap detergent. Farther along I smell food and, sure enough, here's the kitchen. Two pans sit on an immense stove. I lift the lids. Meaty casserole in one; mash in the other. Still warm. Could be our dinner, but where are the catering staff?

I spot a toilet and push the door cautiously, but it's empty and dark. Just beyond is the equally dark restaurant, where the stench of wood-smoke is strong enough to make me cough even though the fire isn't lit. I spent hours in here warming my fingers around mugs of coffee and sitting out snowstorms, but the tables are bare, so I turn down another corridor. The others must be on the floor above, because I can't hear them anymore.

More storage rooms; more locked doors. The light switches are on short timers and occasionally turn off before I've pressed the next one, leaving me in total darkness, having to grope my way along the wall. The silence is creepy. If someone popped out from behind one of these doors, I would just about have a heart attack.

At last a familiar sight: the main entrance onto the glacier. I hurry toward it. Nobody will be out there at this time of night and the door will probably be locked, but if it isn't, I want to taste that ice-tinged air. It's been so long.

It opens. Wind rushes through the gap in a high-pitched, relentless scream. The sound is strangely human. I yank the door shut and stand there breathing hard. I knew this would be the problem if I came back here. Too many doors I'd be better off not opening.

Get a grip, Milla.

Okay. I can do this. Once I get a couple of drinks in me, I'll be fine.

Upstairs, they have a function room where they host weddings and stuff. A useful moneymaker for tiny resorts like this one, especially during the off-season. I've only ever seen it in pictures, but that must be where everyone is, because I've checked everywhere down here.

Here are the stairs. At the top is a heavy fire door, and the air on the other side of it seems even colder. A faint smell. Familiar. What is it? Heather's perfume, maybe.

Voices from the door on the right.

Stop! reads a sign. *The game is on. Phones must be left in the basket.*

I let out my breath. A game. Some kind of quiz, maybe, about snowboarding or what we remember about each other. Something to get us talking about old times. And it's exactly Curtis's style, telling us what to do like this, not wanting any outside distractions from whatever he has planned. I lower my phone into the basket. Except . . .

The sign snags my attention again. *The game is on.* I once said those words to— No. It's a common enough phrase. It doesn't mean anything. I dump my phone on top of the four already there and go inside.

The function room juts out over the mountains, the carpet a thick white pile to mirror the snow outside, the furniture white and silver and no doubt stupidly expensive. Upholstered satin chairs; tables of glass and chrome. The opulence is in stark contrast to the rustic furnishings below. It even smells different. Gone is the fug of woodsmoke, replaced by the scent of fresh paint.

The entire back wall is windows, white velvet curtains tied back with a sash. The view must be spectacular in the daytime, but for now it's total blackness. Not a light in sight. Eerie in our current situation, but otherwise a beautiful venue for a wedding.

If you can overlook how many lives this glacier has claimed.

And how many bodies it still holds.

Don't think of that.

It's so cold in here that I can see my breath. Damp, too. The room probably hasn't been used for months. The others all have drinks. A lone beer sits on a nearby silver tray—Kronenbourg 1664. The glass is icy against my palm. I used to love these little bottles of French beer, sweet and fizzy. Haven't drunk it since the last time I was here.

It's just the five of us still. The staff must be along the corridor. Curtis keeps looking at the door. What does he have planned?

Heather's French-manicured nails curl over my lower arm. "Did you see the game?"

"What game?"

She tows me across the carpet to a tall wooden box sitting on a low table. Beside it are pens, good-quality cream envelopes, and cards. And a printed, laminated sheet. *Icebreaker.* The script is ornate, the sort you see on the order of service at funerals.

And weddings, I remind myself quickly.

> *Write a secret, something about yourself that none of the others will know. Post it in the box. Draw the envelopes out, one by one, and guess who wrote what.*

I glance at Curtis again, amused he's gone to so much effort when we'd have been happy to just drink ourselves stupid. He strides past me to the window, rubs condensation from the glass, and peers out. The fluidity of his movements always reminded me of a male gymnast, and that hasn't changed. He still has the same powerful grace.

I need more alcohol in me before I approach him, so I head over to Brent instead. I'm surprised by the beer bottle in his hand. He never used to drink.

"Been snowboarding lately?" I say.

"Once a year," he says. "All I can afford. I still do a load of skate-boarding."

"I can tell that from the state of your shoes."

His DCs are so worn on one toe that I can see his sock. DC used to sponsor him, but presumably he had to buy his current pair. I'm touched he stayed loyal to the brand, but that's Brent all over.

He was only twenty-one that winter, with the lean frame and all the energy of a teenager. He's filled out a bit now. Hard to say beneath his baggy clothing, but he still looks in pretty good shape. Still wears his jeans halfway down his arse as well.

His dark good looks, courtesy of his Indian father, brought him brief success as a model before his snowboarding career took off. I check him out online now and then, but his Instagram doesn't reveal much. I want to ask if he's seeing anyone—if he has children even—but he might get the wrong idea. I need to know that he's happy.

"So you really didn't invite me here?" Brent asks.

"No," I say. "I told you."

Curtis meets my eye from across the room, looking . . . troubled? Wondering where the staff are, probably.

"You still riding?" Brent says, clearly making an effort to steer the conversation to safer territory.

"Not since I left here," I tell him.

"Seriously? Not once?"

"Busy with work." I can see his surprise. Back then snowboarding was all I could think about, and I always imagined I'd be doing it well into my old age.

The truth is I'm terrified of it. Terrified of who it makes me become and what other lives I might destroy. The moment I fasten into my bindings, nothing else matters.

Brent doesn't know what I did, not all of it. None of them do.

And I intend to keep it that way.

CHAPTER 3

Heather claps her hands for attention. "Icebreaker time."

"Aw, I'm starving," Brent says.

"Me, too," I say. "I found a casserole in the kitchen."

Heather pouts. "It'll be fun. We can eat after."

Was she always this annoying or has being married made her bossier? She tips back the rest of her wine. Maybe she's just drunk.

Brent grumbles, but Heather hands out cards, pens, and envelopes. I look at Curtis again, but he sweeps past me out of the room.

"What are we supposed to write?" Brent asks.

"Something juicy that no one else knows," Heather says.

My throat goes dry. I drain my beer, but it's the kind of dryness that no amount of alcohol will wash away. I know because I tried it when I left here ten years ago.

I chew the end of the pen, straining to think of something funny to reveal, and hear Curtis's voice in the corridor. He has his phone to his ear. Typical Curtis—makes us give our phones up, then uses his. Is he talking to his girlfriend? He sees me watching and shuts the door.

I look down at my card, but I'm too cold and hungry to think straight. In the end I just write: *I have a cat called Stalefish.*

Brent has disappeared. I slip my secret into an envelope and post it in the slot at the top of the box. Where did Curtis get this thing? Apart from being white, it's completely out of keeping with the rest of the room. The flimsy plywood sides have been badly glued together and given a dodgy paint job, and it looks like something my granddad would make.

I need the toilet. The ladies' is the first door down the corridor. The water comes out the tap so cold you'd think the pipes would freeze.

Back in the function room, Brent has produced a large bag of potato chips. I take a handful.

I nod at Brent's snowboard jacket. "Does Burton still give you stuff or did you have to buy that?"

He crunches chips. "I get a discount."

"All right for you. I had to buy myself a whole new kit for this trip." I lick salt from my fingers. I gave all my snowboard gear away ten years ago to a kid who lived across the street. She deserved it more than me.

Curtis has returned from his call and resumed his post at the window, back turned. What's he looking at? There's nothing to see.

Dale comes in with another handful of beers. Brent and I swipe a bottle each.

"Ready to play?" Heather says.

"Just a sec," Curtis says, and ducks out once more.

Heather looks like she's about to combust. I hide my smile. It's as though Curtis did it just to piss her off.

"See any staff?" I ask Dale.

"No," he says. "I reckon we're on our own up here."

"Looks that way," Brent agrees.

"But there was hot food in the kitchen," I remind them.

"Yeah, I saw," Dale says. "I guess they figured we could help ourselves. Send someone up the lift in the morning to make us breakfast, maybe."

"A bunch of guests left unchaperoned? I'm amazed they would allow it," I say.

"Saves on costs," Dale points out.

Brent nods. "Must be hard for a tiny resort like this up against mega resorts like the Trois Vallées."

"What about the game?" I ask. "Did they set that up, too?"

They can't answer. And from the way they're looking at me, they still think I have something to do with it.

"Shall I do the honors?" Heather says the moment Curtis returns. Without waiting for an answer, she opens the flap at the bottom of the box, wrestles out the topmost envelope, and rips into it.

The rest of us pull up chairs. What's she so excited about anyway? What does she think the cards are going to say?

"I'll read them all out, then we'll guess who wrote what, all right?"

She's so twitchy, she's not just drunk. I think she's on something. Then again, Curtis seems equally on edge. He sits stiffly upright, keeping a constant watch of the room.

I can't feel my fingers. I stuff them under my thighs, but my satin chair seat is as cold as everything else in the room.

Heather reads the card and her cheeks color. "*I slept with Brent.*"

She darts an anxious look at her husband as though fearing he'll think it an admission, but he's looking at me, as are Brent and Curtis.

"I didn't write that," Curtis says.

We all laugh.

Everyone except Heather. "We said we'd read them all out before we guess."

She's trying to boss Curtis. Good luck with that.

"I didn't write it either," I say.

The guys laugh some more. Heather glares at me.

Dale puts his hands up. "Don't look at me."

More laughter.

One of the guys must have written it for a joke. Curtis probably.

Heather's opening the next envelope already. Her haste makes me wonder. Was there ever anything between her and Brent? Even if there was, surely she wouldn't advertise it. She and Dale got together pretty early on that winter.

She clears her throat. "*I slept with Brent.*" Her voice is overbright.

More laughter, louder this time, from me, Brent, and Curtis. Dale isn't smiling.

Curtis slaps Brent's shoulder. "No wonder you never made the Olympics. You didn't get enough sleep."

It's good to see Curtis looking happier. His icebreaker is having the desired effect. Warming us up—whether from amusement or embarrassment—despite the frigid air temperature. I'm enjoying seeing Heather squirm. From the expression on Dale's face, if there was ever something between Brent and his wife, it's news to him.

A look passes between Brent and Heather. A wrinkling of Brent's brow that says: *What are you playing at?* Brent thinks Heather wrote it! Heather answers with a slight shake of her head. What does that mean? Not now? Or that she didn't write it?

My brain is boggling. If Brent thinks Heather wrote one of them, does that mean he actually slept with her?

I crane my neck to see the handwriting, not that I would recognize it—we didn't do a lot of writing that winter—but the card Heather holds is written in neat capitals, the way you write when you don't want someone to recognize your penmanship. It's a joke, it must be. A prearranged joke between Curtis and Brent to stir things up. Curtis and Dale always had a problem with each other. Yet Brent's surprise seemed genuine.

I could speak up, insisting I didn't write either of them, but I think I'll wait and see what the next one says.

Heather opens the third envelope. She looks at the card and sucks in her breath. "*I slept with Saskia.*"

Nobody laughs this time. A line has just been crossed.

Despite our differences, I can't imagine why anyone here would write that. As far as I know, only one person present has slept with

Saskia, and I didn't think it was common knowledge. I'm careful not to look in Brent's direction—or Curtis's.

Heather eyes her husband, clearly wondering if he wrote it. If I stick to my assumption that Curtis and Brent wrote the first two, Dale must have written this one. But why the hell would he do that?

Heather opens the next one. Must be thinking it can't get any worse.

But apparently it is, because she blinks and looks up in shock. "*I know where Saskia is.*"

Curtis snatches the card from her hand and studies it, stony-faced. "Is this some sort of joke?"

Nobody answers.

"Did anyone actually write any of these?"

Eyes slide around the room. Heads shake.

Unease creeps through me. A glance at the window, at the total and utter blackness out there, reminds me how alone we are. It's just the five of us. Nobody else for miles and miles. I need to know if Curtis invited us here. Because if he didn't . . .

I look at the door, thinking of all the long, dark corridors beyond. Is someone out there?

Brent breaks the silence. "Let's hear the last one."

Heather opens it and turns pale. The card flutters from her fingers to the floor.

I pick it up. "*I killed Saskia.*"

CHAPTER 4

TEN YEARS AGO

A girl flies high above the half-pipe, white-blond hair streaming out from below her helmet. She's good. On her last hit, she spins one and a half rotations—540 degrees—and brakes to a stop in front of me, spraying me with snow.

I know who that is. Saskia Sparks. She beat me in the British Snowboarding Championships last year, placing third to my fourth.

And this year I'm going to beat her.

My long blond hair, a few shades darker than hers, is pretty distinctive, and if I recognize her, she probably recognizes me, yet if she does, she doesn't reveal it. She simply unfastens her back foot from her bindings and skates across to the tow lift.

I dump my backpack and hurry after her. I've heard stuff about her. The Ice Maiden, they call her.

My lift pass is in my pocket. I tilt my hip to the scanner, wait for it to beep, then push through the turnstile. The lift is pretty basic, weather-beaten plastic T-bars that dangle from a tatty-looking moving cable. I seize the nearest T-bar, slide it between my thighs, and watch the action as it drags me up the slope.

With its naturally forbidding terrain of rugged cliffs, narrow couloirs, and slopes too steep for the average package holidaymaker, Le Rocher holds cult status among expert skiers and snowboarders.

The resort has another big draw, and here it is: the Le Rocher half-pipe. The snowboarder's equivalent of a skateboard ramp, the long white channel stretches up the slope. Built to Olympic specification—a hundred and fifty meters long with walls of snow six meters high on either side—it looks in pretty good shape.

Riders are crisscrossing back and forth, launching out of the sheer ice walls and doing all kinds of crazy shit. It's hard to tell who's who under the hats or helmets and goggles, but there are clearly some big names gearing up for the Le Rocher Open tomorrow.

I wish I'd gotten here earlier. The season started two weeks ago, on the fifth of December, but I was still working. Had to make sure I'd saved up enough to last the whole winter; that way I can focus on my training. I'll never make the UK top three if I'm up all night working some crappy bar job. Anyway. Catch-up time.

Saskia is back at the top already. Is she here for the season or just the Le Rocher Open? She drops in and pulls another huge 540 spin. Really nails those landings.

The first time I saw a half-pipe, the steepness of the near-vertical walls terrified me. It's an illusion. The vert is your friend. Land on it correctly and it's so smooth you don't feel it. But the ice is hard as concrete, so if you screw up, you're in trouble.

Fear tingles through me as I fasten my boots into my bindings. Inside my leather pipe gloves, my palms are clammy. I'm more nervous than usual because my snowboard is new—a Magic Pipemaster 157 from my first-ever board sponsor.

Normally I go easy on my first run, to get a feel for the pipe, but Saskia's the girl I need to beat, so I'm going to try a 540 on my last hit. I ride down the side until I have enough speed, then plunge in. Down the wall, across the pipe floor, then up the opposite wall and into the air.

My front hand finds the heel edge of my board and grips it tight. Backside Air. I soar above the ice, mind pure and empty, seeing nothing, hearing nothing. Only feeling. These precious moments of weightlessness at the top of the arc, suspended by gravity. This is why I juggle three jobs for half the year and push myself to the limit in the gym.

Sinking back to earth, I touch down, all fired up and ready for more. Back and forth from wall to wall like a pendulum. On my final hit, I spin hard and make the 540—just. My fingers shake as I unfasten my bindings. I love this board. I'm going to keep it forever—put it up on my wall so I can show my grandkids.

Saskia's walking up now because there's a queue for the lift, so I trudge after her. The glare off the snow is dazzling, the whiteness of an Alpine winter so different from the gray of an urban one. My eyes are still adjusting.

On her next run she does big back-to-back 540s on her last two hits. Fear swirls in my stomach. I always imagined that once I found sponsors, I could sit back and enjoy myself. How wrong I was. The pressure is tenfold now that I have an image to uphold. I can't let my sponsors down.

I picture the spins in my head as I strap in. I need to go big on the first one to get enough air time to make the second. Here goes.

Crap. I just face-planted in front of all the people eating their lunch at the bottom. Spitting snow, I wipe my goggles and hurry back up. My knee throbs and I don't even want to know if Saskia saw that.

I have to do this. A top-three ranking is the difference between semipro and fully pro, and fully pro means you can train year-round. Unlike Saskia, I don't come from a wealthy family, but I want this more than I've ever wanted anything in my life.

I try again. Another wipeout. My right hand takes the impact and pain zings up my arm. I think I see Saskia smirking as I pick myself up. It takes me four more tries, then, somehow, I manage. And damn it if Saskia doesn't pull a 720. Two complete rotations high above the ice.

The sun blazes down on the half-pipe. Every time I nail something, Saskia raises the bar. I'm pushing it as hard as I dare. If I break something before the Le Rocher Open tomorrow, I'm screwed.

By midafternoon, my water bottle is empty again. I've already trekked to the midstation once to refill it. I leave my board at the bottom of the pipe like last time, among the colorful array of others, and jog across the plateau.

On my way back, I pass a family of skiers—mum, dad, and small child—in agitated debate on the cliff edge. When I peer over, I see why. A tiny blue glove lies on the snow below.

My gaze returns to the family. Strapped to the man's chest is a baby, all bundled up against the elements. Only his little pink cheeks are exposed. And one small bare hand. He must have dropped the glove from the rickety chairlift that rattles overhead. Le Rocher isn't a family-friendly resort and it's the first family I've seen here. They must be locals.

I check either way along the cliff. I've jumped higher ones plenty of times. *If it's not over twenty foot, it's not even a cliff*, according to *Whitelines* magazine. But it will eat into my training time. I look over my shoulder at the pipe, where Saskia will be increasing her lead, then back at the baby and his poor bare hand. Before I know what I'm doing, I've stuck my water bottle into my sports bra and I'm running to the edge. The woman's hand flies to her mouth as I leap.

Midair, a realization hits me. I've only ever jumped cliffs with my snowboard on. This is going to hurt . . .

I plummet through the air. Powder and rocks loom below. As my boots touch down, I tuck my shoulder in and roll, coming to a stop, plastered with snow. I raise my goggles and see the family's shocked faces peering over the cliff at me. Now, where's that glove?

A twinge of pain from my knee as I scramble up. Old injury; it does that sometimes, and today's wipeouts didn't help. I hold up the glove and the parents clap. As hard as I can, I hurl it upward. The man snatches it and shouts out his thanks, and the family disappears from view. Now I need to figure out how to get back up.

After a long sideways hike through deep powder, I'm finally back at the pipe, sweaty and breathless. And all that for a bloody baby glove.

My thermal top is sticking to my armpits and I've drunk half my water already, but at least my snowboard is where I left it. Saskia sits nearby, tilting her face to the sun. She still hasn't acknowledged me, but the moment I pick my board up, she grabs hers and races ahead to the tow lift. I hurry after her, trying to regain my focus.

As we ascend, a figure in a mint jacket busts a huge spin. Shit— that's a girl! You can usually tell female riders from the way they ride— less power, more cautiousness—but this one rides like a guy, fully committed to her moves. How can I compete with that? Hopefully she's not a Brit.

I pull myself together. For now, all I have to worry about is Saskia. She drops in as I fasten my bindings. Damn. She just did back-to-back 720s. I don't think I can do that.

Come on! Your sponsors would drop you if they knew what a chicken you are!

I take a deep breath and plunge in, but my board is sluggish and unresponsive and I'm all over the place. The best I can manage on my last hit is one full rotation. A shaky 360.

Out of control, I speed on down, catch the toe edge of my board, and fall into some poor guy's lap, knocking him backward to the snow.

Brilliant. I've just mown down Curtis Sparks, three-time British half-pipe champion. Saskia's older brother. "I'm so sorry!"

He helps me up. "No problem. You all right?"

"Yeah, are you? I hit you pretty hard."

He seems amused. "I'll live."

I've had a big-time crush on this guy for years. He's not just gorgeous and mega-talented. When asked why he hadn't qualified for the last Winter Olympics, he looked the interviewer in the eye and said: "Because I'm not good enough." He didn't mention having major surgery shortly before the qualifiers. No excuses. His own harshest critic. I loved him for that.

I lift my goggles to see what's up with my board.

"Hey, I saw you in the Brits last year."

"Yeah, I saw you, too," I tell him.

Flustered by the way he's looking at me, I examine my snowboard. "My binding came loose again. Have you got a screwdriver?"

"Let's have a look." Curtis crouches over my board and grasps my binding with large hands. His hair is darker blond than his sister's and really short, his skin golden, pale around his eyes from his goggles.

"Hey, Sass!" he shouts.

And there she is, watching us.

"What did you do with my screwdriver?" he calls.

She comes over with a large screwdriver with a purple plastic handle. I take it. "Thanks."

She raises her pink neon goggles to her helmet but doesn't say anything. She has the most amazing eyes. I've seen them in photos, but they're bluer in real life—even more so than her brother's.

I tighten my binding, putting all my strength into it because I don't want it to come loose again. I had to borrow a screwdriver from some guy at the top earlier.

"Want me to tighten that for you?" Curtis says.

"Do I look like I have a problem with my arms?" It comes out before I can help it. Rude, I know, but would I seriously be up here if I can't tighten my own bloody bindings?

Fighting a smile, he looks me up and down. "I don't see any problems at all."

My cheeks burn. I hand the screwdriver back. And notice a rip in his lower leg. "Oh God, I tore your trousers."

His smile widens. "Hey, don't worry about it. I don't pay for them. You can fall on me anytime."

Is this guy a complete flirt or what? In front of his sister as well!

"It's weird," I say. "Because that's the second time my bindings came loose today." He's making me babble.

His smile fades. "Really?" He turns to his sister.

Why's he looking at her like that?

Saskia smooths her hair over her shoulders. "Must be the warmer weather. The holes in her base have expanded or something."

"You're giving my sister a run for her money today," Curtis tells me, still looking at her. "She's pulling stuff I didn't know she could do."

Saskia's face darkens. Maybe I'm not as far behind her as I think.

She shoves out her hand. "Hi. I'm Saskia."

"I'm Milla."

She breaks into a grin. "I know. Are you coming out tonight? Glow Bar's running a pre-comp party."

I hesitate. "I don't normally go out before a comp."

Saskia tilts her head. "Why? Are you scared?"

I curse inwardly. "No. I'll be there."

CHAPTER 5

In the freezing function room, we pass the "secrets" around. They're all written in the same neat capitals.

"What's going on?" Curtis's voice is dangerously quiet.

A sea of puzzled faces. Dale clenches and unclenches his fists; Brent throttles the neck of his beer bottle. Heather's eyes flit from corner to corner.

Whoever was behind the game, I don't think it was Curtis after all. Nobody could fake that simmering anger, surely, and he wouldn't have said those things about his sister.

He grabs the box and gives it a vicious shake. Wishing he could do the same to us, clearly. Shake us hard enough to get some answers.

Something rattles inside the box. Curtis pushes his hand into the opening at the bottom. A tapping sound. "It's got a false bottom." He flips it back over and puts his eye to the long, narrow slot in the top. "Our envelopes are still in here."

A shocked silence. And we all crowd in to see.

I take the box from Curtis. Halfway down, a layer of wood separates it into two compartments: the top section, where our envelopes are just visible, and the now-empty bottom section. The box hasn't left the room. Could one of us have put the fake cards in without the others seeing, or was it done in advance?

"Let's have a look," Brent says.

I hand the box over. He stomps down hard on it and it splinters.

"What's the point of that?" Curtis mutters.

He's right. I bet the secrets we wrote to share have nothing on the ones Heather read.

Heather snatches an envelope from the floor and opens it. "*I faint when I see blood.*"

Nobody's listening.

Curtis's eyes blaze. "Someone set this up. Who was it?"

He gives each of us a long, hard look. We flinch in turn.

I'm struggling to let go of the idea that he invited me here. Partly out of pride. I was flattered—thought it meant something. *Hoped* it meant something. And if Curtis didn't organize this reunion, who did?

Brent gets to his feet. "Screw this. I need a real drink." The door slams behind him.

Heather has little pink spots in her cheeks. I'll get her alone later and ask her about Brent, because I have to know. If she slept with him, was it before or after she got together with Dale? And before or after Brent was sleeping with me?

Dale steers her to the window and they stand there quietly conferring. Is he asking her about Brent? He must be.

Heather strikes me as unlikely to have orchestrated this. The first three secrets seemed deliberately designed to embarrass her. Or is that just what I'm supposed to think? I sensed a lie earlier, when she told me about her invitation.

I sip my beer, wishing for something stronger—and jump. Curtis is right behind me. Moves like a cat when he wants to, this guy.

"This anything to do with you, Milla?"

"No," I say. "Of course not."

He doesn't look convinced.

"Tell me about your invite," I say. "When did you get it?"

"About two weeks ago."

"Same here." It was pretty short notice, but I dropped everything. *Because I thought it was from you.* We may not have spoken these last ten years, but I couldn't pass up the opportunity to see him again.

"Was it sent to your phone or your email?" I ask.

"Email."

"What address was it sent from?" I should have checked earlier, when he and Brent showed me their invites.

Curtis is looking across the room at Dale and Heather. "M Anderson, something like that. Gmail account."

"I don't have a Gmail account. My invite was from C Sparks. Gmail, too."

I spent so long wording my reply. Should I mention Saskia? Should I offer condolences? I considered phoning him. There wasn't a number on the invitation but there were several on his website. In the end I chickened out. Awkward conversations are easier in person.

Great idea! I wrote. *I'll be there. So good to hear from you. What have you been up to?*

His reply pinged back. *Glad you can come. See you soon.*

I was disappointed but put it down to his being busy. And male. What guy ever writes more than he has to?

I drain my beer. Unlike Brent, Curtis has aged well. He's clean-shaven, the cleft in his chin clearly visible, and he must have been overseas recently, because he has a faint tan. His dark blond hair is a little longer than it used to be, but it suits him. He wears a navy Sparks-brand jacket with white piping down the sleeves. Photos on social media show his whole family wears the brand these days.

Or rather, what's left of his family.

"Did you keep in touch with any of these guys?" Curtis says.

"No," I say.

"Not even Brent?"

Is he asking out of curiosity or something more? "No."

There are so many things I want to ask him. How much time he gets on snow. Where he's living. If he's seeing anyone. I search his face for a trace of the old warmth, or even just a sign he doesn't hate me.

But Curtis is all business. "How about anyone else from that winter?"

"No." I ended up jumping in my car and driving off, leaving the storm behind me. I deleted them from my Facebook. My phone. My life. I feel bad about that now, but I wanted to clear the slate. "But I'm pretty visible online. I'm a personal trainer and I have a blog and a website."

If he's looked me up, he doesn't reveal it. "Right."

"I imagine it's the same with you?"

"Yep."

Curtis is apparently as talented in business as he was at snowboarding, because Sparks Snowboarding, the outerwear company he set up seven or eight years ago, has really taken off. And I love what he's doing with it. Running freestyle snowboard camps in Switzerland every summer, coaching underprivileged kids alongside up-and-coming young stars, and campaigning about climate change, trying to safeguard the glaciers so that future generations can enjoy them.

Across the room, Dale's voice raises, though he lowers it when he sees us looking. Heather shakes her head, her body language defensive. I don't like what I'm seeing. If he lays one finger on her, I'm going over there.

Brent returns with a bottle of Jack Daniel's and a stack of glasses.

I reach for a glass. "Good call. Might warm me up."

Brent pours me a measure, hand shaky as he does so. I sip it and wince. God, that's strong.

Dale and Heather are still arguing. His voice is an angry rumble; hers is plaintive.

"Want one, Curtis?" Brent says.

"No, thanks. So what do you do for work these days?" Curtis asks.

Brent pours himself a hefty measure and knocks it back. "Bricklayer."

I don't know what I was expecting, but it wasn't that.

"Family business." Brent must have seen our faces.

Now that he's told us, I can see signs of it in the broadness of his shoulders, the roughness of his hands. The slight stoop of his back.

I think of his Olympic dreams and something wrenches inside me.

Fame is fleeting for most athletes, but especially so in sports as dangerous as ours. At the heady peak, you're put on a pedestal and hailed as a hero, but one mistake is all it takes. Hitting the lip too fast or too slow; catching a rut left by the previous rider. One tiny error in judgment. Or sheer bad luck. The stakes are so high that if we thought about them we wouldn't jump at all, unless we had a death wish.

We all fall eventually, but somehow Brent's fall seems farther than most. He was Burton's golden boy, the face of Smash energy drinks. For years I scanned the rankings, hoping to see his name, but he disappeared clean off the scene, just like I did. I assumed he must have had a serious injury, but now I wonder. Is the reason he stopped competing anything to do with me? If it was, I don't think I could bear it.

Curtis recovers before I do. "And how is it?"

"It's a job." Brent sounds defensive.

"Have you got a website?" I say.

"Yep."

Curtis and I share a look. So anyone could have found Brent's email, too.

Heather hurries from the room, head down. Should I go after her?

No. She looked upset, and I couldn't cope with the whole tearful-in-the-bathroom bit just now. I never know the right thing to say. When I'm upset, I keep it to myself. That was one good thing about Saskia. She would never do a tearful-in-the-bathroom on me.

I saw Odette cry once, but if I'd received the news she had, I'd have cried, too.

And never stopped.

She will never walk again.

I knock back the rest of my whiskey. I won't think of that. I'll catch Heather when she's calmed down a bit.

Dale stands at the window, bottle in hand. He shoots a look at Brent, then turns his back. What has Heather said?

"How did you two travel out here?" Curtis says.

"I flew in this morning," Brent says.

"Grenoble?"

"Lyon."

"That explains why I didn't see you," Curtis says. "I flew to Grenoble."

I saw the airline tags on their snowboard bags.

"I drove out," I say.

Curtis's eyebrows go up. "All this way?"

"For old times' sake. It gave me some thinking time." *To think about you, among other things.*

Heather bursts back in. "Guys?" She sounds breathless. "Our phones are gone."

CHAPTER 6

Saskia has her arm around me like I'm her new best friend. She smells of perfume, heady and exotic, though she wears no makeup apart from violet eyeliner that makes her eyes look even bluer.

We're in a booth in Glow Bar, six of us, all girls. I had no idea what to wear tonight. Saskia seemed the type who would dress up, but screw that, it's minus ten out there. So I pulled on skinny jeans and two sweaters, prepared to look like a dork, but the girls around our table, who seem to be mainly French, wear jeans and sweaters too, and we all still have our snowboard jackets on. These are my kind of people.

The place is heaving. I'm not into the whole après-ski scene. I came here to train, not to party. I've always found it odd how some visitors to ski resorts spend more time in bars than on the slopes. Still, Glow Bar *is* the only bar in the village.

On the stage, a live band plays thrashy punk rock.

Saskia shouts over it. "Are you here for the season, Milla, or just for the comp?"

"The season," I say. "You?"

"Same."

Nerves skitter across my stomach. All winter, I'll be training side by side with my closest rival. I'll be able to follow her progress, but it will work both ways. I take in her narrow shoulders and hips. She's a couple of inches shorter than me, but height is no advantage in the pipe—a lower center of gravity aids balance. Still, when it comes to power, I'll have the advantage. I'd love to see how she works out in the gym. She must have amazing lower-body strength to ride like she did earlier.

"Have you got sponsors?" she says.

"Yeah."

She waits expectantly.

"Magic snowboards. Bonfire clothing, Electric eyewear." And a muesli-bar brand, but I won't mention that in case she laughs. I drove out with my little Fiat Uno stacked to the roof with the things and I'm sick of them already, but at least I won't starve. My sponsors are product only—they send me stuff; I somehow fund my own training—but I'm not going to tell her that either. "I had a different clothing sponsor two years ago and they dumped me when I busted my knee."

"That happened to me, too," one of the girls says.

Everyone was speaking French earlier, but they switched to English when I joined them.

"We should insure our legs," another girl says. "Like ze football players."

"You know Mariah Carey insured her legs for one billion?" Saskia says.

"Jennifer Lopez insured her bottom," someone adds.

"When are they ever going to fall?" I ask. "I wish I could insure *my* bottom."

We all start talking about which body parts we'd insure.

The barmaid brings over another tray of shot glasses. She hands one to Saskia, who hands it to me. I didn't intend to drink tonight but it's hard to refuse. These girls are all competing in the Le Rocher Open and they're drinking. Saskia's buying. I wait until everyone has one, then knock it back. We all cheer, attracting raised eyebrows from the girls in the neighboring booth, who are German or maybe Swiss, and presumably competing tomorrow, because none of them are drinking.

Two guys lope up to our table, one dark skinned, the other with blond dreads. I recognize them from somewhere.

"Who's this?" says the dark-skinned one, looking at me. London accent.

"Fuck off," Saskia says.

The guys drift off toward the bar. Wait—that was Brent Bakshi and Dale Hahn. And Saskia just told them to fuck off!

Right behind them is Curtis. He flashes me a smile and nods at his sister, frowning when he sees the shot glasses, and heads toward a table of guys—more faces I recognize from snowboard DVDs—to shake hands. Curtis and Saskia are snowboard royalty—their parents are snowboarding pioneers Pam Burnage and Ant Sparks—and they seem to know everyone in here.

Sitting beside me is Odette Gaulin, X Games bronze medalist. The girl in the mint jacket. Her short brown hair curls out from below a Rossignol cap. I'm trying not to be starstruck, but she's actually really nice. She's doing the season here too, I learn; the other girls are only here for the comp.

I lean in toward her. "Do guys get intimidated by you? I mean, you're so good they must do."

Odette waves her fingers. "Pfft."

I wish that band would shut up. I'm losing my voice. "I was seeing this Swiss snowboarder last year and he dumped me because I beat him at arm wrestling."

The girls crack up.

"In front of all his friends," I add.

Odette gives me a high five. This is the vodka talking. I never open up like this normally, especially not to people I've just met, but it feels good to get it out. I didn't realize how much I'm still smarting about it.

A boardercross pro, Stefan never slowed down for me, and I loved riding with him because I had to pull out all the stops to keep him in sight.

"Send him to the gym," the girl across the table says.

"Hire him a trainer!" another girl supplies.

"Feed him steroids!" The suggestions get more and more outlandish.

It's a novel feeling, fitting in with a group of girls like this. Meet-ups with my female friends back home are painful. All they want to talk about is fashion and celebrities. I'm more at home around the bawdy jokes of my brother's rugby mates.

More vodkas arrive. How many is that now? I've lost count. I rarely drink—too busy working or training or both—and never before a comp, but the other girls are still going, and a couple of them are even drinking beers as well, so I knock it back and slam the glass down.

The German girls are talking about us, which I think is exactly what Saskia intends. It's a statement: we're hard enough to drink tonight *and* beat you tomorrow. Which may be the case if you're Odette Gaulin, but not so much if you're me. Yet I don't want to let the group down.

Curtis comes up and says something in Saskia's ear. I can't hear over the music, but I think he's telling her not to drink any more. She waves her hand—she isn't having any of it—and Curtis returns to his table scowling.

"God, he's annoying," she says.

"My brother's super annoying, too," I say. "How much older than you is he?"

"Two years."

"Same as me and my brother."

"I have two big brothers," Odette tells us.

"Poor you," Saskia says, and we laugh.

"Do they snowboard?" I ask.

"No, they are ski racers," Odette says. "Me, I used to race, too. I changed to snowboard when I was fourteen."

"Are they here in Le Rocher?" I say.

"No, they stay in Tignes this winter. Have you been there?"

That starts up a whole conversation about where we've ridden.

The next time Saskia heads to the bar, I see her and Curtis having a heated argument. Jake wouldn't dare tell me what to do. He worked that out years back.

Saskia returns with more drinks. As we down them, the band launches into a cover of a Killers track, "Somebody Told Me."

Saskia jumps up. "I love this song."

The rest of us follow her to the dance floor, and suddenly the whole bar is up and dancing, bodies knocking together in the small space. I'm quite wobbly. Haven't been this drunk in years. I'll have to drink a load of water before I go to bed.

Feeling dizzy, I head to the toilets. On my way back to our table I stumble and a hand grips my upper arm. Curtis.

I curse inwardly. My legs felt shaky enough already and my voice comes out shaky, too. "Thanks."

His eyes seem to sparkle. "Like I said earlier, you can fall on me anytime."

Willing myself not to flush, I nod at his Evian. "You must be the only person in here who isn't drinking."

"I don't drink when I'm training. It messes with my recovery time."

I catch sight of our table. Another round of vodka has arrived. Crap.

Curtis notices where I'm looking. "I reckon you've had enough."

"Excuse me?" I say. "If I need your advice I'll ask for it."

Who does he think he is? It's one thing for him to tell his little sister not to drink, but he doesn't even know me. I wobble off to the bar. I can't let Saskia pay for my drinks all night. She can clearly afford it, but I don't want to take advantage. I have to get at least one round in.

Only I have no idea what brand of vodka we've been drinking and Saskia strikes me as someone who would be picky about such things.

"Same again?" says the girl at the bar before I can open my mouth.

"Yeah," I say, relieved.

Dale and Brent sit farther along the bar. The barmaid chats to them as she fixes my drinks. She's wearing a little black dress and spiky-heeled boots, and they're eyeing up her legs. She's petite and really pretty—long, dark hair; lots of eye makeup. I hear snatches of her accent, thicker than mine—Geordie, from the sounds of it—and warm to her. A fellow Northerner.

Dale says something that makes her roll her eyes. She says something back and he hangs his head, pretending to be shamefaced. Brent laughs and slaps Dale's back.

The barmaid brings my drinks over. I feel sorry for her, having guys chat her up night in, night out—especially ones as imposing-looking as Dale, with his dreads and multiple piercings. She must get sick of it.

Yet as she loads shot glasses onto a tray, I catch her smiling a secret smile and realize my mistake. *She's* the one playing them. And she knows exactly how to do it.

"Here you go," she tells me. "That's ten euros."

I hesitate. Drinks in a ski resort cost a fortune and I was expecting it to be fifty at least. She's made a mistake, distracted by Dale and Brent, but if I don't say something, they'll take the difference out of her wages. "That can't be right."

Irritation crosses her pretty features. "Well, it is."

Okay. At least I tried. I hand her a ten-euro note.

As she rings it up on the till, she glances sideways at the boys and does that hair-tossing, *I'm not interested* thing. I watch in fascination as Dale leans across the bar, sleeves rolled back to reveal his heavily tattooed forearms, and calls out to her. She smiles to herself again and pretends not to hear.

I've never played guys like this. I wouldn't know how.

She stabs a glossy red fingernail at my drinks and says something I don't catch.

"Sorry?" I say.

"That one's the vodka."

What?

A horrible possibility creeps into my alcohol-fogged brain. But Saskia wouldn't do that.

Would she?

CHAPTER 7

PRESENT DAY

We rush into the cold, dark corridor. The basket where we left our phones is empty.

"Who took them?" Curtis's tone is menacing.

"It was brand-new, that phone," Heather says, close to tears. "And it's got all my work contacts."

"Calm down," Dale says. "We'll find it."

Everyone seems equally confused.

I glance either way along the corridor. Did one of these four take them or is someone else in the building? I wish I could think straight. None of this makes sense. I can feel the effect of the whiskey already. Alcohol hits hard at this altitude and I haven't eaten for hours.

"We can work out who didn't take the phones," I say. "Who didn't leave the room? I went to the toilet before we played."

"Did you see if the phones were there?" Curtis says.

I strain to think. "I can't remember."

"I went to get drinks," Dale says. "And I didn't notice either." He looks at Curtis. "Why did you go out?"

"Phone call," Curtis says. "Then the toilet."

"Who did you call?" I ask.

Curtis raises his eyebrow as if that's none of my business.

"Well?" Dale prompts.

"Why is that relevant?" Curtis says.

"It might be," Dale says.

Curtis shoots an angry look my way. "My mum."

"I went out twice," Brent says.

"And Heather went out just now," I say. "Shit. Any of us could have taken them."

"And then what?" Curtis asks.

"Hidden them somewhere, I guess," I say.

Eyes fall on Heather's handbag. She's the only one of us who brought a bag up here.

At thirty-three, I don't own a handbag. I bought one once for my friend Kate's wedding. *Don't you dare bring your backpack, Milla,* she'd scrawled on the bottom of my invite. It was duck-egg blue to match my bridesmaid's dress and I felt ridiculous with it, like a little kid playing dress-up. I donated it to a local charity shop straight after.

Heather's is brown, and from the flashy gold tag on the zip, I'm guessing it's designer. When she realizes where we're looking, she flushes and tips it out onto the carpet. There's a little silver purse, wet wipes, tampons, and a ridiculous amount of makeup. No phones. She looks up, defiant. "Happy now?" She scoops the lot back into her bag.

"The alternative is someone else took them," Curtis says.

Heather's eyes go wide. "But who?"

"You tell me," Curtis says.

Dale puts his arm around Heather and she leans into him. United again, for now at least.

"We need to search this place," Curtis continues. "For the phones. Or whoever it was who took them."

"Okay." Brent downs the remainder of his whiskey and heads to the door. I move to follow him.

"Wait!" Heather shouts. "We don't know who's out there."

"Good point," Curtis says. "I don't think the girls should go on their own."

Dale grips Heather's hand. "I'll stick with Heather."

"I'll stick with Milla," Curtis says.

"*I'll* stick with Milla," Brent says.

Maybe I should be grateful they care, but I'm not. I'm mad. I can't stand this idea that just because I'm female, I'm some pathetic weakling that has to be protected. I'm as strong now as I was then—more arm strength these days, though rather less leg strength—and if someone tried to attack me, I would put up a damn good fight.

I open my mouth to say this. Then I see the tension in Curtis's jaw; Brent's, too. And these two don't scare easily. I think of those dark and deserted corridors. Better to be safe and all that. "How about you both stick with me?"

Curtis nods. "Meet back here in, what, twenty minutes?"

Dale checks his watch. "Okay."

"You go that way," Curtis tells him, pointing left. "We'll go this way. You do the lower floor and we'll take this one."

"You the boss now, are you?" Dale says.

Curtis doesn't answer. He always was the boss, really—not that I usually listened to him.

Dale tugs on Heather's hand and they set off down the corridor.

"Check the ski lockers," Curtis shouts after them. "And look for a landline while you're at it."

We set off the other way. Curtis leads, naturally. Exploring was creepy enough earlier. It's much creepier now. The Panorama building is different in the ski season, when it echoes with the clunks of ski sticks and chatter of the winter visitors. Tonight it's too empty. Too silent.

What would someone want with our phones anyway? I don't know which is scarier—a complete stranger taking them, or one of these guys whom I thought I knew. Whom I once knew, at least.

The first doors on the right are the toilets.

"Shall I check the ladies'?" I say.

Curtis pushes the door. "We all will."

There's a line of four cubicles, all closed. I peer under the bottoms of the doors. If I see a pair of feet . . .

Bang! My heart skips a beat, but it's Curtis, going down the line and kicking each door wide. There's nobody in there. Of course there isn't. Brent riffles through the paper towels in the bin.

We check the men's toilets in the same fashion. An icy draft blows down my neck and I notice the small window is open an inch. I stand on tiptoe to peer out, and imagine a hand dropping our phones, one by one, through the gap into the night. If that's what happened, our phones are gone forever, because this side of the building faces the cliffs. But why would anyone want to do that?

"Was that window open earlier?" I ask.

Curtis swears and yanks it shut. "I didn't notice."

"Me neither," Brent says.

Next door is a cleaner's cupboard that reeks of bleach. We rummage through stacks of paper towels and sachets of soap for the dispensers. There's a mountain of toilet paper. I check inside each tube.

I would rather die than admit it, but I'm glad to have these two with me. Brent especially, because being around Curtis gives me the jitters in a whole other way.

The corridor turns a corner. There are doors on either side, all locked. I tense as we pass each one, braced for someone to leap out.

"What do you reckon they all are?" Brent asks as he tests the last one.

"Offices, maybe," Curtis replies. "Or storage rooms."

The corridor reaches a dead end.

"There's not much up here," I say as we return the way we came. "What about outside?"

"Too dark to look now," Curtis says.

"Can you remember what's out there?" I say. "I can picture a couple of garages for the snowcats." Big ones. The machines that groom the pistes are huge.

"Three, I think," Curtis says.

"There's that hut at the bottom of the tow lift," Brent adds. "And the kiosk."

"And the outside seating area," Curtis says. "With deck chairs. Must be a shed or something where they keep the chairs."

We return to the function room. Heather and Dale aren't back yet. There's a lot more floor space down there than up here.

Curtis shuts the door behind us and lowers his voice. "Reckon Dale and Heather are behind this?"

I stare at him. "But why?"

"No idea."

"I don't think so," I say. "Heather looked pretty scared to me."

"Or is she just a good actor?" Curtis glances at Brent.

Brent shrugs. "Don't ask me."

Curtis aims a kick at the door. "Someone's messing with us and I don't like it."

Brent pours himself another large Jack Daniel's. Interesting to see how these two are handling the tension. Brent's dealing with it by getting drunk, Curtis by getting angry.

"Want one, Mills?" Brent says.

So much for the nostalgia-filled reunion that I imagined. I sigh. "Go on then."

Curtis touches my arm. "Milla."

The sense of déjà vu catches me off guard. One night ten years ago Curtis warned me to stop drinking, and I should have listened to him, but I didn't.

Just like I'm not going to now.

I hold my glass out. Brent must be more rattled than he's letting on, because his hand shakes and he sloshes whiskey all over my fingers. I suck the sticky liquor off and knock the drink back.

I think Curtis noticed that little tremor, because he's eyeing Brent as if trying to assess what he might be capable of.

He's looking at the wrong person.

CHAPTER 8

TEN YEARS AGO

I stagger across the plateau, head throbbing, stomach heaving. Hoping I can make it to the half-pipe without vomiting again.

Huge banners have been erected: *Le Rocher Open*. Bibbed competitors blast out of the pipe, warming up; others stretch or adjust laces and bindings. Faces are tense, riders focused on the runs they're hoping to do. Just like I would be if I wasn't too busy trying not to puke.

I've been attempting to eat ever since I came home from Glow Bar last night, but I can't keep anything down. I'm so angry—mainly with myself. How could I have fallen for it? I'm twenty-three, not a teenager. Peer pressure or not, I should have known better.

Hip-hop booms from a sound system; the sunlight pierces my brain. I shield my eyes, wishing I could curl up in a silent, darkened room and sleep off my hangover.

The guy beside me bites into an overripe banana and my stomach clenches. I can smell it. There are camera crews on either side of me— Eurosport, France 3, a couple more. I clamp my lips together. *Don't vomit again.*

There's a buzz of foreign languages in the queue to sign in. As I collect my competition bib, some of the girls from last night walk past, snowboards under their arms. I lower my head, not wanting to see them laughing at me.

Someone taps my shoulder, and Odette swoops in to kiss me on either cheek. "How are you?"

I raise my eyebrow. "What do you think?"

Her smile turns to puzzlement. "What?"

"The vodka?"

"Vodka?"

"That I was drinking all night?"

Odette's face flushes pink as I explain. She looks around for Saskia in disbelief. There she is, in her white Salomon jacket, way up at the top, about to drop in. Odette turns back to me, words tumbling out of her. Apparently Saskia set it up before I entered the bar, suggesting they drink water shots to faze the competition.

"I'm so sorry," Odette says. "I didn't know."

From her mortified expression, I believe her. "What about the other girls. Did they know?"

"I don't think so."

I can't decide if that makes me feel better or worse.

Saskia zips past on her way to the tow lift. Odette stares after her, like she's struggling to accept her friend would do such a thing.

I've missed half the warm-up time already. I snatch up my snowboard. "Let's get this over with. How's the pipe?"

Odette and I ride the tow lift together.

Curtis is strapping in at the top. He takes one look at me and swears. "I tried to warn you."

"What?" I say. "You knew?"

"I suspected."

Saskia stands with a small group, laughing and joking. Brent is among them. And Dale, lip ring glinting in the sunshine. My anger flares. I march up and tap Saskia on the shoulder.

She turns to face me. Her expression reminds me of my parents' cat when something has aroused his hunting instinct.

"Why did you single me out like that?" I say, aware of Curtis and Odette behind me.

The group falls silent.

I fully expect Saskia to deny it, but she just looks at me, blue eyes unrepentant. "Because I could."

"Scared I would beat you?"

She doesn't answer that. She doesn't have to. I won't beat her today; she's made sure of that.

I'm so mad I want to slap her. I've always played hard—I had to; my brother plays harder than anyone I know. But what he does is overt. This is a different sort of hardness. A female hardness, maybe. Underhanded. And I don't know how to deal with it.

I struggle to keep my anger from my face. "I hope you realize the game is on."

She breaks into a smile. "The game is on."

Curtis beckons her over and the two of them sit, heads close. From the way he's pointing in my direction, he's giving her a hard time. She glances at me once more, then turns her back on me. He's pointing down the pipe now. Pep talk. I'm going to need all the help I can get today, so I strain to hear what he's saying.

"That wall's in full sun, so it's going to soften up fast. Careful you don't catch your edge when you land your spins."

Saskia nods and fastens her board on. He sits there, watching her run. A bearded guy in a competition bib bumps fists with him. American.

I click into my bindings and take deep breaths, trying to prepare my stomach for the up-down motion.

Curtis's words drift across on the wind. "Should stay nice and hard all day."

Funny. He just told Saskia the opposite, or did I hear that wrong?

Half an hour later, I'm flapping with nerves, waiting for my name to be called.

"*Milla Anderson!*"

A calm usually comes over me at this point; everything goes into slow motion and my hours of training and visualizing kick in, allowing me to perform my run on autopilot. This time, though, it's like I'm on fast-forward. I feel dizzy even standing still, so it's hardly surprising that I stuff up my first spin and crash to the pipe floor. My second run is no better. And that's me out.

I force myself to sit on a snowbank and watch the rest of the comp. I'm going to suck this up and make sure I never make the same mistake again.

Curtis is just as smooth and confident on the mountain as he is off it. His clean, powerful moves take him through to the final. Saskia gets through the women's final, nails her back-to-back 720s, and goes on to place seventh. Which is pretty impressive considering this is an international event with riders from all over Europe. Odette wins.

The riders cluster at the bottom exchanging hugs and high fives. Champagne is popped and sprayed over the crowd.

"After-party at Glow Bar!" someone shouts.

It seems like I'm the only one who isn't celebrating. My fingers clench into fists as someone else congratulates Saskia. I pick up my board and creep off.

In four months, Saskia and I will go head-to-head again at the British Championships. And I'm going to beat her then if it kills me.

CHAPTER 9

PRESENT DAY

The door of the function room swings open, making me jump, and Dale strides in, followed by Heather.

Dale looks furious. "Someone's taken our laptop."

Curtis bolts to the door.

"What?" I call.

"I've got a MacBook."

We chase him downstairs and along the corridor. Freezing air blasts my hair back when he opens the double doors. Two at a time, he descends the metal steps. I'm relieved to see my bags where I left them.

Curtis checks his backpack. "Fuck. My MacBook's gone."

I spot the half-open zip of my backpack and rummage through my things in a panic. My wallet and keys are still there. I didn't bring my computer. I do nearly everything on my phone.

The others are checking their bags. Heather paws through layers of clothing.

"Anything else missing?" Curtis says.

"Not that I can see," Brent says.

I'm so flustered, I can't even remember what I packed. "I'm not sure."

"This isn't funny anymore," Heather says. "I want to go down."

Think, Milla. My gaze settles on the security camera aimed at the top of the bubble lift. I position myself before it and wave my arms. "*Hello!* Anyone there?"

Curtis paces the platform. "I can't believe I let this happen. Should have come down here half an hour ago."

I continue waving my arms, hoping the operator will see us, even if they can't hear us, and start the lift running again.

"I haven't backed our laptop up for weeks," Heather tells Dale. "We have to find it."

"You don't have to remind me," Dale mutters.

Curtis turns on him. "What were you two doing down here for all this time anyway?"

"Hey," Dale protests. "Don't go pinning this on us. You left the room twice earlier and you know it."

Heather and Dale certainly had time to go through our bags and hide the computers while they were down here, but potentially any of us could have rushed down and done it.

Or was it someone else?

Either way, this was meticulously planned. Whoever did this installed us upstairs in the function room, correctly assuming we wouldn't drag our bags all the way around the building with us.

"We searched the entire ground floor," Heather tells us. "Then I remembered the laptop."

"Find anything?" Curtis says.

"Whole lot of locked doors," Dale says.

"No staff?" I ask. "Or a landline?"

"We found two empty phone sockets," Heather says. "One in the bar, one in the kitchen."

Empty because someone removed the phones? I can see from her face that she thinks so.

"What are all the locked doors?" Heather asks.

"Find a control room?" Curtis says. "Or a Mountain Rescue room? First-aid room?"

"No."

"Well, then." Curtis goes over to rattle the door of the operator booth. It's locked; of course it is. He cups his hand to the glass and peers through the window.

I join him at the glass. "Any sign of a phone or radio?"

"No." There's frustration in his tone.

Brent comes to see. A crash from behind makes us whirl around. The security camera lies in pieces on the concrete. Snowboard raised above his head, Dale stands beneath what remains of its mounting. I blink down at the remnants, stunned.

"What the hell did you do that for?" Curtis demands.

Dale lowers his board. "Don't want them watching us, do we?"

I battle for calm. "But they might have rescued us."

Curtis picks up the largest of the components. We don't need an electrician to tell us the camera is damaged beyond repair. He tosses it aside. "You've just severed our one potential link to the valley. Anyone see any other cameras in this place?"

"There's probably one in the restaurant," I say.

Dale clears his throat. Somehow I sense what he's going to say.

"I smashed it."

Brent and I exchange looks and I'm pretty sure we're all thinking the same thing. Is Dale the one behind this? But why?

Curtis marches up to him. "Of all the stupid things."

"Oh, get real," Dale says. "If someone's down there watching us on camera, they're in on this. They have to be."

"Right," Curtis says. "We need some answers. We're going through the shit in that game." He nods at Heather. "Did you sleep with Brent?"

I wince. Subtlety was never Curtis's strong suit.

Dale steps up close. "She doesn't have to answer that."

The two men eye each other. Dale is slightly taller—he must be pushing six foot, tall for a snowboarder; Curtis is broader.

"You going to ask me if I slept with Saskia next?" Dale says.

"Did you?" Curtis says.

"Did *you?*" Dale counters.

Curtis seizes him by the shoulders and barges him backward along the platform. A few meters beyond, the platform ends and the ground drops away into the night. A spindly metal barrier is all that stands between them and the cliff.

Brent and I chase after them. Knifelike icicles hang down from the roof above our heads. I'm praying they don't choose this moment to fall. Brent moves in on Dale, so I come up behind Curtis. Risky approaching him while he's this worked up. In theory I know what to do—when your big brother is a rugby player, self-defense is a matter of survival, plus I worked the doors of the Leadmill nightclub for a few years after I quit snowboarding.

Hoping I remember how to do it, I sling my right arm around Curtis's neck, left arm behind his head, to put him in a choke hold. As soon as I feel him give up the fight, I release my grip. Curtis turns my way, shocked and furious in equal measure.

Dale shakes Brent off and says, "And *you'd* better watch it. You're hardly my favorite person right now." Eyes glinting, Dale straightens his jacket and returns to Heather's side.

"We need to keep calm and figure out what's going on," I say, breathless.

"What about the ski lockers?" Curtis asks. "Were they all open?"

"All except one," Dale says.

"Let's see if we can open it," Curtis says.

I shoulder my small backpack and pick up my snowboard bag. They're not heavy; we're only here for two nights, after all. I want my stuff where I can see it. The others are reaching for their bags too, and we drag everything up the stairs.

The locker doors are numbered, a hundred in total, and painted pretty pastel colors. Key rings dangle from their locks. I swing a couple of doors open and check inside. Farther along, Curtis does the same.

"We already looked," Heather says.

I spot the locker that doesn't have a key. Brent tugs at the door.

"I've got a screwdriver," Curtis says.

"Give me a sec." Brent pulls a bunch of keys from his pocket. We watch him slide the keys off the wire key ring and flatten out the wire. He twiddles it in the lock, removing it to adjust the shape.

Dale wanders to the main entrance and seems like he's about to open it.

No. Please don't. I couldn't cope with hearing that sound again just now. Sooner or later I'm going to have to open it again and go out there, but I'm jumpy enough already and I need time to psych myself up.

Dale slips and grabs the wall for balance. "Shit, the floor's wet."

Sure enough, there are damp patches on the floorboards leading up to the entrance.

"Are they footprints?" I say.

"Looks like it," Curtis says grimly. "Did anyone go out?"

Silence. But if they did, their shoes would be wet. As unobtrusively as I can, I check the others' shoes. Am I imagining it or are the tips of Brent's DCs darker?

"Here we go," Brent says, sliding the wire out.

Impressive, but he always was good with his hands.

We crowd in as he swings the locker door open, but the locker is empty. Curtis, who is closest, does a sort of double take, as though something just occurred to him, and looks around sharply to scan our faces. Is he thinking Brent opened that door a bit too easily?

"So where's our phones?" Dale says.

"You tell me," Curtis replies.

I tense. These two look like they're about to square off again.

"Can we eat?" Brent asks.

Curtis turns on him. "We need to find the fucking phones."

"I know, but I'm starving."

Curtis raises his voice. "Do you realize what this means? The lift isn't running, we have no way of contacting anyone. If we can't find our phones, we're stuck here."

"I'm hungry, too," I put in. "Can we discuss this over dinner?" Food might mop up some of the alcohol so I can think straight.

Heather looks incredulous. "How can you think about eating when someone's doing this to us?"

"It's no use being hungry as well as stressed out," I say.

Curtis yanks up his bags and stalks off toward the restaurant. The rest of us hurry after him. He's by the bar as we enter, inspecting the security camera on the floor. We dump the bags in a pile.

Heather nods at her handbag. "Keep an eye on that, could you?" she tells Dale, and bustles off to the kitchen.

I sneak another look at Brent's DCs. "Are your shoes wet?" I ask him quietly.

Brent glances down. "Must be whiskey."

"Right."

"Let's see if I can get that fire going." He heads off to the fireplace.

I reckon I can light a fire as well as any of them, but I want to ask Heather about Brent, so I head to the kitchen.

The herby tomato aroma makes my stomach rumble. Heather peers into the saucepans and turns on the electric rings.

"What should I do?" I ask. I'm no chef. I try to eat healthily, but it's mostly raw foods, just so I don't have to cook.

Heather hands me a wooden spoon and gestures to the casserole. "Stand here and stir that."

She's a flurry of movement, twirling about and opening cupboards at random. How can she move like that in those heels? The last time I wore heels I was seven or eight, playing dress-up. I sprained my ankle, couldn't compete in my gymnastics tournament, and vowed never to wear them again.

I'm desperate to eat something. I peer over her shoulder, looking for a snack, but the cupboards are bare except for a few staples. The commercial fridge, too. It makes sense. They'll stock up next month, ahead of the ski area opening.

"So what do you do for work these days?" I try to keep my tone casual.

"We're sports agents, me and Dale," she says. "I got my law degree and we set up our own agency after we got married."

"Wow. That's really impressive."

Conversation grinds to a halt. I never knew what to say to her. She hardly snowboarded and I had far more in common with Dale. Women like Heather make me feel insecure. The hair, the makeup, the effort to look good at all times. She's exactly how a woman is supposed to be, at least by conventional standards.

And I'm not. I'm like some tomboy who has never really grown up. Still. And for all I pretend I don't care about how I look, deep down, I do care. I worry about it. I worry it turns guys off that I'm not girly and feminine enough. That that's why I'm still single.

Heather rattles about in the fridge. There's never going to be a good time to ask her if she cheated on Dale, so here goes. "I'm trying to figure out who wrote that stuff in the Icebreaker. And I was wondering about you and Brent."

Heather straightens, lettuce in one hand, cucumber in the other. She checks the corridor and turns to me. "What exactly are you wondering?" Her tone is icy.

"Did you sleep with him?"

Her eyes flash. "Did you sleep with Dale?"

"Of course not." I kissed him, though. But I hope that never comes up, because I'm not proud of it. "Well?"

"No." She struggles to hold my gaze.

"I don't believe you," I say.

The guys must have gotten the fire going, because the woodsmoke smells stronger now.

"Believe what you want." Heather opens an overhead cupboard and brings down five plates.

"Never mind," I say. "I'll ask Brent."

She dishes up the food in silence, leaving the lettuce and cucumber abandoned on the counter. This is the second time I've sensed a lie from her today. What else is she lying about?

Woodsmoke chokes my throat as I carry the plates out. The restaurant is just as I remember it. Dark wooden panels and exposed beams; cowhide rugs; black-and-white photos. Flames flicker in the huge stone fireplace; a stag's head juts out above. On the mantelpiece a familiar clock ticks, face yellowed with age.

The lighting is dim, from chandeliers hanging low over the tables. It should seem cozy, but there are too many shadowy corners for my liking just now.

Brent and Dale sit chatting at the table closest to the fire. I dump the plates, relieved to see them getting on again. Dale's on the whiskey too now, and a second bottle of Jack Daniel's sits beside the first.

"Have you drunk a whole bottle already?" I say.

Brent grins. "Free bar. What's not to like?"

I fetch a stack of glasses from the bar and pour myself another measure, knowing I shouldn't, and blink through the smoke to look around. Antique climbing equipment is pinned to the walls: vintage glacier goggles, crampons, a well-worn pair of climbing boots.

A rusty ice axe. Le Rocher's savage summits make it a popular ice-climbing destination in winter. I finger the metal tip. Still sharp as hell.

Curtis kneels by the fire, rummaging through the log pile.

"What are you doing?" I say.

"Looking for the phones."

"I already checked there," Dale says.

Curtis continues rummaging. The smoke is making my eyes water.

Heather arrives with the rest of the plates. "I have to get that laptop back."

"Will you shut up about the laptop," Dale hisses.

Heather always struck me as a strong woman. Back then, she seemed to call the shots in their relationship, but the power balance appears to have shifted.

I sit down next to Brent. The chairs have fluffy sheepskin covers. I want to wrap the sheepskin over my legs like a blanket, but it's tied in place.

"How about Billy Morgan's Quad Cork eighteen hundred?" Brent says as we eat.

"I saw it on YouTube," I say, grateful he's making an effort to lighten the mood.

Dale nods. "And now some Japanese guy landed the first-ever Quad Cork nineteen eighty."

"That's insane," I say. "What's that, like five full rotations?"

"Five and a half," Dale says. "Snowboarding's come a long way."

Heather checks the clock like she's counting the minutes until she can get out of here, and Curtis remains watchful, but with the casserole and alcohol warming my belly and the flames warming my face, I'm starting to relax.

"Can you believe we used to ride without helmets?" Brent says.

"I didn't," Curtis tells him.

"Some of the slams we took," Brent says. "We were lucky we got away with it."

Some of us weren't so lucky, but I'm not going to think about that. Anyway, a helmet doesn't stop you from breaking your neck.

"See that Norwegian guy do a Backside Five Forty Rewind?" Dale asks.

"No," I say. "What's that?"

Dale was the style master, and I used to love discussing tricks with him.

He puts down his glass. "It's like a seven twenty, then you put it into reverse. Imagine stalling your spin midair and going back the other way. It's bloody hard. Try it and you'll see." He lifts his chair onto a nearby table and climbs onto it.

I love these guys. When I go out with my colleagues from the gym we talk about Netflix. I may not have seen this crew for ten whole years, but I still have more in common with them than I do with anyone else.

You don't go pro in a sport for the money, especially not a high-risk one like ours. You're never going to get rich as a freestyle snowboarder, not unless you're Shaun White. No, you do it for the passion. To spend every minute of your life doing it, thinking about it, and dreaming it. None of us are pro, not anymore, but we haven't lost that passion.

Dale leaps off the chair, rotating either way as he drops.

"No," Curtis says. "You've got to rewind a whole one eighty, otherwise it's just a Shifty."

Dale flashes him a look.

"Let's have a go." Brent climbs up and off he jumps.

A sparky excitement stirs inside me. I stand. "My turn."

Heather rolls her eyes, but I feel like I'm twenty again. The chair judders as I climb onto it. I leap into the air. *Umph.* I land hard. I haven't jumped off anything higher than a StairMaster for years.

"We're not getting enough air time." Dale's gaze settles on a section of tree trunk sawn down to make a table. He lifts a smaller table onto it and places a chair on top. The structure wobbles precariously as he climbs onto it. Brent steadies it just in time. Dale leaps high, staggering into our table as he lands and sprawling to the floor.

"Enough," Curtis says. "Stop dicking about."

Dale picks himself up, rubbing his shoulder. "What's your problem?"

"Someone stole my phone and my computer, that's my problem."

"Lighten up."

Curtis leans back in his seat. "You give my stuff back and I'll do that."

He and Dale lock eyes. I notice the empty whiskey glass beside Curtis's plate. I didn't realize he was drinking.

"Haven't changed, have you?" Dale says. "Still annoying as fuck. I knew I shouldn't have come."

"So why did you?" Curtis says.

Dale nods at Heather. "*She* wanted to."

Seriously? I glance at her. Why would she want to come? I always got the impression she hated this place.

"And to answer your earlier question," Dale says, "no, I didn't sleep with your bitch of a sister."

Curtis scrambles up. "There's only one person allowed to badmouth my sister, and that's me. But I choose not to because, unlike you, I have some damn respect."

There's a tense silence.

It seems the mood up here can change as quickly as the weather conditions.

CHAPTER 10

TEN YEARS AGO

Brent and Curtis sit opposite me in the bubble. The wind has really picked up and our little cabin shudders from side to side. I groan and clutch my stomach.

"Don't you go pukin' on my new snowboard pants," Brent says in his thick London accent.

"Yeah, you have to watch her around your pants," Curtis says. "She trashed mine yesterday."

I check Curtis's lower leg. There's no rip. They're new ones. Now that the pressure of competition is over, Curtis and Brent are all smiles. And they have reason to be. Curtis came third, Brent fifth. A good showing for the Brit boys.

Another gust of wind catches the cabin and my stomach heaves. The reek of stale cigarette smoke doesn't help—whoever was in the cabin before us scorned the no-smoking signs.

I climbed in here wanting a few runs to vent my anger. Still, it's probably a good thing they jumped in with me, because they're stopping me from dwelling on my disaster of a day. With Curtis's blue eyes on me, it's hard to think at all.

"I thought you two would be down there celebrating," I say.

"I always do a couple of runs after a comp to wind down." Curtis glances at Brent. "And Brent had this Swiss girl from last night chasing him. Needed to make a quick getaway."

I smile and turn my attention to the boards propped against the window. Brent's is so covered with his sponsors' stickers that I can hardly make out what model it is. A Burton something. The Shaun White pro model, I'm guessing. If Brent keeps riding the way he is, Burton might bring out a Brent Bakshi model next year.

I nod at the Smash sticker. "Do you really drink that shit?"

"Why? Want one?" Brent rummages through his backpack and produces a luminous orange can, which he cracks open and holds out to me.

"No," I say. "Actually, yeah. I've never tried it." I take a sip. "Ugh. It's like mouthwash." I hand it back. "I heard it's got the caffeine of three coffees."

"It's five." Brent stands, his dark hair brushing the cabin ceiling. Cold air rushes in as he slides the window open and drains the can through the gap.

"What are you doing?" I say. "The marmots won't be able to hibernate this year."

"I can't stand the stuff." Brent closes the window and stashes the empty in the side of his backpack. "Don't tell anyone, because they're paying for my season."

I like Brent. He reminds me of one of my brother's mates, Barnsey. "Are they paying you more than Burton?" I ask.

"They're paying more than all my other sponsors put together."

"Seriously?" But it makes sense. Brent's the guy who goes big. He's the perfect figurehead.

"When they told me how much they were offering, I said I'd get their name tattooed on my arse."

"You didn't!"

Brent lifts his jacket and grasps the waistband of his snowboard trousers as though he's about to rip them down. "Want to see?"

Unsure if he's serious, I glance at Curtis.

Curtis throws his hands up. "Don't look at me. Why do you think I've seen his arse?"

Brent laughs and sits back down. He has the cocky confidence that comes from being exceptionally good at a sport—and not just any sport, but one that involves flying through the air at great height. Yet he's funny with it. Not to mention cute, with his ready smile and incredible dark eyes.

I saw him on breakfast TV before I came out here. The female presenter—Anna something, an attractive woman in her forties—asked him what muscles you needed for snowboarding. Pretty much all of them, he told her. She persuaded him to take his shirt off, so he stripped and she was all over him. The male co-presenter practically had to restrain her.

It was a hilarious example of reverse sexism. If you flipped the genders—a male presenter, a female athlete—it would have caused nationwide outrage. As it was, half the audience was laughing at her, the other half was going equally wild. Brent sat back, taking it all in stride.

And yeah, that chest. I got it. Yet he doesn't affect me like Curtis does.

I grip my seat as we're thrown about some more. The bubble slows to a crawl.

"You know Dale asked me for a Smash this morning?" Brent tells Curtis.

"Did he?" Curtis says.

"He went home with the barmaid last night."

"Who, Heather?"

"I don't know."

"Long, dark hair?"

"Yeah."

"She lives with my sister," Curtis says. "Wear him out, did she? Lucky for you."

They laugh.

"Where did Dale come in?" I say.

"Seventh," Curtis says.

The dynamics between Brent and Curtis interest me. They're rivals, but there's friendship as well. Curtis is older—he must be twenty-four or -five, which is getting on a bit for a pro snowboarder. Kids these days are winning major events as early as fifteen years old, and few continue to compete past their late twenties. Soft, young bones don't break so easily. Does Curtis feel threatened by Brent's swift rise? He must do.

I lurch forward as the bubble stops. Crap. We're only halfway up the steep cliff.

"Rumor has it a skier jumped those cliffs once," Curtis says.

I look at the sheer rock face. "Seriously? Would you do it?"

"Not without a parachute."

There's a crackle from the speaker and an announcement in French.

"What did he say?" Brent asks.

"Brace! Brace!" I say.

Curtis laughs. "Sick, Milla."

"What did they say really?" Brent says.

"I don't know," I say. "My French is pretty basic."

"They have a mechanical issue," Curtis says. "'Sorry for the delay.'"

Brent swears. "Anyone got any food?"

I dig through my bag and pull out a muesli bar. "I've got this."

"Cheers."

The bubble swings from side to side like a fairground ride. An icy draft blows through the gap in the window. I hug my knees to my chest. "Bloody freezing in here."

Curtis swaps sides to sit next to me. After a beat, Brent does the same on my other side, so I'm squashed between them. This is pretty intimate, and I sense I'm not the only one feeling that, because we all fall quiet.

The low sun has turned the snow golden. The powder fields above are etched with the wavy lines of a thousand descents. I should be picking their brains about tricks, but I can't think of anything except the pressure of Curtis's leg against mine.

He catches my eye again. "Better?"

"Yep." I need to get out of here. I can't handle him looking at me like that. The last thing I want this winter is a distraction.

The speakers crackle and another announcement comes on.

"No shit," Curtis says. "The wind's triggered an automatic shutdown. They're going to evacuate us one by one from the bubbles. Better get comfy. We're going to be here awhile."

A helicopter buzzes overhead. We crane our necks to see. It hovers above one of the bubbles way down the slope. A man abseils out. I blow on my fingers. This is going to take forever.

"Want my jacket?" Curtis says.

"No, thanks," I say.

"Want mine?" Brent says.

I catch the look that Curtis flashes at Brent. *Back off.* "No," I say. "Do either of you want mine? Good, because you're not having it."

We laugh and it breaks the tension. The flirting stops and we talk snowboarding. Places we've ridden; good days and bad; Terje Håkonsen's record 9.8-meter air at the Arctic Challenge. The sky changes from pink to purple to navy.

"How do you two know each other anyway?" I ask.

"We met at the Burton US Open a few years back," Curtis says. "Rented a place together last season."

"With his sister," Brent adds.

He and Curtis share another look. What's that about? But I don't want to think of her right now. I'm just glad it's these two I'm stuck with and not her.

There's another announcement.

"Not long now," Curtis tells us.

"Is your French fluent?" I say.

"I wouldn't say that."

"And his German," Brent says. "If I'd known I was going to be doing this, I would have tried harder at languages at school."

"Same," I say. "I did the season in Switzerland last year, in Laax, and I had, like, two German phrases."

"What were they?" Curtis says.

I summon my best German accent. "*Ich verstehe nicht.*" I see Brent's blank look. "'I don't understand.'"

"What was your other one?" Curtis says.

"*Wo ist der Krankenhaus?* 'Where's the hospital?'"

Curtis laughs. "Good choice. Actually it's *das Krankenhaus.*"

I aim a punch at his ribs.

There's an angry throbbing above the bubble, and light beams into the cabin.

"Here's the helicopter," Brent says.

A shadowy figure descends from a rope. We hang back as the man forces the door of our cabin open and steps inside. He says something in French.

"Who's going first?" Curtis says.

I put up my hand. "Me!"

I always have this stupid need to prove myself. To show no fear. I blame it on my brother. Jake and his mates would do all this crazy stuff in the woods around where we grew up, and the only way they'd let me hang out with them was if I was the craziest of all. *Go on, Milla. I dare you.* I broke bones trying to keep up with them. Never passed up a dare—and still won't. It's a habit now. Daredevil Milla. People expect it.

The man harnesses me up. "Ees nothing to worry about, okay?"

"I'm not worried," I say. "I've always wanted to do this."

He gives me a funny look, and Curtis and Brent laugh their heads off.

"Go, Milla," Brent says as I begin my descent.

In truth I'm far from calm. The rocks below look super sharp. *Come on, hold it together.* Step by step, I walk my feet down the cliff face. The wind catches me, blowing me sideways. *Whoa.* Clinging to the rope with one hand, I put out my other hand just in time as I'm swung against the rock. I wait for the gust to pass, then continue down.

Ten more meters. At last it flattens off and my boots sink into the snow.

A snowcat has zigzagged the short distance down the trail from the glacier to light up our landing zone. I shield my eyes from the glare of its headlights.

And Saskia steps out of the shadows like a ghost.

I'm so shocked to see her that I nearly tumble backward onto the knife-edge rocks.

"Where did you come from?" I splutter.

She nods to the bubble one down from ours. I catch the triumphant look on her face, and then I understand. She saw me creep off and followed me up here, intending to do a victory lap.

My hands clench at my sides, itching to give her a sharp push.

CHAPTER 11

PRESENT DAY

"You know what?" Dale says. "I'm glad your sister's dead."

Curtis's fist shoots out, hitting him in the jaw. Dale reels backward, hand to his face.

It wasn't a hard punch—I'm sure Curtis could do much worse if he wanted—but I'm shocked all the same. Curtis is usually Mr. Control, although there were occasions that winter when I saw him lose it—all related to his sister. The Superman of British snowboarding and his kryptonite.

Dale recovers and rushes at Curtis, knocking him backward onto a table.

Things turned ugly between Dale and Curtis the night before Saskia disappeared, but as far as I could tell, Heather and Saskia were the ones who started it. Curtis and Dale just got dragged into it. I imagine they went their own separate ways after that—like I did—and their friendship never recovered.

Brent and I jump in. Fists fly and poor Brent gets all the air knocked out of him. I try to get Curtis in a choke hold again but he's wise to me now. Heather cowers in a corner, hands in front of her face.

"How do you know my sister's dead?" Curtis says. "Did you kill her?" From the way he's looking at Dale, it's as though he seriously believes he might have.

A familiar heaviness settles over me.

It wasn't Dale. It was me. I killed her.

I wanted to win so badly that I was prepared to go to any length to achieve it. I've played it over and over in my head these last ten years, only to reach the same conclusion every time. My actions caused her death.

What I did sickens me, yet if I were in that same situation again, would I act any differently? I can't say for sure that I would.

Dale crashes into me, jolting me back to the present. I stagger sideways and topple onto a table with him on top of me. Woozy from the whiskey, I'm slow to react. Brent pulls Dale off by the hood of his jacket. There's a ripping sound.

Dale swears and shoves Brent up against the fireplace. "All right, I'm going to ask. Did you sleep with my wife?"

Dale may have lost the Viking look, but he's still acting like one. I hold my breath. *Say no, Brent, even if you did, or he'll smash you.*

"No," Brent says.

Dale narrows his eyes and turns back to Curtis. "As for you, your sister was out of control. I reckon *you* killed her. Admit it. You were sick of her, just like the rest of us."

Curtis lets another punch fly. Dale dodges and Curtis's fist glances off his shoulder. There are little red circles on Curtis's cheeks. I've never seen him lose it like this.

His anger gets me thinking. Maybe Saskia's death wasn't my fault after all. Did he hit her? Is that how she died? It's hard to imagine because he was so protective of her, but maybe he snapped. Everyone has a breaking point. Even Curtis.

Curtis and Dale are ducking and weaving; chairs and glasses crash to the floor.

Heather wraps her head in her hands. "Stop!"

Brent grips Dale's shoulder. "Cool it."

And Dale punches him in the gut. This is turning into an all-out brawl, and I remember only too clearly what happened the last time these guys brawled.

I have to stop this before someone gets hurt, but what do I do? It's not like we can call the police.

Curtis approaches Dale again. Hoping he won't attack me instead, I step in front of him. "Stop."

Curtis's body heaves against mine.

"The Icebreaker," I say. "It's like someone was trying to stir up a fight. Don't give it to them."

Curtis's jaw is clenched, his eyes furious. It's a standoff for a few tense seconds, until he grudgingly nods. With a pointed look at Dale, he returns to his chair. Still muttering, Dale takes his seat. Brent and I sit, too. We straighten clothes and get our breath back.

"We need to discuss who could have written those secrets," I say. "Because whoever it was really knows us."

"Now, hang on—" Brent says.

"I'm not saying it's all true," I say. "I meant—"

Curtis cuts in. "She's right. It seems to me that there are only seven people who could be responsible. One of them has lost the use of her arms and legs; another has been missing for ten years and declared dead. That leaves us five."

The words hang in the air. Nervous looks all around.

"Anyone heard from Odette?" Dale says.

Under the table, I dig my fingernails as hard as I can into my thighs. He's looking at me, so I shake my head. I've deliberately never Googled her; that way I can tell myself she might have made some miracle recovery. Or regained some use of her limbs at least. Because if she hasn't . . .

"I FaceTimed her last week," Curtis says.

My head jerks his way. "You keep in touch?"

"Hardly. Only once or twice since we left here."

I brace myself. "And how is she?"

The sadness in his eyes tells me all I need to know. "Still in a chair.

She can move her arms but only a little. I thought I might go see her before or after the reunion depending on where she's based these days. But she wasn't up to it."

Heather stands. "Why are we just sitting around? I want to get out of here."

She's looking at Dale as though he can magically transport her down fifteen kilometers of ice and rock back to the resort in total darkness.

"We're not going anywhere tonight," he snaps. "Have to wait till morning."

She looks to the rest of us for confirmation.

"Trust me," Curtis says. "If there was a way, I'd be out of here already."

I chime in. "It's way too dangerous to go out there in the dark. There's crevasses everywhere."

Heather sits reluctantly back down. Silence again. Brent empties the last of the whiskey into his glass and knocks it back. I pick up an overturned beer bottle. There's beer all over the table but I'll worry about that later.

Heather grips Dale's hand so tightly her knuckles turn white. "Why would anyone want to do this?"

Nobody seems to want to state the obvious.

"It's about Saskia, isn't it?" I say, fighting to keep my voice steady. "Someone thinks one of us killed her. Maybe they don't know for certain, or they'd go to the police, but they suspect, so they've brought us here to try to flush the killer out."

I hope my guilt doesn't show on my face.

It's okay. Nobody knows what you did.

I don't know what scares me more: the prospect of being found out, or the possibility that Saskia didn't die the way I imagined but at the hands of one of these four.

From the way everyone's looking at each other, they're all wondering the same thing.

Did you kill Saskia?

Unless, of course, *they're* the one who killed her.

Curtis clears his throat. "Look, we don't even know for sure that my sister's dead."

Dale mutters something.

Curtis jumps up. "What did you say?"

Oh shit. Here we go again.

"Let's call it a night," I say as Curtis pads around the table toward Dale. "It's late and we're all on edge. We'll talk about this more in the morning."

Brent cuts Curtis off. "Time to hit the dorms, bro."

Curtis eyes Dale, then turns on his heel, snatches up his bags, and storms out of the restaurant. Something about the slant of his shoulders gets to me. He looks broken all over again. I glance at Brent, nervous about leaving him in here with Dale, then chase after Curtis, grabbing my bags on the way.

"How many dorm rooms were unlocked?" I say as Curtis pushes through another set of double doors.

"Can't remember."

I brace for the lights to go off, but he bashes every switch he passes and they remain on.

"I don't want to have to share with Heather," I say.

I count the dorm doors as he smashes them open. "One, two." The laundry cupboard. "Three, four. Cool. Heather and Dale can share."

Curtis props the last door open with his foot. "Want this one?"

"Thanks." I drag my board bag inside.

He remains in the doorway. There's an angry red mark on his temple. "You need some ice on that," I say.

Curtis tuts and inspects his knuckles. They're red.

"Have you hurt your hand as well?" I say.

"It's fine." He tilts his head back against the door.

"You okay?"

"Yep."

I watch him take deep breaths.

"Is it me or has Dale changed?" he says.

"He does seem pretty wound up." *Just like you*, I could add, but I don't. I change the subject. "So where are you based these days?"

"London, but I travel a lot. You?"

"Still Sheffield."

He straightens. "Night, Milla. I'll be next door. Just like old times."

I feel a pang of something. Not regret, exactly, but a sense of what might have been.

I chase him into the corridor. This is not the best time to ask him, but I have to know. "Are you seeing anyone?"

I try to make it sound casual, but to my ear, it sounds anything but. Does he pick up on it? He turns slowly and I study his face, yet those blue eyes are as unreadable as ever. I think that's one of the things that drew me to him, combined with the barrier he put up after Brent and I got together. He fascinated me. Still does.

"I broke up with someone a few months ago. Silvi Asplund?" He says it like I should recognize the name.

"I don't follow the rankings anymore."

"Norwegian girl. Rode big air." Curtis leans against the wall. "We lasted a few years, but it was off and on. Ex-athletes aren't easy to live with."

"Tell me about it," I say. "Especially failed ones."

His expression softens. "You didn't fail."

I raise my eyebrows.

"You pushed it more than any of us that winter, Milla."

"That's not true."

"I'm not talking about what you could do. I'm talking about the risks you took."

"All of us took risks," I say.

"Yeah, but most of the tricks I did, I'd been doing for years. Same with Saskia and Brent. We'd tried them out on trampolines, then over airbags at summer camps. You were trying them out over ice."

I hadn't looked at it that way. All I saw was that I was the weakest rider in the group and I was playing catch-up.

"Why did you quit?" he asks.

There's a simple answer to that question. *Because of your sister.* And Odette, of course. But mostly his sister. "I did some stuff I shouldn't have done." I swallow. "And I made some poor choices."

So many poor choices.

Curtis studies me intently and suddenly I'm thinking about one choice in particular—a choice I made in this very corridor, ten years ago. A choice between pursuing my dream of becoming a pro snowboarder and acting on an attraction that promised to be a major distraction.

I wonder if he guesses what I'm thinking. He opens his mouth but the double doors swing open and the others head toward us, dragging their bags. Brent looks at us curiously and pushes into one of the dorms. Doors slam as Heather and Dale enter the room next to it.

I'm about to enter my dorm when Curtis says quietly: "You know they never found my sister's body."

I turn to look at him.

He hesitates. "Tell me I'm crazy, but I smelled Saskia's perfume when we opened that ski locker. And in the corridor."

Goose bumps pop up on my arms as I recall the spicy vanilla fragrance. "I smelled it, too," I say weakly. "I thought it was Heather's."

He checks the corridor and lowers his voice. "I've always had my doubts about what happened to her. There were a load of transactions on her credit card after she disappeared."

I stare at him. "What exactly are you saying?"

Curtis's blue eyes look troubled. "I don't know."

"Do you seriously think . . . ?"

He checks the corridor again, almost as though he expects to see her there.

He doesn't seem thrilled about the idea of his sister being alive. Far from it.

He seems worried.

CHAPTER 12

Saskia's hair is blowing all over the place. Lit up by the headlights of the snowcat, she looks like Medusa.

Brent and Curtis touch down beside us. Am I imagining it or are the boys no happier to see her than I am?

She prowls back and forth, seeking attention like a cat that's been shut inside all day. "God, how boring was that?"

Not boring at all, actually. I was enjoying myself, until you turned up.

"I was so bloody cold." She pulls her glove off. "Feel." Her icy fingers reach into my snowboard jacket to my bare neck.

I jerk away. She advances on Brent.

"Fuck off," he says.

The snowcat toots and we pick our way across the rocks toward it. There's a torrent of French from the driver.

"We're the last ones to be rescued," Curtis translates. "There's a family farther down that he has to drive back to the village. He can only fit four passengers. Do we mind sleeping up on the glacier in the dorms so he doesn't have to make another trip? He'll take us up there."

Brent whoops. "We'll be first on the mountain in the morning."

"I hope they have enough rooms for us all," I say.

The driver opens the door behind the cab and we squash onto the bench seat, boards and backpacks piled across our laps. Saskia is crushed up against me, her perfume thick and cloying in the overheated cabin. Who wears perfume when they're snowboarding anyway? Only her.

The machine claws its way up the incline, tipping us backward. Diesel fumes mingle with the perfume and my stomach tightens again.

"Did you see my last seven twenty?" Saskia says. "I nearly went down."

Somehow her presence has brought all the tension back. It's not just me; the boys are quiet, too—or maybe they're just tired. She tries to get them talking about the comp, but they aren't biting. It's snowing now. The flakes glow orange in the headlights as they blow at the windscreen.

At the top, the Panorama building is all lit up. Curtis starts to get out, but the driver waggles his finger and gives him a long spiel—*crevasses* is the only word I catch—and drives us right up to the main entrance.

"I've never been here at night before," Curtis says as we stomp our feet on the mat.

"Me neither," I say.

A woman in an apron waves us down the corridor. I follow the others into the restaurant, noticing how differently they all move: Curtis upright and purposeful; Brent lazy and loose, trousers halfway down his arse; Saskia light on her feet like a dancer.

The woodsmoke stings my eyes, but the blazing fire is a welcome sight. There's only one other group in the restaurant; it's late already. I tug my boots off and stand before the flames, hoping nobody smells my socks.

Black-and-white photos line the fireplace. Climbers in old-fashioned gear strike jaunty poses in front of familiar-shaped peaks. *Mont Blanc, 1951*, reads one. Dangerous enough at the best of times, let alone in crampons tied on with string.

Curtis leans in close to look at a different photo. "Grande Casse. One of my dad's favorites. He was the first person to snowboard the north face, right after Saskia was born. Mum didn't want him to do it."

"I thought she did all that stuff, too," I say.

"She eased off after she had us."

Typical. My mum was the same, leaving a job she loved as manager of a nursing home to have my brother and me. She returned to work part-time once we were old enough but never got her old position back. Why is it always the women who have to give up their dreams? I don't intend to give up anything for anyone.

Saskia joins us, lifting a pair of vintage glacier goggles from their pin and holding them to her face. "What do you think?"

"Careful," Curtis says. "They're an antique."

She sulkily hooks them back, pausing in front of the stuffed stag's head to stroke its nose before joining Brent at the table.

I've finally thawed out enough to unzip my jacket. My hair snags in the zip. "Damn."

"Here, let me." Curtis's warm fingers descend over mine.

He's so close I can hardly breathe. There's a sweet and musky smell that might be his deodorant, or is it his skin? He wriggles the zip and I brace for him to rip hair out—that's how I do it when this happens—but he's really gentle. A lump forms in my throat.

"There you go." Curtis slides my zip down.

I'm burning up, conscious of his sister and Brent watching us, yet Curtis seems in no hurry to move away. He tucks the rest of my hair carefully over my shoulder.

This guy does something to me. It's not just how he looks—it's how he is. His coolly confident exterior makes me want to crack him open and see what's underneath. Deep down I sense he isn't cold at all. There might even be fire.

Stop. I can't go down that path. This winter is make or break. If I don't reach the top three, I'll have to quit and find a real job.

Saskia gives me a curious look as I sit down next to Brent. Every time I see her, I get mad all over again. I'm going to pretend she isn't here.

Brent swigs from a bottle, long legs outstretched. "Can I get you a drink, Milla?"

I groan. "No, I never want to drink again."

He shows me the bottle. It's only Coke.

"Oh," I say. "No, I'm fine with water." I fill a glass from the jug on the table.

"Aren't you going to ask me?" Saskia says.

Brent takes another swig as though he didn't hear her.

That was interesting. He just blanked her. Blatantly. Why? Do he and Saskia have history?

There's surprise in her eyes. She's clearly not used to being ignored. She stands sharply, chair legs screeching against the floorboards. "Fine, I'll get my own."

I hide my smile as she stomps off to the bar. Brent's smiling, too.

I wouldn't normally be this relaxed around such a good-looking guy, but he's so much like Barnsey. Same mannerisms, same accent even. I feel comfortable with him, as though I've known him for years.

The exact opposite of how I feel with Curtis.

"Hey, Sass." Curtis taps my shoulder.

I jerk my head around. "What did you just call me?"

Curtis grins, shamefaced. "Sorry. It's the hair." He offers red wine. "Want some?"

"No, thanks, I'll stick with water. And tomorrow I'm going to dye my hair pink. I'm not joking."

Brent chuckles. "You're in trouble, bro."

Saskia returns with an empty wineglass. Without saying a word, she whips the bottle from Curtis's hand, pours herself a glass, and sits back down.

The aproned woman comes over with plates of *tartiflette*. Gooey, tangy cheese and soft, buttery potato. Now that my stomach has finally settled, I'm starving. I hold my fingers to the flames while I chew.

"How old were you when you started snowboarding, Milla?" Curtis asks.

"Eleven," I say. "On the Sheffield dry slope. I didn't ride snow till I was sixteen. What about you?"

"Five."

"I was three," Saskia says, even though I didn't ask her.

Lucky cow. No wonder she's good.

"Our parents took us all over the world," Curtis says. "The world's mountains anyway. Mum's from California and we still have family there, so we spent some winters in Mammoth."

I know this, but I don't want him to know I've read up on him. "I remember watching your mum and dad in ancient Burton videos, flying down steep Alaskan slopes."

Curtis smiles. "Did you?"

"You had such a cool childhood."

"Sometimes I got sick of moving around so much."

Saskia yawns.

I turn to Brent. "How about you?"

"Ten," Brent says. "But I skateboarded since I was about six. Dad's a builder and he built this skate ramp in our backyard for me and my brother."

His London accent cracks me up.

"We got some sponsors," he adds. "My brother was really good."

"But you prefer snowboarding?" I say.

He grins. "You can go bigger."

"Was last year your first time at the Brits, Milla?" Curtis says.

"Yeah. I entered the year before but I blew my knee before the comp."

Saskia leans forward. "What did you do?"

"My lateral collateral." It seems like a sign of weakness to be admitting it. "But my knee's great now."

I'm not going to tell her how I worked eighty-hour weeks that summer to fund physiotherapy sessions on top of saving for my next season.

"Saskia busted her ACL a few years back," Curtis says.

Her head jerks his way.

That's a pretty major injury. I wait, hoping he'll elaborate.

Maybe he catches the way she's looking at him, because he leans back in his seat. "It's a snakes-and-ladders game, that's how I see it. You just have to hope you climb up higher than you slide."

The other diners have disappeared and the woman who served us hovers in the background. Poor thing looks exhausted. It's a feeling I know well from summers when I used to work the bar until four in the morning and grab a few hours' sleep before I started my day job.

I lower my voice. "I think she wants us to hurry up so she can clock off."

We finish our plates and she can't snatch them up quick enough. She shows us to the dorms along the corridor. We have a room each.

"Hey, Milla," Curtis says quietly as I'm about to enter mine. "If you get cold in the night, you know where to come."

Saskia turns to look at him, a strange expression on her face.

"I think you'll find my bed's warmer than his," Brent says from his doorway.

I dive into my room before my face burns up.

Athletes are physical people. We have all this energy and sometimes there's some left at the end of the day. So it doesn't surprise me that the boys did that. And I like how they did it. There was nothing leery or threatening about it; they simply put out the offer for me to take or leave.

My legs feel shaky as I stand under the shower. It's no big deal to them—they must have girls chasing them all the time—but I've never been propositioned quite so blatantly by two such hot guys.

And you just know that anyone as talented as those two are at snowboarding would be equally talented in bed.

Water rains down on my head. They're such different people. Brent is like a well-worn pair of skate shoes, comfortable and familiar.

And Curtis is next season's snowboard boots. I've never tried or even imagined anything like them before, but if I put them on I sense I'll never want to take them off.

I close my eyes and tilt my face to the spray. I'm still fragile after my last two breakups. The only kind of hookup I can risk this winter is something fun and casual, and there's nothing casual about the way I feel about Curtis.

But I can't get him out of my damn head.

The water pressure in this place is feeble and the shower does little to warm me up. My teeth chatter as I pull my thermals back on. My feet carry me into the corridor. Sensing I'm about to make a terrible mistake, I lift my hand.

But there's an added complication, isn't there? His sister is my greatest rival. Curtis is the last person I can get involved with.

I walk two paces down the corridor.

And knock on Brent's door.

CHAPTER 13

Memories flood back as I stand in the corridor outside Brent's dorm. The door opens and there he is in his Burton thermal underwear, hair damp from the shower, just like last time, only more unsure of himself.

I feel another wave of affection for him. "Can I come in?"

He steps back, dark eyes wary. "Course."

I want to hug him, but I don't want to give him the wrong impression. I want to know how life's been treating him, but it seems too personal to ask.

Brent and I stand there looking at each other. My stomach is still squirming from what Curtis said in the corridor. We smelled Saskia's perfume.

In this very building.

Were we imagining it? God, I hope so.

The floorboards are icy beneath my bare toes. I should have put my socks on.

"It's just as cold in your room as it is in mine," I say. "Look. I can see my breath."

Brent strips the duvet off the lower bunk. "Sit."

I perch on the thin mattress. He sinks down beside me, careful not to touch me, and throws the duvet around our shoulders. We shuffle backward until we're leaning against the wall.

I came here to get Brent's take on what's going on, but now that I'm here, I'm not sure how to start. I hate this distance between us. I don't know how to be with him anymore.

It used to be so easy. I still remember the slow smile that spread across his face ten years ago when he opened the door to me. The way I didn't have to say anything. He simply led me by the hand to his narrow bunk, climbed in after me, and made good on his promise of warming me up.

His tattoo is just visible below the hem of his sleeve, a little faded now. My finger moves to touch it but I catch myself just in time. I notice his watch—a neon-green G-Shock. "Did your Omega break?"

"I sold it on eBay for a fortnight in Breckenridge."

I'm dying to ask him why he stopped competing but I'm scared I won't like the answer, so I attempt small talk, trying to restore the connection we used to have. "Bummer having to pay for your snowboarding now, hey? It's not the cheapest sport."

His smile looks forced. "Yeah, sometimes I think about moving to France. If I could speak more than five words of French, I might."

His London accent is comforting and familiar.

But the way he's looking at me isn't. He's so guarded. Leaning forward, he pulls a whiskey bottle from under the bed and holds it out. Must have nabbed it from the restaurant. "Want some?"

"No, thanks."

He swigs from it. It's so weird to see him drinking like this.

"Are you still modeling?" I ask.

"Nah. Too old."

Enough of the chitchat. The childish part of me longs to ask him if he slept with Heather, but that would make us feel a million times more awkward, so I'll leave it for another time—or press Heather about it again tomorrow.

I take a deep breath. "So who do you think invited us here?"

Brent gives me a sideways glance. "Assuming it's not you or me, you mean?"

"Did you invite me?"

"No."

"Okay. And I didn't invite you."

His dark eyes flash to my face once more. Shit. He really thought I wanted to see him again. Someone used me to lure him here, just like they used Curtis to lure me.

I pull the duvet more tightly around me. "So who was it?"

"My money's on Curtis," Brent says.

"Really?"

"Think about it. He has the funds."

"Come on," I say. "Look how mad he was after the Icebreaker. Don't tell me that was an act. Anyway, why would he wait ten years to do this? It doesn't make sense."

Brent shrugs.

It seems disloyal somehow to share this with him, but I need him to know Curtis isn't behind this. "He isn't even sure Saskia's dead. He freaked me out in the corridor earlier. Said he smelled her perfume."

"He thinks she's still alive?" Brent shakes his head. "Wishful thinking. Bound to bring back the memories, coming here. Poor guy. You saw how close they were, even though she annoyed the hell out of him. That's why I think it's him pulling the strings here."

"Yeah, but here's the thing. I smelled it, too."

Brent looks unconvinced.

I change the subject. "Did you lot all arrive in the function room at the same time?"

"Nah, I was the first one in there. I checked the restaurant and saw it was empty. The function room seemed the next most obvious place to look."

Interesting how he drew that conclusion faster than the rest of us. Is he the one behind this?

I study him, hating myself for suspecting him. "Clever how they separated us from our bags by making us traipse all around. If we'd known to go to the function room, we might have taken them with us."

"Yeah, I know."

His face reveals nothing.

"So talk me through it," I say. "Who came in next?"

"Dale and Heather. Heather was yapping away on her phone and she was well pissed off she had to leave it at the door. Curtis wasn't going to put his phone in the basket but Heather gave him a hard time about it. *If you're keeping yours, I'm keeping mine.*"

There's a knock on the door.

"Come in," Brent calls.

Curtis appears in the doorway. Hope he didn't hear us talking about him.

"Seen Milla?" he says. "Oh."

He's seen me. Damn. Now he thinks there's something going on between me and Brent. A flashback hits me. He did the exact same thing ten years ago when we spent the night up here, ducking his head into Brent's room in the morning, to ask if he knew where I was.

He looks back at me now, just as expressionless as he was then. I want to tell him that this time it's not how it seems.

"I forgot to say earlier," Curtis says. "Lock your door tonight, okay?"

"Sure," I say.

"Night," Brent calls.

Curtis shuts the door. Crap. He thinks I'm spending the night in here.

I force my mind back to the issue at hand. "What if it's not one of us who set it up? Who else could it be?"

Brent turns thoughtful. "Remember that Julien guy?"

"Julien Marre." That's a name I haven't heard in a long time.

Julien was the main suspect in Saskia's disappearance, incriminated by his own graffiti. He was taken in for questioning and later released. Proved he was in a neighboring resort that day, apparently.

"But why would he do this?" I say.

"He was obsessed with her, wasn't he?"

I study him closely. "You're saying he thinks one of us killed her, so he's brought us here to . . . what, avenge her death? Odd that he waited a whole decade to do it."

"But he *was* odd, wasn't he? I heard you thumped him, by the way."

"Who told you that?"

Brent drags his fingers through his wet hair. "Can't remember. Dale, I think."

"How did he know? The only other person who was there was Saskia."

Brent shrugs.

"Yeah, I thumped him. The dickhead." God, I sound just like Saskia.

"Did he hit you back?"

"No. He was on the ground. I hit him pretty hard."

A short laugh from Brent.

But he's got me thinking. *Is* Julien behind this? It is possible. He had issues with most of us at some point that winter. He hated Curtis and Dale; I know that much.

I push the thought aside for now. "Next question. If one of us killed her, who was it?"

Brent's face hardens. "I should think we all had reason to."

"True."

Brent's gaze meets mine. "Do you think I did it?"

Something about the way he asks it makes me shiver. "Of course not," I say.

But as I look into his eyes, I'm not so sure.

CHAPTER 14

TEN YEARS AGO

I float through the air. It's a whiteout, snowflakes and fog merging as one with the white backdrop. I can't see a thing, but I reach down with my back hand, around my back leg, to grasp the heel edge of my board, then bone out my leg as Dale advised. Stalefish.

They've sprayed the top of the pipe red to help us in today's conditions, so I home in on the red line as I return to earth. Kind of like a jumbo coming in to land at night, except I'm landing on vertical ice. I touch down and speed across the flat bottom to take off again.

Days like this are about holding your nerve and having blind faith in yourself. The minute you lose that faith, you slam hard—as several people have done in the last half hour. The pipe really is bulletproof today with no sunshine to soften it.

In this visibility I don't dare to spin, so I'm working on my straight airs. I've been pushing myself extra hard since my disastrous result in the Le Rocher Open. It was a chance to prove myself to my sponsors and I blew it. Now it all hangs on the British Championships. They're being held here this year, which is partly why I picked this resort to train in.

I reach the bottom and let out my breath. *I survived*. Until next time. Adrenaline rushes through me. How is it that courting death can make us feel so alive?

The fog is so thick I can taste it in my throat, damp and cold when I breathe in.

With a grinding of metal against ice, Dale pulls up beside me. I didn't realize he was behind me.

He gives me a thumbs-up. "You nailed that Stalefish."

"Thanks. Surprised you could see." I rode up the tow lift with him earlier and quizzed him about how to tweak it.

"I'm going to grab a drink," Dale says.

"Me, too."

We stand there glugging from our water bottles. Only Dale could make a fluorescent-orange all-in-one look cool. Little beads of snow cling to his dreadlocks.

"What are you working on today?" I ask.

"My Indies," he says.

"Just that?" An Indy—back hand grabbing the toe edge of your board—is the first grab I learned. It's probably the first grab everyone learns.

Dale smiles. "Style is everything."

A skier spins his final hit, landing backward, an impressive feat in this visibility. Saskia looms out of the fog and speeds past, followed closely by a short guy in a green-and-gray camouflage jacket.

"Who's that?" I say, because he's pretty good, whoever he is.

"Julien Marre," Dale says.

French number one. No wonder.

He and Saskia disappear into the fog. She and I haven't spoken since the comp, but it's impossible to avoid her completely in such a tiny resort. She's been behind me in the lift queue a couple of times and I've braced for her to say something, but she hasn't. Does she feel bad about what she did? She shows no sign of remorse.

Someone lands a flip on his outstretched hands and lets out a scream of pain.

"Fucking hell, they're dropping like flies today," Dale says, and runs up the pipe into the whiteout to warn the riders above.

Curtis sits nearby talking to a photographer. Poor woman hasn't picked the best day for a photo shoot. She's all swaddled up against the cold, only her eyes visible.

Dale returns, and I open my mouth to ask him about *my* Indies, but Heather approaches.

"Hi," I say.

Heather gives me a dirty look. She may be a fellow Northerner but so far that's the only thing we have in common. She doesn't seem to like me. She turns to Dale. "Ready to go?"

"Two more runs?" Dale says.

"I'm freezing," she says.

Hardly surprising in that cropped leather jacket. She's come up to watch Dale, presumably. I've yet to see her with a snowboard on. I don't know what she's doing in a ski resort if she doesn't want to ski or snowboard.

"See you later." I pick up my board.

Brent's sitting on the snowbank, chatting with the pretty Japanese girl who came third in the Le Rocher Open. I nod at them and strap my front foot in.

"Thanks for last night," I told Brent when I woke in his bunk up on the glacier two days ago. "Can we keep this between you and me?"

"Sure."

"Will Curtis—"

"I'll tell him not to say anything."

So we played it cool in front of Saskia at breakfast, and anyone watching us could never have guessed what we'd been doing just hours earlier.

Still, I expected the details of our night together to have traveled all around the resort by now. I know what guys are like—especially at his age. But the occasional secret smile he throws in my direction is the only hint of our earlier intimacy. I'm impressed by his discretion. Curtis has apparently kept his mouth shut, too.

I head down to the tow lift. Looks like Heather's gotten her way, because Dale's strapping on his backpack. Poor Dale. But that's the kind of problem you run into by getting involved with someone out here. I don't want to worry about anything this winter except my snowboarding. Eat, sleep, snowboard. That's all I intend to do for the next four months.

Snowflakes blow sideways at me as I wait for the tow. Some of them find their way down my neck. I squirm and tighten the Velcro on my collar.

As the T-bar yanks me upward, Brent throws himself on beside me, wearing his usual dimpled grin despite today's poor conditions.

We've ridden up the pipe tow together a few times since our night together and kept the conversation to snowboarding. There's none of the awkwardness there sometimes is after a one-night thing and he's been nothing but warm and friendly.

His pipe glove curls over mine on the T-bar. "Want to stay over at my place tonight?"

I look at him in surprise. I thought our night on the glacier was a one-off. But actually I do want to stay over. My body aches from how hard I've pushed it and I want to feel his warm hands and mouth on me again.

I hope he doesn't think this is something it's not.

Two hours later, I ring the bell of the little chalet Brent pointed out to me on our way down. And Saskia opens the door.

She stands on the doorstep, barefoot in ultra-skinny jeans, as though debating whether to let me in. In a tight white sweater, she looks delicate, almost frail, and I marvel afresh at the illusion. There's nothing frail about her riding—or her personality.

Curtis appears behind her. "Good timing. I'm about to dish up."

I remove my snow-covered Nikes and follow them inside.

The others are all here, milling between the tiny kitchen and living room. Heather and Dale; Odette and Julien. This is not at all what I expected. Brent and Julien crouch over a laptop. Brent shoots me an apologetic smile and I can see he didn't expect this either, but he's going with it, so I'll do the same.

There's woodsmoke in the air, mixed with onion and garlic. They can't all live here, surely. Socks, gloves, and goggles fight for space on top of the radiator; wet clothing hangs from everything it can be hung from. There are enough snowboards lying around to stock a rental shop, but there are only three pairs of boots by the fire. Curtis's, Brent's, and Dale's, I think. It was awkward enough facing Curtis up on the glacier at breakfast; I don't relish the idea of a repeat.

"Want a beer?" Curtis calls from the kitchen.

"No, just water," I say, going in. "But I'll get it."

He's muttering and cursing at the stove. I search the cupboard for a glass. As I fill it, he barks at me for a wooden spoon, then berates me for getting the wrong one.

Dale laughs when I emerge. "Keep out of there when he's cooking. I do."

"Yeah, Dale, you're washing up," Curtis shouts.

Heather wrinkles her nose. "It smells like something died in here." She lifts an inside-out snowboard sock from the back of a nearby chair. "This yours, Dale?"

He grins. "Yep."

"So gross." She throws it at him.

Dale catches it easily and tosses it into a corner. I like how Heather's not intimidated by him. He's this strapping, imposing-looking guy but she keeps him firmly in his place.

"Hey, Mills," Brent calls. "This Spanish guy's done a sixty-seven-meter rail slide. New world record."

I head over to him. The jacketed figure on the laptop screen jumps onto a metal rail set in the snow and slides smoothly along it.

"Makes it look so easy," Brent says.

"That's the problem with rail slides," I say. "They look so bloody easy until you try them. I still have the dent on my shin from the last one I did."

Saskia joins us and I stiffen. I'm still furious about the Le Rocher Open, but now that time has passed, I'm feeling a strange kind of respect for what she did. Here, finally, is a girl who plays as hard as I do. And from the way I catch her looking at me sometimes, the respect might just be mutual.

We're watching rail slide fails now, wincing and groaning as the riders fold themselves around an assortment of metal rails.

Curtis comes out of the kitchen, arms laden with plates.

"Curtis spent a whole day doing rail slides once," Saskia says. "Paced out the distance and had me telling him how far he went. Didn't get more than about twenty meters."

It's an impressive distance, but Curtis flashes a warning look at her.

She sidles up to him and slides an arm around his waist. "What? Am I giving away your secrets?"

Seeing them side by side like that, I can't decide which of them is better looking.

Curtis elbows her away but he's smiling. "Here you go, Milla." He hands me a plate of pasta. "Grab a seat before they run out."

If he's sore at me for choosing Brent over him, he shows no signs of it, but the flirting has switched off, just like that. And secretly I miss it.

I sink onto the sofa, plate on my lap. And tense as Saskia sits next to me. One by one the others squeeze on, and Saskia shuffles up close. The nail polish on her bare toes is the exact blue of her eyes.

Dale looks from me to Saskia. "They look like twins."

Okay, now I'm definitely dyeing my hair.

Saskia tilts her head my way. Assessing. "We should go for a ride together sometime," she says lightly.

Forks freeze halfway to mouths and the room falls quiet. The nerve of her, asking me in front of everyone. I'm going to throw the offer back in her face and humiliate her.

Except something in her eyes stops me. Could she actually want to hang out?

"Yeah," I say slowly. "Let's do that."

She pulls out her phone. "What's your number?"

Somehow this is a way bigger deal than when Brent asked for it. I think my winter just got a whole lot more interesting.

CHAPTER 15

PRESENT DAY

My dorm smells of dust and damp. But not, to my relief, Saskia's perfume. Brent's probably right: we were imagining it. It's hardly wishful thinking though—not on my part, at least. More like a guilty conscience.

I turn the catch and tug the door to make sure it's really locked. Whoever left these dorm rooms open for us didn't leave us keys. I hate that we can only lock these doors from the inside. Anyone could have sneaked in while I was talking to Brent. Feeling slightly ridiculous, I check the wardrobe, then the bathroom—behind the shower curtain even—to make sure nobody's hiding there.

Satisfied I'm alone, I sit on the narrow bunk bed. I can't decide which is more terrifying: the notion that Saskia is in the building, alive and well, or the thought of Brent or one of the others having murdered her. The look in Brent's eyes just now really spooked me. The darkness there.

Now that I have a moment, I want to puzzle out the secrets in the Icebreaker. Is there any truth in them? Someone seems to think so, or why would they have gone to all that trouble?

I scan the dorm for a pen, but this is a hostel, not a hotel, and there isn't a pen or a desk or even a chair. I'm lost without my phone. I can't remember the last time I had to physically write something. Usually I just take pictures. I'll be so mad if I don't get my phone back.

I dig around in my backpack. Nothing. The tiny window catches my eye. I huff my breath on it until it's fogged over. Perfect.

The glass is icy against my fingertip. I write our names: *Milla, Curtis, Brent, Heather, Dale.* I'm going to let myself temporarily off the hook and pretend Saskia's death wasn't my fault. Let's say that all the secrets are true and each of us did one thing only.

So one of my friends is a murderer. I glance at the door to check it's locked.

Okay, I need to be objective about this. The first two secrets are easy. Assuming Brent is hetero, and I'm pretty certain he is, the two people who slept with him must be me and Heather. I write *slept with Brent* after our names. Better not let Dale see this.

Strange how sore he was about his wife's alleged cheating. You'd think it happened yesterday instead of a decade ago—before they were married, no less. Still, in a way I get it. Being back here with this group, it feels weirdly as though no time at all has passed.

Anyway, that leaves the three guys. One of them slept with Saskia, one of them knows where she is, and one of them killed her. This reminds me of a Sudoku. And I was never any good at Sudoku—especially not after I've been drinking. The food has soaked up some of the whiskey but not nearly enough.

Okay, assuming Curtis didn't sleep with his own sister, either Dale or Brent must have slept with her. Dale and Heather got together in the second week of the season, so Brent, maybe? He'd had a bit of a thing for her, apparently, the season before I met him. But I asked him back then if he'd slept with her and he vehemently denied it. And it kills me to think of the two of them together. Yeah, she was strikingly beautiful, but she was my archrival.

Dale, then? Saskia might have slept with him just to see if she could steal him from Heather. I chew my lip and write *slept with Saskia* beside Dale's name.

According to the cards, that means either Brent or Curtis killed her and the other one knows where she is.

I think of how Brent was in bed with me.

"You don't have to be that gentle," I told him more than once. "I won't break."

He's just not violent. The only person he's a danger to is himself.

I chew my lip some more, thinking back to the morning of the British Championships. Curtis didn't show at the pipe until a few minutes before his heat. He'd been up on the glacier with Brent and Heather, looking for Saskia, apparently, but what he said didn't make sense.

My fingertip settles on Curtis's name. *Killed Saskia,* I write. I'm going to wipe this off quick in a minute because I would hate him to see. What about what he said in the corridor? It could be a clever lie to throw me off his scent.

So Brent *knows where Saskia is.* Why would Brent know? Did he see Curtis kill her? Did he help Curtis hide her body? Where? They didn't have a car out there, so I don't see how they could have gotten her out of the resort. Which means she must still be here. Somewhere on the mountain.

Goose bumps come up on my arms once again. There are a lot of things about Saskia's last hours that don't add up. I for one never told the full story, and I sense I'm not alone in that.

I stare at what I've written. The letters are running. Water trickles down the glass like tears.

So many assumptions. Have I got it right? This isn't about how we are now. It's about how we were back then. I close my eyes and try to remember.

CHAPTER 16

TEN YEARS AGO

I wake in Brent's bed with his strong, lean frame curled around my back. I'm wearing one of his Burton T-shirts and it smells of him.

I roll over. It's so warm at his place. The radiator beside the bed cranked out heat all night and all he has on is a pair of Calvin Klein boxer shorts. The brands Brent used to model for have been quick to sponsor him, and I wonder if he has to pay for anything right now.

I trace my finger across the packed, tight muscles of his chest. God, that body. An athlete in his prime.

Brent's dark eyes open and he smiles lazily. "Morning."

I continue my exploration, down his taut stomach. "You have the most gorgeous skin." My fingers look so pale against it.

He reaches to the bedside table for his watch, a chunky metal Omega. There's a one-page advert in the *Sunday Times* supplement of him pulling some huge Backside Air wearing it. The retail price is probably more than my entire season will cost.

"What time is it?" I say.

"Eight."

The lifts open at eight thirty, and I'd normally be getting ready for riding by now, but we didn't get to bed till after midnight, sneaking up here once most of the others had gone. I strain my ears for sounds from the kitchen. Is Curtis up?

Brent straps his watch on and I see the tattoo on his forearm again. *Go big or go home.* I touch the letters. "I love this."

"It's to remind me who I am. I never want to get old and boring."

"I can't imagine you ever getting old and boring. You'll still be doing airs when you're eighty. With your walker."

He laughs and pulls me close. I should get up, but it's so warm here in his bed. I snuggle up against him.

He strokes my hair. "Ever done any flips?"

"Not deliberately."

"Do you want to?"

"I have to." I've been aware for some time that I can only go so far with straight airs and spins. To climb higher up the rankings, I need to add some flips to my pipe routine. Saskia can do McTwists.

"I'll teach you," Brent says.

"Cool."

"I'll spot you on the trampoline later if you want."

"Wait—there's a trampoline here?"

"Yeah, at the gym."

"Shit, how did I not know that? I bet Saskia uses it all the time."

"Yep."

I groan into his chest. "I haven't been on a trampoline for years. I did gymnastics until I was eleven. I used to be able to do backflips."

"Should have kept it up."

"Yeah, tell me about it. My parents couldn't afford it." They put all they had into my brother's rugby coaching. It paid off—Jake plays for the Sheffield Eagles—but I still feel stung.

When I was fourteen I got a Saturday job at the local dry slope, so I switched to snowboarding because I could ride for free. I got where I am without help from anyone. It's part of what drives me. My way of giving Dad the finger.

Brent's hand slips under the hem of my T-shirt to my hip. "We'd better get going. Unless . . . ?"

"Will you have any energy left for training?" But my body is already responding.

He grins. "You're talking to the face of Smash, remember?"

My phone chimes with a text.

"I'd better get that," I say. "My brother's having knee surgery this week."

I delve into my backpack for my phone, but the message isn't from my brother. It's from Saskia.

I've ordered you a coffee. See you at the cable car for the first lift up?

Snowboarding with Saskia, or bed with Brent? The decision is easy. I scramble out of bed. "Sorry, I forgot I'm supposed to meet Saskia."

"Saskia?" There's an edge in his voice.

I pull on my clothes. "You have a problem with her, don't you? Is she like an ex or something?" He's shaking his head. "But you slept with her?"

"No."

The vehemence of his answer startles me. She clearly stirs strong emotions in him but I can't work out why. He's dressing too, now.

"I won't have time for breakfast," I say. "Do you have any Smash handy?"

Brent gestures to the crate in the corner. "Help yourself."

"Thanks. See you on the mountain."

"Sure."

I glug it down, wincing at the taste as I hurry out. It's snowed overnight, and six fluffy inches cover the pavement. Cars crawl down the main street, snow chains jingling like sleigh bells. I notice the decorations in the shop windows, the lights strung overhead. And realize suddenly that it's Christmas Eve. I always lose track of time during my winters. The riding is all that matters.

Back at my tiny apartment, I throw on my snowboard gear, stuff a few muesli bars into my jacket pocket, and hurry out again. It crosses my mind that Saskia might have spiked my coffee, but I would taste it and she must realize I'm not that stupid.

Nerves flit in my stomach as I jog down the street with my snowboard under my arm toward the cable car station. I feel strangely like I'm going on a date. Will it be just me and her?

The sun's rays are slanting over the summits, tinting the slopes orange. Saskia is sitting on the top rail of the wooden fence, swinging her boots, with a cup in either hand. I hang back. Do I kiss her, hug her, or what? Why am I so nervous?

She jumps up and settles for a single kiss, lips warm on my cheek in the freezing morning air. Her perfume fills my nose, sweet and strong.

"Here." She hands me a cup.

"Is there vodka in it?" I say.

She laughs and lifts her snowboard from the snow. "Let's go."

The cable car speeds up the mountainside. Saskia and I stand at the Plexiglas, elbows touching as we sip our coffees.

"What perfume is that anyway?" I say.

"Tom Ford Black Orchid. Do you like it?"

I hesitate. It's heavy and exotic, the sort of smell you either love or hate. Rather like Saskia herself. "I'm not sure."

The footprints of a small animal streak the slope below—a snow hare or maybe a stoat. Fir trees droop with the weight of fresh snow. It's deeper higher up.

"Want to go up to the glacier?" Saskia says. "Get some freshies?"

So we jump in the bubble. I don't know if it's the coffee-and-Smash combo or the prospect of us being friends, but I'm buzzing.

You know when you're in an airplane and you look down into a sea of clouds? That's what it looks like from the top of the glacier tow lift today. And what it feels like too, when we ride down. Floating over puffy white clouds.

Back at the bottom of the tow lift, Saskia nods at my snowboard, the Magic logo mostly obscured by snow. "So is it magic?"

"Yeah," I say. "It actually is. Best board I've ever ridden."

"Want to swap boards for a run?"

The thought of my board in her hands makes me shudder. It's my baby. But I can't think of a reason to refuse, so we swap and I rub snow from the nose of hers to see the spec. A Domina Spin 154. Three centimeters shorter than I usually ride. Which makes sense because she's lighter than me. I make a note to lean back more in the powder.

Side by side we speed down, carving out huge turns that spray powder into the air. A snowboard cuts through this kind of snow like a knife through softened butter, but the pleasure is marred by the sight of my board under her feet.

Snow flies into my face as we slap palms at the bottom. I'm relieved to get my board back. We head up the tow lift again.

"Follow me!" she shouts at the top.

I chase her down the other side of the mountain, where I haven't been yet. Powder flies up from her turns, coating my lips and cheeks. We streak downward, jumping and spinning off wind lips. I take a couple of bad wipeouts, but it doesn't hurt nearly as much as falling on the ice of the half-pipe, and I feel invincible.

On the hillside below the pipe later, I spot a cliff and line myself up to jump it. Saskia blasts off after me, landing farther down the slope. Damn.

"Let's do that again," I say.

Rather than riding all the way down to the lift, I whip my board off and hike back up. Saskia puffs uphill behind me. Gasping for breath, I strap my board on again. This time I straight-line to make sure I go farther than she did. She jumps after me, and goes farther still. I remove my board to try again.

We hike higher and higher. This is getting dangerous. I'm already going bigger than I've ever gone.

After another bone-jolting impact, Saskia lands beside me, a fraction farther down the slope.

"Hey!" shouts a voice. Curtis waves from the plateau above. "What are you doing down there? The pipe's epic today."

Saskia and I look at each other, sweaty and breathless.

"Shall we go?" she says.

My annoyance at Curtis's interruption is tinged with relief. If it weren't for him, I can't say how far we would have gone.

If either of us would have ever stopped.

CHAPTER 17

PRESENT DAY

I lie shivering in my narrow bunk. The sheets feel cold and icy. I have two duvets over me but it's not enough. I need another. There was a whole stack of them in the laundry cupboard, but I don't want to go out there to get one.

Questions swim around and around in my head. Who brought us here and why? Did one of my friends murder Saskia? Or is Curtis right, and she's alive and well somewhere in this very building?

A dozen times I've climbed out of bed to check the catch on my door. Without my phone I have no idea what time it is, but it feels like I've been lying here for hours. My last watch broke after I wore it in the gym's Jacuzzi, and I never got around to replacing it—there are clocks all over the gym, and anywhere else I check my phone.

I can't sleep. I'm too cold. I place the pillow over my chest as an extra layer, but it's no good. I'll have to brave the corridor and get another duvet. My dorm is pitch-dark. I grope my way across the floorboards to the light switch. Here it is. Then out into the dark corridor, where I hit the light, too.

The corridor is empty. I let out my breath a little. I don't know what I expected to see. It's the middle of the night. Okay, I'm going to do this as fast as possible. I pass Curtis's door, reach the laundry cupboard, and stretch my hand out. And freeze. Someone's in there. A female voice. Heather. And a male one. But who?

I put my ear to the door, poised to run if I hear them coming out. The rumbling male tone is too quiet for me to tell. It can't be Dale—she'd talk to him in bed, surely. Brent or Curtis, then? Is it Brent? And they're talking about the Icebreaker?

But it could be someone else—Julien. Or some psycho who has brought us here for reasons I can't imagine. My heart pounds. I want to dive back into the safety of my room but Heather's voice raises, like she's upset. Is he threatening her? My palm tenses instinctively against the door. Whatever my feelings for Heather, she's a fellow female.

I press my ear closer to the door. And the light in the corridor clicks off. *Shit.*

As I blink in the darkness, a hand clamps over my mouth. Strong arms grip me, whisk me off the ground, and yank me backward down the corridor. I react instinctively, rolling my right shoulder and punching hard with my right fist under my left armpit.

A male grunt. The arms release me but I'm off balance. I stagger back farther and tumble sideways to the floor on top of him, totally disoriented now. A door clicks closed behind us. I scramble off him, whoever he is, and fumble for a light switch. Here.

The light comes on. Curtis sits there, clutching his chest. We're in his dorm.

"What the fuck were you doing?" I whisper.

He can't speak. He's trying to draw breath.

My heart is still hammering away. God, that was scary.

Curtis stares at me like he can't get over how hard I hit him. "You looked like . . . you were going to open the door," he croaks. "And I didn't want . . . them to know anyone had seen them."

"I wasn't bloody going to. I was trying to work out if it was you or Brent. Or someone else."

"It's Brent."

"Are you sure?"

"I saw them go in there."

Panic over. It wasn't a scary psycho. It was only Brent.

I try to calm my breathing. "What are they doing in there?"

"Beats me."

"Are they having an affair?"

Curtis manages a smile. "I have no idea."

I'm about to go back out to try to hear what they're saying, but there's a click and light floods in under Curtis's door. Curtis puts his finger to his lips. Doors close.

"They've gone," I say.

Curtis struggles to his feet. He's wearing his thermals, a long-sleeved black top in a stretchy fabric that clings to his broad shoulders and tight-fitting black long johns. The red mark on his temple has come right up.

I'm wearing my long-sleeved thermals too, and now that my shock has subsided, I'm shivering again. I wrap my arms around my chest.

He peels a duvet from his bunk and hands it to me.

"Thanks." I drape it around my back.

He stands close, his eyes dark. "I couldn't sleep."

"Me neither."

His room smells of freshly washed laundry, or maybe it's his thermals.

He strokes the back of his neck up and down, looking at my mouth. When he realizes what he's doing, he snatches his hand away, pulls a second duvet off his bunk, and slings it around his shoulders. "What's the story with you and Brent anyway?"

Hope flares. "There's no story. We haven't seen each other for ten years."

He sinks to the mattress. I perch beside him, a careful distance away.

As I've done so many times before, I imagine what might have happened if I'd made a different choice that night. I picture myself as I was back then: Daredevil Milla, super focused and super fit. Just as alone in the world as I am right now, but not nearly as bothered by it. Hardly aware of it even. Hopeful and excited about a future of contests and podiums.

The young Curtis wasn't the player I initially took him for and remained single for most of that winter, focusing instead on his snowboarding. Jacinta Lee—an Aussie pipe rider—was the only girl I saw him hook up with, and that didn't last long.

How would he and I have been together? I suspect the season would have had a very different outcome. Yet it wasn't what I wanted at the time. Curtis is a full-on sort of guy—I saw how he was with Jacinta—and there's no way I could have combined a serious relationship with serious training.

Anyway, what's done is done. But what about now? Are we too scarred by the past to have a future? I catch myself. What am I thinking? Ten years have passed. I don't even know him anymore.

He's looking at my hair. "So you went back to blond?"

"What? Oh. Yeah." I suppose I must remind him of his sister, just as he reminds me of her.

I've always wondered how the loss affected him. From his behavior earlier, there's clearly a lot of emotion there, but does he miss her? Does it stab him in the heart every time he hears her name? Or was it secretly a relief—a huge burden lifted? His life must be so much simpler without her around.

"Can I ask something?" I say. "Why did you stop competing?"

"I was facing a shoulder reconstruction if I kept going." He looks away. "But mainly it was for my mum. I wanted to be around a bit more. And you know. In the mountains, anything can happen. She couldn't have handled losing me as well."

I swallow, wishing I hadn't asked. "It must have been so hard on your parents."

"It tore my family apart," he says quietly. "It's all Mum can talk about, all she can think of. Dad battled for years to have Saskia declared dead. Thought it would help Mum move on. It takes seven years normally to be deemed dead in absentia, but Mum wouldn't have it. Fought it in court, insisting she was still alive. Pointed to the credit card transactions. It got dragged out till last month." His voice cracks. "Mum didn't take it well."

"I'm so sorry."

"She's not convinced it was an accident. There's no proof that Saskia was even on the mountain that day."

"But Brent and Heather saw her up there."

"They *said* they saw her." Curtis searches my face. "Ten years ago I asked you something and I sensed you weren't being entirely honest with me."

I tense.

"I'm going to ask you again." His gaze burns into me and I try my hardest not to flinch. "Do you know where my sister is?"

It's okay—he's not asking the right question. "No."

"Do you think she's still alive?"

"I'm sorry, but I don't." I watch for him to slump a little, but he gives nothing away.

"So what do you think happened to her?"

It's a good sign that he's asking me this, isn't it? It means I guessed wrong earlier and he's not the one who killed her.

Or is he continuing his act to throw me off his scent?

"I see three possibilities," I say carefully. "She had an accident, someone killed her, or she committed suicide."

Pain furrows his face. "But why would she do that?"

I swallow. "I don't know. Either way, I think she's still up here, under the ice."

Curtis studies me for a long moment. "I like to think I can read you, Milla."

"Saskia always could."

His lips quirk. "Could she?"

"But I could never read her. Or you."

His smile widens. "Hey, I said I could read you. I didn't say I under-stand you."

I think he's talking about me choosing Brent over him. To my relief, he never asked me why, and I've never explained, because explaining would mean admitting what I felt for him.

And still feel. That smile gives me jitters in my stomach. It makes me want to cast the duvet aside and climb astride his lap. Except I have no idea where I stand with him.

Especially not now that we have the secrets from the Icebreaker hanging over us.

He seems a lot calmer than he was this evening, so I'm going to ask him about them. He must have been thinking about them. Unless he wrote them, that is. "Are you taking the Icebreaker seriously?"

His demeanor changes. "Someone's certainly gone to a lot of effort."

"But who?"

"God, this bunk is uncomfortable." He lifts his pillow and stuffs it behind his back. "I don't know. But I know this. Whoever killed Saskia—if someone killed her—isn't responsible for the Icebreaker."

It makes sense. If they killed her, they would hardly want to adver-tise it.

He drums his fingers on the mattress. "But why would someone do this? Summon us all here, strand us, and force us to revisit that winter. That's what I'm trying to figure out."

"To bring the killer to justice, why else?" Of course, the obvious con-clusion is Curtis set it up, like Brent said. His family is desperate to know what happened to her, plus they have the financial means to do it.

"What about blackmail?" he says, adjusting the pillow behind his back. "Someone suspects one of us killed her and they're trying to get money out of us."

"Okay . . . I hadn't thought of that." My feet are freezing. I bring my knees up to my chest so I can tuck them under the duvet.

And realize Curtis's blue eyes watch my every move.

"You think I set this up," I say.

He smiles to soften the accusation. "Or Brent."

Here I am in bed with him, the very scenario I've fantasized about since I accepted the invitation to come here, but the Icebreaker has zapped all potential for romance.

"At least you don't think I killed her," I say.

His face hardens. "If anyone killed her, I reckon it was Dale or Heather. Or they did it together."

I nudge him gently to lighten the accusation I'm about to fling back. "And here I was thinking *you'd* killed her." If I'm telling him that, it must mean I trust him, mustn't it? I hope he doesn't take that the wrong way.

Curtis laughs a hollow sort of laugh. "This has been the weirdest night."

Do I? Trust him? I'm not sure.

His laughter dies. He glances down at his left hand and jerks it off the mattress as if he's been burned.

"Milla?" His voice is strangled. "Did you come in here earlier?"

"What? No. Well, when we explored earlier, I might have—"

He's staring down at the bed where his hand was. I realize what he's looking at. Puzzled, I reach for it.

"*No!* Don't touch it!"

I withdraw my hand. There, on the top section of the mattress where the pillow would have been, is a hunk of long hair, neatly snipped. White blond.

A wave of cold passes over me. Curtis lowers his head to study it, getting as close as he can without touching it. And looks up at me with haunted eyes.

"It's not mine." My voice shakes. "It's too pale."

Is someone messing with his head some more?

Or is he right? Could she actually be out there? But why not just announce her presence if so, especially to the brother she hasn't seen in so long? My heart races. The idea that I might open a door and see her standing behind it is utterly terrifying.

I try to think. "Nobody could have known you'd pick this dorm."

Or is there hair under all our pillows? I gulp and make a mental note to check mine when I return to my room.

Curtis is staring at the hair with horrified fascination.

"Did you leave your dorm at any point?" I say.

"Um. Once. No, twice." He's struggling to get words out. "I went downstairs to check the bubble. Yeah. To see if anyone was around. And when I heard the voices. Brent."

He's hardly coherent. There's the time he knocked on Brent's door too, when I was in there, but he's forgotten about that.

If someone's trying to make him crack, so far they're doing a pretty good job.

CHAPTER 18

TEN YEARS AGO

Brent and I sit side by side on the carpet at his place. Seven of us are crammed in front of the telly to watch the new Burton DVD. The fire crackles, the heat of the flames blistering against my forehead. It's New Year's Eve, but with perfect riding conditions and more snow on the way, we elected to have a quiet one.

Everyone cheers as Brent's name flashes up on the screen. Jay-Z's "Young Forever" starts playing. And there's Brent, tanking toward one of the biggest jumps I've ever seen. He flies through the air in a huge 720. And stomps the landing.

I flash him a smile and he presses his knee subtly against mine. My occasional nights in his bed are our little secret still. Nobody except Curtis knows about us, though Saskia suspects. She asked me about him the other day—asked if we were seeing each other. I denied it. I'm not sure why but I don't want her to know about our nights together. It's not like Brent and I are together or anything.

I look over at her and she's watching us. I move my leg away.

On the sofa, Curtis and Odette are side by side, laughing about something. The two of them seem to get on really well. Odette had a bad fall yesterday and she has an ice pack clamped around her wrist.

The doorbell rings.

Dale jumps up. "I'll get it."

He's wearing bright purple, heavily ripped jeans that make my hair, dyed pink the other night in a dodgy kitchen-sink job, seem subdued in comparison. My towel ended up pinker than my hair, but at least nobody else will confuse me with Saskia. Three times people have mistaken me for her now, and it pisses me off.

Dale returns with Heather in tow. She wrinkles her nose at his jeans. She's wearing her tight black dress and kinky boots. Must have just finished work. Brent's eyes follow her across the room; Julien's, too. Curtis keeps watching TV, apparently immune. I shuffle closer to the fire to make room for Heather and Dale on the carpet.

On the screen Brent launches off jump after jump.

"Where's that?" I say.

"New Zealand," Brent says. "Snow Park last August. It was epic. Burton paid for me and Curtis to fly out there."

"Lucky bastards," I say. "Some of us were working. How come you compete at half-pipe anyway? You're so good at jumps you could compete at big air."

Brent doesn't answer.

"He wants to go to the Olympics," Curtis says, getting up to poke the fire.

Brent flushes. He actually does.

Everyone laughs. Everyone except me. Big air isn't an Olympic event. Not yet anyway. Even half-pipe hasn't featured for long—just the last few Olympics.

"Why are you laughing?" I say. "It's fair enough. Doesn't everyone want to go to the Olympics?"

"*I* don't," Dale says.

"Why not?"

Dale snorts. "Corrupt as hell. I'm not playing their game."

I look at Curtis. "Do you want to go?"

"Yeah, sure," Curtis says.

"We went there already," Saskia says.

"What?" I splutter.

"As spectators," Curtis clarifies. "Nagano in 'ninety-eight. Our parents took us."

"Wow," I say. "The first-ever half-pipe event. That must have been amazing."

"It *was* pretty cool." Curtis tosses another log onto the fire, prompting another round of hissing and crackling.

I hold his gaze sometimes, hoping to make him look at me the way he used to, though he never does.

"I watched it on TV," Brent says. "I was fully into skateboarding and I said, 'Right—that's going to be me in ten years' time.' I didn't know the Olympics only runs every four years."

Dale snorts again.

"Are you aiming for the next one?" I say.

Brent smiles awkwardly. So these next few years are just as important for him as they are for me. I have Olympic dreams myself, but I need to climb farther up the UK rankings before I dare voice them.

"How do you get a place there anyway?" I say.

"You have to do the FIS world cups," Curtis says. "To get enough points."

"Bloody FIS," Dale says. "I'd choose the X Games over the Olympics anytime."

The X Games are invite only; I know that much. Curtis has been—he competed last year—but Dale hasn't. It must be a sore spot for Dale.

"Shhh!" Julien points to the TV. His name appears on the screen.

But Dale is still ranting about the FIS—the International Ski Federation.

Julien hunts for the remote with a pained expression. I bite my lip so I don't laugh. And see Saskia doing the same. Her eye catches mine and I clamp my hand over my mouth.

Julien nudges Curtis. "Look."

A smothered sound escapes from behind my hand. I lower my head and run from the room. Saskia follows, and we stand in the tiny kitchen, laughing helplessly.

"Poor Julien," I say.

"Wanker," she says.

We laugh some more. I find it impossible not to like her. And this is how I like her best.

She spots the cask wine on the counter and empties her wineglass into Curtis's basil plant. "Ugh. No wonder this tastes like shit." She pulls a Kronenbourg from the fridge. "Want one?"

"I prefer vodka," I say. "But go on, then. Seeing as it's New Year's."

Bottles in hand, we sit on the counter, close enough that I can smell her perfume. This is the first time I've drunk since the Le Rocher Open.

Pans are piled high in the sink. Brent was supposed to wash up but I suspect he won't. The boys had a full-blown shouting match on Christmas Day after Curtis cooked a turkey, and Heather refuses to stay over because the place is in such a state, so Dale has to stay at hers.

Saskia touches my hair. "I love the color."

"Thanks. I still get a shock when I see myself in the mirror."

She twirls a long pink strand around her finger. "I might have to dye mine."

I give her a sharp look. She laughs, and I realize she was joking.

"Want to come over to mine on Tuesday night?" she says. "We'll have a girls' night."

"Yeah, sure."

"I'll text you the address."

Julien enters the kitchen, remote in hand. "You missed my section."

"Did we?" Saskia says innocently.

Up close, he has the worst case of panda eyes I've ever seen. His nose and cheeks are brown, his eye area white and freckly. He's shorter than Saskia and a fair bit shorter than me, and looks like he's about fourteen, although he's actually twenty-two, according to Brent.

"I rewind it for you, okay?" He tugs her off the counter and tows her back into the living room.

Saskia looks over her shoulder at me, blue eyes sparkling with mischief, and raises her hand to her forehead. *Dickhead.*

Brent slips in as they leave. "Are you staying over tonight?"

"I hope so," I say. "I drank three cans of Smash today and I won't be able to sleep for hours."

Brent's eyes darken. "Fine with me."

It may taste like shit but it seemed to help my riding that day, so I swapped him a box of muesli bars for a crate of Smash and I've drunk half of them already.

He leans in to kiss me but a sound behind us makes us pull apart.

Saskia gives us a curious look and lifts her beer from the counter. "I forgot this."

I still haven't learned if she and Brent have history. As soon as the door shuts behind her, I open my mouth to ask him, but Heather breezes in.

She takes a bottle from the freezer—champagne—and looks at Brent with doe eyes. "My manager gave me this. Could you open it?"

I want to laugh. She must open all kinds of bottles at work every night, yet she asks Brent as though she thinks it will give him personal satisfaction—make him feel more of a man or something.

I reach for it. I'll open it myself and spoil her fun. Except Brent is too fast, taking it from her and opening it capably over the sink. I swear I see him standing a little taller as he hands it back. I watch him watch her hunt for glasses. Not jealous exactly. More . . . curious? Heather brings out a side of him that someone like me never would. I'd rather die than ask someone to help me, guys especially—it's a sign of weakness—yet here's Heather deliberately making herself look weak and somehow putting Brent under her spell in the process.

Until Dale comes in, breaking the moment.

Brent and I return to our patch on the carpet. Saskia and Julien have squashed back on the sofa next to Curtis and Odette, who are deep in conversation. Is Curtis interested in her? I don't see any signs of flirting, but my encounter with Heather has shown me how little I understand about men.

"Have you ever tried a Haakon flip?" Odette asks.

"No," Curtis says. "Have you?"

"Haakon flips?" Julien says. "Zey are so *easy*."

Odette rolls her eyes but doesn't comment.

"I do zem all zee time," Julien adds.

Saskia pulls the throw from the back of the sofa and drapes it over their laps, and Julien seems to forget what he was about to say. Thank God for that.

Dale hands out glasses of champagne. "Anyone hear what the weather's doing?"

"It's going to dump tonight," Curtis says.

"Awesome," Dale says.

"Oh, zis is nothing," Julien says. "You should 'ave been here last winter."

Everyone rolls their eyes this time. Someone shut this guy up, please.

Julien opens his mouth again. And closes it. Saskia is pressed up next to him, with her right hand below the blanket. She's not . . . Is she?

I catch the movement of her arm.

She is.

Right there in the middle of the room. The nerve of her. The others are glued to the telly and nobody except me has noticed. I can't decide whether to be shocked or impressed. This girl is shameless.

Her eyes roam the room and lock onto mine. A tiny smile tugs at her lips.

My insides twist, though I can't work out why.

CHAPTER 19

PRESENT DAY

When I wake in my chilly, damp dorm, my eyes go first to the door to check it's still locked, then around the room to make sure nobody else is in here. Just in case, I scramble out of bed to check the bathroom. My limbs are stiff with cold.

Glad I won't be spending another night in this place, I pull on every sweater I packed, zip my snowboard jacket over the top, and cross the room to the window.

Blue sky; pristine white powder. A familiar excitement stirs, despite my lack of sleep. In the daylight, things don't seem so bad. Whether I find my phone or not, I'm going to get out of here today. If the cable car's not running, it's no big deal—we can snowboard down. Either way, I hope I get the chance to carve up some of that powder before we leave.

The corridor smells of stale woodsmoke. Curtis is in the kitchen, crouched in front of the impressive-looking coffee machine, wearing the dark jeans he had on yesterday and a high-tech purple Sparks fleece with zips everywhere. The mark on his temple has turned purple, too. I want to tell him to put ice on it, because it looks sore, but I'm guessing he'd rather not be reminded of it.

"What's the time?" I ask.

He checks his watch. "Seven twenty."

"It's so weird not knowing what time it is."

The coffee machine peeps. Curtis swears.

"Is it acting up?" I say.

"It's all right. I'm on it."

"Still no staff?"

"No." Curtis presses more buttons. It peeps again and he swears some more.

"You're cheery this morning. Did you get some sleep?"

"Not much."

I peer over his shoulder. "It's run out of beans."

"How do you know?"

"Brains." More like the fact that I've worked at half the cafés in Sheffield.

He turns, furious. I didn't realize he was so wound up or I wouldn't have teased him like that. I busy myself searching for coffee beans. I'm used to dealing with large and cranky males and know enough to keep my mouth shut.

Curtis always had to be in control of everything, so it makes sense that he's finding this hard. The perfume and that hunk of hair in his bed have really gotten to him.

Or is there a more sinister reason for his anger? He killed his sister and he's scared of being found out. Then again, he could be the mastermind behind this, the one who brought us here to solve the mystery of his sister's disappearance. His previous affection for me has turned to hate and what I saw just then was his mask slipping.

I check the cupboard above the sink.

"Sorry," he mutters. "I just want a damn coffee."

I lift down a huge jar of beans. "Here we go. Cappuccino okay?"

"I'll do it." He tries to take it.

"I've used this kind of machine before."

"I was handling it."

I should probably back down but I hate backing down. "You won't know how."

He raises his eyebrow and I hold my breath, aware I might be pushing my luck. It's a standoff. Until he grudgingly steps aside. Careful not to look in his direction, I open the compartment on top of the machine, but I can't get the bloody coffee jar open.

Curtis takes it from me and opens it. "Muscles." He's fighting a smile.

Damn. I turn my back to hide *my* smile. The machine whirrs into action and the kitchen fills with the smell of freshly ground coffee.

"Did you make one earlier?" he says.

"No. Why?"

"When I came in here, I thought I could smell it."

I can tell what he's thinking. His sister was a real coffee fiend. I hand him his cappuccino. "Must be one of the others. Any sign of the phones?"

"No. Look, don't tell the others about the hair—"

He breaks off as Brent shuffles in, hair sticking up and a crease down his cheek from his pillow. "Mornin'."

Do I hug him or not? Brent doesn't seem to know either. In the end, we do, but it's stiff and awkward.

"Coffee?" Curtis asks.

"Yeah, bro."

I turn to the machine before we get into another argument about it.

The three of us sit on the counter, sipping our drinks in silence. God, the tension in this room. Even Brent seems to feel it. His dark eyes have a haunted look that I've never seen before. Natural enough, I guess, after the events of yesterday.

Or is Curtis right? Is Brent feeling the strain because he's blackmailing Dale and Heather? If he is, why are Curtis and I here? Just for show, or does Brent plan to blackmail us, too?

I shift uneasily. There's one thing that springs to mind that Brent knows about, something I'm really not proud of, but he wouldn't do that, would he?

I drain my coffee and jump down. "I'm going to check the bubble."

"I already checked," Curtis says.

But I want to see for myself, and anyway, I need some space. I pass through the double doors into the freezing air beyond and down the metal steps.

The view is breathtaking. The Alps spread out as far as the eye can see, peaks white, valleys green. The little orange cabins hang motionless against the cloudless sky, disappearing briefly over the cliffs, then continuing across the plateau below. You can't see Le Rocher village from here—it nestles deep in the valley.

I turn my attention to the operator booth and test the door. Still locked; I expected as much. I cup my hands to the window. There's a complicated-looking control panel and various monitors. I'm pretty sure that even if we broke in, we wouldn't be able to get it running. It must need some kind of key.

Never mind. We'll make our own way down. On snowboards until the snow runs out, then on foot. It'll be a fair walk because the snow line was pretty high up, but we should be able to do it in half a day.

Footsteps on the stairs behind me. It's Dale. Game-show-host Dale, who smells of expensive aftershave and looks like he reads GQ these days, rather than *Whitelines*, in his smart jeans and charcoal knit— possibly cashmere—although the hood of his snowboard jacket is ripped from the fight yesterday and he has the beginnings of a black eye.

He glances around. "Still locked up?"

"Yep." I step around him to return upstairs.

He catches my right arm. "Did you invite us here, Milla?"

"No." I wriggle my arm but he has a strong grip.

"So why does my wife say you did?"

There's something about this place. It's as though the wildness of these mountains is creeping into us. Or maybe it's just that we're so far from the rest of civilization. We're unpoliced up here.

"I don't know. Let go of me."

If anything, his grip grows tighter. "Give me an answer first."

My heart is thumping, but in situations like this, you can't show fear. "I could hurt you," I say. Offense is the best defense—according to my dad and brother at least.

He doesn't even blink. "I could hurt you more."

As we square off I search for a trace of the Dale I remember—the glimpse of a tattoo; holes in his ears and lip from where his piercings used to go. But there's nothing. It's as though he never existed.

CHAPTER 20

TEN YEARS AGO

Saskia hasn't changed out of her snowboard trousers. She rustles about, making juice. Odette and I lean against the counter. None of us wanted to drink, so it looks like our girls' night will be a tame one. Fine by me.

"What are you putting in it?" I ask.

Saskia turns to me with laughing eyes. "Beetroot, carrot, spinach, and lemon."

Does she sense it makes me nervous when she hands me drinks? I suspect she does. She's bought me coffees on the mountain a few times now. My budget doesn't extend to buying hot drinks, so I haven't returned the favor, but she doesn't seem to care. Maybe it's her way of making up for the Le Rocher Open.

She dumps a scoop of beige powder into the blender. "And maca."

I study the container.

"Supposed to help muscle recovery," she says. "Curtis got me onto it."

I sniff it. "Does it taste like shit?"

Odette dips her finger in. She's wearing a wrist brace from her fall a few days ago. "It's not too bad. Try it."

I taste it. "Yuck."

Saskia buzzes the juice. "You won't notice it in here."

Odette reaches for another pot. Super greens. "Put some of this."

"No, no. I want her to actually like it." Saskia sloshes the brown liquid into glasses and we carry them to the sofa.

The apartment is small but it's way nicer than mine, with a pale wood floor and colorful rugs.

"Do you live here as well?" I ask Odette.

Her fair skin has caught the sun today. "No," she says. "I have an apartment above the ski rental shop."

"It's just me and Heather," Saskia says.

"Is Heather working tonight?" I say.

"Yeah, thank God." Saskia leans forward to put her empty glass on the coffee table, sweater riding up to reveal her slim back. She fascinates me. So small, yet so damn strong.

Magazines are strewn across the coffee table. I glance through them, hoping for some kind of character insight. French fashion mags mix with snowboard and trashy UK celebrity ones. Which doesn't tell me much, and anyway, some of them might be Heather's.

I gesture to the snowboards propped against the wall. "So are all those boards yours?"

"All except that one." Saskia points. "That's Heather's."

"No way, you have, like, five boards."

They can't all be from her sponsor—anyway, two of them aren't even Salomon. And with an average price of five hundred quid a pop, boards like that don't come cheap.

I turn to Odette. "How many do you have?"

"Three."

"How many do *you* have?" Saskia asks me.

"One," I say, wishing I hadn't asked. "But that's all I need because it's magic."

And they laugh.

I catch Saskia watching me as I drain my juice. Maybe the fascination works both ways.

She props her bare feet on the coffee table. Her toenails are silver tonight. "I have a question for you, Milla. Which is better—snowboarding or sex?"

I expected something like this; it's a girls' night, after all. And while I love talking snowboarding with Odette, I'd rather not discuss my progress in Saskia's presence, so I'm happy with the way she's changed the subject.

"Depends who I'm with," I say.

There's a naughty sparkle in Saskia's eye. "With Brent."

"I told you," I say. "I'm not seeing him." He and Curtis are in Italy today for a comp. I make a mental note to ring him later to find out how they fared.

Saskia raises her eyebrow.

"Anyway," I say, "I like both."

Odette smiles. "Yes, one for daytime, one for nighttime."

"Don't be boring," Saskia says.

She seems snappy with Odette tonight, as though she'd rather have me to herself. Or am I flattering myself? Three's always an awkward number. Of our little trio, Odette's the serious one, Saskia's the fun one, and I often find myself tugged between the two. Tonight I'm veering toward Saskia.

"Why not both at once?" Saskia says. "Find a quiet place on the mountain."

"In the bubble lift, maybe?" I say.

Saskia smirks. "Are you speaking from experience?"

I laugh. "No! Your turn now. Which is better?"

I'm dying to hear what she'll say. Men turn their heads wherever she goes, yet she shows no interest in any of them, apart from maybe Julien, whom I suspect she only puts up with for his snowboarding advice. I presume that like me, she prefers to focus on training.

"Yeah," she says. "You're right. I need both."

"With Julien?" I press.

She laughs and looks away.

I'm about to ask Odette but the buzzer rings. And it's bloody Julien. I watch Saskia greet him—a cool kiss on either cheek.

Odette frowns. "It's a girls' night."

"Oh, what does it matter?" Saskia says.

You'd think Julien and Odette would be friendly, with both of them being French, but Saskia's the one who always talks to him. Odette doesn't even kiss him tonight but merely nods at him instead.

Julien says something in French.

"We're speaking English tonight," Saskia says.

"You see my inverted seven twenty today?" he asks.

We listen to him for a bit. It would be interesting except his English is so broken, I struggle to follow. Saskia interrupts to ask Odette about an upcoming competition in Switzerland. Julien seems unconcerned with Saskia's lack of interest. He can't take his eyes off her. Like she's his muse or something.

I turn to Odette. "I saw you land some huge nine hundreds today."

Odette waves her fingers. "Not huge. I saw you grabbing your seven twenties."

"I screwed up most of them." We're doing that thing women do. Putting ourselves down.

Saskia yawns. She doesn't talk herself up like Julien does, yet she doesn't put herself down either. Wouldn't feel the need. She rubs her neck, easing it one way, then the other.

"You hurt it?" Julien jumps up to stand behind the sofa. He sweeps Saskia's hair aside and starts working his fingers into the tops of her shoulders. The intent look on his face reminds me of my parents' cat when he kneads someone's lap.

I stifle my laughter and glance at Odette to see if she's noticed. She's watching them with a strange look in her eye. Until she sees me looking.

Her expression clears and I'm not sure if I imagined it.

For a moment I thought I saw hatred.

CHAPTER 21

PRESENT DAY

Dale's grip tightens around my arm. Some guys couldn't hit a girl—
Brent, for example. Curtis probably reckons he could if he had to, but
I'm not too sure. Looking into Dale's cold, gray-green eyes, I believe he
could.

Suddenly I think of how he went for Saskia at Glow Bar ten years
ago. My mind races ahead of me. Did he attack her again after that and
kill her? Is that what happened to her? If so, I'm in real danger here.
He thinks I invited him here to trap him, so he'll be like a cornered
animal.

Damn. And now I've lost the element of surprise. What do I do?
Game-show-host Dale scares me. I want Viking Dale back.

I look down at his hand. His nails are neatly trimmed and he has
thick blond hair on his wrist.

*The best fighters do everything they can to avoid a fight, Milla. But if you
can't avoid it, hit first and hit hard.*

My dad taught me how to fight. Tough guy, my dad. Smart as well.
I could hit Dale left-handed, or better still, knee him in the balls—and
I totally want to—but he would hit me back and we'd both end up
hurt. I'll try another option first. "If you don't let me go right now, I'll
tell your wife you kissed me."

It's low of me to use that against him. *I was the one who initiated* the kiss. But I don't care. I'm mad. If this doesn't work, I'm going to knee him and run.

He releases my arm.

I used to have a lot of respect for Dale. He was this fun, easygoing guy with a unique sense of style—in his snowboarding, his fashion sense, and life itself. Should I tell him about Heather in the cupboard with Brent last night?

No. I need to hear Brent's side of things first. Or better yet, focus on getting out of this place. I climb the stairs, fighting to calm my breathing.

"Hey," Dale calls.

I turn.

"Sorry."

Seriously? You do that, then think you can apologize and all will be forgotten? I'm not convinced he's even sorry, but I nod and continue upward, holding my breath until I reach the relative safety of the kitchen.

Heather's in there, sleek as ever in skinny white jeans and the heeled boots she was wearing yesterday. Her eyes narrow when Dale walks in shortly behind me.

No, Heather. I didn't kiss him. Not this time.

Dale goes straight over to her and puts his arms around her—to reassure her, stake his claim, or both, I can't tell.

I sense Curtis's eyes on me. Do I look as flustered as I feel?

"Is the bubble running?" Heather asks.

"No," Dale says.

"And I have a feeling it won't be," Curtis adds.

Heads turn his way.

"If someone went to this much trouble to get us up here, they aren't going to let us go so easily."

"If only we had our bloody phones," Heather says.

"That's why they took them, isn't it?" Curtis says. "They wanted us stuck here."

A shiver runs through me. What else do they have planned for us?

"We fly out tomorrow night," Heather says. "Back at work on Monday. What are we going to do?"

"Have some breakfast?" Curtis says.

Heather swears.

"Then we make our own way down," Curtis continues. "Good thing whoever planned this wasn't smart enough to take our boards along with our phones."

Dale clears his throat. "Heather doesn't have a snowboard."

Shit. I hadn't thought of that.

Curtis looks hopefully at me and Brent. "Got a spare?"

Brent and I shake our heads.

Curtis eyes Heather's boots. "Tell me you've at least brought some other footwear."

"Yeah," she says.

"That's a relief."

She glances awkwardly at her husband. "My strappy heels."

Curtis puts his head in his hands.

And he's right. We have a problem.

"I told you," Dale says.

Heather looks mutinous. "If I'd known we were bloody mountaineering down, I wouldn't have bloody come."

Hardly mountaineering, I'm about to say. Then I remember the top section of the route down. One of the resort's many black runs—extremely difficult, for experts only—it's steep and riddled with rocks. With snowboards on, our biggest concern would be the patchy snow cover and the risk of damaging our boards. Without a snowboard, though, Heather *would* basically be mountaineering in places.

This is bad.

"What size are you, Heather?" I say.

"Five."

"I'm a seven. You can always wear my Converse with a couple of pairs of socks."

Heather nods.

I shoot Dale a look. *Hope you feel guilty for threatening me now.*

"What about you, Milla?" Curtis says.

"I'll keep my snowboard boots on." My new ones that I haven't yet broken in. I wince at the thought of the blisters.

All of us—even Dale—look at Curtis for his verdict. Having spent practically his whole life in the mountains, Curtis is easily the most experienced person present.

He shakes his head. "I don't like it. The snow will be icy as hell after having the sun on it all summer. Even in Converse, she'll be sliding around all over the place until we reach the bottom of the snow line."

"We could put a rope on her," I say.

"There's rope in that storage room near the main entrance," Dale says.

He and Curtis must still be sore at each other—quite literally— over last night, but they're managing to put aside their differences. We're pulling together, all equally keen to get out of this place.

"Ever done any climbing?" Curtis asks Heather. "Hill walking even?"

Heather shakes her head, her face pale.

Curtis turns back to Dale. "Cliffs all over the place. If she slides, she could pull one of us clean off the mountain. Keep it as a last resort. First we need to exhaust every other avenue."

"Like what?" I say.

"Like breaking into the lift operator booth. If we can get the bubble running, we're halfway down. If not, there might be a radio or some kind of emergency button. We need to check around outside, see what's out there. Might be a radio in the tow lift shack."

"Whoever did this must be some kind of psycho," Heather says shakily.

Curtis pauses a beat. "Has anyone seen or heard anything to suggest there's someone other than the five of us up here?"

His eyes meet mine briefly as he scans the room, and I notice how he worded that. He didn't mention the perfume or the hair, but I think that's what he's getting at.

The others are shaking their heads.

Curtis hasn't suggested splitting up. Why? He could ride down with me and Brent, say, leaving Heather here with Dale until the resort staff start the lifts running. Is it the possibility of his sister's presence that's stopping him?

"Right," Curtis says. "Eat up, then we'll get to work." He gives Dale a pointed look. "Unless anyone's got a better suggestion."

Dale raises his hand to his head in an ironic salute.

And Curtis strides out of the kitchen.

Heather glances at Brent and once again I wonder what went on in that laundry cupboard.

Dale says something in her ear; she nods and nuzzles his jaw. Their marriage may not be perfect, but he's still there for her. What's it like to have that? To have someone who always has your back? I don't know because I've never had it. Through choice, but even so. Sometimes I wonder if I'm missing out.

I turn away and pour myself a bowl of Chocapic. Haven't had it since that winter. The others pass the box around and we carry our bowls into the restaurant, where chairs are overturned and the floor is strewn with broken glass from last night's fight.

There's an awkward silence as we eat. Heather is trying to catch Brent's eye.

Don't do that, Heather, or Dale will see.

Out the window the sun blazes down on the glacier, the glare so bright I have to shield my eyes to look at it. A few hundred meters up the slope are the remains of various jumps, presumably from the summer camp Burton runs here every August.

Sadness fills me. In a different life we would be out there enjoying ourselves—instead of stuck in here suspecting terrible things about each other.

I need to get it through my head that this is not the nostalgic reunion I had hoped it would be.

And these people are no longer my friends.

CHAPTER 22

TEN YEARS AGO

Adrenaline pumps through my veins. Today is backflip day. It snowed overnight and they haven't cleared the pipe, so we came up to the glacier to build a jump.

You are entering a high mountain area. Danger: crevasse, avalanche! Proceed at own risk! The warning signs are repeated in six different languages, but we duck under barriers and hike into the powder.

The fresh snow glitters in the sunshine. This is perfect timing for me, a chance to try new tricks with a softer landing. If I can nail backflips over a straight jump, I can move on to McTwists in the pipe.

There are seven of us up here today. Dale and Curtis work with shovels—collapsible ones they brought up strapped to their backpacks; the rest of us use our hands and snowboards to shape the jump. Cold seeps through my snowboard trousers as I kneel on the snow, gripping my board by its bindings to slide it back and forth across the takeoff.

Curtis straightens, face red with exertion. "Looks good to me. Everyone happy with that?"

He and I walk up together, sinking in up to our knees with each step. The air's thin up here and I'm gasping like a woman in labor. He's panting too, which makes me feel a bit better.

"You need to go to the gym more," I say.

"Shut up. I didn't see you there last night."

"I was at physiotherapy." My knee's been flaring up since I jumped the cliff to save that baby glove.

I check over my shoulder to make sure Saskia's not within hearing distance. She's way back, with Odette and Julien. "Saskia can do Mc-Twists, yeah? She did one in the final at the Brits."

"Yeah," Curtis says.

"I haven't seen her do any here yet."

"She had a bad slam at the Hintertux summer camp. Knocked herself out. That's when she started wearing a helmet."

"Has she tried one since?"

"Not that I know of."

"Interesting." If I can land some backflips today, she's not going to be happy.

The snow gives way under my boot. Curtis yanks me backward. There's a glassy blue crack right where I trod.

We peer cautiously into it. It's a deep one—bottomless, they call it—that continues downward as far as you can see.

"Big crevasse just here, folks," Curtis shouts to the guys below.

I check around me for more. Problem is most of them are hidden beneath thin layers of snow—snow bridges—so you can't tell they're there until you step on them.

"Go on," I tell Curtis. "You can lead."

He laughs and tests the snow ahead with the tail of his snowboard. We continue slowly up. At the top we strap our boards on, wheezing for breath.

Curtis pulls his helmet on. Of our little group, only he and Saskia wear them. I probably should, but they're not cheap and I haven't gotten around to buying one.

I hear Saskia quizzing Julien in French as they reach us. Odette walks behind them, looking pissed off.

"Who's going to be the guinea pig?" Curtis says.

"Me!" I say immediately. I'm the weakest rider of the group and I need to show them I can keep up.

Straight-line, I tell myself. *Because they're all watching.*

Down I speed, into the hollow, then up the takeoff and into the air. The jump throws me higher than I expected, but I hold my nerve and grab my heel edge, pushing out the tail of my board so I'm flying through the air with my board perpendicular to my direction of travel. Method grab. You know if you've got it right because you feel it. And I feel it.

Gravity tugs me downward. I release the grab. It's a big drop and I'm going to feel the impact. My body weight slams down through my quads. I ride it out, glad of all those leg presses.

Cheers drift down from the top. As I unstrap, Curtis sails off, then Odette, with Methods that make me see how I could improve mine. I watch where they land: only a couple of feet farther than me, ha!

Saskia jumps next, then Julien and Brent, and I smile because they do Methods, too. Dale does one, holds it as he rotates 180 degrees, and releases his hand to grab Indy before he lands. I'm not surprised Oakley picked him up. He has style of his own.

"Pah! Double grabs," Julien says to no one in particular. "I don't like them."

I walk back up alongside Odette. I was over at her place last night and we stayed up late watching French snowboard DVDs. Odette's different when Saskia isn't around—more relaxed, and I guess I am, too. She didn't say where Saskia was and I didn't ask, sensing they'd had some sort of falling-out. We discussed our goals for this winter: the comps we plan to enter, the tricks we hope to learn. If she were a Brit, there's no way I would have shared that sort of stuff with her, but she's so far ahead of me it didn't seem to matter.

Julien and Saskia are right behind us. Saskia's French must be better than Julien's English, because they're speaking French again. From the way he's pointing at the jump, he's giving her advice.

"Does he sound like an arsehole in French as well as in English?" I ask Odette quietly.

I expect her to laugh but she doesn't even smile. "Yes."

She really doesn't seem to like him, but it makes sense. They're both incredible riders, yet while Julien takes every opportunity to tell people how incredible he is, Odette just keeps her head down and rides. If Curtis hadn't mentioned it, I'd never have known she came second in an FIS world cup at Vars this week.

"What are you working on today?" Odette says.

I hesitate. "Backflips, hopefully." Now there will be no chickening out.

"Your first time?"

"Yeah. I'm so nervous."

Her gloved fingers grip my arm. "Don't worry. You will do it!"

Brent's strapping in at the top.

"Backflip time," I say quietly. "Any last-minute tips?"

"Don't land on your head." Brent grins. "Nah, you did great on the trampoline. Full commitment, though. You don't want to get halfway round and decide you don't want to do one."

From the way he walks, all slouchy and relaxed in his low-slung trousers, you'd never guess Brent is an elite athlete. You'd think he's a stoner—or just plain lazy. Then you see him with his snowboard on.

He blasts off the jump with a massive 720. He seems to feel no fear. I envy him. My palms are sweating inside my gloves. Saskia is quizzing Julien again as they strap in. I can't wait to see her face if I pull this off.

Curtis gets to his feet. "You going?"

"No, after you," I say because I'm not quite ready.

Curtis speeds down and pulls a smooth backflip. Everyone cheers.

Now I really have to do one. I race downward. Speed is important—I need enough air time to get my board around. The moment the nose of my board reaches the end of the takeoff, I tip backward.

It's kind of like going around the loop in a roller coaster. Except that rather than just sitting there, safely strapped in, I have no idea what's going to happen. My field of vision goes blue, then white. If I hit the ground just now I'll break my neck for sure. Then I see blue sky again and I'm touching back down with my board beneath me.

The cheers are louder than they were for Curtis.

Curtis gives me a nod of respect when I join him. "Nice."

I shrug it off like it was nothing special. Inside, though, I light up. I'm not sure why, but praise from Curtis means more to me than praise from any of the others. It's as if he's my brother and my dad rolled into one. By impressing him, it's like I've achieved the impossible and impressed them. Stupid, I know, especially since my feelings for him are far from fraternal, but I will treasure this moment.

Saskia launches off the jump and I can't hide my smile when she spins again. I've raised the bar and she can't reach it.

Curtis sees my face. "Be careful with my sister."

"What do you mean?" I say, startled.

"Just . . . Be careful."

"Are you asking me to go easy on her?" I say. He better not be.

"No. But she doesn't like to lose."

I laugh. "Does anyone?"

Curtis opens his mouth as though he's about to say something, then clamps it shut.

That gets me wondering what else she's done. But we have an understanding now. She's not going to do anything else underhanded.

"Don't worry," I say. "I play hard, too."

Just then, Julien flies off the jump with some kind of weird corkscrewed spin. This is what I love about freestyle snowboarding. It's not like cycling or running, where races are won by hundredths of a second and it takes a photo finish to decide. Our sport is so young that riders are landing new tricks all the time—tricks people never thought possible or even imagined. Just think what they'll be doing ten years from now.

Brent slaps my back when I catch up with him. "Good one, Mills."

Five backflips later, I'm feeling pretty smug. Every time I land one, I tell myself I'll quit while I'm ahead. Then I see the look on Saskia's face and make myself do another.

This is how I'm going to beat her. Not through dirty tricks, but by sheer hard work, nailing new maneuvers one by one. I have a panel of experts on hand to ask advice from and three more months before the Brits in mid-April. I can do this.

Brent and Dale sit at the top eating muesli bars—mine. Good thing someone likes them. I still have twenty boxes of the things. Setting my board down, I sink to the snow beside Brent and tear into a muesli bar of my own.

A feminine gasp makes me turn.

Saskia stands nearby, hand cupped to her mouth. "I'm so sorry, Milla."

Dread slides over me. My snowboard isn't where I left it.

I scramble to my feet. It'll be behind me. Or even racing down the slope, where it'll eventually hit a soft patch and come to a stop.

But it's not.

"It was an accident," Saskia says. "I caught it with my toe." She points to a hole in the snow.

I rush over. Just visible, some thirty meters down a narrow crevasse, is my precious snowboard.

I look at her and catch a hint of a smile, which she quickly wipes.

So much for our understanding. She may not realize it yet, but this means war.

CHAPTER 23

Brent taps the window of the operator booth. "Tempered glass."

He and Curtis are all kitted out in their snowboard gloves and goggles. The lock on the booth door is a decent one and Brent wasn't able to pick it. They confer about the best way to break in.

The rest of us hang back. As soon as I get a chance, I'm going to slip away and search the dorms—for our phones or a clue about who's doing this.

The wind has picked up. The little orange bubbles creak as they sway back and forth. I don't hold out much hope for the men getting the lift running. Ski lifts must have decent security these days, and whoever brought us here must have guessed we'd try to access the booth.

Brent picks up his snowboard. "Let's try this."

Dale and Heather are farther down the platform, talking in low voices. Another argument, from the sounds of it. He sees me looking and shushes her.

"Back in a minute. I'm going to the bathroom." I race upstairs and down the corridor into Dale and Heather's dorm.

Dale has packed a lot lighter than Heather, so I'll start with him. I rummage through his snowboard bag. Snowboard trousers, gloves, goggles, sweaters in muted shades, and cargo pants. Mostly his old sponsors' brands and all newish. Underwear—a Calvin Klein man these days, I see. The old Dale would never have splashed out on designer boxers. He'd have saved his money for snowboarding. A Ziploc bag of screws, a couple of board tools. Nothing personal. No phones.

I check under the pillows and mattresses, and pat down the duvets of all four bunks. Have to be quick. The wardrobe is empty. Heather's suitcase lies open on the floor. Clothes galore—mostly black and expensive looking, all neatly folded. I press the pile, feeling for the hard edges of a phone. Nope.

There's a jumble of lacy underwear in one corner. It's weird to see another girl's underwear and I can't resist picking a couple of pieces out. A tiny black gauze G-string and a matching bra that's little more than nipple covers with straps.

I stuff them back in. Bathroom next. Among the makeup in Heather's cosmetics bag are pale blue pills in a foil packet. Again, I have the urge to look closer but I don't have long, so I zip it up and check Dale's sponge bag. Shit—someone's coming!

I dive into the shower cubicle and pull the curtain across just as the door creaks open.

"Now go wash your face." Dale's voice. "And pull yourself together."

Heather's crying. "We're never going to get out of here. This is all your fault. You should never have taken her credit card."

Whose credit card? Mine? Have they been in my dorm?

"Keep your fucking voice down," Dale says. "She didn't need it, did she? What do her parents care about a couple grand? They're loaded."

Oh God. I think they're talking about Saskia. So was it Dale who used her credit card, not Saskia?

"She owed us," Dale says. "And I didn't hear you complain about spending it."

Muffled sobs. "If this comes out I could lose my law license. We'd lose everything."

"Don't you dare go to pieces on me now," Dale hisses. "Nobody knows. We got away with it, so why are you still going on about it?"

"Did we? Or is that why we're here?" Heather sniffs. "Because some-one suspects."

"What, Milla, you mean?" Dale says.

"Or someone pretending to be her. You shouldn't have stolen it."

"We'll be down from here by the end of the day. All you have to do is keep your mouth shut till then."

Heather starts crying again. I'm bristling at how Dale's talking to her. There's no affection. He sounds angry and bitter. Curtis is right. Dale has changed.

"I'll get you your tablets," he says.

There's a draft as someone enters the bathroom. The shower curtain flutters. I hold my breath. My wrist still remembers the clench of Dale's fingers. If he did that to me down there, what would he do if he caught me in here?

I hear the tap running. The curtain flutters again. Has he gone?

Heather sniffs some more. "Thanks."

"We need to get back out there," Dale says.

A click as the door shuts, then silence. I slump in relief. That was close.

My mind is reeling. Does this mean they didn't kill her? If they did, they'd be freaking out about that rather than the credit card, surely. But I can't rule it out. One of them could have killed her and the other one doesn't know.

Better get on with the search. I've checked everywhere in their dorm. All is quiet in the corridor, so I creep out. Who next—Curtis or Brent?

I hurry three doors down to Curtis's dorm. It's a lot neater than mine—I might have known he would make the bed—and it smells faintly of musk, his deodorant perhaps. I want to get this over with as fast as possible because I would hate for him to catch me in here.

His navy-and-white Sparks Snowboarding bag lies on the lower bunk, partly open. I unzip it all the way around and peel back the flap.

The floorboards seem to wobble beneath me and I have to grip the bunk before I fall down.

There on top of the folded pile of clothes lies Saskia's lift pass.

My hand shakes as I pick it up.

He shouldn't have this.

You have to scan your pass at the bottom before you enter the cable car, and again to enter the bubble. Saskia would never have made it past the eagle-eyed lift attendants without it. Yet Heather and Brent said they saw her up on the glacier, and Curtis said he saw her gear up there. Did they really, or are the three of them in this together?

All those accusations Curtis made. The perfume, the hair, his questions about whether she's still alive. Was it to cover up the fact that he killed her? I don't want to believe that, but I can't find any other explanation.

Saskia looks as gorgeous as I remember in her photo. Her stunning blue eyes gaze at me like she's trying to tell me something.

Where are you, Saskia, and why does Curtis have your pass?

CHAPTER 24

TEN YEARS AGO

"I hate her," I whisper in Brent's ear.

Below her pink neon goggles, Saskia's mouth twitches as though she knows I'm talking about her. Her long, white-blond ponytail curls around her neck like a snake.

"Chill," Brent says.

"But I loved that board."

I thought she liked me. That's what hurts most of all. That I was stupid enough to be taken in by her. She only befriended me so I would let my guard down.

"Let it go," Brent says. "You're on fire with your riding right now and that's because of you, not your board. She can't take your talent away from you."

We're sitting at the bottom of the half-pipe, eating our lunch. My new board is identical to the one I lost but I still mourn the old one. And every time I look at Saskia, I relive the moment I realized it was lost forever.

It's another sunny day and Brent wears a back-to-front Burton base-ball cap. He slides his arm around my shoulders and pulls me close.

I tense. Brent looks super cute in that cap, but until now he and I have limited this kind of stuff to behind closed doors, and no one except Curtis knows about us.

And they're all here today. Odette and Saskia sit nearby, friends again, apparently, after their earlier falling-out. Curtis is chatting with an Aussie girl who was pulling big airs earlier. Julien stands dwarfed by a trio of French freestyle skiers. Even Heather has graced us with her presence. She's been sulking at the bottom of the pipe with a camera all morning. Dale's clothing sponsor dropped him—budget cuts—and he needs some decent shots to send to prospective sponsors.

I chew my baguette, feeling awkward.

Saskia's the first to notice. She raises her goggles to her helmet and watches us through narrowed eyes.

With his free hand, Brent lifts his cap off and places it on my head, the right way around. "I like you, Milla. Girls get all clingy with me usually, but you don't." His dark eyes study me like he's trying to make sense of it. "You make *me* get clingy, which is fully weird."

Saskia nudges Odette and they both look over at us. Why do I feel so uncomfortable? I like Brent. I love watching him in the pipe, rocketing into the air and hanging there with super-tweaked grabs. Knowing his incredible body will be mine to play with later.

And he's the sweetest guy. He turned up on my doorstep this morning with a spare board for me to borrow. I didn't like to tell him how my doorbell rang last night and I opened the door to find a Magic Pipemaster 157 leaning against the wall. I'd presumed it was from him, but I now suspect Curtis, even though he denied it.

Still, despite how great Brent is, I'm not up for a full-blown relationship. I force a smile and slip out from under his arm. I'll have to talk to him about this, but not now, in front of everyone. "I'm going back up."

"Go for it." Brent flashes his dimples.

Glad he doesn't seem to realize anything is wrong, I hand his cap back, stuff the rest of my baguette into my backpack, and glug from my water bottle. I'm craving another Smash, but I'm drinking way too much of the stuff. It provides a short-term energy boost, but it hangs about in my system and I've been struggling to sleep.

What I see when I lower my water amazes me. Saskia stands in Curtis's arms with her face pressed into his chest. Is she upset? He lost it with her up on the glacier yesterday but he holds her tight now, murmuring something. What's he saying to her?

Saskia nods and pulls away from him. As she heads toward me, I scrutinize her face. I'm not convinced she was truly upset. She was just playing him.

She picks up her board. "I'll walk up with you, Milla."

I try to think calm thoughts as she walks up the side of the pipe beside me. I need to blank her out and direct my anger into my riding. I'll get my revenge when I smash her at the Brits.

"You're not still mad about your snowboard, are you?" she says. "I told you it was an accident."

Like hell it was. But I have no way of proving that.

She nudges my elbow. "So. You and Brent, hey? I thought so."

"What about you and Julien?" I counter tersely.

"What about it?"

"Are you together?"

She laughs. "No. I'm just using him like you're using Brent." Her ponytail blows sideways, lashing me across the cheek.

"What?" She always manages to say the last thing I'd expect. "I'm not using Brent."

But she has me questioning myself now. *Am* I using him?

No. Brent and I have fun together. It's simple and easy and there's nothing wrong with that. This is just another way Saskia's trying to get under my skin.

Her lips curve into a smile. "I've seen the way you look at my brother."

"Sorry?" I check behind us to make sure nobody else is within hearing distance.

Saskia's smile widens. It terrifies me that she can see through me like this. How can I beat her when she can read my mind?

CHAPTER 25

Saskia smiles up at me from the lift pass.

Something—a draft or a tiny sound that only my subconscious registers—makes me look up. And there in the doorway is Curtis.

Fear flickers through me as he approaches. What's he going to do to me? I hate myself for being scared, but being grabbed by Dale earlier made me realize:

1. How little I really know these guys.

2. That the normal rules don't apply up here.

Curtis stops a foot away. He must be feeling all kinds of emotions—hurt that I searched his stuff, guilt that I discovered the lift pass, and panic that I'm onto him—but his expression is as unreadable as ever. Wordlessly he takes the pass from my hand. He stares at it. Flips it over. Looks up.

Shock, that's what I see. And suspicion.

"Where did you get this?" he says.

"From your snowboard bag."

He blinks. "Did you put it there?"

"What?" Of all the things I was expecting, it wasn't that. A direct attack, straight off, so fast he hardly had time to plan it. "Of course not."

Curtis looks back down at the pass, flexes it, holds it to the light at an angle. Smells it even. The photo is printed directly onto the plastic.

He rubs a fingertip over her face. "It looks used, like it's her actual pass from that winter."

His acting skills are incredible, if that's what he's doing. He's utterly convincing.

I take the pass from him. Here in my hand is one little piece of the puzzle of Saskia's disappearance, but I have no idea what it means. According to the resort computer, there was no record of Saskia's having used her pass on the day she went missing, so how come Brent and Heather saw her on the glacier? A glitch in the system, the police decided, but the presence of the pass now disproves that.

"If she'd gone up the mountain that day, she would have had this on her," I say.

Curtis levels his jaw. "That's just what I was thinking. So where's it been all this time?"

"You're saying it hasn't been with you?"

"Yeah, that's what I'm saying. Where did you find it exactly?"

"On top of your clothes."

He folds his arms across his chest. "It wasn't there this morning. Someone planted it. Between when I left my dorm and when I came in just now."

I notice how he worded that. He isn't prepared to let me off the hook just yet.

"It would have taken, what, five seconds?" he says.

"But why?"

"Blackmail, like I said last night."

I want to believe him, but I'm just not sure.

The stony look in his eyes turns thoughtful. "Or maybe it's a clue. Someone wants me to dig for answers."

I cringe inwardly. There's one particular thing I'd like to remain buried.

"Can I have it?" Curtis asks.

I hesitate. And tuck it into my jacket pocket. "I'm sorry. It has massive implications. I'll have to tell the others."

He nods, his face tight.

He's offended that I don't trust him.

"I searched Dale and Heather's dorm as well," I say, to show it's not personal.

Curtis's eyebrows go up. "Yeah? So have I. When did you do it?"

"Five minutes ago." I'll bring up Saskia's credit card later. I want Brent there when I do because Curtis is going to flip. "What about you?"

"While you lot were eating breakfast."

"Risky. Find anything?"

"Just a whole lot of hairspray."

"Think Dale wears it as well now?" I say.

Curtis laughs and the mood lightens.

Until he says: "I searched your dorm, too."

Pain lances through me. Now I know how he feels. "Fair enough."

He pulls a silver-and-blue bracelet from his pocket and looks up at me.

I'm flushing. "What?"

"It's Saskia's."

"I know. She gave it to me."

He narrows his eyes. "When?"

I force myself to hold his gaze. "Back when we were friends."

He studies me a moment, then hands it back. I don't want it—didn't even want it to begin with—but I stuff it in my pocket with the lift pass. I'll throw it in the first crevasse I find. I only brought it to the reunion thinking he might like it as a memento of his sister, but the moment is lost now.

We head down the corridor.

"Any luck with the operator booth?" I ask.

"We got in, but we couldn't get the bubble running. None of the buttons on the control panel are working. Either the power's off or someone disabled it."

"No radio?"

"No. But you could see where it was supposed to go. Someone had taken it."

We find the others in the restaurant.

"Let's search outside," Dale says before I can mention the lift pass.

Curtis nods at Heather's heeled boots. "Someone's going to have to stay here with your wife."

To protect Heather from danger, or to protect the rest of us from what she might get up to if left in here alone? I suspect the latter. Curtis doesn't seem to like Heather much; I noticed that ten years ago. When Heather and his sister lived together, they had repeated fallings-out and more than once Curtis had to intervene.

"I'm happy to stay with her," Brent says.

Dale steps forward. "No you fucking won't."

I see Curtis hide a smile.

"You and your bloody shoes," Dale hisses at Heather.

She flinches.

I don't like how Curtis and Dale are ganging up against her. Dale clearly wants to check outside but there's no way he's going to leave his wife alone with Brent.

"I'll stay too, if you want," I say. "Curtis and Dale can go."

If there are phones to be found out there, I trust Curtis to find them. Anyway, I want another chat with Heather.

Dale nods grudgingly.

"Okay," Curtis says. "We'd better gear up. Did you bring your avalanche transceiver and a harness?"

"Transceiver but not a harness," Dale says.

"There's some in that storage room."

"Do we need them?"

Curtis raises his voice. "Are you kidding? The ski patrol haven't blasted the slopes for months, we've got all these unstable layers. It's one huge avalanche waiting to happen. And as for the crevasses . . ."

Glaciers *are* particularly dangerous this time of year—a mass of crevasses and not enough snow yet to cover them. During the ski season, resort staff scrape snow over the smaller ones and rope the others off.

"Keep your hair on," Dale says.

Curtis turns back to us. "While we're gone, I've got a little job for you lot." He reaches into his jacket pocket and pulls out a long stream of keys, laying them on the table one by one like a magician.

Dale snatches one. "That's my house key. Aw, that's just plain rude, man."

"Sorry," Curtis says, though he doesn't sound it. "Had to be done. We need to see if they fit any of these locked doors."

"When did you get them?" Dale says.

"While you all were eating. I couldn't risk someone hiding them."

Dale slams the key down and walks off.

On the table I can see my apartment key, my car key, and even the tiny key on a separate ring that fits my bike lock. Curtis would have had to fish through the inner pocket of my backpack to find them among my emergency tampons and the condoms I packed, just in case, with him in mind.

It's like another punch in the gut.

After half an hour of trying to jam keys into doors, I give up. "Who wants another coffee?"

Brent and Heather are sitting close in the restaurant when I carry the cups out. They fall silent as I approach—which tells me exactly what they were talking about. I pull up a chair. Brent rakes his fingers through his hair; Heather drums her perfect nails on the table. It's so weird to think of the two of them together. She's my polar opposite. I hope she has the sense not to tell Dale, or Brent will be in real trouble.

We sip our coffees. Brent's hair is sticking up at all angles from so much raking. I want to rake *my* fingers through it and straighten it for him, but it's not mine to rake anymore. He's not my Brent either—not the guy I remember. The light has gone from his eyes.

I think back to the long, dark months after I quit snowboarding. There was a gaping hole in my life. I felt aimless and lost. Didn't know who I was anymore. All I knew was I had to plug the hole before the will to live bled out of me. I turned to alcohol at first, but it only made me feel worse the next morning.

My brother dragged me to the gym one night and I slowly clawed my way out of the darkness. Sometimes, when I work my body so hard I'm nearly blacking out, I feel okay about myself. As though if I could only push myself a little harder—run a bit faster or lift another five kilos—I might feel happy again.

Anyway, I get why Brent hit the bottle, and I don't hold it against him. But God, I miss him. The old Brent.

I turn my thoughts back to our situation. "Can I ask you something, Heather?"

She looks at me over the rim of the mug.

"The day that Saskia disappeared. Why did you go up the mountain?" It's always struck me as odd that she was up here that day.

"I wanted to watch the competition," she says, as though it should be obvious.

"Even though Dale wasn't in it?"

"Yeah. Why not? I'd lost my job, didn't have anything else to do."

Brent sips his coffee, saying nothing.

"But the competition was at the half-pipe," I say. "So why did you go all the way up to the glacier?"

"I saw Brent in the first cable car." She glances at him. "We got to chatting."

"What about?"

"How am I supposed to remember? Saskia was in there too, but I didn't want to talk to her. When we got to the midstation, Brent said he was getting the bubble up to the glacier for a warm-up run, so I went up there with him."

There's something about her story that I don't quite buy. Heather came up to the midstation sometimes on her afternoons off, tottering about in her unsuitable shoes and sunning herself on the sun deck, but I never saw her on the glacier. For one thing, she didn't dress for it. A leather jacket doesn't cut it in minus twenty.

Brent drains his coffee and wanders over to the bar.

Heather continues. "Saskia was in the bubble in front of us and we got in an argument at the top."

"About . . . ?"

"The fight in Glow Bar. She stormed off. Then Curtis turned up looking for her, complaining about how he'd wrecked his shoulder because of her." Her eyes flit to the doorway as though she's scared Curtis will catch her talking about him. "I tell you, he was scary mad. I've never seen him so mad."

"Right." This is a different version of events than the one I heard from Curtis ten years ago. And it doesn't paint Curtis in a good light.

"Know what he said?" Heather checks the doorway again and lowers her voice to a whisper. "*When I find her, I'm going to bloody kill her.*"

CHAPTER 26

TEN YEARS AGO

The gym smells of sweat and deodorant. It's busy tonight. I spot the Aussie girl that Curtis was talking to at the pipe and head to the vacant leg-press machine beside her.

She must be sponsored by Roxy, because all her clothing carries their heart-shaped logo. I check how much she's pressing—100 kilos— and set myself up with 120. She flashes me a smile as I sit down.

Curtis is doing pull-ups opposite, T-shirt lifting to reveal toned abs. He swings down and drapes himself over an empty machine next to the Aussie girl. "Did you meet Jacinta, Milla?"

"No," I say. "Nice to meet you."

"You ripped in the pipe earlier," she says.

"So did you." She's a way better rider than I am. I'll check her out next time I'm online because I want to know where she is in the rankings.

"I love your hair," she adds.

Curtis sits there while we do leg presses. I can tell from his body language that he likes her. And I get the attraction; she's pale and leggy, like a young Nicole Kidman, and—much as I hate to admit it—she seems really nice.

When she adds another twenty K, I hop off my seat and add another fifty. My quads are going to hurt tomorrow because I'm leg-pressing nearly three times my own body weight. Five . . . six . . . Curtis raises an eyebrow. I think he knows exactly what I'm doing. Seven . . . eight . . . nine . . . My legs are shaking but I manage the last one and pause to mop my forehead.

Saskia does squats with a medicine ball across the gym, watching us in the mirror. Watched in turn by Julien, I notice, who is on the weights bench beside one of the strapping freestyle skiers I saw him with this afternoon.

"I got some footage of you earlier," Curtis tells Jacinta when she finishes her set. He brings his video camera to the pipe sometimes and we take turns filming each other. "We're watching it at my place tonight if you want to come over. In fact, come for dinner."

Her eyes light up. "Awesome."

Curtis turns to me. "Are you coming, Milla?"

I can't bear to see him looking at Jacinta like that for much longer, but I need to speak to Brent, and anyway, I want to watch the footage. "Yeah, sure."

Brent calls Curtis over to spot him and Curtis gets up, giving me a flash of hairy pale thigh in his gym shorts. I launch into another set of leg presses. I'm regretting making it so heavy—I'll hardly be able to walk tomorrow—but Jacinta is still going and I can't give up before she does.

Freshly showered, I stretch out on Brent's bed. I love this feeling—the burn of muscles pushed beyond their limits. My entire body throbs. I've pressed every last bit of energy out of me.

The door opens and Brent returns with a towel around his waist, face still flushed from the gym. I lie back, enjoying the view as he dries himself. Now I need to find some way of broaching the topic of our relationship.

"How come Dale wasn't at the gym tonight?" I ask. "He wasn't there last night either."

"He had a fight with Heather yesterday."

"What about?" I'm so nosy.

Brent laughs. "How would I know?"

"Does she realize how much she's affecting his training? What's she even doing here? I've seen her snowboard, like, once."

"She was studying in Lyon for a year for her uni degree. Law and French. Got a job at Glow Bar over her uni holidays and ended up meeting Dale."

I'm intrigued that Brent knows this. He has a soft spot for Heather, I think. "What about her course?" I say.

"Deferred it, I guess."

"They're screwing up their futures, both of them."

Brent shrugs. "Anyway, tonight was her night off, so he took her out to dinner. They'll be here later."

That gives me the perfect opening. "That's why I swore off relationships this winter."

Brent gives me a curious look.

"I promised myself I would focus on my snowboarding, nothing else."

He dries his hair, taking that in.

"Are you okay with that?" It's a bit late to ask, I guess. I should probably have brought it up earlier. Still, casual sex is what most guys dream about. I shouldn't feel guilty.

"Whatever you want." He tosses his towel into the corner, pulls on boxer shorts, and throws himself on the bed beside me.

I glance sideways at him. Still damp, his hair clumps together in dark spikes. Is he really okay with it? I think so.

He pops two tablets from a foil packet beside the bed—painkillers for his shin splints—washes them down with the bottle he keeps there, and lies back.

I trail my fingers over his pecs. He smells soapy clean and his skin is still warm from his workout—mine, too; I'm only wrapped in a towel.

He touches my cheek. "You've got panda eyes."

I grin. "I know. I look ridiculous."

"By the way, Curtis told me I should keep an eye on Saskia."

"What do you mean?"

"You two are neck and neck at the moment. She's after your blood, apparently."

I think of Curtis's words on the glacier—*she doesn't like to lose*—and a shiver of unease runs through me. "Am I supposed to be scared?"

"Hey, I'm only telling you what he said."

I want to laugh it off, but Curtis doesn't seem the type to worry about something unnecessarily. I search Brent's face and my unease deepens. He's taking the warning seriously.

"Tell me why you don't like her," I say.

Brent rubs his jaw. "You know how she is with Julien? That's how she was with me last season. I shared a place with her and Curtis, re-member?"

"She flirted with you?"

"Played with me, more like. Nice one minute, impossible the next. I liked her to start with."

At least I'm not the only one she fooled.

"She stirred up so much shit between me and Curtis that winter," Brent says.

"Why would she do that?"

"Who knows. Gets off on it, maybe. Curtis knows what she's like, but she's family, so he'll stand by her no matter what. It took me half the season to see her for who she was. Poor Julien still hasn't worked it out. She uses people."

Shame pricks me when I remember her accusation earlier. *Am* I us-ing Brent?

"You can't trust her, Milla."

"What else can she do to me?"

"I don't know. But you need to watch out."

But I'm onto her now. Surely there's nothing else she can try. "Okay, so how do I go about beating her?"

Brent shakes his head. "You never rest, do you?"

"I'm serious."

"Okay, you either go bigger or you get more technical with your tricks. Preferably both." He looks thoughtful. "You could try a Crippler. No. Maybe not."

It's a flip, I know that much, but the name alone has put me off ever considering it. "What's that exactly?"

"It's kind of between a backflip and an inverted five. I'll show you one in the pipe tomorrow. But I don't know. If you get it wrong, you land on your face."

"Cool. I'll look them up on the Internet. See if I can find a YouTube vid. So how do I go bigger?"

Brent hitches up the hem of my towel and traces a zigzag line on my bare thigh with his fingertip. "This is your line in the pipe, right? And this is mine." He traces a zigzag with much wider angles. "I'm hitting the wall at maybe forty-five degrees?"

"Okay." I've noticed this, but I've never really thought about it before.

"I get fewer hits, but they're big because I'm traveling way faster than you are when I take off."

"Right." So my route across the pipe is costing me too much speed. I picture Saskia's line and compare it to mine. Does she take a steeper line? I'll watch her tomorrow.

Brent's hand hasn't moved from my thigh. And it feels good. Our eyes meet.

I force thoughts of Saskia aside. "Want to zigzag a bit higher?"

———————

I smooth my hair down as Brent and I enter the living room. The others are all there, crammed in front of the fire. My stomach wrenches at the sight of Jacinta next to Curtis on the sofa.

"We were waiting for you," Curtis says.

Heat rushes to my face.

Brent grins. "Want a beer, Mills?"

"Yeah, go on then," I say.

"After that workout?" Curtis says. "No, get her a Super Mag."

"A what?" I say.

"Magnesium blend," Curtis says. "Muscle recovery drink."

I'd normally refuse on principle because I hate being told what to do, but Jacinta looks like she might be drinking it, and after that workout my poor quads need all the help they can get, so I grudgingly agree and Brent heads to the kitchen.

"You should have one, too," Curtis calls after him.

"Yes, Dad," Brent calls back.

I climb over Julien and settle on an empty patch of carpet. The fire crackles and spits. I smother a yawn. I lay awake for hours last night, body exhausted, mind still buzzing from excess caffeine. I vowed I wouldn't drink any more Smash, but I was so tired this afternoon, I had to. Maybe sleeping tablets would help. That way I'd get the best of both worlds. Energy by day, sleep by night.

Brent returns with a glass in either hand and sits behind me, pulling me backward into his lap. So much for keeping this casual. Dale and Heather sit nearby in a similar position. Heather is checking her phone, looking bored. I feel sorry for her, actually. If she's studying law, she must be really smart, yet she's stuck here in a room of smelly snowboarders.

"Everyone ready?" Curtis says. His laptop is connected to the TV. He points the remote and drapes his arm along the top of the sofa. Not touching Jacinta. Yet.

I sip my drink. Brent is muttering about it but it's not too bad. Like flat lemon soda.

Brent is up first, busting his trademark Backside Air. He sails so high it must have caught whoever was filming by surprise, because they've cut off his head. I note his line as he crosses the pipe floor. Lower down he slams his spin and everyone winces in unison.

"Aw, that looked brutal," Dale says.

"I over-rotated." Brent's grinning but I saw the bruise on his hip earlier.

The footage continues and Odette drops in, followed by Curtis. I'm up next, and as always I'm devastated by how little air I get compared to all the others. I note my line. There's the problem. That's my goal for tomorrow.

Saskia appears at the top of the pipe. Until a gloved finger covers the screen, obscuring the view. *My* glove. The first time Saskia filmed me, she did the same thing to me.

From her perch on the sofa, Saskia's head turns my way.

"The game continues," I say softly.

Curtis's expression darkens, so I hide my face in my drink.

The finger retreats from the screen as Jacinta drops into the pipe in her pink Roxy jacket. I hate that she's better than me.

Curtis leans sideways on the sofa to say something in Jacinta's ear; she nods and whispers back. Inside me, something twists and writhes. He's giving her advice.

I can tell she's into him from the way she tilts her body toward him. The way she looks at his mouth when he speaks. I can't watch. Yet I can't not watch either.

Curtis lowers his hand to his lap. Her hand is nearby and he hooks her little finger with his. I turn away.

On the screen, a beginner skier has somehow strayed into the pipe, apparently lost. Dale does a massive spin, comes down blind, and almost lands on top of him.

"Fuck off!" on-screen Dale shouts, and the room erupts with laughter.

God. Curtis and Jacinta are kissing. She pulls away with a soft laugh, then goes back for more. I don't blame her. Curtis smiles through the kiss and touches her jaw. Whispers something in her ear. She nods; they stand and head upstairs.

I catch Saskia staring after them. Looks like I'm not the only one who's jealous.

CHAPTER 27

Over at the bar, Brent lifts bottles one by one to study the labels.

Please don't start drinking, Brent. I need you sober and prepared for what might be about to go down. It's not even noon yet, and we have a long day ahead of us.

I turn back to Heather. She's lied to me before. Is she lying again? Yet her story has a horrible ring of truth. When it came to his sister, Curtis's emotions always ran high. I've seen him lose control over Saskia-related issues several times already this weekend.

"What happened next?" I say.

"We couldn't find Saskia, so we figured she must have ridden down to the half-pipe."

I study her body language, trying to decide if I believe her. She's really jumpy, eyes flitting from me to the doorway to Brent, but that's not necessarily a sign of dishonesty. It could be a sign of fear.

Fear that Curtis is onto her.

That she might be about to meet the same fate as Saskia.

Across the restaurant, Brent pours a large measure of something into a glass. *No, Brent.* He downs it and crosses the room to the window.

Heather toys with her teaspoon. "The competition was about to start, so I got the bubble back to the midstation and left Brent and Curtis on the glacier to ride down."

"I don't remember seeing you watching the comp," I say.

"I only stayed for the first few heats, then I got too cold, so I went home."

She jumps hard as Curtis and Dale stomp in, pink cheeked, leaving a trail of snowy footprints in their wake.

"Find anything?" I say.

Dale shakes his head. "Waste of time."

"We didn't bother breaking into the lift shack," Curtis says. "You could see through the window the space where the radio would normally be."

Dale eyes Curtis, flexing his fists. "Someone had taken it. Same as downstairs."

The time outdoors clearly hasn't improved their moods.

Brent leans his forehead to the glass. "Fuck."

I need to tell Curtis about the credit card, but I'm getting visions of him pounding Dale's face to a pulp, and it's not as though we can call an ambulance if they hurt each other. We're hanging on a precipice, and one wrong word could tip us over the edge.

"So I'm mountaineering, am I?" Heather says shakily.

Dale kicks over a chair and Heather flinches.

"Must be something we can do," Dale says. "I hot-wired a car one time. Maybe we could try to hot-wire one of the snowcats."

Curtis snorts. "Be my guest. Even if you get one started, do you seriously reckon you could drive it down the black run?"

I can see Heather cringing at the prospect.

"I'd rather take my chances on foot," she says.

Brent stalks back and forth in front of the window like my cat does when he's desperate to go out.

Curtis looks my way, and I realize he's waiting for me to tell the others about the lift pass. Shit. They're going to turn on him. This is going to be the final straw.

I finger the sharp corners of the pass in my pocket. If I tell them,

Dale will take it as conclusive evidence that Curtis killed his sister, and Heather will side with her husband. Brent has tried to stay neutral so far, but I sense he's reached the breaking point and this could well sway him. And I'll be caught in the middle.

I consider Curtis's story. What if it was planted on him, like he said? To make us turn on each other? Exactly like the Icebreaker itself.

"Are you looking at *him?*" Dale says suddenly.

Heather splutters. "What? No."

Dale grips her by her upper arms. I step over to them. Brent starts in our direction, too.

Dale raises his chin. "Don't even think of it," he tells Brent.

"I wasn't looking at anyone," Heather says in a tiny voice.

"Back off," I tell Dale. Talk about possessive. He never used to be this wound up.

Nor did Curtis and Brent. A dangerous energy buzzes in the room. It really is as though the savageness of the terrain outside is infecting us.

I slide my hand from my pocket. I'm going to keep quiet about Saskia's pass for now because I can't risk starting another brawl. We need to keep calm and work together to get safely down from here.

Curtis checks his watch. "We need to get going so we're down before dark."

"What about the lift shack at the top of the tow lift?" Dale says. "Might be a radio up there."

"I doubt it," Curtis says. "Not when they've removed the ones down here."

"Yeah, but they might not have bothered to take that one. It'll only take us a few minutes to check."

"We haven't got a few minutes," Curtis snaps. "We don't know how long it's going to take to get your wife down the black run."

Dale shoots Heather a poisonous look.

She stares down at her feet. Right now, it's hard to say who she seems more scared of, Curtis or her own husband.

"Look," I say. "If it's any easier for you, Heather, I'll lend you my snowboard and I'll go on foot."

She has no concept of how big a deal this is to me. I've just passed up the first chance I've had to snowboard in ten years. But the poor girl looks like she's about to puke on her boots.

"Thanks, Milla," Dale mutters.

I'm not doing it for you, arsehole. I'm doing it for her.

But Heather wraps her arms around her chest. "I don't remember how to do it. It's ten years since I was on a board and I was never any good even then."

The rest of us exchange looks. The prospect of guiding a nervous beginner down a rock-riddled black run is none too appealing.

Curtis sighs. "Who's up for trekking up to that lift shack?"

I suck in the thin, cold air of the glacier. The Alps spread out below me like spiky white teeth. To the east: Italy. A hundred kilometers north: Mont Blanc. I feel like I'm standing on top of the world.

God, I missed this. The brilliant whiteness. The familiar weight of my snowboard tucked under my arm, the way other women carry handbags.

"Won't be long," Dale tells Heather.

She nods and adjusts her scarf.

Dale was going to stay down here with her but she must have seen the longing on his face—or more likely she was happy to get rid of him.

"Go," she told him. "I'll sit at the bottom and watch."

I was amazed that she would offer but I'm not complaining, because all kitted up with his snowboard and goggles, Dale looks like Viking Dale again.

Brent, too, looks more like his old self. He nods at the half-melted jumps, smiling his dimpled grin. "You thinking what I'm thinking?"

"Definitely," Dale says.

For a few minutes I'm going to pretend everything is just as it used to be and we're all still friends.

Curtis is clearly dubious about Heather being left on her own, but he doesn't argue. He'd rather have Dale with him, I imagine, than down here with Heather and possibly up to no good.

"Careful where you step," Curtis says. "We're sticking to the line of the lift. Single file."

"Got it," Dale says.

We trudge up the slope. The kiosk is all shut up, the deck-chair area swamped with snowdrifts. The little plastic button seats of the tow lift dangle from the cable, creaking as they swing in the breeze.

"Wish we could get the lift running," Dale says. "Save us a walk."

The powder is over our knees in places. I wade up behind Brent, more out of breath than I care to admit. Dale is just in front. He glances over his shoulder and I look back, too. Heather's still there, perched on a snowdrift beside the main entrance.

Above, steep peaks loom. I suppress a shudder at the thought of all that snow sliding down on top of us. We all wear harnesses and avalanche transceivers. I gave my old transceiver away with the rest of my snowboarding stuff, but my brother still goes snowboarding every year and luckily he had one I could borrow. I'm glad I thought to bring it with me.

Unzipping the neck of my jacket, I peer down at the little blue box strapped to my torso and check the screen. The last thing you want is to be buried under the snow, wondering if you switched the damn thing on.

"Aw, how good does that one look?" Brent says as we draw level with the largest of the jumps. He starts to head over.

"*No!*" Curtis shouts. "It's not safe. Stick to the lift line."

Brent huffs and turns around.

"Perfect for a backflip," I say as Brent reaches me. "We'll hit it on the way down." I expect him to laugh, but he doesn't.

"Sure you're up to it?" he says. "If you've not ridden since—"

"Oh, don't start." This overprotectiveness reminds me of why I ended things with him. I was actually joking about the backflip, but now I'm going to have to try one.

Dale turns. "Always liked to play it dangerous, didn't you, Milla?"

Something about his tone bothers me. I stare at his mirror lenses, wishing I could see his eyes. Was that a gesture of respect—an attempt to renew our friendship?

Or was it a threat?

Now that I think about it, it's odd that he was prepared to leave Heather on her own. It's as though he *knows* nothing bad will happen to her.

Because he and Heather are the ones behind all this.

If so, what exactly does he intend to do with the rest of us?

CHAPTER 28

TEN YEARS AGO

I watch intently as Saskia drops into the half-pipe. "Does she still go bigger than me on her first hit?"

"Hard to say," Brent replies.

I sigh. "I'm going to take that for a yes."

Brent and I sit at the bottom on a snack break. Last night was cold and clear, and the pipe still hasn't softened. He's bashed his knee, I've tweaked my wrist, and we both hold wads of snow against our injured parts.

A gasp goes up as someone hits the deck hard. Shit—that was Curtis. He dusts snow off his jacket, then scrambles up.

"He's trying Haakon flips," Brent says. "He was doing them on the tramp yesterday."

Jacinta is waiting at the bottom of the tow lift. Curtis adjusts the strap on her helmet and they ride up together. They've barely been apart all week. I turn away. But if he has to date anyone, I'm glad it's her. She's lovely.

Saskia is watching them too, and she doesn't look happy. Wants all her brother's attention for herself.

Odette drops in and flips high above the lip. McTwist—a big one. I sigh again. "How can I compete with that?"

"She's not doing the Brits, is she?" Brent asks.

"No, thank God."

"So don't worry about it. Not yet."

"I could train twelve months a year and I still won't be able to ride like that. My survival instinct's too strong."

"Chill, Mills." Brent slides an arm around my back.

I push his arm away. "You wouldn't understand. You don't have a survival instinct."

Brent just laughs and I want to punch him.

I watch Odette finish her run. A few rare women like her can override the fear, but as much as I try, I just can't do it. I'm landing small McTwists now when the conditions are right—but the fear is ever present. Holding me back. It's so frustrating.

The one consolation is Saskia can't override it either. She's McTwisting again—my attempts have pushed her into it—but I can tell she's as scared of them as I am.

I cram a handful of nuts into my mouth. I'm training so hard that I struggle to replace the energy I use, so I've taken to eating nuts all day long, even as I go up the tow. Sleeping tablets are helping me settle at night, but then I need a Smash in the morning to wake me up.

Curtis is back at the top already. I watch nervously, suspecting he's going to try another Haakon flip. I find it difficult enough to watch him as it is—Brent, too. Some of the positions they put themselves into. Upside down with their heads swinging perilously close to the ice; spins that seem like they won't stop in time for them to land.

Brent falls a lot because he pushes the limit so damned hard. Curtis rarely falls but when he does he drags himself up, Terminator-like, and tries again until he nails it.

He plunges in now, spins sideways through the air, and goes down again.

Brent groans. "That would've hurt."

Curtis lies there, a hand pressed to his shoulder.

"Should we check he's okay?" I ask.

Brent bites into a muesli bar. "Just wait."

Sure enough, Curtis struggles upright and sideslips down, testing if he can rotate his shoulder. Still nursing it, he heads to the tow.

"You watch," Brent says. "He'll try it again."

"Should we stop him?" I say. "He's going to break something."

Brent laughs. "Bit of advice. When he falls, don't go near him, don't even look at him, or he'll bite your head off."

Just like my brother when he loses a rugby match.

Julien drops in. Back-to-back flips on his first two hits.

"I thought Dale was going to punch Julien earlier," Brent tells me.

"Really?" I say. "Why?"

"He made some comment about Dale's nose grabs. And his jacket. In the same sentence. Guy doesn't know when to keep his mouth shut."

My laughter dies as Curtis drops in again. I almost can't bear to watch. He flips sideways above the ice, catches his edge on landing, and goes down with a crunch.

When it's clear he's not getting up, Brent and I hurry over. He's clutching his shoulder, face twisted with pain.

Brent removes Curtis's snowboard, hooks an arm around his waist, and hoists him upright. "Come on, bro. Let's get you to the cable car."

I hang back, sensing Curtis won't want me to see him like this. Anyway, Brent looks like he can manage.

Jacinta hurries over. "Crap, did you fall again?"

"I'm fine," Curtis says through gritted teeth. "See you after training."

Saskia watches from the top of the pipe, apparently unconcerned.

"Back in a bit," Brent says, and the two of them walk off.

Ten minutes later, Brent reappears alone.

"Is he all right?" I ask.

"Popped his shoulder a couple of times last winter," Brent says. "Thinks he felt it come out and go back in just now."

Poor Curtis. I wonder how long he'll have to sit out for.

Saskia rides past on her way to the tow. I glance at her, expecting her to ask about Curtis, but she heads straight by. Seen it all a million times before, I guess.

Brent and I head up the tow together. My goggles have misted up. The foam's wet after so many falls. I search my pocket. Damn. "Have you got a goggle cloth?"

"Sure." Brent hands me one with the Oakley logo.

He's riding in his back-to-front baseball cap again. When we reach the top of the lift, he lowers his goggles over it. "I'll show you a Crippler."

"You don't have to," I say.

He frowns down the length of the half-pipe.

"Seriously," I say. "I'll look on YouTube." I couldn't cope with seeing him fall as well.

"I'm just trying to remember how to do them. It's been a while."

He speeds off down the side of the pipe and plunges in. My breath catches as he flips on his second hit. A few hours ago he was inside me, looking down at my face with more tenderness than I wanted to see. And now he's upside down, twisting his body through a crazy diagonal, high above the ice.

Emotions flash through me. Pride. Envy. Guilt—he's doing this for my benefit—and terror.

Mainly terror. If he doesn't get his board around in time . . .

He gets his board around—just—and I breathe again.

Odette laughs softly as she straps in nearby. "Cripplers are scary."

I didn't realize she was watching me. "Hi, Odette." I'm flushing now.

"So you are together with Brent. Yes?"

I hesitate. "It's a casual thing."

"He rides well. And can he beat you at arm wrestling?"

I manage a smile. "We've never actually tried. But yeah, I reckon he'd win." I try to pull myself together. "Nice McTwist earlier, by the way."

"Thanks."

I should ask her if she's tried a Crippler but I'm still breathing hard.

I didn't want to feel like this about anyone out here. Friends with benefits; that's all Brent and I are supposed to be.

A few runs later, I'm walking up the side of the pipe behind Saskia when Jacinta drops in and pulls one of her huge 720s. Good thing I won't be competing against her this winter. Saskia will, at an FIS world cup event next week. I could have entered, but after my shameful performance at the Le Rocher Open I'm giving international competition a miss until next year and focusing purely on the British Championships.

Jacinta zigzags back and forth and speeds up the wall toward me. From the position of her upper body I can tell she's gearing up for another big spin. A small black object tumbles into the pipe. Jacinta swerves around it, but an instant later she's airborne. Her spin goes off-axis and she returns to earth, board and legs still over the flattop. Her thigh meets the lip of the pipe with an appalling crack.

She screams and slithers to the pipe floor. Oh shit. I sledge down the wall on the seat of my pants to see if she's okay. Saskia joins me and we crouch over Jacinta, who is in too much pain to speak. I wave madly to the people at the bottom for help.

The back of my mind is processing what I saw. That black thing. What was it? I look around but I can't see it.

Whatever it was, though, it came from Saskia's hand.

CHAPTER 29

PRESENT DAY

I trudge up the slope toward the lift shack, eyes glued to the back of Dale's jacket. I hope I'm wrong about him. Anyway, it's three of us against one of him, so what's he going to do?

This is taking longer than I expected. I forgot how hard it was to walk through deep powder. Curtis is powering ahead, almost at the shack already. I glance down at the Panorama building. Heather's still there.

"Where did you ride last winter?" Brent asks Dale.

"I didn't," Dale says. "Me and Heather were too busy setting up the business."

"And how's it going?"

He hesitates a beat. "Tough, actually. Barely covering overheads."

Okay, so Dale is clearly short of cash. Curtis raised the possibility of blackmail. Is that what this weekend is about? Is this whole reunion a desperate scheme that Dale has hatched up to extort money from one of us? What if they can't or won't pay up? What would Dale do then?

Curtis reaches the shack and disappears inside. At least the door's open. With a jolt, I remember it was Dale's idea to walk up here. I watch him nervously, hoping he doesn't try anything.

As the rest of us get to the shack, Curtis emerges. And he looks murderous. Something flaps in his hand—a sheet of paper.

Across the middle of the sheet are three words. Written in neat capitals, just like the secrets in the Icebreaker.

THE GAME CONTINUES.

A tremor runs through me. "That's what—"

"I know," Curtis says.

"What?" Brent asks.

"It's what Saskia and I used to say to each other," I reply.

"Oh, come on," Dale says. "Are you serious? It's not her doing this."

Curtis steps toward him. "And you know that how?"

Dale puts his hands up. "It's just not logical. I know she's your sister, man, but stop and think for a second. Like, where's she been hiding all this time?" He looks to Brent for help. "And why would she want to mess with us?"

Pushing past us, Curtis raises his goggles to his forehead, eyes sweeping the slopes as though he's looking for her.

"I take it there's no radio?" Dale calls.

Curtis doesn't answer. Squinting into the distance, he hikes up for a better view.

With a hiss of exasperation, Dale heads to the lift shack.

I turn to Brent. "What do you think? Is there a chance—"

"No. It's not her." Brent's response is instant, just as it was the last time I raised the possibility. And that niggles at me. Why's he so sure? He can't know that. Unless . . .

"So who is it then?" I watch his face, what I can see of it below the goggles.

"I told you," he says flatly. "It must be Julien."

"You really think so?"

"Who else? He was all over her that winter. Probably reckons one of us killed her and wants to punish us for it."

"Why wait ten years?"

Brent has no answer. But I remember the angry scene with Julien the night before Saskia disappeared and I'm not convinced Julien's behind this.

A movement down the slope catches my attention. What . . . ? I shield my eyes from the sun. The Panorama building sits still and silent. The main entrance is obscured from view behind the largest of the jumps, so we can't see Heather's perch from here. I thought I saw a moving figure, but there's nothing now. It must have been Heather. I look up at the sky. Or the shadow of that cloud.

Dale comes out of the shack empty-handed. "Better get back down."

He's looking down the slope at the Panorama building. Maybe he's finally realized it was risky to leave Heather on her own.

Brent eyes the jumps, clearly planning his line already.

Curtis has returned. He gives the paper one last look, then stuffs it in his pocket. "Strap in."

The still air rings with the clicking of snowboard bindings. The sound triggers a million memories, and excitement rushes through me. I rachet up my bindings and for the first time in ten years I feel alive. I'm going to push all this shit from my mind, just for a minute.

Curtis lines himself up with the topmost jump and soars off it into the air.

Brent whoops. "All right!"

I'm tingling with fear—a good sort of fear. Some people choose drugs to get this feeling, and arguably that might be safer, but I've always preferred to get it from sports. Here goes. My board hisses over the ice, picking up speed. Wind blasts my face, flapping the legs of my snowboard trousers. The high I get from pushing myself in the gym is nothing compared to this.

I reach the end of the takeoff and pop upward. There's a familiar and oh-so-sweet stomach-dropping sensation as I sail through the air. I grab the toe edge of my board and bone out my front foot. Indy. And release the grab to land smoothly.

"Take it easy, Milla," Curtis warns as I pull up beside him.

"Just for a moment, I was happy," I say. "Why did you have to go and spoil it?"

"We're on our own up here. If something happens, you're screwed."

I'm pumping with adrenaline. "I don't see you taking it easy."

"Yeah, but I'm still snowboarding regularly. You said you're not."

"It's like riding a bicycle."

"God, you are *so* like my sister. Just sometimes." Must have seen my face. "Anyway, don't go thinking you're getting helicoptered off if you break something."

"I'm aware of that."

Curtis glances up at Dale and Brent, who are crouched over Dale's board, fiddling with the bindings, and lowers his voice. "Why didn't you tell them about the lift pass?"

"I don't know."

Curtis studies me thoughtfully. "Do you—" His jaw drops.

I turn to see Brent flipping through the air, grabbing his board upside down. He stomps the landing and brakes hard, spraying us with snow. There's a huge grin on his face. I give him a high five. This, finally, is the Brent I used to know.

"Keep it safe," Curtis calls.

"You telling me how to ride now, bro?"

"Am I the only one who's aware of what's going on?" Curtis shouts, clearly out of patience. "If something happens to one of us, it affects all of us."

Just then, Dale flies through the air with some crazy corkscrewed spin.

Curtis throws his hands up. "Oh, for fuck's sake!"

I can see his point—it *is* dangerous out here—but it was just as dangerous in the Panorama building with the way these guys keep turning on each other. Better that we let off steam up here for a couple of minutes before we prepare for the long trek down.

Still muttering, Curtis rides down to the next jump. And casually backflips.

Okay. This is my chance to be the fearless wild child I used to be. And it might be the last chance I ever have to do a backflip, because who knows if I'll ever return to the snow? Brent adjusts his goggles beside me. I don't tell him what I'm about to try because he won't like it.

Dale lets out a shout. "Where's Heather?"

I shield my eyes from the sun, straining to see. She's not there. "Maybe she got cold and went in."

"*Heather!*" Dale's shout echoes around the valley. He races down, bypassing the rest of the jumps.

Brent sighs. "Better get down there."

He and Curtis ride after Dale.

I look down at the jump. Dale's at the building already, removing his snowboard. I know I should scrap my backflip, but it will only take me a few extra seconds. Soon I'll be back home doing the same old same old and I have this one tiny opportunity.

I race down, relying on muscle memory to guide my body through the motions. When I reach the end of the takeoff, I tip backward, tucking tight to make sure I get my body around. As I return to earth, I realize I've flipped too hard. I'm going to land on the tail of my board. In a desperate attempt to correct, I lean forward. The nose of my board embeds itself into the snow and comes to a sharp stop. My upper body keeps rotating, but my legs don't budge; they're locked in place.

Fiery pain rips through the back of my knee. For a moment it's all I'm aware of. I clutch my knee as though that will somehow limit the agony. When the surroundings swim back into focus, I see Brent and Curtis peering down at me, panting for breath.

"What's the damage?" Curtis says.

I gasp out the words. "I think it's my lateral collateral." It was the same sort of fall the last time I ripped it.

Curtis glances at the building. Dale's not there. Must have gone in already.

"Go," I say. "I'll catch up with you."

"Want a hand?" Curtis says.

I shake my head and struggle upright. Gingerly I shift weight onto my bad leg. Waves of pain. I bite my lip so I don't gasp. Both of them reach out to me.

"I'll manage," I say. "Just go."

Curtis explodes. "Why do you never let anyone help you?"

He and Brent hurry down to the building.

That's all I need—him ripping into me. "Oh, and you do?" I shout after him.

Using my board as a crutch, I limp after them. The hot ache in my knee becomes a savage sting every time I put weight on it. *Blank it out. You've done it before.*

By the time I reach them, Curtis and Brent have pulled off most of their kit and replaced their snow-covered boots with their skate shoes. I prop my snowboard against the wall beside the others.

Dale runs out of the building. "I can't find her."

"Have you checked your dorm?" Curtis says.

"She's not there." Dale looks frantic. "Did any of you see her come in? She might have gone down a crevasse."

We exchange looks. The golden rule on a glacier? Never take your snowboard off. With your board on, your weight is spread over a larger surface area. Without one, the risk of falling down a crevasse increases massively. When we walked up, we stuck to the line of the tow lift, knowing that a few months earlier at least, resort staff would have kept it clear of crevasses. But Heather would have no clue about that, and unlike the rest of us, she wasn't wearing a transceiver or harness.

"I'm going to check around out here." Dale heads off toward the garages.

"We'll look inside," Curtis calls after him.

"You managing, Mills?" Brent says.

"Yep."

Curtis watches me struggle to get my boots off, without saying a word. I can tell it's killing him.

"You don't have to wait for me," I tell him.

"All right," Curtis says. "You check upstairs, Brent, and I'll check down here. I'm sure she's in there somewhere."

"I'll be in my dorm," I call as they race off.

I scoop up a handful of snow and press it to my knee. There's a mountain of kit by the door. I rummage through harnesses, gloves, and goggles for my shoes. Here they are. My socks are soaked now, but I grit my teeth and hobble inside. I need to get this leg elevated.

I turn down the corridor toward the dorms. Curtis must have just been down here because the lights are on. I sniff the air and my stomach lurches. I think I smell Saskia's perfume again.

My senses prickle. Someone's behind me.

I turn as fast as my knee will allow, but nobody's there. Spooked, I limp on. Not far now. I can't wait to get behind a locked door. A rustle from behind makes me spin around again. Shit—that hurt. I clutch my knee. But the corridor is empty.

"Hello?" I call.

A thud of footsteps from upstairs. That must be what I heard. Brent's up there. This building plays tricks on my mind. I continue past Brent's dorm and the laundry cupboard.

The lights click off. Total darkness. I hate that stupid timer. Where's the bloody switch? Still clutching my ice pack in one hand, I pat the wall with the other. The ice is melting and dripping everywhere, making the floorboards slippery, and the last thing I need is to fall again. I creep forward, groping my way along. There has to be a switch somewhere.

A draft rushes in behind me. Was that a door opening? I turn, eyes straining into the blackness. "Hello?"

Is someone in the corridor with me? My fingers flap for a switch. Yeah—here!

As the light comes on, something disappears around the corner. I stifle a gasp.

I didn't see that. I couldn't have.

It looked like a flash of white-blond hair.

CHAPTER 30

TEN YEARS AGO

I text Curtis. *How's Jacinta?*

Broken femur. They've taken her down to Grenoble.

I'm so sorry.

Poor Jacinta. That's her season over.

I lie awake for half the night debating whether to tell Curtis about his sister's role in the accident. I'm almost certain the black thing, whatever it was, came from Saskia's hand. Yet I couldn't swear to it; it happened so fast. It might just have blown past her in the wind. And if it *did* come from her, she could have dropped it accidentally. My gut tells me she dropped it deliberately, but even so, she probably only intended to distract Jacinta and make her bottle out of her spin.

Anyway, telling Curtis wouldn't achieve anything. Saskia would say it was an accident and the damage is already done. Hopefully she's learned her lesson.

At the pipe the next day I can't get the accident out of my head. Every time I'm about to jump, I find myself looking around to see where Saskia is, to make sure she can't drop something onto *me*.

Okay, she's coming up the tow, so I'm safe. Deep breath. Come on, focus!

With ten weeks to go until the Brits, I've pushed aside the idea of trying a Crippler for now. It was scary enough watching Brent do one yesterday. Instead, I'm trying to go bigger, so I'm dropping in from farther and farther up the pipe. Of course, Saskia soon caught on and now she's doing the same.

This time I drop in from twenty meters up and nearly lose it on my way down the wall. My first hit shoots me higher than I expected; I flap my arms like mad for balance and somehow I land it. A few more speed wobbles and a sketchy spin on the last hit. I skid to a stop, amazed I'm still upright.

Brent drops in above. Such an aggressive line; no wonder he goes so big. I count the rotations on his final hit. One, two, three. I think. He spins so fast it's hard to tell.

"Was that a ten eighty?" I say when he pulls up alongside me.

He grins. "Yeah. I was going for a twelve sixty, but never mind."

"You went huge. Don't you get scared?"

"Only when I'm watching you."

"Shut up."

"I mean it, Mills. You were way on the edge on that last run. Cool it a bit, hey?"

"*What?* You're the last person I expected to hear that from."

"Sorry. Um, I'm going to grab a snack if you want to—"

"No."

He heads off to his backpack.

Odette pulls to a stop beside me. "Are you okay?"

I blow out my breath. "Brent just told me to cool it. Such a bloody hypocrite."

"It's hard riding with someone you care about. But you have to separate it. Otherwise . . . Pfft. They are holding you down like an anchor."

It's so true. And how can you bust big air with an anchor?

"We go up again?" Odette says.

"No. You go. I need to psych myself up." I want to watch Saskia and see where she drops in from.

"Okay," Odette says. "Cross your fingers. I will try my inverted spin."

Odette and I spotted each other on the trampoline yesterday.

"Good luck," I call as she rides off.

Dale sits on a snowbank drinking a Smash. I regret ever trying the stuff. I've cut down to a single can a day now and I'm aiming to quit altogether. Once you get into the habit of not sleeping, it's hard to break. I think I need stronger sleeping tablets.

Here comes Saskia. I strain to see. Damn—she still goes higher. I look the other way as she rides past me to the tow. Curtis is right behind her. Whatever he did to his shoulder, he's not letting it hold him back.

"You should go for a Tail Grab on that last spin," he calls to Brent as he rides past. "You'd be able to hold the grab longer."

Curtis ranked number one in the UK last year and Brent ranked number two, but the way Brent's riding this year, he might reverse that. Why's Curtis helping him? But if Brent thinks there's anything odd about it, he doesn't show it. He just nods thoughtfully, like he's picturing it in his head, and bites into his apple.

I chase after Curtis and throw myself onto the T-bar beside him. I want to see what he's playing at.

"Thought you'd be down at the hospital," I say.

"Jacinta didn't want me to miss training," he says.

"How is she?"

"Yeah, not too good. She'll fly home when she's fit to fly. It was a bad break."

"That's awful. What about your shoulder?"

"I got it checked out while I was there." Wry smile. "Handy, that."

"And how is it?"

"Not that bad."

Which basically means it's hurting like hell but not enough to stop him from riding.

I nod in Brent's direction. "Can I ask something? Why did you do that?"

"Do what?" Curtis says.

"Help Brent."

Silence.

"The boy's got balls," Curtis says finally.

"Yeah, but you're competing against him."

He shrugs. "I guess it's how I play this game."

"Does Brent help you?"

"We discuss tricks, yeah."

"You play the game a lot differently from how your sister plays it." *And from how I play it*, I think, but don't say.

Curtis's jaw tightens. "I like to think so."

My goggles have misted up again. Gripping the T-bar between my thighs, I pull my glove off and search my pocket for my goggle cloth. "Do you have a goggle cloth?"

"Here."

Someone has dropped their sunglasses in the middle of the tow track. One-footed and no-handed, I steer around them. My board skids out from under me.

Curtis grabs me by the waist. "I've got you."

Damn. As much as I try to pretend my crush has gone away, it hasn't. It's stronger than ever. "Thanks."

It was a mistake to get on the lift with him. I need to focus. We're nearly at the top. I take slow, deep breaths, trying to clear my mind.

"You okay?" Curtis says.

I smile. "Yeah. I'm trying to go bigger than your sister."

"I noticed." He's not smiling.

"Let me guess. You're going to tell me to cool it as well?"

"Who told you to cool it?"

"Brent."

"No. Go for it. Just . . . watch your back around my sister, okay?"

I stare at him. "What do you mean by that?"

He presses his lips together as though he regrets saying anything.

I wish he'd tell me what's going on. I think of his previous warnings to me. How he told Brent to keep an eye on her. Does Saskia have a history of more than just obnoxious pranks? Has she hurt someone else?

Right, that's it. I'm going to confront her.

She's strapping in at the top of the pipe, so I head over to her. "Can we talk?"

She seems surprised. "Sure."

We've hardly spoken since she kicked my board into that crevasse. Curtis glances our way as he straps in. I look around for somewhere we can go where we won't be overheard.

"Want to ride down to the chairlift?" she says.

"Yeah, great," I say.

"Where are you going?" Curtis calls when we ride off in the opposite direction.

"The chair!" I shout.

Saskia and I swoop down the red run. The slope is deserted. I did this run with Saskia a month ago, back when I thought we were friends. I hate to admit it given everything she's done, but I've missed riding with her.

She pulls a 180 over a mound; I streak after her and pull a 360. She sees and 360s a lip to the side of the slope. I attempt a 540 and fall. She laughs.

There's this notion that it isn't cool to be competitive if you're female, and around other women, even Odette, I find myself trying to hide my competitive streak. With Saskia, though, I let it out. She's so unafraid to be herself, it makes *me* unafraid. In her company, as angry as she sometimes makes me, I feel like I'm the truest version of myself.

If only we could have been friends. Maybe we would have been if we were doing a team sport instead of an individual one. Or would we still be competing with each other, because that's just how we are?

We reach the bottom of the chairlift, gasping for breath. There's no queue, so we go straight through the turnstile. That was such fun I want to do it again. Damn. Now I have to bring up the accident.

A three-man seat trundles toward us. It snowed lightly earlier and the black PVC seat backs look like they've been sprinkled in icing sugar.

"Hey!" someone shouts.

I look around.

Curtis races down the slope toward us. "Wait!"

Saskia tugs my arm. "Come on."

I hesitate, but Saskia yanks me forward and the chair sweeps us up.

"See you at the top!" I shout to Curtis.

Saskia hasn't lowered the safety bar, so I reach for it.

"Wait," she says. "Let me take my jacket off. I'm sweating."

So I leave the bar raised and sit back in the seat. It's a warm day. It's only early February but it feels like spring already. Saskia ties her jacket around her hips and sits back beside me.

Curtis lets out a shrill whistle from the chair behind.

I turn. "What?"

"The safety bar!"

"Is he for real?" Saskia mutters.

I lower the bar and it swings down across our laps with a clunk. I turn to Saskia. Let's get this over with. "What was it you dropped onto Jacinta yesterday?"

To my shock, she laughs. "Is *that* what you wanted to talk about?"

I study her, hoping her amusement is due to surprise rather than the demise of Jacinta's season.

She reaches into her pocket and pulls out a black scrap of cloth. "You mean this?"

I notice the symbol in the corner—the white lightning bolt of Electric eyewear. "Hey, that's my goggle cloth."

"I found it in the pipe where poor Jacinta fell. You dropped it right on top of her."

"*You* dropped it!" I say.

She laughs again. "Why would *I* drop *your* goggle cloth?"

My mouth opens. Her actions caused Jacinta to break her leg, yet there's not a shred of remorse. It's almost as though she's happy about the result. "You're unbelievable. You must have . . ." God, I can hardly get words out. And how the hell did she get hold of it?

She glances over her shoulder at her brother on the chair. "It's my word against yours. If you keep quiet about it, I won't say anything either. Who do you think he'll believe?"

I witnessed just now how protective Curtis is of his sister. He might have told me to watch out for her, but if it comes down to choosing a side, he would quite possibly believe her. Blood is thicker and all that. And it's *my* goggle cloth after all.

Then I think of the text message I sent him yesterday. *I'm so sorry. You could easily construe that as guilt.* My friendship with Curtis means so much to me. Even if Saskia described it as though I'd dropped the cloth as a silly prank, I'm not sure he'd ever forgive me for breaking his girlfriend's leg.

Saskia stuffs it back in her pocket. "I'll just keep this. Evidence."

CHAPTER 31

PRESENT DAY

My knee throbs. As fast as I can, I limp down the corridor. Face your fears head-on; that's what snowboarding taught me. I turn the corner, terrified of what I'll see.

The corridor is empty. I let out my breath. It was just my imagination.

Or my guilty conscience.

The corridor branches and I turn left. "Heather!" I call.

"Milla?"

Heather's voice, so faint I can hardly hear it.

"Where are you?" I shout.

"Here . . ." A series of thuds from farther down the corridor.

I follow the sound and push the door two doors down. Heather bursts through the gap and tumbles into my arms.

"The door . . ." She's shaking so much she can hardly speak.

"Hey," I say. "You're okay."

"It wouldn't open."

"It opened fine just now. Maybe it was just stuck." I push the door wide. "See?"

The room is some sort of staff changing room with cubbyholes for shoes and clothes, and a shower and toilet. I don't remember seeing it before. Maybe I didn't switch on the light.

Heather wraps her arms around herself, still shaking. Definitely not acting this time. That's one scared woman.

"Why did you come in here anyway?" I say.

"I needed the toilet." Her eyes sweep the corridor. "So I went to our dorm. And on my way back, I saw someone."

"Who?"

"I don't know. But there was someone in the corridor with me."

"Brent or Curtis, you mean?"

"No. It wasn't one of us."

My heart thumps again. I'd just about convinced myself my eyes were playing tricks on me. But if Heather saw it, too . . . "Were they male or female?"

"I didn't get a good look. I just ran and hid in here."

I sniff the air. The smell is so faint I'm not sure if I'm imagining it. "Can you smell perfume?"

She sniffs. "No, why?"

"Curtis thinks Saskia might be the one who brought us here," I say.

"No." Heather shrinks back against the wall. "It can't be."

She's gone so pale that for a moment I think she's going to faint. I grip her arm. "Deep breaths."

"But she's . . ." She finds it hard to say. "Dead. Isn't she?"

"Apparently." I'm not at all sure anymore.

Heather falls into a stunned silence. I can't tell if it's ghosts in general that scare her or the notion of this one particular ghost.

"Anyway, Dale's freaking," I say. "You better go and tell them you're alive."

Her eyes dart either way down the corridor. "Will you come with me?"

"You'll be faster without me." I explain about my knee. "Go on. I'll catch up when I can."

Reluctantly she heads off.

My knee is on fire and I'm desperately thirsty. There's a glass by the sink. I limp over to it, flinching as the door slams behind me. The glass doesn't look too clean, so I run the cold tap and scoop water into my mouth with my hands. The water pressure in here is even worse than it is in my shower. Only a trickle comes out.

When I've drunk two handfuls, I lean against the wall, psyching myself up to limp back to my dorm.

As I turn to leave, someone crashes through the door.

A tiny scream bursts out of me.

Curtis grips my hips. "Hey, it's me."

I'm breathless. Shock, combined with the feel of his hands. "I found Heather."

"Yeah," he says. "I saw her just now."

I haven't pulled away and neither has he. Like me, he still wears his snowboard jacket, and the Velcro fastenings on our collars are close enough to snag together. I can smell his skin—sweat and sunscreen.

"How's your knee?"

I smile. "Hurting."

He smiles, too. "You had to do that, didn't you?"

"Yep."

"Do you regret it?"

"No."

His hands tighten on my hips and something inside me tightens, too.

"I've got a knee brace in my dorm," he says. "But I don't know what the hell we're going to do, because now you can't ride down. You make me so mad, Milla."

He doesn't seem it, though. Not anymore. There's warmth in his expression, the most there's been since we arrived here. And something else.

I walk him backward until he's up against the tiles.

"Milla."

I'm glad he's still holding me because I wouldn't trust my legs just now. "What?"

"What are you doing?"

"What does it look like?"

The desire in his eyes has mixed with turmoil. He swallows. "There's something I haven't told you."

Dread coils in my stomach and just like that, the mood is broken. I pull away from him.

There's only one thing I can think of that he might be keeping from me.

Did he? Kill her?

Please tell me I'm wrong, but what else could it be?

Curtis always seemed like he had stronger morals than anyone else. If he killed her—his own sister—what hope do the rest of us have? If I can't trust him, I can't trust anyone. Ever.

He steps toward me. "Forgive me, Milla."

What's he going to do to me?

I yank the door, but it doesn't open. Watching him over my shoulder, I tug harder. Shit. Unlike the dorms, this door doesn't have a catch. Somebody must have locked it with a key. "Did you lock it?"

"No. Milla, listen."

Through my panic I strain to think. He couldn't have locked it because I'd have seen him do it. Without taking my eyes off him, I pound on the door.

"Stop," Curtis says.

Heather's voice. "Milla? Curtis?"

"In here!" I thump on the door.

It opens with a creak. Heather stands there, gasping for breath. Was she the one who locked it?

"Quick," she says. "Brent's hurt."

CHAPTER 32

TEN YEARS AGO

I ring the bell at Brent's place.

Curtis opens the door with the sleeves of his hoodie rolled up and flour all over him. "Brent had to go to Risoul. Photo shoot for Smash tomorrow. He forgot to tell you."

"Oh." I step back from the door.

"Stay," Curtis says. "I'm making pizza."

"Um. Okay." I follow him into the kitchen.

He's walking stiffly, favoring his left leg.

"Are you hurt?" I say.

"It's nothing. I'm always falling to pieces by this time in the season."

"Brent's got painkillers. I'm sure—"

Curtis cuts me off. "I don't believe in them."

On the counter, dough is rolled out in neat circles. I should have guessed he'd be making pizza from scratch. His nose and cheeks are tanned from a run of sunny days; he's worked up a sweat from cooking and his hair is damp. I watch him deseed a red pepper, fingers fast and confident. I know somehow that being in bed with him would be very different from being in bed with Brent. How would those fingers feel on my skin?

Curtis glances up and catches me looking. Heat rushes to my face.

Like his sister, he has an uncanny ability to read my thoughts. I bloody hope he couldn't read what I was thinking just then.

"Wine? Beer?" he says, neutral as ever.

"I'll stick with water." I help myself to a glass.

Curtis nods at the mushrooms. "Chop them, could you?"

I search for a knife. "On the mountain earlier. When you chased me and Saskia down the slope. You looked rattled."

He shifts his feet.

"Why?"

He shrugs. "I don't know. But maybe . . . Now that we're in the lead-up to the Brits, it might be better not to ride with her. Just in case."

I laugh uncertainly. "Why? What else do you think she's going to do?"

He stares down at the pizzas, clearly mega-uncomfortable with the topic of conversation.

I remember something. "The safety bar."

Curtis's head jerks up.

A chill passes through me. "You don't think she would . . ."

When you spend as much time sitting on chairlifts as we do, you don't always bother to lower the safety bar. It's no big deal. I've never even come close to falling from one. The seats tilt backward, so it would be almost impossible to fall.

Unless you were pushed.

"No," Curtis says. "Of course not."

But he clearly *did* think that. Or at least considered it a possibility.

I slice the mushrooms thinly. "Put it this way. I won't be getting on any more chairlifts with your sister."

We chop in silence. Is Curtis right? She kicked my board down a crevasse and her reckless behavior caused Jacinta's accident. But would she really go that far? There were rocks below the lift. If I fell, I might have died.

Curtis's phone rings. He checks the screen and frowns. "Hi. When?

No, that's right before the Burton US Open. They'll have to send a photographer out here."

He hangs up.

"Your agent?" I say.

"Yeah." He looks really stressed.

"Hard being famous," I tease.

He snatches the knife from my hand. "If you're going to do it like that, we might as well eat frozen pizza."

I look down at the mushrooms, with no idea what I did wrong.

Curtis opens the fridge, pulls out more mushrooms, and chops them in half so fast they fly into the air. "Like that. See? Otherwise they go floppy."

"I'd rather have frozen pizza and do without the hassle."

"Trust me, it'll be worth it. Grab some basil, will you?"

I browse the little jars of dried herbs on the counter. Here we go. *Basilic.*

"Fresh!" he says in an exasperated tone.

I pull leaves from his basil plant and chop them. The smell fills the kitchen.

"Stop!" Curtis shouts.

"What now?"

"Never chop them. It ruins the flavor. Tear them."

I slam the knife down. *If we were together, I would tell you to shut up, shove you up against the wall, and kiss you. Or skip the wall and drag you straight upstairs.*

His fiery energy is a pain in the kitchen, but I'm pretty sure it would be explosive in the bedroom.

"Don't look at me like that, Milla." He says it so quietly I almost don't catch it.

I gulp. "Sorry."

He turns his back on me. "I only have so much control."

I think that means he feels it, too. My body is coiled with tension. It's been building all season, and with the Brits just over two months away, it's going through the roof.

Curtis blows out a long breath, back still turned, and gestures to the living room. "You'd better go in there. I'll finish the pizza."

My feet carry me toward the sofa. He's right—I can't look at him like that. I wouldn't do that to Brent or Jacinta, and neither would Curtis. He and Brent somehow manage to maintain their friendship, despite being neck and neck in the rankings, but if anything happened between me and Curtis just now, it would jeopardize that.

I shift wet clothing aside and sit down. The socky smell is particularly strong today. Three pairs of snowboard boots lean against the radiator. I lift an issue of *Whitelines* from the coffee table. Curtis is on the cover, jumping what looks like a bottomless crevasse. I'm flicking through the pages, hoping there's an interview, when I hear Saskia's voice.

"What's for dinner?"

Great. Just what I need.

"Uh, pizza," Curtis says.

"Yum," she says.

Did he invite her or has she just invited herself? I can't tell.

She enters the living room. Her face falls when she sees me, although she recovers quickly. "Hi."

"Hi." I should make small talk, for appearance's sake, but I'm picturing her beside me on the chairlift. With her right hand slipping behind my back.

Saskia peels off her snowboard jacket and slings it to the sofa, narrowly missing my legs. Her helmet and gloves come off next. She releases her hair from its ponytail and it cascades in waves down her back. Would she seriously have pushed me?

Something occurs to me then. It works in Saskia's favor if I'm unnerved by her. Was that Curtis's intention? To try to intimidate his sister's closest rival?

Saskia pulls her pipe gloves from her snowboard trousers, perches them on top of the radiator, and leaves the room. I hear the lock slide across the toilet door.

Her lift pass lies on the floor near the coffee table. It must have fallen from her pocket. I climb off the sofa. The pass is halfway to *my* pocket when a sound in the doorway makes me look up.

Curtis stands there. "What are you doing?" he says quietly.

I don't answer.

His brow lowers. "Don't."

How does he know what I was planning? Am I really that transparent? "What?"

"You know what."

I hate that he's caught me. I glance at the toilet door to make sure Saskia's still in there. "She cost me half a day of riding when she lost my snowboard." Not to mention stealing my goggle cloth to sabotage poor Jacinta. "Why shouldn't I even the score?"

He doesn't answer.

"Are you her minder or something? She'd be able to get a replacement. She'd just have to produce her ID at the ticket office."

"You know she'll retaliate." The toilet flushes behind him. Curtis closes the distance between us. "Give it to me."

I hold it out of reach.

A little muscle in his temple tightens. "I don't want to fall out with you over this, Milla."

"So stay out of it. Or help me beat her."

His face twists. "You can't ask me to do that. She's family."

The toilet door opens and Saskia prowls into the room, raising her eyebrows when she sees us together. "This looks cozy. Am I interrupting something?"

Behind my back, I let the pass fall to the floor and head to the front door. "Actually, I'm not hungry."

CHAPTER 33

PRESENT DAY

Brent sits at the foot of the stairs that lead up to the function room, rubbing his head.

I ease myself to the step beside him. "Are you all right?"

"I've had worse."

Curtis stands with his palm over the light switch, ready to press it when it goes out.

"What happened?" I say.

Brent blinks. "I don't know."

He smells of alcohol. "Did you have anything else to drink?" I ask.

He frowns. "No."

I shoot a look at Curtis. Did Brent fall because he was drunk? I can tell Curtis is wondering the same thing. Then again, Brent pulled a backflip just minutes ago, so he can't be *that* drunk.

"He was just sitting here when I found him," Heather says.

I saw Brent concussed a few times that winter, and he was usually up and riding again pretty fast. This time looks worse than that. His eyes are glazed and unfocused; he's looking around like he doesn't know what's going on.

"Did someone push you?" I say.

Brent grips his forehead. "I don't know."

Did Saskia push you?

But it could have been Heather or Dale. Even Curtis. Curtis was the one who sent Brent upstairs, after all; he could have pushed him before he found me in the bathroom. I glance at Curtis again, still shaken by our earlier conversation. He looks back, sorrow in his eyes.

Brent hauls himself up and staggers sideways.

Curtis grabs him. "Hey, take it easy, mate. Maybe you should sit back down."

"I'm all right," Brent says.

But he's off-balance, gripping the rail for support.

Curtis remains at his side, ready to grab him again. He checks his watch and swears.

"What time is it?" I say.

"Nearly two. We need to decide if we're going or staying."

"Going, I hope," I say. "I don't want to spend another night in this place."

"But your knee. I was thinking me and Brent should ride down and get them to turn the lift on for the rest of you. But now . . ." He glances at Brent. "Maybe me and Dale."

Shit. I don't trust Dale and I can tell Curtis doesn't either. Come to think of it, where is Dale? I check either way down the corridor.

"I don't like the idea of leaving you here," Curtis says. "But what choice do we have?"

Right now, I'm not sure which of them I'm more scared of. I don't trust any of them.

Heather stands to one side looking tense. "I don't think we're here alone. I saw someone in the corridor," she says to Curtis. "While all of you were on the glacier."

"I think I saw someone as well. Just for a second, turning a corner." I squirm as I say it aloud. "And it . . . I'm sorry, Curtis, but it looked like your sister. I swear I saw long blond hair." After what Curtis told me in the bathroom, I'm not sure if it was her or her ghost. Or just my overactive imagination.

Curtis closes his eyes. "Shit."

"Whoever it was, they locked me in that bathroom," Heather says.

I remember how the door acted up on me as well. Maybe there's something wrong with it.

"God, my head hurts," Brent says.

"How much did you have to drink?" Curtis says.

"Hardly anything. It's not that. Just let me splash some water on my face."

There are toilets on the left. Curtis helps Brent along to them.

Heather wanders down the corridor. "Dale?" she calls. "Where are you? *Dale!*"

"Have you seen him since you came in?" I say.

"No." She reaches the corner and stands there, apparently reluctant to let me out of her sight.

Curtis and Brent come out of the toilets.

"The water's off," Curtis says.

"What?" I say.

"Let's try the kitchen," he suggests.

I brace for a painful walk, but he slings an arm around my back with a look that dares me to protest. I can't help flinching. I feel weird about his touching me now.

The kitchen tap is a trickle that soon dries up. Curtis tries the hot tap and nothing at all comes out.

"Pipes must have frozen," I say. That would explain the miserly dribble of water in the bathroom earlier.

"How cold do you reckon it is out there?" Curtis asks.

"Minus ten, maybe?"

Curtis nods. "Cold, but not that cold."

He's right. The Panorama building is designed to withstand low temperatures. One time I rode up here it was minus thirty. It's odd that the pipes would freeze now when strictly speaking it's not even winter.

"Somebody turned the water off," I say.

The game continues.

Did Saskia mess with the water? From Curtis's expression, I can tell he's thinking the same thing, although once again, of course, it could have been any of us. Or someone else—Julien?

"If one of you ducks out and gets some snow, I'll melt it," I say.

"I'll go." Curtis seizes a saucepan.

"Good thing we've got power," Brent says. Looks like he's coming around a bit.

Curtis stops dead. "Anyone bring a flashlight?"

The three of us shake our heads.

"I have a small one," Curtis says. "But if we're leaving anyone up here, we need to find more. Now. Or even candles."

There are miles of windowless corridors in this place. I bite my lip, thinking of how dark they'll be if the power goes off.

Curtis ditches the saucepan and runs off down the corridor. Brent jogs after him.

"Hey, are you okay?" I call, but Brent's gone already.

Heather stands in the doorway, arms crossed protectively in front of her.

"Did you see any flashlights or candles?" I ask.

"I don't know," she says. "I just want to get out of here."

Right now, I'm grateful to have her with me. I check the kitchen cupboards for candles but there aren't any.

Why do you always feel extra thirsty when you have no water? I hold a glass under the cold tap but the thin trickle dries up before it's even half full. I knock it back. Someone goes past—Brent.

"Hey," I call. "If you're feeling up to it, could you get me some snow? I'm desperate."

"Sure." He lifts the pan that Curtis discarded.

"Wait!" I pull out another. Snow is mostly air, so I don't think a panful will melt down to much water.

Brent takes it and heads off.

Curtis strides in, small Maglite in one hand, knee brace in the other. "Here, put this on."

"Thanks."

"Want a hand getting it on?"

"I'll manage." After what he said earlier, I'm scared to look him in the eye. I raise the leg of my snowboard trousers and wrap the brace carefully around my knee over my thermals.

"We need to talk."

"Yeah," I say, though I'm not sure I want to.

Curtis pulls a foil packet from his pocket. "Take these."

Painkillers. Generic ones with British supermarket packaging. "Are they yours?"

"Yep."

As subtly as I can, I check the foil is intact. "I thought you didn't believe in them."

"I don't."

"Right." And somehow that seems to define who he is. Who I *thought* he was at least. The guy who brings painkillers to a reunion even though he doesn't believe in them. Whether he does it because he cares for others weaker than himself or simply out of a compulsive need to be prepared for anything, I'm not sure.

I prize a couple out and swallow them down dry.

He starts opening cupboards.

"What are you looking for?"

"A flashlight. Candles. Whatever."

"I already looked."

"I'll try the restaurant." Curtis hurries out.

Brent is taking forever to fill those pans. At last he returns, badly out of breath, with the pans stacked one on top of the other and heaped with snow.

"You were out there for ages," I say.

He sets them on the electric hob. "I wanted to get it from where nobody had stepped."

I scoop a handful to press on my knee and turn the rings up as high as they will go. "Is your head okay?"

He rubs it. "Bit achy still but I'm managing."

Curtis comes in with an armful of tealight candles in small glass holders and a lighter, which he dumps on the counter.

"Cool," I say.

"Find a flashlight?" Curtis asks Brent.

"No," Brent says.

Curtis turns to Heather. "Did Dale bring a flashlight?"

"I don't know." Heather doesn't seem to know anything just now.

"Where is Dale anyway?" I say.

"Did he come back from checking outside?" Curtis asks.

"I was out there just now and I didn't see him," Brent says.

"I haven't seen him either," Heather says. She's in a total panic now. Her eyes dart from corner to corner.

Curtis turns to Brent. "You check their dorm and in the building, and I'll give him a shout outside. Be careful."

They're back a few minutes later. Dale isn't in his dorm.

"I've shouted my head off out there but he's not answering," Curtis says. "This is getting ridiculous. We're running out of time."

"Was he wearing his transceiver?" I ask.

"No," Curtis says. "That's what bothers me. He left it by the door with his harness and his board. We better go and look for him. Milla, you stay here."

"I'll get my boots on." Brent hurries off.

Curtis nods to the lighter and candles. "Keep them on you in case the power goes off," he tells me. He glances at Heather, who is slumped against the wall, and tugs me into the corridor. In my ear he whispers: "Watch your back."

"What?" I whisper, startled.

"Heather's only little, but you never know with women."

I watch him disappear down the corridor, thinking of the day Heather and Saskia buried me alive.

CHAPTER 34

TEN YEARS AGO

Heather packs the final clump of snow into place over my head. The cold presses in around me, cutting through the fabric of my snowboard jacket and trousers. I blink into the grayish half-light and take slow, deep breaths, hoping I'm never in this situation for real.

I've lost some good friends to avalanches. Doreen Clavette, the French number five in the half-pipe, was swept away while freeriding this summer. There was nobody up there looking for her—the guy she was riding with was buried, too. Is this what their final moments were like? How long did it take them to die? No, I don't want to know.

I touch my fingertips to the ice. The girls will be looking for me by now. Saskia and Odette, with their transceivers in search mode, pacing the snow above and homing in on the signal from the transceiver strapped around my neck.

As the person least likely to ever be doing this for real, Heather's doing the burying. Highlight of her winter, I should think, burying me. She bristles when Dale and I talk snowboarding. Hates that we get on so well. Anyway, the current snow depth up here on the glacier is ten meters, so it was easy enough.

Hang on. Is my transceiver even on "transmit"? I was playing with it before I climbed in here. Damn. The snow is packed too tightly around me for me to open my jacket and check.

Panic creeps in. I want out of here. Where are they?

This drill was Saskia's idea. It's a whiteout up there. The visibility was too bad to ride the pipe, so we came up to the glacier intending to build a jump but soon realized we wouldn't even be able to see it.

"No point having transceivers if we don't know how to use them," Saskia said. "Who's up for being buried? Milla?"

"No, thanks," I said.

"Why? Scared?"

The satisfied glint in her eye compelled me to open my mouth. And like an idiot, I rose to the bait. "Fine, I'll do it."

Daredevil Milla strikes again. Why did I have to do that?

Uneasily I think of Curtis's warnings. But Saskia has kept her distance from me for weeks now—he must have said something to her—and it's not as though she can get up to anything, not in front of him and all the others.

It's freezing in here. My hands are so cold I can hardly feel them. I should have put my gloves on.

Saskia and Odette are taking forever. What's taking them so long? Curtis is down the slope, timing them. Naturally we had to turn this into a competition—girls against boys. Saskia's idea again. *Come on, girls. Where are you?*

I can't hear anything. How much longer will the air last?

Pull yourself together. Brent's going to be buried next. He won't panic. He's not scared of anything. I try to control my breathing, sucking in slow breaths through my nose. If I have to, I can bust my hand out and wave it around and they'll come and pull me out.

Light. From a hole above my head. I laugh in relief as Saskia's face peers down at me.

"Nothing here," she says.

The snow is slammed back into place.

What's she doing? She saw me. Didn't she?

It's darker than it was before. Has she piled more snow on top? Fear flutters across my stomach. What's she playing at?

"Hey!" I shout. But I can't hear them, so I'm guessing they can't hear me.

I raise my arms and push upward. The snow grazes my fingertips; ice chips fly into my face. I blink them from my eyes, cold wetness coating my eyelashes, and punch again, but the snow is solidly packed. Is it my imagination or is it getting hard to breathe?

Why isn't Odette doing something? I suck in gulps of air. *Stop. Breathe slowly. Make the air last.*

Curtis and Dale won't let this go on for too long, will they? Actually they will. The longer the better, so they smash us with their faster time. Brent can't help me; he went off to the kiosk for a snack. Will Heather even remember where she buried me in this fog? Even if she does, she won't be in a rush to rescue me.

This was such a stupid idea. There's no need for me to be down here at all. Why didn't we just bury a transceiver like everyone else? I summon all my strength and try again, pushing upward with both hands. Snow showers over my head and into my mouth. I cough it out, really panicking now.

And a terrible realization hits me. Saskia planned this.

CHAPTER 35

The dead black eyes of the stag stare into the restaurant. Its pale fur is matted, its antlers lined with dust. I can't shake the feeling that it's watching me.

The only sound is the rhythmic tick of the clock on the mantelpiece and the crackle of flames. It took me ten minutes to get the fire going. Everything in this place is damp.

Heather flits about the room like a trapped bluebottle. "Where the hell is he?"

I'm worried, too. Dale's no idiot, but in this sort of terrain, accidents happen even to the best of them. He could be lying somewhere injured, buried under a slide or having fallen into a crevasse.

Unless this is some devious plan cooked up by him and Heather, in which case Curtis and Brent are the ones in trouble. Or is Saskia out there? In which case, they're all in trouble.

Out the window, the sky is gray, the peaks navy. The last of the light has nearly gone. One thing's for sure: we won't be getting down from here today and I'm dreading another night in this place.

I toast my fingers by the flames but I can't stop shivering. Below Curtis's knee brace, I have my homemade ice pack. The ibuprofens have done nothing to dull the pain. Alcohol would help but I want to keep a level head until the men return.

"That bloody clock does my head in," Heather says.

"It's the stag that does *my* head in," I say. How many situations like this have those dead eyes seen? Before the Panorama building was erected, a simple wooden hut stood in its place, a refuge for climbers of decades past. You can see it in some of these photos. Did the stag live there, too? It looks old enough.

Heather paws through the wood in the log pile.

"What are you doing?" I ask.

"If we could find the phones, we could call for help."

We've looked there at least twice already but I don't point that out.

"Argh!" Heather snatches up the clock and hurls it against the wall. It crashes against the wooden panels. Glass showers the floor. I didn't know she had such a temper.

I see my chance. At a weak moment like this, she's more likely to tell the truth. "You know I didn't invite you here, right?"

She nods.

"So who did?"

She chews her lip. "I don't know."

"I'm trying to figure out who set up the Icebreaker," I confide. "I need to know if you and Brent—"

She starts to protest.

"It's just that if you did, we need to think about who else knows about it."

Heather glances over her shoulder to the corridor, then snaps her head back to me. "Yes. I slept with him. Happy now?"

"Okay." I won't ask if it was while I was with Brent, even though I'm desperate to know. I can't lay any claim to Brent. I told him I didn't want a relationship and he's still the least possessive guy I've ever dated. Not that you could call what Brent and I did dating. The only time we ever saw each other on a one-on-one basis was in bed.

And one time in a dark and very steamy steam room.

But what would make Heather cheat on Dale?

Now that she's admitted it, the dam has broken. "See, I thought Dale cheated on me," she says. "With Saskia."

"Seriously?"

"I went to meet Dale at the gym and they came out of the trampoline room together. She had this smug smile on her face."

"Wait, was this the day before the Brits? I remember that. I was there in the gym when she asked him to spot her."

Dale wasn't keen, but Saskia bribed him—said she'd buy his drinks for the rest of the winter—and she was probably only smiling because she'd learned how to do Cripplers.

"Anyway, Dale went to get changed," Heather says. "And I asked her what she was smirking about. She . . . not exactly said but . . . insinuated she had had sex with him right there in the gym."

Did they really, or was Saskia just messing with her? Saskia always did love to mess with people. I'm inclined to think she didn't sleep with him, but I don't want to tell Heather why I think that.

"When I confronted Dale, he denied it and stormed off. But . . ." Heather looks at me like she wants reassurance.

"If they slept together, I never heard about it."

She checks over her shoulder again and lowers her voice. "Anyway, that was the night I slept with Brent."

"Right." So Brent didn't cheat on me, because I split up with him the day before.

"I went round to Dale's place to try to talk to him, but Dale wasn't there, only Brent." Heather struggles for control and continues in a strained voice. "He gave me a hug and I poured it all out. Somehow I started kissing him. He asked if I was sure I wanted to do this, then he took me upstairs."

A tear rolls down her cheek.

Good old Brent. The perfect shoulder to cry on. Followed by the perfect revenge shag. It was bloody risky—presumably Dale could have turned up at any moment—but Brent always was a risk-taker and I knew he had a soft spot for her. Still, I'm surprised at him. He and Dale were mates. I guess he was upset about our breakup and Heather caught him at a weak moment.

"Who else knows about that?" I say.

"Saskia. Nobody else."

A jolt passes through me. Curtis seems to think his sister's behind all this, and what Heather's just told me fits in with that idea.

"It was really bad timing," Heather says. "Saskia was in the street when Brent showed me out. She saw Brent hug me on the doorstep and put two and two together. Asked me outright."

Yeah, somehow that doesn't surprise me. Saskia was astute like that.

"I denied it, but I guess I was too flustered to be convincing. She laughed her head off."

I can just picture Saskia doing that. Poor Heather.

"I nearly slapped her right then." Heather's hand clenches at her side. "*Leave it*, I told myself. *Walk away.* I had to work that night, so I went back to my place to get changed."

"So what happened at Glow Bar?" I say. "Why did you two start fighting again?"

Heather sighs. "I accidentally knocked Saskia's drink over and she thought it was deliberate. Said she was going to tell everyone that I'd shagged Brent. I said I'd tell them she'd shagged Dale first. It got really nasty."

"Right," I say slowly. Things are falling into place.

Heather continues. "Saskia said of course she didn't sleep with Dale. *Poor Dale*, she said. *I'm going over there right now to tell him about you and Brent.* She kept taunting me."

"That's why you hit her?"

"Yeah."

"And did she tell him?"

"No. Not as far as I know."

"And you didn't tell him yesterday?"

Heather hangs her head. "He'd divorce me."

"Really? Over something that happened ten years ago?"

"You don't know what he's like," she says quietly.

But I noticed earlier how possessive Dale is. Maybe she's right. She knows him far better than I do. "Does Curtis know?"

"Not unless Brent told him."

Questions churn in my brain. Does this have anything to do with Saskia's disappearance? I always wondered why Brent and Heather were on the glacier that day. Was the real reason they went up because they wanted to talk in private? It's a long way to go just to do that, but the bubble lift *would* be a perfect place to make sure nobody overheard them. Except Saskia . . . what? Interrupted them? And used what she knew to blackmail Brent to spot her as she practiced Cripplers? Brent's a nice guy. He might have been prepared to miss the warm-up at the Brits to protect Heather. But what happened after that? A tragic accident?

Or something else?

Anyway, I've just learned two things.

1. Heather can lie—not just to me but to her husband as well.

2. Brent and Heather know how to keep their mouths shut. What else are they keeping quiet about?

CHAPTER 36

TEN YEARS AGO

I'm sealed into my cold, dark tomb, still trying to claw my way out. The ice feels like granite against my fingertips. I'm scratching and scraping and I must be losing skin—my fingers are too numb to feel it—but I'm not getting anywhere.

My breaths get faster and faster; the sides of the tomb close in around me. I can't breathe. Am I digging in the right direction? *Think!* I try to focus, but it's so dark I'm no longer sure which way is up.

A bitter taste rises up my throat. I'm going to vomit. I gasp for air but nothing comes in.

"Help!" I scream. My hands thrash in front of my face. I have to get out of here. I don't want to die like this.

Snow tumbles into my open mouth. I cough it out.

A chink of light. The chink becomes a hole, and Curtis's face peers in at me. He lets out a shout, then two pairs of arms dig down. Curtis and Dale. I should help them but I'm shaking so hard my arms won't do what I say.

At last the hole is big enough. Curtis leans in and hauls me out. I lie gasping on the snow. He unzips his jacket and drapes it over me. Like a shroud. I shove it off. I can't cope with having anything covering me. I just want to breathe.

Saskia's voice. "There's something wrong with my transceiver."

"There's something wrong with you!" Curtis shouts.

I hear Odette's calm tones but don't catch what she says.

Figures walk to and fro—Saskia, Curtis, Dale. I suck in beautiful gulps of air. Brent must still be at the kiosk.

"And how come *you* couldn't find her?" Curtis says.

"Saskia wanted to do it on her own," Odette replies.

I should get up. I hate their seeing me like this—so weak and vulnerable. But I don't think I can move.

Curtis kneels beside me. "Want some water?" He produces a bottle—his bottle—and holds it to my lips. I gulp a mouthful and let my head drop back to the snow.

Odette leans over me. "Are you okay, Milla? Saskia's transceiver, it wasn't working."

I don't believe that for a minute but I can see that Odette does. She's that sort of person—always believes the best of people.

Curtis pulls a protein bar from his pocket and rips it open. "Eat."

I shake my head. I can't stomach it. Snowflakes drift down from the sky onto my face. Burying me again. I shudder and haul myself upright. Everything goes dark but I plant my feet firmly and take deep breaths until the feeling passes.

My backpack sits on the snow nearby. I pull it on. "I'm riding down."

"Wait—" Curtis says.

But I want to put as much distance between myself and the glacier as possible. Between me and Saskia and everyone who saw that.

Snowflakes fly at my goggles as I ride into the whiteout. One by one, black piste markers loom. They're the only way I can tell I'm moving. I follow them down. The piste is deserted. Nobody except us is stupid enough to have come out in this weather.

She could have killed me. But what am I going to do? What *can* I do?

My legs are shaking twice as much as they normally would by the time I reach the midstation. I intended to ride the cable car straight down, but now that I'm here, that seems like the ultimate admission of defeat. What would I do down there anyway? Pace the floor in my tiny apartment? I'm so wound up. Maybe I can ride this feeling out.

Blindly, I head to the bubble lift. There's no queue, and I dive straight into an empty cabin.

As the door starts to shut, Curtis throws himself in. He leans his board against mine, shrugs off his backpack, and sinks to the bench opposite. I press my hands to my lap, willing them to stop trembling. I don't want him to see me like this.

"You okay?"

"Yep." Glad of my mirror lenses, I turn to the window.

"She went too far."

I turn back to him, stunned that he's finally spoken out against her.

He stares down at his snowboard boots, jaw tightly set, body rigid. Pity briefly overrides my anger. How many situations has his sister dragged him into over the years? Was she like this at school? I can just imagine her: the Beautiful Bitch, queen of the sixth form. The girl that all the guys had the hots for, and all the other girls wanted to be friends with, because they were terrified of what she would do to them if they weren't.

What can I do to get back at her, except outride her at the Brits? "So help me beat her," I say.

Curtis lifts his gaze. "Why do you want this so much, Milla?"

Something—either the feeling of coming close to death or the relief of having survived—makes me open up. "You know the happiest day of my life?"

"The Brits last year?"

"No way. I fell on the last-but-one hit and embarrassed myself. And I didn't win. No, my happiest day was school sports day when I was about twelve. I won the four-hundred-meter, eight-hundred-meter, and the final leg in the one-hundred-meter relay, one after the other. And I wasn't even in the school running club. I just wanted to win more than any of the other girls."

Curtis sighs. "Talk me through your pipe run."

I scramble my thoughts. This is *so* not the best time but it might be the only chance I get. "Okay. So I drop in, Backside Air, Frontside Indy . . ." Hit by hit, I list each trick. It's no secret; he sees me doing it every day.

"First thing you've got to fix is your boot grabbing."

I hang my head. Boot grabbing, when you grab your boot instead of your snowboard, is not cool.

"You're doing it when you grab your fives and sometimes your threes."

Curtis takes my riding to pieces, listing half a dozen more things I need to improve. I listen, devastated. Wishing I had a pen to make notes. No wonder Saskia has stayed ahead of me. Brent and Dale have given me advice, Odette too, but nowhere near as in-depth as this. My ego is taking a slamming.

"Brent suggested I try a Crippler," I say when he finishes.

Curtis's eyebrows shoot up. "Has a female rider ever done one?"

"Not in competition."

He thinks about it for a moment. And frowns. "No. Not yet anyway. What you need to do before that is fall."

"What?"

"You're too scared of falling."

He's dead right, I'm scared. Falls break bones. Falls end seasons. End sponsorships even. I know this from experience. But it's hardly helpful to have it pointed out.

And I *hate* it that he's noticed. "I don't want to break something this close to the Brits." They're only two weeks away.

"Yeah, but it's holding you back. Find yourself a big jump into deep powder and make yourself fall. It won't be as bad as you think. Then you can think about Cripplers."

I look at him uncertainly. Falling is risky, even with a powder landing. Whose side is he really on? Is he genuinely trying to help me or has his brotherly loyalty kicked back in?

CHAPTER 37

PRESENT DAY

Heather paces up and down in front of the window in the restaurant.
If I hadn't hurt my knee, I'd be pacing, too.

"What if they don't come back?" she says.

"They'll be back," I say.

It's pitch-dark out there now. Where are they and why haven't they found Dale? I glance at the table again to check the candles and lighter are there in case the lights go out. Privately I'm freaking out just as much as Heather is. Curtis and Brent could have fallen down a crevasse during the search. Should I go and look for them? But what if the person who's messing with us—Saskia, Dale, or someone else—has hurt them? And they're lurking out there, waiting for me to go out?

I strain for something to talk about. "So how is it being married?"

Heather comes over. "It's . . . okay."

"Right."

She backtracks, telling me about their friends and relatives and their new agency, but I can tell the original answer is the truest one. That it's just okay.

She lets out a shuddery breath. "Look, I need my pills. They're in my dorm. Will you come with me?"

"Sure," I say, but I'm immediately on guard. *Watch your back.* Is she plotting something?

I'm still wearing my snowboard jacket and trousers. I stuff the lighter and a candleholder in my jacket pocket and haul myself upright. We slap every light switch we pass as we go down the corridor.

"Does it hurt a lot?" she asks as I limp alongside her.

"Yep." No point lying. I'm gritting my teeth so as not to gasp with every step.

The double doors swing shut behind us.

And the lights go off.

Heather squeaks. Bracing for her—or anyone else—to attack me, I fumble for my lighter and candleholder. I'm straining to picture the layout of the building. If someone comes in the main entrance, I'll limp this way as fast as I can and lock myself in my dorm. If they approach from this direction, I'll turn left and left again . . . and then what?

I can hear someone—Heather, I hope—patting the wall.

"I can't find a switch," she says.

"Don't bother. The power's out." I flick the lighter on and see Heather's pale face. My hand is shaking so much I'm struggling to light the candle.

Stop panicking, Milla. It's not helping.

At last I have the candle lit. I check either way down the corridor. It's just the two of us. "Let's get your pills quick and get back to the restaurant," I say. "It'll be lighter in there with the fire."

We reach her dorm.

"They're in the bathroom," she says.

Holding the candle in front of us, I limp inside. In the bathroom, Heather rummages through her bag and slides out the foil packet. She looks up and screams.

I lurch backward. She points a shaky finger to the mirror. A word has been scrawled on the glass with red lipstick. *GUILTY.*

Heather looks at me with terrified eyes.

What does it mean? Who is guilty—Heather or Dale—and guilty of what? Heather's breaths are loud and fast in the candlelight, as are my own. I whip back the shower curtain and raise the candle to light up the corners of the room. There's nobody there.

The wardrobe.

I glance around for something to use as a weapon but there's nothing suitable.

"Hold this," I say, and give Heather the candle. I don't trust her, but right now I don't have much choice. I want both hands free. If there's somebody in there, I'm going to hit first and ask questions later.

Heather sticks close as I approach the wardrobe. I yank the door open. It's empty. I take the candle back.

With trembling hands, Heather pops two tablets from the foil and swallows them. She catches my eye. "I get anxiety attacks."

"Let's get out of here."

Candle lighting the way, we head back down the corridor. *Guilty.* It could be about stealing Saskia's credit card. Or part of a blackmail plot. I'm feeling really shaky by the time we reach the restaurant.

"I need to eat something." I limp into the kitchen.

Heather follows me in. My knee throbs and I should be elevating it, but Heather's in no fit state to do anything. I light more candles so I can see what I'm doing and check the cupboards for something that doesn't require cooking. There's a can of tomatoes and several of tuna. Funny. I could have sworn there was more in here yesterday.

I grate cheese, keeping a close eye on both Heather and the doorway. My knee makes me vulnerable. I'm pretty sure I can take her on if I need to, but her *and* Dale?

Heather dashes into the corridor. I follow her out.

"I heard something," she whispers. "Just then. Didn't you?"

"No." The corridor is dark and silent. "Maybe it was just the pipes."

"There's someone else in the building."

I check over my shoulder into the shadowy restaurant. "What sort of noise was it?"

"A creak. Like a door shutting."

"Maybe it was the wind," I say, trying to sound reassuring.

We return to the kitchen. Away from the fire, my teeth are chattering, but I leave the ice pack on. I need to limit the swelling in case I have to walk down from here.

A distant bang. Heather gasps and grips my arm.

Voices in the corridor—Curtis and Brent.

Heather dashes out. "Did you find him?"

The answer is obvious. Dale isn't with them.

Curtis can hardly meet her eyes. "Sorry." He clicks the flashlight off and we crowd into the candlelit kitchen.

Heather turns from him to Brent in disbelief. "You have to keep looking."

"It's not safe," Curtis says. "I'm sorry, Heather, I really am. But we're tired. We're making mistakes."

He and Brent look wrecked. I know they wouldn't give up easily. Brent pulls his hat off and runs his fingers through his damp hair.

"Where's a fucking phone when you need one?" Curtis mutters.

Heather snatches the flashlight. "Okay, I'll go myself." There's hysteria in her tone.

I zip up my jacket. "I'll go with her." There's no way she can go out on the ice alone in the dark. With my knee like this, I won't get far, but if I hadn't insisted on doing that backflip, Dale might not have been out there on his own in the first place.

Curtis blocks the doorway. "You'll end up in a crevasse."

Heather tries to push past him. "We can't leave him out there."

"I put my foot through a snow bridge just now, Heather," Brent says quietly. "Curtis had to grab me. The snow gave way under us both and it was scary."

"He could be holed up in the snow somewhere," Curtis adds. "We'll go back out at first light."

I glance at Brent and he shakes his head a fraction. I don't rate Dale's chances either. It probably gets down to about minus fifteen at night up here at this time of year.

I turn back to Curtis. Does he still think Dale and Heather are up to something? That Dale has disappeared on purpose? When I get a quiet moment I'll ask him. Still, Heather's desperation is pretty convincing. She fights and struggles to get past.

Brent reaches for her and she collapses into him. He shoots me an awkward look over her shoulder. It's so odd seeing him hold her.

"How's your knee?" Curtis says.

I shrug. No point complaining. "Got any sports tape?"

"Yeah. But I'd stick with the knee brace and keep ice on it for the next twenty-four hours."

"I meant for the trek down tomorrow."

Worry flashes across Curtis's face. "It's a bloody long way with a blown knee."

He slumps against the wall beside me and I watch his chest rise and fall. He looks utterly spent.

Brent is still trying to console Heather.

"How long ago did the power go out?" Curtis asks.

"Maybe twenty minutes?" I say. "Where would you turn it off?"

"I had a look while we were out there. The electricity cupboard's on the exterior wall of the building. Big padlock on it."

So either someone else was out there with them—or one of them turned it off.

Heather flails at Brent's chest. "This is your fault. You forced us to come here."

Brent lowers his voice. "No. I told you that last night."

"I don't believe you," Heather says.

"Wait," I say. "How did Brent force you to come?"

Heather glares at Brent and turns defiantly to me. "He blackmailed me."

CHAPTER 38

TEN YEARS AGO

The ice presses in around me, crushing my chest. I can't breathe. I flap my hands, desperate.

"Hey, hey." Brent's voice rumbles into my consciousness.

I open my eyes. It's not ice; it's just the duvet. Brent's not-been-washed-all-season, safe, warm duvet. I inhale the musky smell and try to control my breathing.

"You okay?"

"Bad dream."

"Come here."

I bury my face in his chest. That was so real. I don't know if I can face going up the mountain today. What's Saskia going to do to me next? Because if I keep doing what I'm doing, I have to face it: there *will* be a next time.

I feel like I'm at a crossroads. I have two options: distance myself from the group, keep my head down, and train on my own, avoiding Brent's place when Saskia's there. Or fight back hard.

I can't let her win.

But have I got the strength to fight?

"Better?" Brent says into my hair.

"Yeah."

He climbs out of bed and draws the curtains. His face lights up.

"There's a foot of fresh. Want to head up to the glacier for some freshies? The pipe'll be buried."

I can't help shuddering at the word *buried*.

Le Rocher's cobbled main street has been cleared, snow piled high on either side. A thick white carpet covers everything else in sight. Inches teeter on top of road signs; half a meter is stacked up on roofs and balconies. Parked cars are barely visible.

Brent, Curtis, and I walk down the center of the road. The little stone church is swamped by snowdrifts, its wrought iron cross and railings covered with a thick white frosting. Shopkeepers use snowblowers to clear their shopfronts.

It's the first of April today but it feels colder than it was back in February. I zip my jacket up to my chin. I went to the doctor recently for stronger sleeping tablets. They hit hard and I still feel woozy and off-balance this morning.

"I've got to call in at Sport 2000," Brent says. "Cracked my high-back yesterday."

Curtis and I sit side by side on a snowdrift outside the shop while we wait. The smell of chocolate drifts from a nearby patisserie and my mouth waters.

"Have you heard from Jacinta?" I say.

"Yeah, phoned her last night," Curtis says. "She's getting the cast off in two weeks and she'll start rehab, ready for the Aussie winter."

"Great. Say hi from me."

"Will do."

A man chases a woman down the street with a snowball. I have to laugh. They must be in their fifties. There's something about fresh snow that brings your inner child to the surface.

A distant boom echoes across the valley and my laughter dies. That's the ski patrol, blasting the slopes to set off avalanches that might other-wise bury people. They have their work cut out for them today. They can't let anyone up there until they're sure it's safe. I gaze at the snow-swamped slopes. After what happened yesterday, I feel like I've lost my nerve. I never want to be buried again.

A louder boom makes me flinch. My eyes search for the dust cloud that would signify an avalanche.

"So of all the sports in the world, why half-pipe?" Curtis says. "Why not running? Or something else?"

Does he sense how I'm feeling? I think he might. "It's probably be-cause of Spider-Man."

He splutters. "What?"

"When I was little, my brother and I were fascinated with how Spider-Man could stick to walls. We used to try it. Put a mattress on the floor next to the wall and run at it, hard as we could. Then I tried half-pipe and the walls are about the height of a two-story building and, you know. We do sort of stick to them."

Curtis laughs. He must think I'm so weird.

"How about you?" I say. "Why half-pipe?"

He turns thoughtful. "When you ride the park you get, what, four or five jumps max? Big air you get one. In the pipe you get ten or so hits in the space of less than a minute. The adrenaline's like nothing else. My head's pretty busy normally, I'm thinking of a million different things, but while I'm in the pipe, my head's empty. I'm in the zone. Us-ing the force or something." He breaks off. Grins. "I couldn't have this conversation with anyone else."

"Likewise."

He holds my gaze a moment longer than he should do. I'm glowing right now.

Brent comes out and Curtis scrambles to his feet. He doesn't talk to me in the same way when Brent's around. A male respect thing, I guess.

"So long, Luke," I say under my breath. "May the force—"

"Shut it," Curtis mutters.

It's funny to think that if Curtis and I had hooked up that night on the glacier, we'd probably have had some awful breakup by now and wouldn't be speaking to each other. By turning him down, I've ended up getting to know him in a way I wouldn't otherwise have done. So it worked out for the best, after all.

It doesn't stop me from wanting him, though.

We enter the cable car. Damn. Saskia is in there already with Odette. Curtis nods to Odette and heads to the far corner without saying a word to his sister.

But Brent strides right up to her. "Why are you such a bitch?"

No, Brent. Don't do this.

The cabin falls quiet. I look on, helpless.

Brent lifts his hand as though he's about to grab her. "Leave Milla alone. Got it?"

Saskia arches her eyebrow and looks like she wants to laugh. Brent's hardly a threatening guy.

Curtis starts to push his way over.

"I can't believe I ever used to like you. You're just a spoiled, insecure brat and everyone around you knows it." With that, Brent lowers his hand and returns to my side.

I let out my breath. That was awkward. Brent hates confrontations, so I'm amazed he would do that for me. "Thanks," I whisper. "But I can fight my own battles."

Across the cable car, Saskia's smirk has faded somewhat. Did he get to her? I think he actually did. Behind her bravado, she's human after all.

Odette pats her on the hip. And her hand lingers. *Whoa.* Are they *together?*

Saskia darts a look at me, as though she can hear what I'm thinking. The spark returns to her eyes and her lips curl back into a smile. She knows I saw.

My head reels.

You don't own friends. That's what Mum always told me when I was little. But Mum's wrong. There's always a hierarchy of loyalties. I thought Odette was *my* friend just as much as Saskia's, yet all along she belonged to Saskia alone.

Now that I know, I wonder how I didn't realize earlier. The signs were all there. The secret little smiles they send each other; the way they always sit together. I knew Saskia spent a lot of time at Odette's place but I thought it was to avoid the rest of us.

Why do they hide it? Because they're both in the public eye? Or they don't want their families to know?

All our conversations about grabs and flips. I was flattered by Odette's interest, but she was probably feeding it straight to her girl-friend. I feel betrayed.

Odette flashes me an apologetic smile but I don't smile back.

The cable car swings into the midstation.

When I get out, Saskia is waiting for me on the platform. She leans in close and whispers in my ear. "Don't worry. I'll get him back."

Brent, Curtis, and I ride the bubble lift up to the glacier, leaving Saskia and Odette behind, and I force my thoughts to snowboarding. The conversation with Curtis earlier, whether deliberate on his part or not, reminded me what got me into half-pipe riding. That feeling of sticking to the wall and defying gravity. I could never get enough of it and I still haven't. I can't let Saskia scare me off.

That's why I have to keep fighting. And to have a chance of making the top three, I need to fight with everything I've got.

Curtis's advice about falling plays through my mind as we build a jump, because this is the perfect time to try it out. To deliberately fall goes against anything I've ever done, but Curtis is right. My fear *is* holding me back.

I ride down and fly Superman-style through the air, landing splat on my front. The air wheezes out of me, but it's not as bad as I expected. The powder is so soft and pillowy it's like sinking into a frozen cushion.

Brent is at my side in an instant. "Are you all right?"

I laugh weakly and pull my snow-covered goggles off my face. "Yeah."

From way up the slope, Curtis gives me a nod of approval. It's snowing again, fat wet flakes that settle on my cheeks like kisses. I haul myself upright and head back to the top.

And make myself fall again. And again.

Poor Brent doesn't know what's going on.

"I only said to try it once," Curtis says quietly the fourth time I do it.

"I'm still scared," I tell him. "And I'm going to keep falling until I'm not scared anymore."

CHAPTER 39

I stare at Heather. "You said your invite was from me."

She's crying so hard she can barely speak. "The first one was."

I'm confused. "The first one?"

Her eye makeup is running down her cheeks in black streaks. I hand her a napkin from a stack on the kitchen counter.

She blows her nose on it and takes a shaky breath. "We got an invite from you but we didn't want to come back here, so I emailed to say we couldn't make it. A few days later I got another email." She fights to compose herself. "From Brent."

Brent frowns and shakes his head. "No."

"What did it say exactly?" I ask.

"*Be there or I will tell,*" Heather says. "Just that."

Brent shoots her a panicked look.

"It's okay," I tell him. "I know you slept with her."

Brent's head jerks my way. His mouth opens. And closes. And opens again. "All right, I slept with her. It was ten years ago, for God's sake. What does it matter now?" He glances at Curtis and Heather. "But I don't know anything about this email, I swear."

Once again, my brain is boggling. So everyone got an invite from me, except me. I got one from Curtis. We all accepted, except Heather. When she declined, she got an invite—or rather a threat—from Brent.

Does that mean Brent was behind this weekend all along? Did he invite me and Curtis, making it look like we invited each other? But why?

I feel like I should believe Brent over Heather, but I can't put aside the look in his eyes in his dorm last night.

"So how do you explain the email?" I say.

Brent rakes his hand through his hair and darts another look at Heather. "Well . . . someone knows we hooked up and used it to black-mail her to come here."

I want to believe him but I'm just not sure. "Who knew about the two of you?"

"As far as I'm aware, nobody."

Saskia knew, I think, but I don't say it. The pain is making me light-headed. I lean against the wall. Several more hours before I can take more ibuprofen.

Heather starts crying again. Brent reaches for her.

She slaps his hand away. "This is your fault!"

"Hey, hey." Brent tries to calm her down.

Curtis leans against the wall beside me, head tilted back, eyes closed. I can't tell if he's thinking or just plain exhausted.

My stomach rumbles. I need to eat something before I pass out. Summoning the last of my energy, I straighten and slop the tuna-tomato mix onto plates. Gordon Ramsay would have a fit—it looks like dog food—but I don't think anyone here will care.

The mood as we sit by the fire is very different from how it was last night. We eat in silence, slumped over our plates. The wind has picked up, rattling the panes. I picture Dale out there somewhere. Once the sun sets, the temperature plummets.

Heather's grief has died down to quiet sobs that make her shoulders shake; her food sits untouched in front of her.

Curtis drags up another chair. "Keep that knee elevated."

I try to lift it. Pain radiates up my thigh. I gasp and drop my foot back to the carpet.

Curtis crouches. "Let me." He lifts my foot carefully, watching my face.

"Thanks." I still feel weird about his touching me. I want to talk to him but I'm waiting for a moment when Brent and Heather aren't listening.

Brent's drinking brandy tonight. He pours himself another large glass.

"Sure that's—" Curtis begins.

Brent cuts him off. "Don't say it." He downs the brandy and refills the glass.

"You need to eat something, Heather," I say, but she doesn't seem to hear me.

"Hey, what happened to the clock?" Curtis says.

"Don't ask," I reply.

He kneels and sweeps the broken glass to the wall with the sleeve of his snowboard jacket. To the left of the fireplace, two rusty nails protrude from the wall an inch apart. I don't recall seeing them yesterday. Did something used to hang there? I strain to think. A photo, maybe? Has someone taken it?

Heather's voice is a furious whisper. "We're here because of what you did," she tells Brent.

From the corner of my eye, I see Brent glance up to check if Curtis or I heard. Curtis didn't hear—he's still dealing with the broken glass—and I pretend I didn't either.

"Shh," Brent whispers. "Careful."

What the hell is it that Brent doesn't want her to say?

CHAPTER 40

TEN YEARS AGO

I flip through the air and plummet back to earth, no idea which way up I am. Down . . . down . . . Is the trampoline even underneath me anymore? I brace for the worst.

There's a ripping sound from my T-shirt as Dale yanks me upright. The trampoline rebounds beneath us, throwing us together. His inked arms steady me as I stagger for balance. We've worked up a real sweat and he's stripped down to just a T-shirt, too.

"You were all right until you grabbed," he says.

I'm trying to land a Crippler. It's a long shot, but it's the best chance I have of making the top three. Brent usually spots me but he's being interviewed for *Snowboard UK* ahead of the Brits in two days' time. I almost asked Curtis, but spotting someone on a tramp can get pretty intimate, and I don't trust myself not to do something I shouldn't.

The right decision, definitely. Dale's had to grab me over and over. The trampoline's a bit small for this sort of thing, and even after the flips I land, I nearly stagger off the side afterward.

"What am I doing wrong?" I say.

Dale mops his brow. "It throws you off your spin when you grab. Want me to demonstrate again?"

"No." He's already demonstrated dozens of times, flipping sideways through the air in a smooth and stylish movement. He makes it look so easy. I'm not even wearing my snowboard yet, just grabbing an imaginary one. I'll put it on later when I figure this out. *If* I figure it out.

"Try some more without the grab, maybe," he says.

"All right."

"Wait a sec." Dale peels his T-shirt off.

I try not to stare. A large tribal tattoo covers one of his shoulders and snakes across his well-muscled pecs. If it were Curtis bare-chested in front of me, close enough to feel the heat radiating from him . . . Yeah, good thing it isn't.

I wait for Dale to move backward, then jump three times, building up height. He jumps in time with me so we don't double bounce. On the fourth jump, I spring hard upward. Even with my head upside down, I can tell it's gone wrong again. As I rotate, I clip Dale with my hand and hear him grunt.

He grabs me as I come down. My feet scrabble for purchase.

"Sorry," I gasp.

He's gripping my waist, still. Our bodies are flush together, his chest damp and solid against mine. Wider than Brent's. More like Curtis's.

"Did I hurt you?" I say.

His cheek is red. Without thinking, I touch it. Soft stubble brushes my palm. His gray-green eyes jerk to my face, pupils a fraction dilated. Something sparks inside me, and before I know it, I'm kissing him.

For a second, he kisses me back, lip ring digging into my bottom lip. We fly apart. It's hard to say who pulled back first, but Dale looks about as shocked as I feel.

"Sorry," I say. "I shouldn't have done that."

"Yeah," he says. "You shouldn't have."

I feel terrible now.

Still, that's one seriously loyal guy. Whereas I imagine most women would freak out if someone suddenly kissed them, I'm pretty sure most men are unable to resist, whatever their relationship status. Or maybe that's just me being cynical. I've only ever been in one serious relationship—at least I thought it was serious until I came back early from the Brits two years ago with ripped knee ligaments, only to find one of my so-called friends at my so-called boyfriend's place.

Dale rubs his lip ring as though he's trying to wipe away the kiss. I'm pretty confident he won't tell Heather. She would kill me, of course, but she would want to kill him even more, and he must realize that.

He looks at me. "I can't do this."

"Fair enough," I say.

He climbs down from the trampoline.

Damn. Now I don't have anyone to spot me.

I flip through the air and plummet back to earth, no idea which way up I am. No trampoline below me this time. I slam into the powder, side-on.

Fiery pain burns my chest. It feels like my lungs and stomach have flown out through my mouth. I gasp for breath but it's not happening.

Panic sets in, even though I've done this several times already today. My mouth and nostrils strain for oxygen. *The pain . . .*

At last I'm sucking in air. I run a mental check of body parts. All good. Everything's still working. My head took a decent whack. At least I had a soft landing.

Brent peers down at me. "That's it. No more."

He and I are up on the glacier, way out to the far side. We built a makeshift quarter-pipe so I could practice my Cripplers in deep powder. If I'd tried that in the pipe, I wouldn't have gotten up from it.

There's snow in my pants, my sports bra, and just about everywhere else. I shake out the worst of it. "Don't worry. I'll get it right next time."

"I'm sorry," Brent says. "I can't watch."

"Thanks a lot. I didn't think I was that bad." My goggles flew off when I landed. Where are they? Way over there. I stand up, mildly dizzy, and trudge off to retrieve them.

Brent chases after me. "I'm serious, Milla. You're going to break something. You have to stop."

"You're the one who suggested Cripplers."

"Yeah, well, I wish I hadn't."

I wipe my goggles. "One more try. Maybe two."

"You're not even wearing a helmet."

"Says the guy who rides in a baseball cap even after you knocked yourself out twice this month."

He pulls his cap off and rakes his hand through his hair. "I can't let you do this to yourself."

"It's my risk. I decide. I have two more hours until the lift stops."

"You need more time on the trampoline."

"I haven't got more time."

"Why are you pushing it this hard? You're riding great."

"Yeah, but I want to win."

Brent shakes his head. "Winning's not everything. There is other stuff."

"Like what?"

"Family, friends. *Life*."

I'm getting mad now. "Well, my family's a bit of a sore point. I'm not soft and girly enough for my mum, but I'm too soft and girly for Dad and my brother. And my friends back home don't get why I even like snowboarding. So you're right. Winning *is* more important to me than all that stuff right now. But I'm not good enough."

"Know what my dad says to me? 'Do your best, that's all you can do.'"

"Know what my dad says to me? 'Try harder, Milla.'"

"Fuck your dad. You should be doing this for you, nobody else. If you fall and smash yourself up, you're the one that's going to suffer." Brent reaches for me but I shake him off. "This is you at your peak, so enjoy it. In ten years, you'll look back and wish you could still do all this."

"You don't get it, do you? This is my last chance. If I can nail a Crippler here, I can try it in the pipe tomorrow and do it in the Brits the next day. If I can't, that's it. I'll have to go and find a real job."

"So you're going to keep trying until you break your neck?"

If I stand here arguing about it for much longer, I'm going to lose my nerve. "Have I ever told you to go easy?"

Brent sighs. "I know, and I'm sorry, but I care about you."

"Well, don't. Okay? It wasn't part of the deal."

He's quiet for a moment. "Look, I don't know what we have but we have something. And I care. Simple as that."

"So let's call it quits. Whatever 'it' is. We're just friends. Now you don't have to help me. You don't even have to watch. I just need you to stay around for ten more minutes because if I have a bad fall I'll be stuck here and nobody will know."

"Let me get this right." His voice is small. Hurt. "You're breaking up with me over this? Because I care?"

I look up the slope at the jump, exasperated. Fear is setting in now. "It's hardly breaking up. It wasn't even a relationship."

"I can't stop caring, Milla. And I actually thought you cared about me, too."

I haven't got time for this. "What am I doing wrong? Do I need more speed?"

Brent shakes his head and straps his board on.

"Brent!" I shout.

He rides off.

I march back up the slope. With or without him, I have to do this. I strap in and look around. A trio of figures slalom down the piste, half a dozen more ascend the tow lift, but none of them are looking my way and they're not even in hearing distance. I'll wait until they come nearer.

I've always prided myself on not needing anyone, but it occurs to me now that this is not entirely true. Sometimes, even in an individual sport like snowboarding, you do need someone.

Nobody's looking this way still. I'm itching to jump but it's just too risky. Argh! I fling myself to the snow. Of all the days for this to happen. How am I going to face my family if I can't beat my result from last year—or even worse, if I rank lower?

I can imagine their responses.

Told you so, Milla.

Toughen up.

Cold seeps through my jacket and trousers. Soon I'm shivering, but I lie there anyway.

The hurt on Brent's face weighs on my mind, eating away at me. I never made him any promises, so why do I feel so guilty?

It's no good; I'll have to talk to him. Swearing inwardly, I fasten on my snowboard and ride down. When I reach the half-pipe, though, I don't see Brent anywhere.

Odette approaches. She kisses me on either cheek. "You weren't training today?"

I feel weird around her now that I know she's with Saskia. "I was on the glacier trying Cripplers."

"Cool. And can you do it?"

"I'm getting there." I don't want to say too much. She'll tell her girlfriend. "Brent and I ended things."

She touches my arm. "I'm sorry."

"Probably for the best. Like you said, he was my anchor."

She looks at me in sympathy. "In another sport, ski racing perhaps, it would be different. But with half-pipe, the chance of injury is so high."

"You and Saskia seem to manage it," I say before I can stop myself.

"Actually I am terrified for her." Odette turns to look for her.

And there she is, coming up the tow lift.

"Why do you keep your relationship secret?" I say.

"She doesn't want anyone to know."

"Right." I sense Odette's sadness about this. "Hey, did Brent turn up just now?"

"Yeah, he did one run and fell and hurt his knee. He went down a few minutes ago."

"What?" Panic rushes in. "Is he okay?"

"He walked to the cable car. So I think it's not so bad."

But is it bad enough that he can't compete? Smash is the main sponsor of the British Championships this year and Brent's their star rider, his airborne image on billboards around the resort. He's acting like it's no big deal but I know he's feeling the pressure.

With a jolt, I remember Saskia's threat. *I'll get him back.* Is that what happened? Did she cause him to fall? I long to ask Odette if Saskia was anywhere near him at the time but I don't dare. I'll go down and ask Brent for myself.

Saskia reaches the top of the lift and glances my way. I couldn't swear to it, but it looks as though she's gloating.

CHAPTER 41

This place is doing my head in. Brent sits beside Heather in the candlelit restaurant, either to comfort her or to stop her from saying whatever it is he doesn't want her to say. I'm trying to figure out what that could be and all sorts of things are going through my mind.

Ugly things.

Things that are much worse than just a one-night affair.

What was Brent doing while I was with Heather and Curtis in the bathroom? Did he fake banging his head? He recovered quickly enough. He took ages to fill those pans up, too. Is it possible that he did something to Dale out there, then shoved him down a crevasse?

The fire is fizzling out. Curtis gets up to put more wood on. Come to think of it, Curtis disappeared for a while as well, supposedly looking for flashlights, and Dale was hardly his favorite person. I know Curtis has a hot temper, but does he hate Dale enough to kill him?

Could Curtis and Brent be in this together?

The black eyes of the stag bore into mine. My gaze shifts to the two empty nails beside it. What used to hang there? Does it matter? I don't know.

I don't know anything anymore. My knee hurts too much for me to think straight. I'm trying to remember how long it took last time until

I could start walking on it, but it depends how badly I've torn it and if it's just the lateral collateral or other ligaments as well.

The lights come on again.

"Well, that's something," I say.

Curtis snorts. "Yeah, but how long are they going to stay on for?"

"True." At least I know it wasn't him or Brent who turned them on.

"Someone's playing with us," Curtis says.

But who? Dale?

"And I think it's my sister." Grim-faced, Curtis checks the doorway, as though she might appear there.

I replay what he said to me this afternoon in the bathroom. If he killed her, why does he seem so sure it's her? I look around at the others to see what they make of this.

Heather stands. "I'm going to bed."

I don't think she heard him. Or maybe she's in too much shock about Dale to deal with anything else. Her eyes are red from crying. I can't imagine how hard this must be for her. That is, if this isn't some mysterious scheme cooked up by her and Dale.

I lift one of the candleholders. "Here, take this in case the power goes off again. Have you still got a lighter?"

She pats her pocket. "Yeah." She eyes the corridor uncertainly.

"I'll come with you." I brace myself to get up.

But Brent gets to his feet. "I'll take her."

He snatches up the brandy bottle as they leave.

Curtis grips his forehead. "Am I losing my mind to think my sister's out there?"

I check the corridor to make sure Heather's gone. Curtis is going to flip when I tell him, and Heather has enough on her plate right now. "You know the credit card transactions? How much was spent?"

"About three grand."

"In France or the UK?"

"France, and right across Europe in shops and restaurants. Mum and Dad didn't know what to do. If it was her or someone else. They gave her that card for emergencies. Her sponsors weren't paying her anywhere near as much as mine were. You know what she's like. She has expensive tastes."

I notice the tense he uses. *She has expensive tastes.* He really thinks she's still alive. I must have misunderstood him earlier. He didn't kill her. But what else could he be keeping from me?

He sighs. "Dad stopped the card eventually. My parents nearly split up over it. Mum didn't speak to him for weeks."

"Couldn't they trace the transactions?" I say. "From security cameras or something?"

"The police did their best, but the restaurants didn't have cameras. A few of the shops did, but the images were poor. Could have been anyone."

I take a deep breath. "You're not going to like this," I tell him. "It wasn't Saskia. It was Dale."

Curtis looks at me, stunned. I tell him about the conversation I overheard earlier.

Good thing Dale and Heather aren't here right now. Rage is coming off Curtis in waves. He's doing his best to hold it in but the little muscles in his jaw clench; his foot taps a rapid beat on the floorboards.

"It's weird, though," I say. "Wouldn't they have needed her PIN number?" At least if they were using the card in France and Switzerland.

A bitter laugh from Curtis. "She'd written her PIN on a bloody Post-it note that she kept with the card. Left it lying on her kitchen counter. I gave her a hard time about it but it was still there the next time I went round. She was clueless sometimes. It wasn't her money, so she didn't care."

He's silent for a moment. "So Dale stole her credit card. But that doesn't explain how we smelled her perfume. Or the lock of her hair or how her lift pass turned up like that."

"What are you saying? That she chose to just walk away from her life and disappear?"

"Maybe."

"Was she happy?" *Tread gently*, I warn myself.

He looks thoughtful. "I have no idea."

"Did your family know about her and Odette?"

"What?"

Shit. He doesn't know. Her own brother. Yet somehow it doesn't surprise me. Saskia had all these different sides. I never knew which was the real her, so maybe Curtis didn't either.

"Odette and Saskia," I say. "They were together."

Curtis frowns. "No. No way."

"Trust me on this."

He blinks rapidly. "I knew Odette was gay, but—"

"How did you know?"

He hesitates. "I asked her out at the start of the season and she told me straight out."

I file that away to digest later.

"So you're saying my sister was . . ."

"It's not for me to label her, but she and Odette were definitely a couple."

"Are you sure?"

"Positive."

Curtis stares into the flames.

"How would your family have reacted?" I say.

No response.

"Curtis?"

His face twists. "She didn't tell me."

"Would your family have a problem with her dating a woman?"

"Um. No. They'd be fine with it. Shit, how could I not know?"

Without the clock, there's total silence.

"So you think she disappeared of her own accord for ten years," I say. "Then returned to . . . do what exactly?"

He turns away to the blackness beyond the glass. "That's what worries me."

Unease runs through me. "If she wanted to mess with us, why would she have waited a full decade?"

"I never understood half of what she did."

Saskia's voice rings through my ears. *I'll get him back.*

I never did find out for sure if she caused Brent's fall before the Brits. He said his binding came loose; that's why he fell. He removed his board briefly for a snack and I'm guessing she tampered with it. That was the problem with her. She was so damn clever it was impossible to pin anything on her.

Curtis gets to his feet. "Look, I'm wiped out and you're in pain. Nothing more we can do right now." He reaches into his jacket pocket for his Maglite. "Keep this on you. I'll take you to your dorm."

As I haul myself upright, my gaze settles on the empty pins on the wall. And suddenly I know what used to hang from them.

That ancient ice axe.

CHAPTER 42

TEN YEARS AGO

The clock in my head is ticking extra loudly today. This is it. The last day of training before the Brits. But I'm not ready.

Every time I reach the top of the pipe, I think about trying a Crippler and something stops me. I'm pretending that it's common sense. That if I injure myself today and can't perform tomorrow, my sponsors will quite rightly find a more productive athlete to back.

Deep down, though, I know it's fear.

The pipe is rammed. All week, British snowboarders have been flying or driving in from wherever they were training this winter, and they're all here today, pushing their limits. A couple of girls whom I met at the Brits last year come over to say hi, including Claire Donnahue, reigning British number one; Brent is cranking out huge airs, sore knee strapped up; Curtis seems to have nailed his Haakon flips; Dale smashed his wrist and headed down early to see the physiotherapist.

But I'm only dimly aware of it all. I came close to landing a couple of my Crippler attempts yesterday, and I think I know what I did wrong. Should I? Shouldn't I? I could try just one . . .

But what's this? The lift operator is roping the pipe off because it's four o'clock. Damn. I've been so busy thinking about Cripplers that I haven't focused on the rest of my run. In a daze, I walk over to where I left my backpack.

Curtis is chatting with Nate Farmer, who came third in the Brits last year, behind him and Brent.

"Heard you've got some new tricks," Nate says.

Curtis feigns surprise. "Did you?"

I notice he doesn't answer one way or the other.

Nate smiles. "I guess we'll see what you've got tomorrow."

Curtis shrugs. "Too icy to try much."

When I know full well that icy conditions won't deter him.

Odette approaches, short hair hidden beneath her Rossignol helmet. "How was your day?"

I force a smile. "Not too bad. I'm still in one piece."

She's gone out of her way to be nice to me since Saskia buried me two weeks ago.

Sensing she's about to ask what I'm planning in the comp, I gesture to Curtis and Brent. "Which of them do you think will win tomorrow?" From watching their runs earlier, I'd be hard-pressed to say.

"It depends what the judges are looking for," Odette says. "If they prefer the technicality of the tricks, then Curtis. If they want size, perhaps Brent."

Saskia comes over to get her backpack, looking smug. With good reason. She's going to beat me tomorrow, unless she screws up badly. Which she won't. She's nearly as consistent as her brother, damn her. I thought that by wanting it enough I could make it happen. But she wants it just as much as I do and she had a ten-year head start.

She's stayed well away from me these last two weeks. Curtis had a word with her, I presume. Then again, she could just be biding her time.

"All ready for the Brits?" she says to Odette.

"Yeah, maybe," Odette says.

Alarm bells start to ring. "But she's not competing," I say.

"Oh, but she is," Saskia says.

All the air seems to rush out of me. "She's not a Brit."

"I need the points," Odette says.

I stare at her. "What?"

"It's a tiny comp and the prize money is nothing," Odette says. "But internationals can enter. We don't get a British ranking, but we get FIS points. I missed a few comps this year when I hurt my wrist, so I need the points."

If I felt sick before, now I really want to vomit. So much for me making the top three. This is bad. Really bad.

On paper, the result won't affect the British rankings because she's not a Brit, but it'll affect the rankings in my head and, more important, how it looks to any potential sponsors watching.

There's a hard edge to Saskia's smile and I realize she's not happy about this either. How long has she known?

Numbly I pick up my board and follow our little gang for what has become a daily ritual: the race back down to the resort. For the boys, it's harmless fun, but for us girls, it's personal. Odette always wins, no surprises there, but Saskia and I are pretty evenly matched in the speed stakes. I have Stefan, my boyfriend from last year, to thank for that, and I guess she has her brother.

The top of the piste is the informal start line. Saskia and I shuffle into position.

I need to fight back. It's that or slink off home to cry. "Did you see my Crippler earlier?" I ask brightly.

That wipes the smile off Saskia's face. She exchanges looks with Odette and turns back to me, disbelieving.

Brent is fastening his bindings nearby. He hasn't said much to me since I broke up with him yesterday, but after a moment's delay, he reaches out to bump fists with me. "Yeah, you nailed it, Mills."

His glove meets mine and I give him a look of silent thanks.

Saskia stares. It's a false victory, but it's the only one I'm going to get.

She taps Curtis on the shoulder. "Will you spot me on the tramp later?" she asks sweetly.

He looks from her to me and Odette. "No. Ask one of your friends. Or haven't you got any?"

Saskia lowers her goggles, sour faced. She wants to try Cripplers, clearly, but doesn't want any of the competition there to witness it. Which now includes Odette.

Hmm. If I can pile the pressure on and make her believe I'm going to do a Crippler tomorrow, maybe she'll risk something she shouldn't.

"Everyone ready?" Curtis calls. "Go!"

This is a black run. I point my board down the fall line, weight on my front foot. We're bombing down: Brent and Curtis; me, Saskia, and Odette. My trousers flap; the wind roars in my ears. The boys pull ahead as always, with Odette right behind them. So far Saskia and I are about level. My tired quads scream in protest as I swerve around a fallen skier.

The piste curls off to the right. Curtis carves around in a powerful racing turn. Brent keeps going straight, jumping the small cliff at the bottom, like he always does. Just because he's Brent. I hate cliff drops and normally follow the others down the piste, but today I'm feeling reckless. Or desperate, more like. The piste is busy with holidaymakers; the powder might be faster. So I scrape in a speed check and head for the cliff.

Before I can change my mind, I'm airborne, plunging downward and leaving my stomach behind. The impact of landing wrenches my knees and nearly sends me over the nose of my board. Leg muscles on fire, I lean back and ride it out.

Brent disappears into the fir trees ahead. I chase after him. The trees are covered in thick white coats. In their shadow, the air is colder and pine scented. The powder is shades of purple and up to my knees. Snowboarders dream of such conditions, but I'm too focused on the race to enjoy it.

Trees come up thick and fast and it takes all my concentration to dodge them. Branches scrape my cheeks; snow tumbles onto my head and shoulders. Any minute now I'm going to see the piste again. There!

I strain to see the off-white of Saskia's jacket. Shit—she's nearly at the bend already. The piste narrows to single file for a few meters just here, with a rocky outcrop on one side and a big drop on the other. Saskia and I are going to hit it at the exact same time, only I'm going to hit it from above.

She glances sideways and sees me. I'm not pulling out. She'll have to.

Except she's not going to; I can tell. My board's going to take all the impact, and since I'm coming at her from above, her board is going to slide off the track.

We close in and I brace myself for the impact. Just before our boards make contact, something yanks me hard backward by the scruff of my jacket.

What the—? My board swerves below me and I tumble to the powder. Another figure wipes out nearby.

And of course it's Curtis. How did he even get behind me?

He rips his goggles off. His cheeks are an angry red that I know isn't just from the cold.

I feel my own face flaming, too—anger and shame in equal mix. My hands are shaking. I would have pushed her. I really would have.

He hauls himself upright. The movement makes him grimace and touch his shoulder. Oh God. Did I make him hurt it even more?

"Why, Milla? Why did you have to do that?"

I could tell him how Jake thrashed me at every sport we ever played and became a rugby star even before he finished school. How Dad didn't notice me after that because it was all about Jake. How I need to show them I'm good at something.

But it's no excuse.

Curtis shakes his head. "You're just as bad as her."

There's nothing I can say because I know he's right.

And the worst thing of all? Saskia is a speck in the distance, streaking past the finish line. She's beaten me, yet again.

CHAPTER 43

With Curtis's arm around my waist, I limp out of the restaurant.

Picturing the rusty blade of that ice axe.

I want to tell Curtis about it, but what if it was him who took it?

"Wait here," he says, and enters the kitchen.

He opens a drawer. And looks up at me in shock.

"What?" I say.

"The knives. They're all gone."

"What?" I limp over to look. "Shit. They were here earlier while I was making dinner."

Curtis slaps his palm down hard against the counter. The sound makes me jump. So someone has taken the axe and a whole stash of knives and left the rest of us unarmed.

A terrible thought strikes me. "I hope they haven't taken our snowboard stuff as well."

"Good point."

We hurry along the corridor. So far the power has remained on, but I'm braced for it to go out again. We reach the main entrance, where I'm relieved to see our things are still there. I cram my gloves and goggles, harness and transceiver into my pockets, tie my boots together and sling them around my neck.

Curtis fits his and Brent's snowboard boots into the bindings and lifts both boards. "Can you manage?"

"Yep." I pick my board up. As I do, I catch sight of Dale's board, leaning alone against the wall. And that's when it really hits me.

Curtis is looking at it, too.

"We're not going to see him again, are we?" I say shakily.

He presses his lips together. "I don't know."

Silent and somber, we head to the dorms. When we reach my room, I dump my snowboard on the floor and cautiously push the door, cursing once again that I can only lock it from the inside. Anyone could have been in here. Could still be in here, even.

"Wait." Curtis strides in, checking the wardrobe and bathroom. "All clear."

"Thanks," I say sheepishly.

He studies me for a moment, and maybe he picks up on my fear, because his gaze softens. "First thing tomorrow, we'll be out of here. Bang on the wall if you need anything."

I lock the door behind him. All senses still on alert, I look around, but everything seems just as it was when I left it.

Relax, Milla. Nobody can get in.

With that axe, someone could presumably hack through the door, but at least I'd hear them. Then what? Shout for help?

What if nobody came?

I glance at the tiny window. In a worst-case scenario, I could probably smash the glass by throwing something at it and escape that way. Somehow. Bad leg dragging behind me. Is it big enough? I pull back the curtains. And almost scream.

Written across the fogged-up pane are three words: *I MISS YOU.*

My skin crawls. It's not her. It can't be her.

I stare at the message. It's written in capitals like the secrets in the Icebreaker and the *GUILTY* on Heather's mirror. Brent came along the corridor not long ago. It might have been him. I hope it's him. I have to know. Steeling myself to go back out, I sweep my door open and check the corridor.

Brent opens his door, brandy bottle in hand.

"Did you write on my window?" I say.

He blinks. "What?"

I limp inside and the door clicks shut behind us. "Someone wrote *I miss you.*"

"It wasn't me."

The air rushes out of me. It can't be her. She wouldn't miss me.

Not after what I did.

Brent's staring at me. "You think it's Saskia."

"I don't know."

His expression hardens. "Do you miss her?"

Guilt floods me. "Brent . . ." I know exactly what he's talking about.

He slugs more brandy. "Night, Milla."

We don't hug; we're beyond that now. I just limp out. Our relationship is damaged beyond repair. I damaged it. Damaged him.

Back in my room, I scrub the writing off the window. Someone— either Saskia herself or someone else—is slipping ghostlike around this building. The catch on the door doesn't seem enough anymore. I search for something I can jam underneath it, just in case. My tube of sunscreen is the best I can manage.

Brent's voice rings through my head as I lie in my cold, narrow bunk. *You're breaking up with me because I care?*

He's a sweet guy—who was barely an adult back then—and he did nothing wrong. Saskia was right—I used him. Snowboarding does something to me. It turns me into this demon who doesn't care about anyone else. I saw that today out on the glacier, when I was more bothered about my backflip than looking for Heather.

I stare into the darkness and think of Stefan.

It's not the arm wrestling. It's you, Milla. You have to win every bloody argument. Every bloody conversation even.

I think of Vinny, a martial arts trainer at the gym, whom I was seeing until a few months ago. *I'm tired of trying to keep up with you, Milla.*

It's not just snowboarding, is it? It's how I am.

Brent's voice again. *Winning's not everything.*

But for me, winning *is* everything. When I want something, I go all out to get it, no matter what the consequences. Friendships don't figure, or other people's feelings. And while that may be what it takes to reach the top in a sport, it causes problems in the rest of your life.

That's why I don't have any real friends. It's why all my relationships go wrong. And now I'm paying the price. I'm completely and utterly alone.

Odette's face floats before my eyes. I sink lower into the blackness. She's still in a chair, Curtis said, and can't move her arms much. But technology is so advanced these days. Does she have some kind of independence?

I can't believe Curtis looked her up and I didn't. Some friend I am. She said she never wanted to see me again, but that was right after the accident. Now that she's had so much time to come to terms with it, she might feel differently.

I owe it to her to try again.

Except I don't know if I'm strong enough to face her after what I did. Curtis's voice. *You're just as bad as her.*

I curl into a ball. Pain shoots up my leg, but I deserve every bit of it. I'd hoped this reunion would give me a chance to repair some relationships, but I screwed up too badly and they're irreparable. Brent's still hurting over our breakup; Curtis suspects me of something terrible—and I *did* do something terrible; and Heather and I are so different, I can't relate to her.

As for Dale, my selfish insistence on trying a backflip delayed the others in the search for Heather. And may well have caused his death.

I press my knuckles into my eye sockets. I can't bear to think about him out there. But I won't cry, not until I'm safely down from here.

My secret is eating me up. It's time to come clean. I throw the duvets off and hobble once more into the corridor. And knock on Curtis's door.

Footsteps, the click of a catch, and the door swings open. Curtis stands there in his long-sleeved black thermal top and trousers. I force myself to meet his gaze. *Tell him.* I open my mouth, but I can't find the words.

Curtis gives me a long look—part sad, part exhausted. Part curious. It's freezing here in the corridor. I wrap my arms around my chest. He steps back from the door and gestures to the bed.

It's not what I expected, but my feet make the decision for me. I limp across the floorboards and ease myself into the narrow bunk. The duvet flops against my cheek, soft and smooth; the mattress is still warm from his body heat.

Curtis clicks the light on in the bathroom, turns the bedroom light off, and climbs in with me.

CHAPTER 44

TEN YEARS AGO

Glow Bar is packed. Lights flash, music thumps, laughter rings out. The Brits have invaded. I push my way through the rainbow of snowboard jackets to the bar. I didn't want to come out, but it would have looked defeatist if I didn't. Oh crap. There's Curtis at the bar and he's spotted me.

Reluctantly I join him. "How's your shoulder?"

"Not too bad."

Has he forgiven me for earlier? I can't tell because he's looking at something over my head. I turn and of course it's his sister.

In a glittery silver corset top, she sits in a booth with Odette. Julien's trying to drag them onto the dance floor. Odette looks like she wants to slap him, but Saskia is laughing—teasing and flirting with him at the same time. She's been stringing him along like this all winter. It makes me nervous to watch because one day he's going to snap, surely. And perhaps Curtis thinks the same, because he's poised to race over.

"What do you make of Julien anyway?" I say.

"No comment," Curtis says, and I laugh.

Heather finishes serving someone. I wave but she doesn't notice and begins serving someone else.

Across the room, Saskia has convinced Julien to sit down. How effortlessly she plays him.

"You know, there's a lot I admire about your sister," I say grudgingly.

Curtis looks wary. "Like what?"

"She doesn't care what anyone thinks of her."

"And that's a good thing?"

"Women are too paranoid about what people think. I know I am, and I hate it, but I can't help it. Your sister doesn't give a shit."

"I wouldn't say that's a good thing."

"It's a male thing."

His brow wrinkles. "Is it?"

"Yeah. Guys don't care that much. You focus on what you want, you know? But when a girl's like that, people call her out on it. It's sexist, but that's how it is."

Curtis stiffens, hand braced on the bar. Over people's heads, I see Julien on his feet again, looking agitated, but Saskia smiles sweetly and he seems to calm down.

Curtis turns back to me. "You know she's never had a serious relationship."

"No?"

"She's never brought anyone home to meet my parents."

Because she dates women? Does he know? He must do, surely. He's her brother. But it's not my place to say anything. "Are your parents strict?"

"No. Not at all."

"How many girlfriends have you introduced to them?"

Curtis counts on his fingers up to ten, then keeps counting. Jealousy flares inside me until he grins. "Only joking. Maybe three."

"What was it like growing up with her as a sister?"

"Why all the questions?"

I shrug. "Just curious."

He rubs his jaw, clearly reluctant to answer, and I'm struck once again by his brotherly loyalty. *Forget it*, I'm about to say, but before I can, he speaks.

"It was a fucking nightmare." He smiles to lighten the words. "I may be older than her but I learned early on not to mess with her."

"Yeah?"

"Me and a mate stole her clothes one time when we were at the local swimming pool. We must have been about seventeen. It was my mate who suggested it. I knew it was asking for trouble, but I didn't say anything. Anyway, she had to walk back home through town in her swimsuit."

I smile, imagining it. "So she was, what, fifteen? Yeah, that would hurt."

"Anyway, she got me back. That's the thing about my sister. She always gets you back."

"What did she do?"

"Nothing obvious. But everyone at school started whispering about me behind my back. And nobody would come to the end-of-school dance with me." He laughs. "That had never happened before."

I laugh too, picturing handsome high school Curtis bewildered and alone in his school hall.

"It took me halfway through summer until I found out why. She'd spread the word around school that I was this S-and-M fiend."

I laugh hard this time. "And are you?"

He raises his eyebrow.

My laughter dies and a shot of heat rushes through me, even though I'm pretty sure he's just mucking with me.

He's fighting a smile. "Anyway, we made a truce and she's pretty much left me alone since then."

Probably because it's convenient having her big brother run around behind her, sweeping up the pieces and digging her out of all the shit she stirs up. But I don't say that. There are clear limits about what others can say, and that's a line I don't want to cross.

"Hey!" Curtis waves his hand and catches Heather's attention.

"What can I get you?" Heather seems distracted tonight and her eyes look puffy. Has she been crying?

"An Orangina and . . ." Curtis looks at me.

"Same for me."

Curtis must be wondering why I'm not ordering anything for Brent. Or maybe Brent told him what happened. Do they talk about stuff like that? I glance at Brent, who stands among a bunch of guys I don't know, and a stab of loss hits me. The loss of a friend.

"Actually, get me two," I say.

Curtis pushes ten euros across the bar.

"No . . ." I hate guys buying drinks for me. I pull out my wallet, but it's too late; Heather has taken the note and I don't have the energy to fight. "Thanks."

Curtis picks up his Orangina.

"Wait," I say. "I need your advice about tomorrow. Should I play it safe or go for it?"

He hesitates. Have I overstepped by asking for his help this close to the big comp?

"Brent said you've been trying Cripplers," he says finally. "Did you land any?"

I double-check that Saskia and Odette aren't within hearing distance. "No. But I came close a couple of times."

Curtis presses his lips together. "What time's your heat tomorrow?"

"Ten a.m."

"The pipe's going to be hard as nails."

My shoulders slump. He's right. The snow won't have had time to soften up.

He searches my face. "Why do you want this so much, Milla?"

"I told you before. I like to win. You of all people should understand that."

"I think you want it more than I do."

"My brother's a rugby star." My voice catches in my throat. "I want to show people I have talent, too."

His tone softens. "You do have talent. You don't need a competition to prove that."

I bite my lip so I don't cry.

"When I compete, you know who I'm really competing against?" he says.

"Brent?"

"No. Myself."

"What?"

"I'm trying to ride the best I possibly can. Screw everyone else. Yeah, I'm trying to beat them, but I can't control what they do. I can only control what I do. Forget my sister. Forget your brother. Just compete for you."

I can see the logic in his words, and his method obviously works for him, but he hasn't spent his whole life playing catch-up. He was born in the lead. I don't have that luxury. I swallow hard. "You wouldn't get it. You're the older one."

Something hits me then. Curtis found fame as a snowboarder right about when my brother found it at rugby. Is he the reason Saskia's the way she is? I feel a wave of sympathy for her. Much as it terrifies me to admit it, she and I are so alike.

Curtis tenses again. Across the room, Julien's face is all red. "I'm going over," Curtis says, and hurries off.

I pick up my Orangina.

"That's bullshit, you know," says a voice in my ear.

Startled, I turn to see Dale beside me at the bar. This is the first time he's spoken to me since our kiss. "Sorry?" I say.

Dale nods at Curtis's departing figure. "Curtis Sparks is one of the most competitive people on earth. Plays real mind games. You can't trust a word he says."

CHAPTER 45

PRESENT DAY

Curtis and I lie face-to-face in his narrow bunk. The fabric of his thermal top is soft against my hands, the sheets smell of him, and this feels so good I want to cry.

Tell him. But all I can do is gaze at him.

From the tension in his jaw, I sense that he, too, is fighting with himself about something.

"What do you want?" His voice is soft and low.

I'm so nervous, I'm shaking. When I don't answer, he lifts his hand to my face as though he can't help himself and drags one of his broad fingers across my bottom lip. "This what you came here for?"

My throat tightens. I don't know if it's because of the intense look in his eyes or because I've wanted him for so long. Or because of all the times he's been there for me, whether I wanted it or not. But my voice would crack if I tried to speak.

Curtis must be puzzled by my behavior. He's never seen me at a loss for words before. "Want me to kiss you?" he whispers.

My throat tightens further.

He brings his face to mine until we're so close his breath warms my lips. And that's it—I can't think about anything except kissing him. My lips part, ready.

But he doesn't close the distance. "I'm not going to kiss you until I know you want me to."

I grab his head and pull him to me. He rolls me back against the mattress and kisses me properly—hard and deep. He tastes of toothpaste; his skin smells of woodsmoke. His fingers curl through mine to bring my hands up to either side of my head and he flattens his palms against mine, holding me down to the mattress.

I knew he'd be like this. He's taking control, like he always does.

Stubble scratches my face, a delicious contrast to the slick heat of his mouth. I've never been kissed with such intensity. Maybe I'm not the only one who's wanted this for a whole decade.

I could fall so hard for this guy. But not here, not now, with all that's going on and this secret hanging over me. This is terrifying. I want to run from the room.

Curtis comes up for air, eyes intent on my face, reminding me just how good he is at reading me. I blink up at him.

"You okay?"

"Yeah."

"Tell me to stop." He waits a moment. When I don't speak, he lowers his head and kisses me much more gently—my forehead, my cheeks, my chin. Everywhere except my lips. And I can't not do this, because I want him so damn badly. He kisses his way from my jaw to my throat, still holding me down. Which gets to me big-time.

When his lips return to mine, I open my mouth to let him in, except he teases me, giving me his tongue only briefly, then swapping it for his fingertip. I wanted to see him lose control, but *I'm* the one who's losing it, bucking underneath him and trying to tug my hands free because I need more.

At last he lets me have his tongue. I'm sucking in air through my nose and it feels like we're underwater. From the way he's breathing, his control might finally be slipping.

He wouldn't kiss me like this if he knew what I did to his sister.

I need to tell him, before we go any further. But he'll hate me.

And it feels so good.

When I finally get a hand free, I pull at his thermal top. He breaks the kiss to sit up astride me and peel it over his head. I take in his torso in the half-light. These are not the pumped-up, unbalanced muscles of the bodybuilders I see in the gym but the strong, functional muscles of an athlete. Even now, ten years on.

He looks down at me with faint amusement as I explore.

I slide my fingers over the taut, smooth skin, tracing the mounds and hollows. And the scars. He's beautiful.

"Can I?" He reaches for the hem of my thermal top.

"Yeah."

He lifts it off. My nipples are tight in the cold air, and when he touches them with a fingertip they tighten more. He snatches his hand away and sits upright over me, shoulders rising and falling.

What just happened?

"I need to tell you something, Milla." His thighs grip my sides. "I tried to tell you in the bathroom earlier."

My mouth goes dry. I think I know what he's going to tell me. But it doesn't make sense. Unless it was all lies. How he thinks she's still alive and out there, and asking me who I thought killed her. Telling me the lift pass was planted. My stomach turns. He must have taken it from her pocket as some sort of sick keepsake.

His blue eyes look down at me, apprehensive. "Before I tell you, I want you to know I'm so sorry for what I did."

There's only one thing he can mean. Images flash through my mind. His large hands tightening around his sister's throat. Or stabbing her with one of his large kitchen knives. Or pushing her off a big drop. Or—

He glances at the door. "Just don't tell them, okay?"

There's a wild look in his eyes. What's he going to do to me after he tells me? Will he dispatch me the same way he did her? Out there in the ice?

I shove him off me. Pain surges through my knee as I struggle out from under him and limp to the door, still topless.

Curtis comes up behind me, holding the door shut. "Milla."

"Let me out."

"Please."

I catch the desperation in his voice. His sister had a way of finding our trigger points. She liked to push people to their limits, just for fun, to see what happened. After twenty years of it, it's understandable that he might snap.

I turn to face him. "You don't have to tell me." My voice sounds shaky. If this comes out, he'll be locked up for life. It's better if I don't know.

"I do. I should have told you earlier." He swallows. "You're going to hate me, but I hope there's a chance you'll understand. Okay . . ." He takes a deep breath.

I want to press my hand over his mouth. Once he tells me, I'll have to report him.

Won't I?

CHAPTER 46

TEN YEARS AGO

I watch Curtis push his way across Glow Bar to deal with Julien, feeling completely mixed up and no closer to knowing what I should do tomorrow.

Is Dale right? Can I trust anything Curtis has said, or has he been on his sister's side all along?

Dale is still trying to get Heather's attention. He doesn't normally have to wait for his drinks in here but she seems to be ignoring him tonight. They must have had another fight. Hope she hasn't found out I kissed him. That's the last thing any of us needs.

I carry the Oranginas across the room to Brent, unsure if he'll even accept a drink from me anymore. "I wanted to wish you good luck for tomorrow."

Brent takes the bottle with a sad smile. "You too, Mills."

"Thanks. I'll need it."

"You know I never wanted to hold you back."

"I know." I sip my Orangina. It's loaded with sugar and I should stick to water, but our little group has acquired a real addiction to the stuff this winter.

Curtis's voice carries over the music. "She's not interested, get it?" he tells Julien. He switches to French, presumably repeating the message to make sure he gets it across.

"So you're up against Odette?" Brent says.

I groan. "Don't remind me."

"Don't worry about it. It doesn't affect the British rankings."

"It affects how it looks to all the spectators." I change the subject. "You know when Curtis gives you snowboarding advice? Do you trust him?"

Brent's answer is instant. "Yeah, why?"

"Just . . . Don't you think it's odd that he would help you? It could turn out he's helping you beat him. You don't think he'd tell you something . . ." I search for the right word.

"Deliberately give me the wrong advice, you mean? Nah. He's not like that."

"But he's so competitive."

Across the room, Julien has disappeared and Curtis is talking to a couple of guys I don't know.

"What you've got to understand about Curtis," Brent says, "is he knows a lot of people and he seems like a friendly guy but he's got walls a mile high. There's an inner circle and everyone outside of that is a potential opponent. If you're in his inner circle, the guy would kill for you."

"Right," I say slowly.

"But you've got to earn that trust."

"And you did?"

Brent nods. "Took a while, but yeah."

"Is Dale in the inner circle?"

"Nah. Dale pisses him off."

"Yeah, I've noticed that." Two strong personalities fighting for dominance. "What about me? Am I in the inner circle?"

Brent looks away. "Hard to say."

In other words, no. The answer hurts, but I sense the truth in it. I may have made the inner circle briefly, after Saskia buried me, but the race earlier today blew my chances.

I sip my drink, wondering who'd be in *my* inner circle. My brother makes my life hell when he wants to, and I have issues with both of my parents. Brent and I were close, but not anymore; and Odette, but again, not anymore. Snowboarding has distanced me from my friends back home. My fault entirely, because whenever I've had to choose between snowboarding and them—twenty-first-birthday parties, engagement parties, or whatever—I've chosen snowboarding.

So nobody. I don't have an inner circle.

All around me, groups of friends laugh and chat. How has it come to this? The eve of the most important competition in my career so far and I'm friendless and alone.

Brent nudges my hand. "Want me to come over in the morning and we'll ride up together?"

"Yeah, great." A spark of hope. Maybe this will work out. Brent and I will stay friends.

Heather bustles about collecting empties from Saskia's booth. She knocks over Saskia's half-full bottle of Orangina. Saskia says something and Heather draws herself up, furious. Silver top gleaming, Saskia gets to her feet, too. They argue, and Heather looks madder and madder, though I can't hear what they're saying over the music.

Odette stares at Saskia in shock, then scrambles to her feet. She shouts something in French at Saskia and runs from the bar.

What on earth did Heather say?

Saskia leans in close to say something in Heather's ear.

Heather slaps her across the face. "You bitch!" It's loud enough that I hear it.

Saskia slaps Heather back hard enough to make her stagger sideways.

Before I can so much as blink, Dale comes crashing across the room from the bar to barge Saskia backward. She stumbles over a chair and the two of them tumble into a booth with him on top of her.

Curtis jumps in to haul Dale off. The crowd scatters as he and Dale grapple. The music stops; the bar falls silent.

"You need to keep your sister under control," Dale shouts.

"She's not a dog," Curtis retorts.

"I don't know about that," Dale says.

Curtis's fist shoots out so fast I hardly see his arm move. Dale staggers, clutching his jaw, then rushes forward. He punches Curtis, who ducks, so Dale only manages to clip his ear.

Three burly bouncers pile in. Two of them grab Curtis's arms and bend them behind his back at a savage angle. Curtis stifles a groan and his face goes white. Oh shit—his bad shoulder.

Dale tries to hit Curtis again and when the third security guy gets between them, Dale hits him instead. Other security guys appear from nowhere, a man in a suit barking something in French at their rear.

The bouncers bundle Dale and Curtis toward the back exit. Dale nurses his hand. He must have hurt it pretty badly because he doesn't put up a fight.

Heather casts a worried look in Dale's direction, but the man in the suit beckons her over.

"What the fuck just happened?" Brent says.

"I have no idea," I say. "And I'm stone-cold sober."

"Better go and see where they're taking them." Brent heads off.

Saskia's the only one left at the table. Perfectly composed once again, she catches my eye and shrugs like it's no skin off her nose.

I push my way through the crowd to the rear exit, following Brent, but a security guy blocks my path. I'll have to go out the front.

The man in the suit is having a word with Heather. Telling her off, clearly, because she's hanging her head.

Saskia grabs my arm as I pass her. "They'll be fine. Stay."

"Do you think?" I say.

"They're big boys."

The security team troops back in. Curtis, Brent, and Dale are probably halfway down the street already.

Saskia indicates the seat beside her. "Sit."

I hesitate. What does she want now? Saskia's the last person I want to hang out with, but maybe this is a golden opportunity. I still haven't come up with a decent game plan for the Brits. If I can get a sense of how much risk she intends to take tomorrow, I can gauge how much *I* need to risk.

Reluctantly I sit down.

"Know why they didn't throw me out?" Saskia says.

"Why?"

She nods at the largest bouncer, who surveys the room, arms folded over his wide girth. "They're hoping to see some more. A proper cat-fight, you know? Rip each other's clothes off and that."

Heather walks out the exit with her leather jacket on, looking distraught.

"I think she's been fired," I say.

"Serves her right, the silly cow," Saskia says.

I look around. The others have all gone. Now it's just me and her.

CHAPTER 47

"It was me," Curtis says. "I'm the one who invited you here."

Once again, the floorboards shift beneath my toes, only this time it's as though the ice under the building has cracked and the whole place is caving in.

I have to get out of here. Pain rips through my knee as I whirl to the door, but it's nothing compared to the pain I feel inside.

"Mum's never gotten over Saskia's disappearance," Curtis says quietly. "She's had three breakdowns so far."

I unlock the door. I'm bare from the waist up but I don't care.

"The day we got the legal declaration of Saskia's death, Mum tried to kill herself."

My hand hesitates on the doorknob. That was just two weeks ago. No wonder Curtis is struggling.

"This was a last resort. One final attempt to find out the truth. Because she'll do it again."

Slowly I turn.

Curtis looks almost as broken as he did when the Mountain Rescue called off the search for his sister. "If we found a body, it would give Mum some closure. We could, you know"—his voice cracks—"bury her. Or at least learn what happened to her. It's the not knowing that's the worst. Mum imagines all this terrible stuff, like someone kidnapped her or something, when it was probably an accident. I thought maybe I could bring her a little peace of mind. But I never intended *this*."

I look for my top but can't see it, so I fold my arms across my chest. "So what did you intend?"

"A fun weekend. A chance to catch up and talk about old times." He peels a duvet off the bed and drapes it over me. "Here, have this or you'll freeze."

I hug it around me, the fabric smooth and cold against my bare breasts.

"The plan was to get you all drunk and see if I could get some answers. Or even a clue. A reason. Anything. I sensed back then that there were things you weren't telling me, but after so much time had passed, I thought you might be ready to talk." He rubs his bare biceps. "Maybe I'd learn something and maybe I wouldn't, but at least I would have tried. Want to sit?"

I shake my head. All the lies he told me. I feel sick.

He pulls a duvet around himself and sits cross-legged on the bed.

"The Icebreaker?" I say.

"Nothing to do with me." He must see my skepticism because he's quick to add, "I mean it. I don't have a clue where it came from. My plan for getting answers was nowhere near as devious."

"Did you take our phones?"

"No. I sent the invites and paid for our accommodation but that's all, I swear."

My knee hurts. I perch at the far end of the bunk. "Why bring us all the way out here?"

"See, I thought about doing it in the UK, some bar in London or something, but with the way things ended up, I didn't know how keen everyone would be to see each other. I figured if I invited you all here, you wouldn't be able to resist."

"Wouldn't be able to leave, more like."

"That wasn't meant to happen. I mean, I knew we'd be the only guests up here, but I thought there'd be staff around."

"Why did you pretend the invites were from me?"

"I'd emailed Brent a couple of times, years back, but he never replied. I was in a bit of a state because of Mum. And yeah, I knew it wasn't right but I was desperate. I thought if it appeared to be from you, Brent might come. And there was no way Dale would have come if he thought it was from me. Anyway, Heather still said no."

"So you blackmailed her. *Be there or I will tell.*"

He looks away. "Yeah."

"How did you know about Brent and Heather?"

"I heard them. I was in bed having a power nap before Glow Bar. Wasn't hard to recognize Heather's voice."

"So here we are." I need to push aside my hurt and focus on puzzling this out. "Who did you speak to at the resort?"

"Some guy called Romain, because the director was away. I wasn't sure if they'd let us up here this time of year—the weather's pretty unpredictable—but I phoned up and explained what I wanted and they got back to me with a quote."

"Did you meet with anyone in person?"

"No, I did it all by phone and email. The resort office was all closed up when I walked past yesterday, but Romain warned me it would be. Said everything would be set up and ready for us. The minute we climbed out of the bubble and nobody was here, I sensed something was wrong."

"So why didn't you say anything?"

Curtis looks sheepish. "It would have defeated the whole purpose of bringing you here. I thought I'd play along with it until I figured out what was going on. Anyway, the Icebreaker sort of worked in my favor."

"So how do you explain everything that's happened since yesterday?"

Curtis glances at the door and lowers his voice. "Someone's stepped in and taken over."

"Someone at the resort?" As I say it, I realize the problem with this idea. The Icebreaker. Whoever wrote the secrets was no stranger. But how . . . ?

"Think about it," Curtis says. "This is a poor area; no industry and most of the work is seasonal. The director was away. Can't be many staff on the books this time of year. Easy enough to bribe one of them. I don't reckon you'd even have to pay that much. As far as they know, we're only up here for the weekend, so it wouldn't be that big a deal to turn off the cable cars and play a few mind games."

The expression jolts me. Why did he have to say that?

Wanting to believe him, I study his face. "Leaving people stranded up here? They'd lose their job."

"If it's a contract worker they haven't got much to lose. Maybe the deal was we'd phone when we want a ride back down or we'd make our own way down, who knows." He frowns. "This thing has my sister written all over it."

The pain in his eyes seems genuine. "But why would she do this?" I'm cringing a little as I ask that, because I know at least one reason why.

"I'm not sure." He stares into the shadows for a moment before his gaze returns to mine. "Anyway, I'm so sorry."

I don't know where to look. If nothing else, he lied to me about the invites.

But at least he finally told me. He has more guts than I do. In a way, I can understand his actions—his family always meant so much to him—and even why he suspects me. He's witnessed me at my ugliest and he's right that he doesn't know the full story of Saskia's last hours.

"Why tell me now?" I say.

"I was waiting until I knew for sure."

"That I didn't kill her?"

"Yeah."

"And you know now? Well, that's something."

He doesn't answer.

I stare at him. "You *still* suspect me. Yet you kiss me like that?"

He shrugs, sadness in his eyes. "I like you, Milla. I always did. Some of the stuff she did to you . . . I thought about it a lot over the years and figured if it was you who . . . hurt her, it was probably either an accident or self-defense. And if it was, I could live with that."

He searches my face. Now would be the time for me to come clean. But there's a knock on the door.

Curtis swears.

"Better get it," I say.

He scrambles off the bed and opens the door a crack.

"I heard a noise."

Crap. That's Brent's voice.

"And Milla's not answering her door."

"Uh . . ." Curtis glances over his shoulder at me.

I pull the duvet to my chin. "It's okay. Open the door."

Curtis sweeps the door wide. Brent jolts when he sees me there. I've hurt him all over again.

"I didn't hear anything," Curtis says.

"Me neither," I say.

Brent hovers in the doorway, clearly uncomfortable. "It was like a door shutting. And Heather's not in her room either."

Curtis and I exchange looks. My heart starts pounding again. Straight out of one drama and into another.

"Come in," Curtis says.

Brent shuffles in and I smell brandy fumes. Has he drunk the whole bottle? Smells like it.

Curtis locks the door behind him and pulls a hoodie over his head. "Want to get some clothes on, Milla?" He tosses me my thermal top and two of his sweaters.

"Should I go out so you can change?" Brent says stiffly.

"No," I say. Nothing he hasn't seen before, and both guys must be thinking that, though I'm grateful neither of them points it out.

My bad knee has stiffened up. I hoist my leg carefully to the ground. Brent turns his back as I dress. Curtis's clothes are huge on me but at least they're warm.

"You can look now," I say.

Brent rakes a hand through his hair. "So what do we do?"

Curtis looks guarded. "I guess we search for Heather."

Brent nods.

I notice how easily he's prepared to follow Curtis's lead now. Brent's scared.

And that scares me. A lot.

"Should we have weapons or something?" Brent says.

I suck in my breath.

Curtis pauses a beat. "What sort of weapons are you thinking?"

I catch the way Curtis is looking at him. It's a test to see how quickly he responds. If he has already armed himself.

"Plenty of sticks and spades outside," Brent says.

And ice axes.

Brent's dark eyes meet mine. "And ice axes."

God. I picture a shadowy figure standing behind one of the many closed doors, ice axe raised and ready.

I open my mouth to tell them the one in the restaurant is missing. But Brent's still looking at me. Did *he* take the axe? Or the knives? My judgment is shot, but if he took them, it's better if he thinks we don't realize.

"Got anything in your room?" Curtis says.

"My screwdriver," Brent says.

"Go get it."

Brent disappears.

The instant the door shuts, Curtis leans in close. "Do you trust him?"

I hesitate. I know every inch of Brent's body, but do I really know *him?* Now, ten years on? I can't forget that look in his eyes last night. "Do you?"

"I'm not sure." Curtis rummages through his backpack.

"You know that ancient ice axe on the wall downstairs?"

"Yeah?"

"It's gone."

Curtis's head jerks up. "Since when?"

"I only noticed at dinner." I feel bad now for not mentioning it earlier.

He swears and pulls out a large screwdriver with a purple plastic handle—the very one I borrowed from him ten years ago. "Here, take this."

"What about you?"

"*Take it.*"

I take it.

"Listen, if it's my sister out there, you stay away from her, okay? Let me deal with her."

There's a nightmarish quality about this. The idea that she would come back from the dead and hatch this elaborate plan. To do . . . what, exactly?

Curtis throws a worried look at the door. "Brent should have come back by now. Do you trust me, Milla?"

"I—" I don't know. "I need time to take in what you told me."

"Look, from now on, I will do my best to be totally honest. But you need to trust me. Once we go out that door—"

There's a scream from the corridor. A piercing female scream.

I yank the door open and dive out, sore knee nearly giving way beneath me, to see Heather wielding the missing ice axe.

So she's the one who set this up. Her and Dale.

Brent stands a few meters down the corridor from her, arms raised, screwdriver in one hand. Whose side is he on?

Heather swings around, wielding the axe in my direction. It may be old but it could still do some serious damage. I raise the screwdriver. Ice axe versus screwdriver. I don't fancy my chances.

Curtis is somewhere behind me, armed only with his bare hands.

Why is Heather doing this? Where's Dale, and who has all those knives? I want to look behind me down the corridor but I daren't take my eyes off Heather. I'll have to trust Curtis to have my back.

Heather's eyes lock on the point of my screwdriver. "Stay back!"

Her knuckles are white on the handle. I sense that if I make a single movement, she'll swing.

The lights go off.

CHAPTER 48

TEN YEARS AGO

Saskia's face flashes before my eyes in the darkness, lit up in green and orange as we dance on the stage at Glow Bar.

That Killers track is playing again. I've heard the song so many times this winter. The strobe lights reflect off Saskia's silver corset. Every guy in the place is watching her, though she seems completely unaware of it—or maybe she doesn't care?

She and I seem to be playing a game of Last Woman Standing. So far I'm doing okay in that I haven't consumed any alcohol; then again, I don't think she has either. I'm clearly not going to get her drunk enough to affect her performance tomorrow, but perhaps I can tire her out. I had an early night last night, and juggling three jobs has given me plenty of practice at functioning on just a few hours' sleep. Hopefully she won't hold up as well.

She'll still beat me.

We dance until the music stops. Security herds us toward the exit. Saskia and I exchange looks as we step onto the street.

Tension crackles between us. Tomorrow we'll be archrivals. My attempts to scope her out earlier went nowhere. She gave nothing away. But I can't see either of us taking first or second. Odette will probably win, followed by Claire Donnahue. Claire was blasting it in the pipe today. I didn't see her tonight. She must have stayed in—smart girl.

Anyway, unless Saskia screws up or by some miracle I land a Crippler, she will take third. Some of the other girls were busting serious moves earlier, too. I doubt I'll even make fourth. My only hope is to try a Crippler. Or at least make Saskia think I will.

We approach Saskia's place. Someone is outside, crouching by the mailbox. Julien. What's he doing? He straightens when he sees us. There's something in his hand—a marker pen. He's written something in French across her name on the mailbox panel.

"What does that mean?" I say.

"'Frigid bitch,'" Saskia says.

Julien sniggers. I stride up to him and thump him hard in the gut. He goes down. Finally a benefit of having a big brother. Jake and I scrapped all the time and I learned from a young age that if I was going to hit him, I needed to do it properly so I at least had time to run to Mum.

Saskia's looking at me with new eyes. "Why did you do that? You don't even like me."

I'm not even sure myself. "I was the only person who didn't hit anyone tonight. I felt left out."

She lets out a peal of laughter. Julien still hasn't gotten up.

Saskia pulls out her door keys. Damn. I'm supposed to be tiring her out. I remember what Dale said about Curtis earlier. Mind games. I've never been the sort of person to play them, but it's that or slink off home to cry. What would Saskia least expect right now? Since we're so similar, logic suggests that what would surprise me would also surprise her.

Friendship.

"I just realized," I say. "You've never seen my place. Do you want to?"

She turns suspicious. "I should probably get some sleep."

"Why? Are you scared about tomorrow?"

It worked on me before and it works on her now. She tosses her head and holds out her arm. I link my arm through hers and we continue along the street. I check over my shoulder to make sure Julien isn't following. He's still lying there, wheezing.

Snowflakes drift down silently around us.

Saskia peers up at the sky. "It'll be heavier farther up."

"I hope they groom the pipe."

"They'll have to."

Our feet—mine in Nikes, hers in cute fur-lined boots—slip out from under us. Black ice. We giggle and cling to each other for balance.

"That's all I need," she says. "Break my ankle before the Brits."

It's clear the Brits is all either of us can think about.

"I hope it's not snowing tomorrow," I say. "I don't fancy trying a Crippler in a whiteout."

I'm a rubbish liar—my brother always told me that—but Saskia gives me a sharp look and I sense her uncertainty.

I steer her across the road. "Here we are." I stick my key in the lock and sweep my apartment door open, feeling sheepish.

She steps inside. "Oh."

I laugh. "That was my reaction, too, when I saw it."

Sixteen square meters, with a double bed that pulls out from the wall. The kitchen—tiny fridge and electric hob with two ancient rings—is in the corner by the door, and you can only access the bathroom if the fridge door is shut. It was all I could find that late in the season.

We sit on the bed since I forgot to pack it into the wall earlier. I can still smell burnt rice from last night's dinner.

Saskia's looking at me like she's wondering why I brought her to this dump.

I search for something to say. I've never been any good at this female-bonding thing. Then again, I suspect Saskia isn't either. We're more at home competing with each other than being nice to each other.

I spot the silver-and-blue chain around her wrist. I've seen her wearing it a few times now. "I love your bracelet."

She gives it a disinterested glance. "Odette gave it to me. You can have it."

"No, it's okay."

But she takes it off. "It's yours. I don't like it anymore."

And I sense the bracelet isn't all she's talking about. I watch, help-less, as she puts it on my bedside table.

Her eyes light on one of Brent's Burton T-shirts scrunched on the pillow and she turns to me with a naughty smile. "Do tell. Is he good in bed?"

"Is Odette?" I counter immediately, because I'm not going to tell her anything about Brent. I shouldn't ask about Odette either, and if any-one else were in the room, I wouldn't.

Saskia's eyes sparkle. "What about you? Are you good, Milla?"

Nerves bubble inside me. We're playing a game of one-upmanship, just like we do on the mountain.

I raise my eyebrow, feigning nonchalance. "What do you think?"

She reaches across to touch my hair. Studying me intently for a sign that she's fazing me—or daring me to take the game further, I can't tell.

"Seriously," she says. "Because my brother would love to know."

There's envy in her tone, as though her brother's desire is the one thing she can't compete with me for, but the reference to Curtis jolts me. Next she'll start asking how I feel about him. I need to shut this game down fast before I give anything away. One last killer move to knock her out of the ballpark.

I cup my hand to her jaw. "Maybe I am."

I expect her to pull away but she doesn't.

"Show me," she whispers.

Okay. She's fazed me.

But I can't let her see that. There's only one logical next move that I can think of. I lean in and kiss her. I feel her surprise in the form of a tiny jerk, then she kisses me back.

And I'm plummeting through the air with nothing beneath my feet. It's the same stomach-dropping feeling I get when I overshoot a jump. I thought she would pull away. Instead she's taken the game to a whole new level.

I've never kissed a girl before. Not on the mouth like this. Her lips are so much softer than Brent's, and she kisses differently, too. But she's with Odette. She'll have to pull out before I do.

Then again, when have I ever known her to pull out of anything?

Through my lashes I see those intense blue eyes, so like her brother's, studying me. I push her back to the bed and kiss her harder. She unzips my snowboard jacket, so I unzip hers and pull her sweater over her head.

Laughing, she strips me down to my bra. "Go on, then." She indicates the zip of her corset.

My hand shakes as I open it. Her slim fingers slide across my bare stomach. She knows exactly where and how to touch me, and to my shock, I seem to know how to touch her—she's responding at least. What about Odette? I feel guilty, but it'll take more than that to stop me now.

I tell myself I'm doing this to win the competition—the private one she and I are locked in right now and the public one tomorrow. I tell myself it's because the eyes gazing up at me could be Curtis's.

The truth might be simpler. All winter, I've had this strange fascination with her, and here I am, closer than I ever imagined. Crazy as it sounds after all she's done, I think in this moment I love her. Just a bit.

CHAPTER 49

PRESENT DAY

It's pitch-dark in the freezing corridor. All my senses strain for the whoosh of air that would precede the descent of a blade.

"Nobody move!" Heather shrieks.

I back away from the sound of her voice, arms up to protect my head—though what protection my arms would offer against an axe, I'm not sure.

Something rustles behind me. I jump hard enough to send a jolt of pain through my knee.

"Put the axe down." Curtis's voice. How does he manage to sound so calm?

I back into him and he gropes along my arm for the screwdriver. I let him take it from me. Guess that means I trust him after all.

He steps around me and moves forward toward Heather. What's he going to do to her?

"Why have you brought me here?" Heather cries. "What do you want from me?"

The desperation in her voice registers. I grope forward until I touch Curtis's shoulder. I don't want him to hurt her. "Curtis, it's not her."

"Milla," Curtis warns.

I push past him, hoping I've got this right.

"No, Milla," Curtis says.

I ignore him. "Heather?" I hear the wobble in my voice. "Brent heard a noise and you weren't in your room."

Silence.

"Brent?" Once more my voice wobbles.

"Here." Brent sounds distant. "I've found two switches but nothing's happening. Power's off again."

Hands grip my shoulders, making me jump anew. "Where's that flashlight?" Curtis whispers in my ear.

"Um. In my dorm. On the floor near my bunk."

"I'm going to get it." He hands me the screwdriver back. "Don't move."

There's a draft behind me as he leaves.

"Heather?" I say. "You're scaring us."

No answer.

"Curtis has gone to get his flashlight," I say.

For long seconds, the only sound is our breathing.

Another draft behind me and the corridor lights up. Curtis stands in the doorway of my dorm with the Maglite. Heather shrinks back against the wall, fingers tight against the axe. Brent is farther down the corridor.

I step forward, hand outstretched and visibly trembling. "Heather."

The axe slips through her fingers and drops to the floor. She sinks to the floor after it, sobbing loudly.

Brent slumps, clutching his chest. "You scared the shit out of me, Heather."

I would crouch beside her, except I can't bend. All I can offer her is my shaking hands on her shoulders.

"Come here." Brent hauls her to her feet and holds her tight.

"I found . . ." Between her sobs, Heather's trying to say something.

"What?" I say.

She sucks in a noisy breath. "A room." She points a shaky finger down the corridor.

"What kind of room?"

She's crying too much to speak. I look helplessly at Brent.

"Can you show us?" Brent says.

She chokes back a sob and nods. Brent picks up the axe and hands Heather his screwdriver. Curtis stiffens but says nothing. Heather leads us down the corridor. Curtis follows, lighting up the way. I limp along behind them, gritting my teeth at the pain, with Brent at the rear.

Our shadows bob along the wall. Four figures. One with an axe.

I hope that flashlight has plenty of battery left. Heather takes the left-hand branch, passes the bathroom I found her in earlier, and stops at the next door down.

I could have sworn this one was locked before. And when she pushes the door open and Curtis shines the flashlight in, I know I haven't seen this room before.

"Shit," Curtis breathes.

CHAPTER 50

TEN YEARS AGO

A pounding at my apartment door wakes me. Saskia stirs in bed beside me, topless and quite possibly as naked as I am.

"Milla?"

Oh shit. That's Brent's voice. I scramble out of bed and search for clothes.

I expect Saskia to be as horrified as I am at being caught like this, but she doesn't move. I fish my sweater off the floor and pull it over my head. "Put some clothes on."

Her eyes gleam. "Why?"

"Because I want you to."

She lies there, smiling the smile I've seen so many times this winter.

"Milla!" Brent calls. "Come on! I need a piss."

Saskia smothers a laugh.

"Just a minute!" I toss Saskia her corset and knickers and step hurriedly into my jeans.

Brent rattles the door. "Hurry up."

Saskia still hasn't moved from the bed. Defeated, I open the door. Brent has his snowboard with him and he's wearing all his gear. He dumps his board and backpack on the carpet, rushes in, and freezes midstride when he sees her.

She's in the middle of the bed, bare breasts visible above the duvet. She waves a dainty hand. "Hi, Brent."

Brent turns to me, stunned beyond speech. He takes another look at her and dives into the bathroom.

"Get dressed," I tell her. "Please."

She stretches her arms above her head and yawns. "In a minute."

The toilet flushes and water gushes from the taps. Saskia waits until Brent emerges from the bathroom, then stretches again and climbs out of bed totally naked.

Poor Brent doesn't know where to look. She scoops up her silver corset and knickers and puts them on, making a show of it. I catch Brent watching, despite himself, and I don't blame him. She really is stunning. Not model thin—slimmer than me, certainly, but toned and strong with it. Her skin is smooth and tanned. The tan must have come from a tube; my arms and legs haven't seen the sun for months.

Brent forces his gaze to me. In a strained voice, he says, "We were going to ride up together?"

He's looking at me as though I'm a total stranger.

CHAPTER 51

The room glows amber in the light of Curtis's flashlight. There's a long desk down the center, with half a dozen monitors down either side.

"The control room," Curtis says.

There's that smell again. Perfume. I look at Curtis and see him notice it, too. He goes pale and grips the wall for support.

At the far end of the room is a mattress. With a pillow and a couple of duvets. My heart starts beating faster. Someone's been sleeping here. But who? I glance at the doorway and Brent must be thinking the same thing because he checks either way down the corridor. He may be drunk, but he's holding up well.

Curtis stares at the mattress with haunted eyes.

I turn to Heather. "How did you find this room?"

"I told you, I heard a noise." She chokes back another sob. "I thought it might be Dale, so I went to look."

"And this door was open? Like, wide open?"

She nods.

"When did you take the axe?"

"This afternoon while you lot went to the lift shack. I was scared." Her eyes flit to mine and I sense she means scared of Curtis. "I decided I'd put it in my room in case I needed it."

"Did you take the knives, too?" Curtis says.

"What knives?" Heather says.

Curtis and I exchange looks. So the knives are still out there somewhere.

My knee doesn't like my bending it. Carefully I reach down to press my palm to the mattress. "It's cold." That's a relief.

"Maybe staff sleep here sometimes," Brent says.

I don't know if he's trying to convince us or himself. It's true that resort staff might occasionally have to stay up here—the Mountain Rescue guys, for example. This mattress alone doesn't prove Saskia or anyone else is currently in the building.

"But who unlocked the door?" I say. Because someone clearly did, and if it wasn't Saskia or a stranger, it was one of us. Dale, even.

Below the desk is a bar fridge. Brent opens it and we peer inside. Milk, cheese, ham. A couple of ready meals. On the desk above is a microwave. A plastic Carrefour bag beside it contains cereal, bread, and fruit. A bowl and plate and cutlery sit nearby.

A chill runs over me. "Next door," I whisper. "That bathroom. You don't think . . . ?"

Curtis blinks like he's coming out of a daze. He steps into the corridor. We creep out after him. He shines the flashlight on the handle of the room next door, hanging back as though afraid to touch it. I'm afraid, too. Is someone in there?

Is Saskia in there?

Brent tries the handle, still gripping the axe in his other hand. The door opens and Curtis sweeps the flashlight around the walls. The bathroom is empty, the exotic vanilla smell far fainter than it was this afternoon. I'm about to follow the others in when I remember how the door jammed earlier. Not wanting to risk it happening again, I remain in the doorway, propping it open.

Search complete, we return to the control room. Brent walks down the line of the monitors, moving each mouse in turn, but the screens remain blank. "No power."

My mind races. Did someone leave this room unlocked deliberately because they wanted us to find it? Or was it an accident?

"Heather said she heard a noise," I say. "Maybe someone was moving about down here and Heather disturbed them, so they had to leave in a hurry."

"And they turned the power off so we couldn't use the computers," Brent finishes. "Could be."

"So where are they now?" I say.

"Plenty of other rooms to hi—" Curtis breaks off. "What the hell?"

The faint sound of music. Where's it coming from?

Curtis turns to Brent. "Give me the axe."

Brent pauses a beat. And hands it over.

Curtis bolts from the room. Left in the dark, the rest of us have no choice but to hurry after him. Around the corner, the music is louder. Oh God, I know this song. It's the one Saskia used to love: the Killers' "Somebody Told Me." Heather sucks in her breath, clearly recognizing it, too.

We reach the stairs that lead up to the function room and once again I smell perfume. Dread pools inside me. The music is coming from up there.

Two at a time, Curtis bounds up the stairs, Brent right behind. Dry-mouthed, I haul myself up after Heather. What will we find—will it really be her? And if it *is*, what exactly does Curtis intend to do to her? He shoves through the fire door at the top and it swings closed behind him, plunging us into darkness again, but Brent kicks it open, holding it in place until Heather and I reach him.

In the function room, the music is deafening, the scent of perfume stronger than ever. Curtis stands in front of the low table. Lit up by the glow of his flashlight is a tiny boom box. It's running off a battery, it must be, because it's not plugged in.

I glance around the room into the dark corners. There's nobody here but us.

Heather clamps her hands over her ears. "Make it stop!"

Curtis raises the axe.

"No!" I shout.

Curtis looks my way, his face demonlike in the flashlight's blaze. I limp forward to jab the stop button. The music cuts off. I open the lid and lift out the CD, hoping we might learn something from it, but it's an unmarked disc. I slot it back in the machine to see if there's anything else on it, but there's just the one track.

I haven't seen a boom box for years. Do they even still sell them? Remembering our lack of batteries, I check the boom box's battery compartment, but they're way too big for the flashlight.

Curtis pushes past Heather and Brent and out the doorway. We follow him along the corridor. He opens every door he passes—the toilets, the cleaner's cupboard—until he reaches one that doesn't open.

"Hold this." Curtis hands me the flashlight.

Before I realize what he's about to do, he grasps the axe in two hands and swings it at the door. It takes half a dozen blows to make a big enough hole to see through. He snatches the flashlight from me and shines it in. Swears and hands the flashlight back. Its glow is weakening by the minute but I daren't point that out.

Curtis's shoulders are heaving; sweat glistens on his forehead. I reach out to touch him and think better of it. He wrenches the handle of the next door down, then takes the axe to it. The rest of us stand back as he hacks his way through that door and the following one.

The flashlight is about to die; my leg aches; I'm so tired I'm nearly asleep on my feet. And if I'm tired . . . Curtis stumbles as he swings the next blow and strikes the doorway instead of the door.

Cautiously I touch his shoulder. "Enough."

He slumps with his forehead against the wood. The axe slips to the floor.

"Look," I say. "It would take all night to hack through every locked door in this place. There's nothing we can do right now except lock ourselves in our dorms and get some sleep. Tomorrow at first light we get out of here."

Without a word, Curtis heads back along the dark corridor and down the stairs. Brent picks the axe up before I can, so I limp after Curtis, lighting the way.

When Curtis reaches his dorm, he swings the door wide. "You're in here, Milla."

It's not a question. I limp inside. And turn to look at Heather. "I don't think Heather should be alone right now."

"I'll stay with her," Brent says.

I glance at Curtis. Imagine if Dale turns up in the night and catches them together.

Or does Brent know full well that Dale isn't going to turn up? I glance down at the axe in Brent's grasp.

"All right." Curtis shuts and locks the door behind us and stands there with his back to the wood. In his eyes: guilt, frustration, misery. He's taking all this on his shoulders, blaming himself for bringing us here. Bringing *me* here in particular. I want to reach for him and relieve him of some of the burden, but the set of his jaw makes me hang back. I'll give him time to cool down.

Minutes pass. At last he lifts his gaze. "Where do you want to sleep?" He gestures to the far bunk. "Over there? Or with me?"

And just like that, the outside world doesn't exist anymore. There's only me and him.

The hurt of his betrayal is creeping back up, but the answer is easy. "With you."

Curtis considers the bunks for a moment, then lifts two of the narrow mattresses from the wooden bases to the floor. Side by side they take up the entire width of the room.

He looks at me. "We should probably get some sleep."

I step up to him. "Are you telling me to keep my hands off you?"

For the first time all night, a flicker of a smile crosses his face. "Maybe."

"You should know by now that I don't take orders from you."

His smile makes a reappearance. "Oh, I know." He takes the flashlight from my hand and sets it on the floor in the corner, still on. "Lie down."

I peel off my sweaters and ease myself to the mattress.

Curtis sinks down beside me. Pulls the duvets over us, then clicks off the flashlight. "Save the battery."

I reach into the blackness to touch his face.

"Milla."

"What?"

His voice is raw. "You don't want me like this."

I grope my way down his body until I locate his hands, one by one, and lift them above his head, pinning him down like he pinned me down earlier. To provoke him. Because that's the only obvious way to reach him now. Curtis isn't the sort of guy who will allow himself to be pinned. I just hope I can handle his response.

"I'm warning you, Milla."

Ignoring him, I slide my free hand down his chest to his waistband, still holding him down with my other, and burrow under the layers of clothing to the smooth, bare skin of his stomach.

His breaths are loud in the darkness. For long seconds he doesn't react. Then, just as I hoped, he wrenches his hands free and flips me onto my back.

"Kiss me," I whisper.

Silence. "My head's a mess."

"I know. So is mine." I trace his mouth with my fingertip. "Kiss me anyway."

CHAPTER 52

TEN YEARS AGO

Saskia's soft lips brush mine. I catch Brent's horror-struck look over her shoulder and jerk away.

"Thanks for last night," she says.

"I don't understand," Brent says. "Are you two together?"

"No," I say.

"Yes," Saskia says.

Brent snatches up his snowboard. "I'll see you up there, Milla."

"Wait!" I shout.

But he leaves without looking back.

Saskia smirks. "Oops."

Last night, I may have loved her, but now I'm back to hating her. It would have been bad anyway, Brent's finding us like this, but she's just made it a million times worse—and she knows it.

I have to wipe that smug look off her face. "I'm going to tell Odette exactly what you did to me last night."

I watch her, hoping for a reaction, but all I see is curiosity. She's wondering what last night meant to me, or if I have it in me to tell Odette.

No. It's more than that.

She *wants* me to tell Odette.

Right before the Brits, preferably, to knock her off her game and give Saskia a chance of beating her. For a moment I have to grip the wall. I thought I was playing her, at least to start with, but all along she was playing me. Yet somehow that's not what stings the most. *Last night meant nothing to her.*

"Heather and Julien are right," I say. "You're a shallow, self-centered bitch who doesn't care about anyone except yourself."

Still smirking, Saskia wriggles into her jeans.

I turn my back on her. Heather and Dale; Curtis and Brent; Jacinta. She's hurt us all. I can't let her get away with it. Except she will, won't she? She always does.

Hardly aware of what I'm doing, I make coffee. Behind me, she continues dressing. I shouldn't do this, but I'm going to.

I hand her the coffee and wait until she finishes it.

"I hope you break your neck," I say.

Her smile falters. Something flickers across her blue eyes. She zips up her snowboard jacket and heads out the door.

Did I finally get to her? I'm not sure. Even after our earlier intimacy, I'm no closer to understanding her.

My heart is still thumping when I enter the cable car. I shouldn't have done that. Not before a big event like this. I went too far.

Oh shit. Odette's the last person I want to see right now. I cringe as she steps forward to kiss me on either cheek. Can she smell her girlfriend on me?

"Have you seen Saskia?" she says.

I gulp. "No."

"She was meant to have breakfast at mine." Odette looks worried, and I remember how she stormed out of Glow Bar last night. I still don't know what they were fighting about.

Over her head, I scan the line of people waiting to board the cable car. Is Saskia among them? Whatever happens, I need to get to Saskia before Odette does and tell her I didn't mean what I said this morning. Odette can't find out about our night together. She'd be devastated.

"You look so nervous," Odette says.

My cheeks flame. Her gray eyes always seem to pick up on things that nobody else picks up on.

She steers me to the window. "Don't talk anymore. Look at the mountains and find your focus. I always do this before a competition."

I was wrong yesterday. Odette isn't like Saskia. I can tell she feels bad about gate-crashing a British contest. Like she said, she's only doing it because she needs the points.

At the midstation we walk across the plateau to the pipe. Saskia isn't there, nor are any of the others, which is weird. We sign in and collect our bibs. British flags flap alongside French ones.

"Let's warm up," Odette says.

I can't focus. Where is everyone? They're missing the warm-up. If Brent's late, he'll be in huge trouble with his sponsor. The Smash girls are here in full force in their bright orange jackets, handing out cans of the drink to everyone who'll accept them. Odette keeps checking the clock on the side of the lift shack and I can tell she's as puzzled as I am.

Just before the first heat is due to be called, Curtis shows up at the top of the pipe. He has his board on—must have ridden down from the glacier. Odette and I hurry over to him.

"Where are the others?" I say.

Curtis looks around. "Isn't Brent here?"

"No."

He seems preoccupied. "He was on the glacier. Said he was coming. Heather was with him."

"Heather?" I say.

"Was Saskia there?" Odette asks.

"Apparently." Curtis looks away. "But I didn't see her."

Guilt blasts me once again. There's only one reason Saskia would have gone up there. To try a Crippler over powder. A desperate last-minute attempt because of my lie yesterday.

How did Brent end up going up there with her? Did she bribe him to spot her like she bribed Dale? After this morning, I can't see Brent helping her even if she paid him. Unless he helped her as a way of getting back at me. But Brent isn't like that, is he?

And why was Heather there? She never goes to the glacier.

"What about Dale?" I say.

"He's in the hospital," Curtis says.

"*What?*"

"Broke his hand in the fight last night. A bad break, according to Heather, so he's waiting to see a specialist this morning."

"That's awful." So that's the end of Dale's season—and quite possibly some or all of his sponsorship deals.

"*Urgent call for Brent Bakshi!*" the commentator says. "*If Brent is here, could he please sign in and collect his bib.*"

I look around. The crowd at the bottom hush as they, too, look around for him. Where the hell is he?

"*We're also waiting for Curtis Sparks and Dale Hahn.*"

I nudge Curtis. "You'd better sign in."

Curtis doesn't seem to hear me. He stares off into the distance. I can't see the clock from here, so I look around for someone to ask and there's Claire Donnahue, snowboard and helmet plastered with Casio stickers.

"Do you know what time it is?" I say.

She pulls back the cuff of her glove to reveal a silver Baby-G. "Nine thirty."

"Thanks." Half an hour till my heat. I turn back to Curtis. "You *are* competing, aren't you?"

He unzips the top of his jacket and slips his hand inside to touch his shoulder. Wincing, he heads off to talk to the guy at the sign-in desk.

He returns without his bib.

"Aren't you competing?" I say.

"Nope."

I look at him in shock. "The bouncers last night?"

"They finished it off, but it's been playing up for a while."

Another wave of guilt hits me as I remember how he yanked me during yesterday's race. "God, I'm so sorry."

"It's not the end of the world."

But from the look on his face, it *is*.

His sister has clearly done something, because he's in utter turmoil. He gazes up at the glacier. Shadow spreads up the slope as a cloud drifts by, and the mountain bruises violet before my eyes. What exactly went on up there?

CHAPTER 53

PRESENT DAY

I pat the mattress behind me. Curtis isn't there. Hot pain spears my knee as I sit up. I bite back a scream.

"Morning."

And there's Curtis by the window. Thank God.

But he looks worried. "Clouds are coming in."

"Snow?"

"A full-on storm, I reckon."

I stand and stagger off-balance as more pain zings up my leg.

Curtis is across the room in an instant to steady me. "You okay?"

"Yeah."

He puts his mouth to my ear. "If we were anywhere but here, I'd still be in bed with you."

His kisses are gentle now, but they weren't last night. Every part of my body remembers the pressure of his.

He pulls away, regret in his eyes. "How's the knee?"

I roll up the leg of my thermal trousers to see.

"Jesus."

My knee is one and a half times its usual width.

"Can you bend it?"

Gingerly I try. Shit, that hurts. "Pass me the ibuprofen, could you? Oh crap. There's only two left. Got any more?"

"No," he says ruefully. "Sorry."

"Brent might."

Curtis raises his eyebrow. True; Brent's not a first-aid-kit kind of guy. I wash the pills down. The tiny amount of relief they provide is going to run out in about six hours.

Curtis is wearing his snowboard stuff already.

I hobble over to the window. Curtis is right. Those clouds look menacing. "I need clothes from my dorm."

"I'll come with you," Curtis says.

Screwdriver in his hand, he opens the door and we brave the corridor. My room looks just as I left it. I pull on my snowboard jacket and trousers over my thermals. And my snowboard socks, trying not to look at my blisters. My stomach rumbles.

"I would kill for a coffee right now," I say.

"The power's back on."

"Really?"

Curtis clicks on the light to show me.

"Why . . . ?"

"Either they needed it on, or they're playing with us."

We exchange looks. His sister loved playing with people.

It's taking all my concentration to blank out the pain of my knee. "So what's the plan?"

That's the good thing about Curtis. I know he'll have one.

"We search for Dale, but quickly. Because if he's been out there overnight . . ."

"Yeah."

"Then we figure out if you can make the trek down. If you can't, we could split up. Two of us head down and the other two wait for them to get the lifts going."

There's an obvious problem with that idea. He and Brent would have to go, leaving me here with Heather, and we're still not sure about her and Dale's involvement in this.

"Or I could go down on my own," Curtis adds.

"No. No way." In terrain like this, you ride with a buddy, because there are all kinds of dangers. Crevasses, avalanches, cliffs. The snow cover will be patchy, with jagged rocks poking through, and when that snowstorm hits, he won't be able to see a thing. Plus we don't know who might be out there. If he gets in trouble, nobody will know.

I pull the knee brace over my snowboard trousers. "I can make the trek."

"Let me and Brent do the search at least."

"No. I'm sticking with you."

"Okay." Curtis seems relieved. "But we need to get a move on because we don't want to be stranded halfway down when that storm hits."

I ease my poor feet into my snowboard boots, bending my bad knee as little as possible. The insoles are damp and icy—should have put them by the fire last night—but at least the cold takes my mind off the blisters. I fasten my harness and pull my goggles over my forehead. My transceiver is still in my jacket pocket.

Out in the corridor, Curtis knocks on Heather's door. "Hey, it's us."

Brent opens the door, hair sticking out in all directions, dark circles around his eyes.

"You get some sleep?" Curtis says.

Brent pulls a face. "Put it this way: if I had some Smash, I'd drink it."

"Didn't Smash go bust a few years ago?" I say.

"Yeah," Brent says. "Should have come up with a better flavor."

"How's Heather?" Curtis says.

Brent swings the door wide. They've done the same thing that Curtis did with the mattresses—positioned them side by side on the floor. Heather is curled in a ball on the nearest one, tear-stricken and anguished, hands clenched around the duvet. Did Brent arrange the mattresses like that so he could hold her? I'm touched—yet not surprised. Brent's a really sweet guy. And he possibly has more affection for her than her husband has.

Heather's eyes open. And close again when she sees it's only us. She rolls to face the other way.

Curtis beckons Brent into the corridor. "Did she sleep?"

Brent lowers his voice. "Nah, she's a mess." He rubs his eyes. "So what's the plan?"

"Storm's coming in. We search for Dale fast and get out of here." Curtis glances at me. "If Milla reckons her knee will hold up."

"It'll hold up," I say.

Brent looks dubious. "It's a long way. And what about Heather?"

Curtis and I exchange looks. Shit. Back to square one. She can use Dale's snowboard now, I guess, but it won't be easy.

Brent tests the light switch. "Power's on. How about I see what's going on with the computers?"

"You'll need a password, surely," Curtis says.

"It's worth a try," Brent says. "If I get in, I can email the resort and we'll get the lift running."

"It's too risky going down there on your own," I say. "We need to stick together. And you can't leave Heather up here."

"I'll take her with me," Brent says. "And the axe."

Curtis nods. "All right. We'll come and find you, but be careful, yeah?"

Curtis and I pick up our snowboards. Screwdriver in one hand, board in the other, he helps me down the corridor.

"We need to eat something." Curtis leads me into the restaurant. "Sit here and I'll see what I can find."

I open my mouth to protest. And sigh. "Okay." I can't have been upright for more than five minutes but my knee feels more swollen already and I need to save it for the long trek down.

He hesitates, clearly reluctant to leave me. "There was that stash in the control room."

"Just grab whatever's fastest."

"I'll check the kitchen."

The stag looks balefully into the restaurant with its creepy eyes. I can't bear it. I limp over to the fireplace, hoping it's not screwed in place. Up close, its eyes don't even match. One is glossy dark brown, the other black, as though it broke and someone did a bad repair job. I grasp either side of the wooden plaque. Good; it moves. Something snakes out the back of it. A cable. Roughly level with the stag's left eye.

Once again, the floorboards shift beneath me. I peer into the shiny black eye. Is that what I think it is?

CHAPTER 54

TEN YEARS AGO

Odette's fingers twist and coil in her lime-green pipe gloves. "She's been training for this all winter. Where is she?"

She's so fraught about Saskia's absence that it's hard to believe she scored a 9.4 in her last run. From the way she keeps looking at me, it's as though she senses I know more than I'm letting on. She mustn't find out what I did.

I can't believe Saskia didn't show. I went too far this morning. I think about the state she might have been in after she left my place. Curtis sits on a snowbank at the side. Odette goes off to question him again.

Brent hasn't shown up either. Why? Please don't let it be because of me.

I watch the men's semi-final without really seeing anything. Odette hurries back over, shaking her head.

"And at the top of the pipe, the girls are gathering for the final!" The commentator sounds like he drank multiple cans of Smash for breakfast— or picked up his commentating skills from watching horse racing.

"We have Claire Donnahue in red, Odette Gaulin in green, Milla Anderson in blue . . ."

I have no idea how I reached the final. I'm running on automatic pilot.

"Are you doing a Crippler?" Odette asks.

The four other girls look my way.

"Probably," I say.

Odette checks up the slope, looking for Saskia even now. "She should be in this. Do you know something, Milla? If you do, tell me, please."

Can I trust Brent and Saskia not to say anything? Brent, maybe. Saskia, not so much. Should I at least tell Odette that I saw her this morning? Because if it comes out later, it will look suspicious. I open my mouth. "Last night—" I begin.

"*Odette Gaulin!*" the commentator shouts.

Oh shit. That was bad timing. Or maybe good timing, because it saved me from having to answer.

"What?" Odette says.

"I'll tell you later," I say.

"Tell me what?"

She looks worried now. I shouldn't have said anything. "Go."

She turns reluctantly and checks her bindings. Shakes her head like she's trying to clear it. And drops in.

"*Massive Tail Grab!*" the commentator shouts as she lands her first hit. "*And she stomps it!*"

Speeding across to the opposite wall, Odette launches upward and flips upside down.

And catches the lip of the pipe. With her face.

A gasp bursts out of me and most of the spectators, but the worst is yet to come. Her body is still directly above her head and tipping in the wrong direction.

It's sickening to watch. I can see what's going to happen but I can't do a thing except sit there, fingers clenching into fists, as her pale neck bends backward to an impossible degree. Until her body does a terrible sort of flip-flop and slithers down the wall to the pipe floor.

"*Oooh! Horror slam for Odette Gaulin!*" the commentator shouts.

CHAPTER 55

PRESENT DAY

Curtis enters the restaurant with a banana in either hand. "Will this do you for now?"

I put my finger to my lips. He sees the stag's head and frowns. Silently I show him how the thin cable runs down the wall between the wooden panels, across the top of the mantel shelf, then down to a power socket above the skirting board.

"Is it a camera?" Ridiculous that I feel the need to whisper. If someone was watching us, they'll have seen me lift it.

"Probably."

"Would it have sound, too?"

"Could well do." Curtis grips the wooden plaque, clearly tempted to rip the thing from the wall, though in the end he leaves it hanging there and tugs me over to the doorway.

I lean in close. "A normal security camera wouldn't be hidden like that."

"No."

"Do you think there's more?"

He closes his eyes. "Could be all over the place. They could watch it from their laptop, or a phone or whatever."

"But why?"

"I don't have an answer for that yet. But I'm guessing that's why they turned the power back on. The battery probably only lasts a few hours." He picks up his snowboard. "Come on. Sooner we get this search over with, the sooner we can get out of here."

"Shouldn't we warn Brent?"

Curtis bites his lip.

"He needs to know." Even if Curtis doesn't trust Brent, I do. I think.

Curtis hands me the bananas. "Wait here. I'll be right back." Snowboard under his arm, he jogs off.

I continue down the corridor, past the ski lockers, to the main entrance, peeling my banana on the way. I want to see what the weather's doing on this side of the building.

The glass panel is frosted over on the inside. I dump my snowboard and the bananas and pull my gloves from my pockets.

Curtis races toward me. "I said wait. Why can't you ever just listen to me?"

"I knew you'd catch up to me," I say.

His face is red. "I'm trying to get us out of here in one piece. I need to know you'll do what I tell you."

"You say 'jump' and I jump. That what you want?" It's not the time and place for us to be having this conversation, but I can't help it.

Little muscles twitch in his jaw. "Yeah. Sometimes."

"What if I say 'jump'? Are you going to jump?"

From the look on his face, it's never occurred to him that it might work both ways. "Okay." His voice is softer now.

I shove his banana at him. "I'll believe it when I see it."

We bite into our bananas, watching each other. When I finish it, I toss the peel on top of the ski lockers, wipe my hands on my snowboard trousers, and kiss him on the cheek. He catches my hands and kisses me properly. We pull apart with sheepish faces. Our first fight.

We put on our transceivers and gloves. Dale's transceiver is on the floor beside his orange Oakley goggles. I try not to look at them.

Screwdriver at the ready, Curtis pushes the door. A freezing wind blasts us backward as though it doesn't want us to go out. We lean into it and step outside.

The vast expanse of the Diable glacier spreads out before us. Curtis and I are the only color in an otherwise black-and-white landscape. I feel exposed, and judging by the way he's gripping that screwdriver, so does he.

Our snowboards are no use for moving about on the flat, so we leave them propped against the wall where we can see them.

"Let's do a quick circuit." Curtis's breath forms a white cloud as he speaks. "Stick close."

The snow crunches underfoot as I limp up the slope behind him. The air has an extra chill to it. I pull my hood up and tuck my chin into my collar. The search feels futile. If poor Dale was out here all night, he'll have frozen to death hours ago.

"That wind's really picked up," Curtis shouts as another gust knocks us sideways.

The sky is overcast, the sun a burning white ball trying to battle its way through. A losing battle—darker clouds are marching in from the east. The snow is on the way; I can feel the dampness against my cheeks.

We pass the garages where they keep the snowcats and test each door in turn, but they're locked, all of them. The sheds, too. My senses prickle. Is Dale out here? Is anyone else? I check over my shoulder but nobody's there.

My knee throbs. The wind is blowing the top layer of snow about, making it difficult to see where we're treading.

Curtis slows.

"You're quiet," I say.

He stops. Turns. "Why did you come to me last night and not ten years ago?"

Oh God. But he has a right to ask. I strain for words. "I felt something for you back then that . . ." Shit, this is hard.

"I knew you felt something," he says. "I felt something, too."

I take a deep breath. "I couldn't have mixed a relationship with you and taken my snowboarding where I wanted it to go."

He takes that in. "Fair enough."

"Could you?"

For a moment, the only sound is the roar of the wind. "I don't know. I didn't get a chance to find out."

A tightness chokes my throat.

"What about now?" he says. "Can you mix me with your life now?"

I swallow. "I hope so. Can you mix me?"

He raises his goggles and gives me a look that just floors me. "Yes."

If it wasn't so cold, I'd be flushing. I can't hold back my smile and neither can he.

He lowers his goggles. "Better get on with this," he says gruffly.

We head on up the slope. I should tell him about me and Saskia, but what exactly can I say? How it started as a fucked-up, twisted attempt to attack her? I'll have to explain how, for me at least, it changed into something else. I've thought about that a lot over the years, and I'm still trying to make sense of it.

I'd never met anyone like Saskia before and I probably never will again. Yeah, there was a lot wrong with her, but there was a lot to admire as well. Her strength of character and sheer balls. How she didn't need to be liked; that in particular is what made me like her. Love her, even. In a way.

Was that why I kept going? Or was it purely a physical thing? Athletes like to push their bodies, to test what it feels like when we do new things. If something feels good, we keep doing it. And it felt good with her. Can I seriously tell her brother that?

"Crevasses." Curtis's voice snaps me out of the moment.

We head cautiously over. The dark rock faces of the peaks above look down on us as though they know something we don't. Braced for what I might find, I peer into the first glassy chasm. Nothing. I let out my breath and hear Curtis do the same.

We head back down the slope and out to the right, along the top of the cliffs and toward the black run that leads back down to the valley. I doubt Dale would have come all the way out here, but Curtis points to another crevasse ahead. The wind buffets me, blowing me off-balance.

Curtis slows as he nears the crevasse. And stops dead.

My stomach lurches. *No. Please, no.*

CHAPTER 56

Odette lies crumpled and still in the bottom of the half-pipe. People rush up the pipe toward her. I stare at her, willing her to move.

"*And Milla Anderson is up next,*" the commentator says, far more subdued than he was a minute ago. "*But we'll suspend the action until we see how Odette is.*"

I want to go down to her, but they'll call my name as soon as the pipe is clear.

An official speaks into his radio, and not long afterward two men ski across from the midstation towing a sledge between them—the Blood Wagon, they call it. I watch them check her. This is all my fault. If I hadn't opened my stupid mouth, she'd never have fallen. I distracted her at a crucial moment.

They're strapping her down in preparation to load her onto the sledge. Nausea rises up my throat. If I hadn't spent the night with her girlfriend, she wouldn't have fallen. I have to go to her. I sideslip down the center of the pipe.

Blood is gushing from her nose. I reckon she's broken it. The men are busy, so I pull my glove off, hunt in my pocket for a tissue, and clamp it to her face to try to stem the bleeding.

Odette's gray eyes flutter open. "I can't move." There's panic in her voice. Her speech is funny—sort of woolly.

"Are you in pain?" I say.

"No. I can't feel anything. I can't move my legs."

"Don't worry. They're strapped down."

I stand back to let them secure her in a neck brace. I need to get back up there but she's holding my gaze as though I'm the only thing stopping her from falling into an abyss.

The men are saying stuff to her but she doesn't seem to hear them. "I can't move my arms."

"They're strapped down, too," I say. "Just relax."

The men talk into their radios.

Her eyelashes flap like the wings of a trapped bird. "My fingers. Are they strapped down?"

I glance down the length of her body. Her green pipe gloves lie still at her sides.

They're not strapped down.

CHAPTER 57

There, in the depths of the ice, lies Dale. He's on his back, face gray, eyes closed. Still as a marble statue.

Curtis swears softly.

Dale must be twenty meters down. Did he die instantly or did he lie there battered and broken from the fall, his shouts for help unheeded as he slowly and agonizingly froze to death? There's no way of knowing.

Curtis slumps. "We should have found him."

I touch his sleeve. Even if he and Brent had found Dale last night, and by some miracle he'd survived the fall, I don't see how they could have gotten him out of there. "You did everything you could."

He puts his head in his hands. "We had our differences. But . . . God."

I blow out a long, slow breath and turn back toward the Panorama building. "We have to tell Heather."

How am I going to tell her? She'll go to pieces.

"Milla," Curtis says sharply. "Don't move."

Midstride, I freeze. "What?"

"Stay where you are."

My heart thumps. Slowly, I turn my head.

Curtis is crouched on the snow near the crevasse, screwdriver in one hand, a chunk of something thin and white in the other.

"What's that?" I say.

"Polystyrene." He hurls it aside and reaches into the snow to pull out another jagged piece.

Hairs prickle on the back of my neck. I blink, struggling to make sense of it. There's only one explanation that comes to mind and it's one I don't want to accept.

Curtis voices it for me. "It's a trap. Someone put this over the crevasse with a thin layer of snow over the top."

A cold feeling rushes over me. "An artificial snow bridge," I say. "When someone steps on it, they fall in."

Dale's death wasn't an accident.

"Directly between here and the piste down," Curtis says grimly. "Someone wanted to make damn sure we couldn't get—"

It happens so fast I don't have time to react. The snow around Curtis opens up and he sinks in up to his knees. He throws himself sideways, hands grappling for purchase.

I start toward him.

"No!" he gasps. "Don't!"

So I remain where I am, watching helplessly as he claws his way out of the hole.

Cautiously he climbs to his feet. "Shit, I lost the screwdriver."

Our only weapon is now a distant speck halfway down the crevasse. Still, it's better than Curtis being down there. He creeps toward me, planting his feet with care.

He's still breathing hard when he reaches me. "I'm going to follow our footsteps back to the building. Walk behind me. There might be more traps."

"Wait," I say. "I should go first. I'm lighter."

"Just do it." His tone is harsh.

I remember our argument earlier. Okay, I'll follow him. That way I can grab hold of his jacket if he looks like he's falling. I tighten my knee brace so I'm as ready as I can be to take his weight.

We creep forward. I test every step as I place my feet, expecting the snow to crumble beneath me at any moment.

"Who the fuck would do that?" he mutters.

"Is Heather off the hook now at least?"

"I don't know. Her and Brent. There's something going on."

A memory pricks me. "In the kitchen last night," I say reluctantly. "Heather said something and Brent hushed her up, like he didn't want us to hear."

His head snaps around. "I missed that. But I've caught some looks between them. It sounds crazy, but could they be having an affair? And they wanted to get rid of Dale?"

"No," I say, not wanting to admit a similar notion crossed my mind yesterday. "What happened ten years ago was a one-off."

"What's to say they didn't continue seeing each other in secret when they got back to England? Or they ran into each other at some point, after she'd gotten married maybe, and hooked up again. Perhaps she was scared of what Dale would do if she left him for Brent. Dale's a pretty forceful guy."

Was, I think, but I don't say it.

"I'm not saying Brent and Heather are responsible for the Icebreaker," Curtis says. "But they might have seen this situation as a chance for Dale to have an accident."

"No way. Brent wouldn't do something like that."

"So maybe it was Heather's idea."

"But setting up a trap like that . . . It's insane." And it seems borderline insanity for Curtis to be suggesting it. I remember how he crumbled last night when we smelled his sister's perfume. He's fighting to hold it together but he's under immense strain right now.

Then I remember how Dale threatened me yesterday morning. How quickly he could turn physical. And how Brent was unaccounted for yesterday afternoon around about when Dale disappeared. It *is* just possible.

"Shit," Curtis mutters.

"What?"

"They've got the axe."

We continue toward the building.

Curtis lowers his voice as we near it. "If I'm right, we need to pretend we know nothing about this or we put ourselves at risk. And if I'm wrong, they need to know what we just found."

"So what do you suggest?"

"We need to test Brent."

"How?"

Curtis looks over at the trap. "Only thing I can think of is we send him walking over there and see what he does. If he knows about it or if he keeps walking."

"It's too risky."

"We have to know."

I look at him in dismay. I've hurt Brent so much already and this is going to hurt him yet again.

Curtis points to the sky. It's snowing already—tiny fine flakes that you can hardly see against the white backdrop. The clouds have darkened since I last looked. The weather changes so fast up here.

"And we need to do it right now," Curtis says. "Because that storm's about to hit."

CHAPTER 58

TEN YEARS AGO

Every athlete knows the risks of their chosen sport. We take what precautions we can, then tuck the risks away in the backs of our minds and try not to think about them anymore. Thinking about them would affect our performance.

But when I see Odette lying there in her narrow hospital bed, surrounded by machines, with tubes snaking out from under the sheets in all directions, I'm confronted with what half-pipe snowboarding can do to us.

In a split second it has broken a strong and healthy body to the point where it can no longer perform basic functions. Where the arms and legs, despite their rock-solid muscles, can no longer move.

I rode down in the cable car with her. They wouldn't let me ride in the ambulance, so I jumped in my car and drove down the valley. I'm glad I pulled out of the comp. Otherwise she'd have no one. Her brothers are at a ski race in Austria and the hospital hasn't been able to get hold of them yet; her parents are driving across from the other side of France, but the heavy snow forecast all over the Alps will delay their arrival.

I look down at her motionless body. Her poor nose is a swollen mess and two black eyes are rapidly developing, but it's her other injuries, the ones I can't see, that worry me most.

The doctors think she's broken her neck.

And all I can think is: *I caused this.*

By the time I leave the hospital, it's dark outside and snowing hard. So much for spring. It's a slow drive up the hairpins back to Le Rocher. Halfway up, my tires are sliding about so badly I have to pull over to put snow chains on.

When I finally arrive at my place, cold and wet, I lift my phone from the table and see ten missed calls from Curtis. I'm out of minutes on my phone, so I hurry out again. The cars in the main street are backed up behind a snow plow, engines revving, wipers flapping.

There's a lone figure in the distance heading the other way. I'd know that walk anywhere. "Brent!" I call.

He doesn't look around. Because he didn't hear me? Or because he doesn't want to talk to me? I can't tell. I continue down the street, hoping Curtis is still up.

He yanks the door open, breathless. His face falls when he sees me. "Have you seen my sister?"

"No."

"Where've you been?"

"In the hospital with Odette." My feet are soaked. I stomp the snow off my shoes and follow him inside.

"How is she?" he asks.

Words choke in my throat. "Bad."

He closes his eyes briefly. "I don't suppose Saskia showed up at the hospital?"

"No."

Curtis swears. "I think something's happened to her."

"Have you tried her phone?"

It's a long shot, because like me, Saskia rarely takes her phone up the mountain.

"No answer," Curtis says.

"So she didn't show at the Brits after I left?"

"No."

Guilt rushes over me. This morning I wanted to hurt her. *I hope you break your neck.* And now it looks possible that I *did* hurt her. I shouldn't have done it.

Curtis is looking at me curiously. "What? Do you know where she is?"

"No."

"When did you last see her?"

My cheeks heat some more. "Early this morning. She stayed at my place last night."

"Yeah?"

I can see his surprise. "We were the last ones to leave Glow Bar." I choose my words carefully because I don't want to have to lie. "We were getting on pretty well for once, so we walked up the street together. Julien was outside her place. He'd written something on her mailbox."

Curtis's face darkens. "That was him?"

"Yeah. Anyway, I invited her to my place and she ended up sleeping over. She left about eight."

"If Julien's done something to her—" Curtis swears and reaches for his jacket. "I'm going to pay him a visit."

I catch his arm. "Not a good idea." I can see how mad he is.

His eyes narrow.

"Seriously," I say. "You'll be done for assault. Call the police."

"Fine." He shakes his arm free and pulls out his phone.

I wait on the sofa. He's speaking French, so I can't tell what he's saying but it sounds like he's arguing.

He swears and hangs up. "They told me to wait two days."

"Have none of the others seen her?" I say.

"Every time I call Dale or Heather, Dale rants down the line at me about how she's screwed his and Heather's lives and hangs up. And Brent's being weird."

"Yeah, why didn't he show at the Brits?"

"Said he'd rolled his ankle."

Curtis looks dubious and so am I. So far this season Brent's had a concussion, shin splints, and a whole load of other injuries and it's never stopped him from riding. Besides, he was walking just fine when I saw him a few minutes ago.

So what could have kept him from competing?

All our months of training and I never foresaw this outcome. That Odette would be the only one of our group to manage even part of a run in the final—and look how that ended up.

Curtis is pacing the room.

"Have you called the Mountain Rescue?" I say.

"Yeah, but it was nearly dark by then," he says. "They got hold of the resort office and there's some discrepancy about her lift pass. The resort computer has no record of her having gone up the mountain."

"But you saw her," I say.

"Brent and Heather saw her. I saw her stuff."

From the way he glances away, I sense there's something he isn't telling me.

He paces the room. "What do I do? I don't want to put people's lives at risk searching for her in the dark if she's not even up there." He sighs and shakes his head. "Maybe she's just gone off in a huff somewhere. You never know with my sister."

CHAPTER 59

PRESENT DAY

Curtis grasps the door of the Panorama building.

"Wait," I say. "I don't want to do this. I trust Brent."

"Well, I don't," Curtis says. "He's not the same guy he was ten years ago. He and I used to be good mates but he can't look me in the eye anymore."

I don't want to admit my own doubts. "But there could be other traps. What if you're wrong and he dies?"

"What if I'm not?"

A movement catches my eye through the glass panel in the door. I rub frost off the glass and see Heather in the corridor.

With the ice axe.

I duck below the glass, dragging Curtis down with me. Ow, my knee. I clutch it, gritting my teeth.

"What?" Curtis says.

"I just saw Heather with the axe."

Curtis raises his head a fraction to look. "Are you sure?"

I peer cautiously through the window. The image is vivid in my memory, yet the corridor is empty. Doubt creeps in. Did I really see her or has this place driven me out of my mind? "Pretty sure."

"Okay, this is what we're going to do. I'll creep down there and see what's going on. You wait here. If Heather or Brent come down the corridor, you duck round there." He gestures to the side of the building. "And hopefully they won't see you."

"No," I say. "I'm coming with you."

"Oh, come on!"

"I'm not your responsibility. I talked Heather down last night. Hopefully I can do it again."

Muttering under his breath, Curtis pushes the door. I begin to pull off my gloves.

"No. Keep it all on," he whispers.

He's right. I gulp, imagining us chased onto the snow by a mad axe woman. Our snowboards lean against the wall by the door. I glance at mine, making a mental note to grab it on my way out, if I need to. I can't run with my knee like this, but with my board on I have a chance of getting away from her. If I can somehow cross the flat and the trap—or traps—to where the incline begins.

After that, it all depends on Brent's role in this. I couldn't outride Brent ten years ago and I certainly can't outride him now.

As we tiptoe down the corridor, I hear voices.

"I think they're in the monitor room," Curtis whispers. "I'll go round the other way. Come at them from behind. They won't be expecting that. Just stay back, okay?"

I nod, although I have no intention of doing that. Curtis heads off down the right-hand corridor. I creep forward past the ski lockers.

"We have to find Dale." Heather's voice is shrill. "Why aren't you looking for him?"

"I told you," Brent says. "Curtis and Milla are out there looking."

"I don't believe you. You don't care about him. I think you've done something to him."

"Jesus, Heather. Put that thing down. You're scaring me."

"I bet they've gone down the mountain." Her voice raises. "You're going to leave Dale here."

Brent keeps his voice low and calm. "There's no need for this. Curtis and Milla are out there, I swear. I'll go and help look for Dale, too. That what you want?"

Someone steps into the corridor. I push the nearest door on the right—thank God it opens—and dive inside as fast as my knee will let me. It's the storage room where they keep the ropes and harnesses. I peek out through the gap in the door.

Brent and Heather are heading this way, Brent in front, Heather right behind with the axe. I open the door another inch. Brent's eyes widen when he sees me. He waves me back and shoots a nervous look over his shoulder at Heather. I retreat behind the door while she passes and peep out again to watch them continue down the corridor.

Brent opens the main entrance and the wind whistles in.

"I can't see them." Heather waves the axe around, movements unpredictable, as though she herself isn't sure what she'll do until she does it.

Brent backs away. I hold my breath for him.

"They might be behind the garages," he says.

Heather steps out. She'll struggle out there in her heeled boots.

"You need your scarf and gloves," Brent says. "I'll run in and get them for you."

She doesn't argue. Brent shuts the door behind her and jogs back down the corridor toward me. "She's lost the plot," he says. "Did you hear her?"

Curtis runs toward us.

"It's okay," I call.

He reaches us, breathless, and I fill him in.

"She thinks I've done something to Dale," Brent says. "What do I do? It's not safe for her out there."

I look pointedly at Curtis. Brent's on our side; we have to tell him about the traps.

Curtis hesitates. "Dale's dead."

Brent stares. "What? How?"

"Crevasse." Curtis searches Brent's face, clearly still not sure about him.

"Shit," Brent says.

I check the corridor to make sure Heather's still out there. "Any luck with the computers?"

Worry clouds Brent's face. "No, but there's something you need to see." He throws another look at the main entrance, like he's not sure what to deal with first, then leads us into the control room.

He points to the screens. I suck in my breath. You'd expect the majority of the screens to show the views from the mountain webcams, but only a couple show the slopes. The rest show the rooms in here. The function room, the kitchen. And the dorms.

I stare at the rumpled sheets on Curtis's bed with a sick feeling in my stomach. "That's your room."

"I know," Curtis says, his expression black.

Would they have seen us . . . ? The lights were out, but would the cameras have some night vision? I push the thought aside. "Who's doing this?"

"Beats me," Brent says.

I remember guiltily that he still doesn't know Curtis is the one who invited us.

"Is there anyone else it could be apart from my sister?" Curtis says, his tone weary.

"I reckon Julien is behind this," Brent says.

I consider that for a second. But I'm still not convinced. The last time I saw Julien with Saskia, he was furious at being rebuffed by her, and I can't see what would cause such a sudden turnaround. Curtis opens his mouth.

I notice blood on Brent's wrist. "Shit," I say. "You're bleeding."

Heather's wild movements must have accidentally nicked him.

Brent glances at it. And topples sideways.

Curtis catches him just in time. "Faints when he sees blood. Doesn't go out for long." Curtis heaves him into a chair. "Come on. Wake up."

Curtis's face changes. I realize where he's looking. There's Heather on one of the screens. Heading straight for the crevasse.

I bolt for the door. Pain flares through my knee.

"Wait!" Curtis says sharply.

Something moves in the bottom left corner of the screen. Another figure, in pale clothing that nearly blends into the snow. I stand there frozen.

"Who the fuck is that?" Curtis says.

Brent is coming around. He raises his head.

The figure has their back to us and wears a jacket with the hood up. He or she is small—not much taller than Heather. Heather cowers, ice axe slipping from her fingers. There's an exchange between them, a heated one, from the looks of it, because Heather shies away, both hands raised protectively.

The figure lifts an arm as though directing her forward.

God. The trap's right there. And Heather clearly knows nothing about it because she walks forward as directed.

No, Heather! Don't go any farther!

I turn to Curtis in alarm. "We have to stop her."

"No time," he says bleakly as she takes another step.

"*Stop!*" I shout, but of course she can't hear me.

One more step. And Heather sinks clean through the snow.

Gone. Just like that.

I blink, hardly able to process it.

Brent struggles to his feet.

Curtis grabs him. "No."

"What do you mean?" Brent says, straining for the door. "We have to help her."

"I'm sorry," Curtis says. "But there's no way she'll have survived the fall."

Brent tries to break free. "Let me go, you fucker. We can't just sit here."

Heather's fall plays over and over in my head like a stuck record as Curtis and Brent grapple. I clench my fists. Suck in jagged breaths. Curtis is right, though. We saw how deep that crevasse was. We need to put poor Heather out of our minds for now and focus on this situation we're in, or we'll be joining her.

"Who *is* that?" Curtis says, watching the screen over Brent's head.

"It's that bastard Julien," Brent says, voice muffled by Curtis's shoulder. "It has to be."

"Julien's dead," Curtis says, eyes intent on the screen. "He died in a car accident last year. I read about it on—" He lets out a strangled gasp.

I see the screen and realize why. The hooded figure has turned to face us.

To reveal flowing white-blond hair.

CHAPTER 60

TEN YEARS AGO

It's been four days since Odette's accident. The sight of all those tubes coming out of her doesn't get any easier, but I've been driving down here every day to visit her. It's the least I can do. I put her here. If it weren't for me, Saskia would have been at the comp and Odette wouldn't have fallen.

She still hasn't regained movement in her arms or legs. She's broken her C2 vertebra. The worst kind of spinal injury. Doctors are waiting on scan results to see how much damage she's done to her spinal cord.

I stroke the back of her hand even though I know she can't feel it.

"Where's Saskia?" she asks. It's the first thing she always asks me.

"I'm sorry," I say. "I don't know."

The Mountain Rescue called off the search this afternoon, but I can't bear to tell her that. Saskia's disappearance is now a police matter.

"Curtis says their parents will fly here?" Odette says.

"Oh, did he visit you? Yeah, they arrived yesterday and joined the search."

I met them this afternoon when I called in at Curtis's place to see if there was any news. I wish I could have met them under different circumstances.

A doctor approaches Odette's bedside. From his somber expression and the way he holds the clipboard up between us as if it's some kind of shield, I sense bad news.

The doctor says something to Odette in French. *Parents.* He's asking where her parents are. They went to the canteen for something to eat. Which Odette tells him, presumably, because he edges out of the room. He'll wait until her parents return.

Odette shouts and he pauses in the doorway. She wants to hear the news. I'd be the same if it were me lying there. Desperate to know.

The doctor returns to her bedside.

"Should I go out?" I say.

Odette's eyes dart my way. "No. Stay."

The doctor glances at his clipboard as though trying to delay the inevitable. At last, in a low and serious tone, he speaks.

And Odette's face crumples exactly like Curtis's and his parents' faces did this afternoon. The doctor pats Odette's arm and says something else.

A single word bursts from Odette's lips. Then she clamps them tight and closes her eyes. The doctor nods and heads past me to the door.

Odette's lips are quivering and trembling as though a terrible sound is trying to escape. A tear rolls down her swollen, bruised cheek. I stand there, no idea what to say. No point asking if she's all right because she clearly isn't.

Through clenched teeth she says: "Go."

"Okay," I say. "I'll come back tomorrow."

"*No.* Don't come back."

"You don't mean that?"

Odette closes her eyes again.

I chase the doctor down the corridor. "What did you just tell her?"

The doctor turns and hesitates, clearly confused by the dilemma I present. Does it breach patient confidentiality if he translates the prognosis I've just heard?

The beeping of his pager distracts him. He glances at it.

"I'm so sorry," he calls in English as he rushes off. "With time, she may regain some upper-limb function, but she will never walk again."

CHAPTER 61

"Fuck." Curtis sinks to the floor of the control room. "Fuck."

"It's not your sister," Brent says.

Warning bells ring in my head. How can he know that?

Curtis's face is white, eyes fixed to the figure on the screen. "Ten fucking years. Why would she do that to us? To my mum?"

"Listen, bro," Brent says urgently. "Whoever that is, it's not Saskia."

Why is he so sure?

"She didn't try once to contact us," Curtis mutters. "Where was she for all this time?"

"You're not listening!" Brent shouts. "I'm telling you, it's not Saskia!"

The desperation in his voice silences us. A terrible feeling grips me and somehow I know what Brent's going to say next. It's what I read in his eyes two nights ago.

Then he says it. "It can't be her. Because I killed her."

Curtis's head jerks from Brent to the screen. "What? No. That's her."

I stare at the screen. It certainly looks like Saskia. And yet . . .

Brent kneels before Curtis. His voice cracks. "I'm so sorry, bro."

Curtis's gaze flits between Brent and the screen. I can understand his turmoil. Half of him is trying to take in what Brent has just said. The other half longs to believe that's his sister out there, alive and well, though he's horrified by what she's just done.

And what it would mean. To have vanished for ten years, then returned to do this to us, you'd have to be some kind of psycho.

Yet isn't that exactly what Saskia is?

Brent bows his head. "I'm so, so . . . sorry." He's choking up.

The figure on the screen steps forward and disappears from view. Coming our way. I want to hear this, but she—whoever she is—is going to be here any minute.

"We have to go," I say.

But where?

Ride down. That's the best option. And hope we're faster than her. A wave of pain from my knee reminds me of the problem with that idea. I tug Curtis's arm. "I need that sports tape. Now."

Curtis doesn't budge and I don't know if he even heard me. "Keep talking," he tells Brent.

Brent looks at him, anguish in his eyes. His voice trembles; his hands, too. "The morning of the comp, I turned up at Milla's place. And found her and your sister in bed together."

Curtis turns to me in shock.

Oh God. That's probably the worst possible way he could have found out.

"I walked down the street in a daze," Brent says. "And Saskia caught up with me a few blocks away. She was laughing. Know what she said?" He takes a shaky breath. "*It's the first time all winter Milla's been satisfied.*"

"Not true," I say.

I can totally imagine Saskia saying that. She'd vowed to get back at Brent for humiliating her in the cable car and here was the perfect opportunity. Brent's distress would amuse her no end. She'd sink her claws in, keen to see if she could hurt him further.

Brent continues, clenching his fists. "*How does it feel to be dumped for a girl?*"

"I didn't," I protest. But we can't get into this right now. I check the corridor. Nothing. I shut the door but can't lock it. Damn.

"It's not that you left me for a girl," Brent says. "But her. After what she did to you. To all of us. I cared so much about you, and you chose your worst enemy instead. How was that supposed to make me feel? And she was gloating about it." He studies his hands as if they belong to a stranger. "The next thing I knew, I'd pushed her." He breaks off. Shoves the side of his hand into his mouth.

A realization hits me. The hunch of Brent's broad shoulders. It wasn't caused by carrying bricks.

For a moment, the only sound is his muffled breaths as he fights for control. "I didn't mean to hurt her. Well, I did. But not to kill her. It was icy. Her foot slipped out from under her; she fell backward hard and cracked her head on the cobbles." He shoves his hand back in his mouth and bites down hard. Closes his eyes.

Something wrenches inside me. But at the same time, I can understand why he pushed her. There were times when *I* wanted to push her. She seemed to bring out the physical anger in all of us.

Brent's eyes open. He stares at Curtis. "Say something."

But Curtis just sits there like it's too much to take in.

I put my ear to the door. Is she coming?

Brent rocks back and forth, watching Curtis with terrified eyes as he chokes the words out. "She wasn't moving. I panicked. It was only eight and the lifts weren't open for another half hour. No one was in the street. I didn't have my phone on me but we were right outside her and Heather's place, so I dragged her inside. She was breathing. I think. I told Heather to call for an ambulance." He breaks off. Looks from Curtis to me. "Heather said they'd lock me up."

Curtis's jaw tightens, eyes intent on Brent.

"We . . . argued about it." Brent swallows. "Heather hadn't slept since that fight in Glow Bar and Dale was still in the hospital. It got heated. I left the room to calm down and when I went back in, Heather was bending over her." His voice catches again. "Holding a cushion over her face."

I clutch the wall. So they both did it. Heather and Brent.

"I grabbed the cushion. Asked her what the hell she was doing. Heather said, *She's a monster! Look at what she's done to us all!*" Brent stares ahead, eyes unfocused, as though reliving the horror of what he witnessed, and continues shakily. "If she wasn't dead before, she was now."

He bows his head. Curtis and I wait.

At last he continues. "We had to get rid of her. Only thing I could think of was to take her up to the glacier and find a crevasse. Do you remember her massive snowboard bag?"

I hear Curtis's sharp intake of breath.

Her blue Salomon wheelie bag. I can picture it exactly. Saskia brought it up the mountain sometimes when she needed to take more than one board up. People often took snowboard bags up there, especially when there was a comp. It's useful to have a spare board in case you damage one. We used to leave stuff lying around all over the place and I never had anything stolen.

"We squeezed her into it," Brent says.

A strangled sound bursts out of Curtis.

Brent continues. "It had wheels but it was heavy and I'd need help with doors and stuff, so I made Heather come with me. In the bubble, Heather was losing it. Reckoned she saw the bag move."

Again that strange sound from Curtis. He doubles over, head in his hands.

Words tumble out of Brent like he's rushing to get the story out before he breaks down completely. "There was a skier in the bubble with us. I told Heather to shut up, she was just seeing things. We reached the glacier. Hardly anyone was up there, they were all at the pipe getting ready for the comp, so we dragged the bag off to a quiet spot. I was going to open it and check if she was alive, but before I had a chance, you came jogging across looking for her, Curtis."

Curtis moans and clasps his head. His gloved fingers grip his hair so tightly I'm surprised he's not pulling it out. He mentioned seeing his sister's stuff. He must be thinking how close he came to finding her.

How he may even then have had a chance to save her.

"We didn't want you to see the bag, so we ran over to you." Brent hesitates. "You were pretty angry."

So far this is matching up with what Heather told me. Maybe she was telling the truth after all. *When I find her, I'm going to bloody kill her.* Did Curtis actually say that?

"Heather panicked," Brent says, "and told you Saskia went in the building a minute ago, so we went inside with you to pretend to help you look. We only left the bag for ten minutes, I swear, but when I went back for it, it was gone."

Brent slumps, as though all the life has now left him.

My heart is in my mouth. Is Saskia dead or not? Maybe she was still alive but unconscious as they took her up the lift. Then, as they reached the top, she slowly came around. I picture her opening the zip, crawling out of the bag. And sneaking away . . . where?

"It was me." Curtis's words are muffled.

"What?" I say.

"I did it. I killed her."

I look at him in shock. Desperate for it not to be true.

Curtis slides his hands from his face. "That night at Glow Bar. What a train wreck. She'd destroyed everything. Dale and I were out of the comp, Odette was upset. And you, Milla. You were prepared to break your neck to beat her. It was all too much. I wanted to hurt her like she'd hurt all of us."

I stare at him, trying to reconcile the man in bed with me last night with one who apparently . . .

"But how?" The word sticks in my throat.

"I went to the half-pipe first, saw she hadn't signed in, and thought I'd catch her at the top of the cable car. Make her realize what she'd done. As I got over there, I saw her board bag in one of the bubbles, so

I chased her up to the glacier and saw Brent and Heather. We split up to search the building and I went out on the sun deck and spotted her bag on the snow. I headed over to it but still couldn't see her. Her bag was right near a crevasse." He meets my eyes. "It was the only thing I could think of to get back at her. I remembered what she did to your board . . ." He screws his eyes shut. "And I shoved it in."

Oh shit.

"If I'd known she was in there—" Curtis breaks off. He sits, still and silent, as if paralyzed by what he's done.

I shoot a look at Brent. "She was already dead."

Brent takes the hint. "Yeah, she was dead, bro. Definitely. I didn't see her move. Heather was hysterical."

But I hear the doubt in our voices. Curtis sits there pressing his knuckles into his eye sockets. He's never going to forgive himself.

Yet if Saskia went down that crevasse, who's out there doing this to us? Maybe she somehow slipped out of the board bag, hid nearby, and watched Curtis kick the empty bag in. And crept away, dreaming of revenge . . .

The door smashes into my back, throwing me against Curtis. Fire shoots through my knee. I look over my shoulder and the blood drains out of me.

There in the doorway is a girl with white-blond hair.

CHAPTER 62

PRESENT DAY

It's her. Back from the grave and full of vengeance.

I draw in a breath as my brain processes the sight before me. The face. The features.

It's not Saskia.

It's Odette.

And she has a gun—some kind of rifle, which she's pointing at us. Which she must have pointed at Heather too, I realize. Not her arm.

"Stay where you are." Her voice is cold, her eyes as well.

Jesus, it freaks me out to see her with that hair. It was light brown back then but now it's blond. The exact white-blond that Saskia's used to be, only it doesn't suit Odette's sallow skin. It just looks odd.

"But your injury," I say weakly. The only clear thought in my suddenly whirling mind. "They said you'd never walk."

I glance at Brent and Curtis to see if they're as stunned as I am.

"Doctors give you the worst-case scenario," Brent says. "And they don't always know. Necks and backs are funny."

The rifle swings his way, cutting him off. "A year in a hospital bed until I could use my arms." Little drops of spittle fly from Odette's mouth. "Two years with the leg braces. Five years more of rehabilitation. Nothing funny about that."

Brent backs into the corner. Curtis and I are still on the floor.

Suddenly I'm doubting Curtis again. "I thought Curtis FaceTimed you recently?" I say. "He didn't seem to know about your recovery."

"Pfft. What did he see? A harness. A headset. A chair. Easy."

Like Brent, I'm flinching away from the gun, but Curtis doesn't move. He's in a dark place right now.

Odette wears a white camo jacket and matching trousers. Was she out there on the glacier earlier watching us? We'd never have seen her.

"Everything this weekend. All of this was you? But how?" I say.

She waves her fingers. "My brothers work the lifts here now, so it was simple. They would do anything for me. We are the only ones who know you are here."

The liftie at the foot of the cable car. That's why he looked familiar. I only met her brothers briefly at the hospital. Her other brother must have been running the bubble lift. I didn't even notice him.

"But why, Odette? We were friends that winter, all of us. Why would you do this?" My mind is still spinning.

She gestures to Curtis and Brent. "Because you killed her! I guessed it was one of you. I did not guess it was three of you." She inclines her head in the direction of the glacier. "Then *he* robbed her!"

Keeping the rifle trained on us, she slips her hand in her pocket and brings out a phone. "I heard everything. I recorded it."

She stabs buttons and I hear Brent's voice.

I didn't mean to hurt her. Well, I did . . .

She stabs it again and it stops. "Every room is bugged. There are sound detectors that start recording when they hear a noise."

She's wearing Saskia's perfume and violet eyeliner as though she's tried to morph herself into her dead girlfriend. Which is seriously creepy. There's even something Saskia-like about that look in her eyes. Or is it just hate that I see?

"All the time I was in the hospital I blamed myself. Why would Saskia go to the glacier before the competition? I thought it was because of me. I upset her with my angry words in Glow Bar, so she went up there to take stupid risks. She was fragile. Maybe you did not see that, but I did."

Her easy familiarity with her weapon keeps me locked to the spot. I tense up every time she moves, scared she's going to spring. She doesn't, though. She doesn't come anywhere near us—can't risk our trying to wrestle the rifle off her.

"My brothers, they were worried about me. My oldest brother quit ski racing and moved into my apartment in Le Rocher so he could visit me regularly. Finally I left the hospital. The first thing I see on my bed-side table when I come home is Saskia's lift pass. She must have left it when she was at my house before Glow Bar. And she couldn't have gone up the mountain without it. At Le Rocher, they are strict like that. So if she wasn't on the mountain, how can she just disappear? It is not nor-mal. I said to myself: I think someone has hurt her."

I squeeze Curtis's gloved fingers, but he doesn't react. It's as though he has turned to stone. The shift of his chest as he breathes is the only sign he's alive.

"I took the pass to the police." Odette's voice raises. "They said it wasn't enough to prove anything. I was so angry. I asked myself, who could have wanted to hurt her? I made a list."

In the corner, Brent shifts his leg, though he stills it when she swings the rifle his way.

"I decided one of you must be *responsible*." Odette hisses the word out. "But what could I do? I had no proof. So I put my anger into my rehabilitation. Both my brothers were living with me by then because I needed a lot of help. It isn't easy to find work in this valley, and the only job they could find was for the lifts. So life continued."

The rifle swings to Curtis.

"Until you phoned. They only have a few staff here in November and you spoke to my brother Romain because the director was away.

Romain phoned me immediately. I saw the news online that morning. Saskia was officially dead and you wanted to celebrate!" The look in her eyes is pure malice.

Curtis blinks. "No. I—" He breaks off.

"It wasn't right," Odette says. "So I formed a plan."

"The Icebreaker?" I say.

The rifle swivels in my direction. "I wanted to . . . how do you say? *Semer la pagaille*. Provoke you. Make you think about Saskia and only Saskia until you cracked and confessed what you had done. I stole your phones, put hair under your pillow, sprayed the perfume. Left messages on your windows and mirrors. But getting answers was harder than I expected. I had to improvise."

"The power, the music," I say. "The bathroom door that you could only open from the outside."

She nods.

"And you hit Brent," I say.

"I pushed him," she says, correcting me. "I was behind him on the stairs and I dropped the keys. I thought he heard me. I had to get away without him seeing."

"And that trap in the snow?"

For the first time she looks a little sheepish. "I had to make sure you couldn't leave before I learned the truth."

"But any one of us could have fallen into it."

She turns defiant again. "As it turns out, that didn't matter, because none of you were innocent."

"Did Dale walk into it by accident?" I ask, unsure I want to know.

Odette hesitates. "I called him over. He was surprised to see me. Very surprised. But I told him Heather had fallen down there and he went to look."

My fingers clench. How could she?

Her eyes blaze. "I loved Saskia and he stole from her. Heather, too. I pointed my gun at her because I wanted her to say to my face that she spent Saskia's money. Instead she told me so much more. About that morning. 'The cushion . . ." Pain crosses her features before her anger returns. "I promised myself I will hurt whoever hurt her. Dale and Heather hurt her." She pauses a beat. Glances at each of us to check she has our full attention. "Julien hurt her."

"What do you mean?" I say, resolutely shoving images of Dale and Heather's final moments from my mind. "The writing on her mailbox?" Photos of Julien's graffiti somehow ended up in the media as Saskia's disappearance became national news.

"My brother brought me the newspaper in hospital and I knew immediately it was Julien. How dare he? He had to pay for that." A ghost of a smile, which vanishes just as fast.

My stomach drops away. "The car accident? That was you?"

I glance at Curtis, but he seems to barely be following.

The rifle swings back to me. "And you, Milla. You were my favorite. I felt bad I had to involve you in this. I was almost sure it wasn't you who had killed her. I missed you these last years."

I remember the message on the window in my dorm and now it makes sense.

Odette's eyes narrow. "I was wrong about you. You didn't hurt her, but you hurt *me*."

"I know," I say. "I'm so sorry. The Crippler."

"What?"

"At the Brits. The one that made you fall. You tried it because I'd told you I was going to."

She frowns. "It was a Haakon flip. It was always part of my routine."

"Oh. But I distracted you right before your run."

She looks at me like she has no idea what I'm talking about. "I do not blame you for the Brits. I blame you for Saskia. She was mine. You knew that. You have . . ." She searches for a word. "Polluted all that I had with her."

I try to process it. All those years I thought I'd caused her accident.

She'd kicked me out of the hospital and I thought that was why. Maybe she'd just wanted time alone to process what had happened to her. Still, I can't ignore my role in the tragic chain of events. If I hadn't slept with Saskia, Brent wouldn't have pushed her, she'd have been there at the Brits, and Odette might not have screwed up her flip.

Odette's expression hardens. "I thought Saskia slept with Dale. Heather said this in Glow Bar. That's why she slept with Brent."

I picture Odette's face as she ran out of the bar that night. So the secret in the Icebreaker referred to Dale. Mentally I check off the other secrets. She knew Heather and I had slept with Brent. The final two—I know where Saskia is and I killed Saskia—had to just be fishing. Assumptions that she made, just like I did, on the basis that whoever did it was unlikely to have acted alone.

"But I was wrong." Odette stabs the rifle at me. "Saskia did not sleep with Dale. She slept with you. We were friends, as you said. How could you do that?"

Her anger seems fresh. Shit. Because she's only just found out from listening to Brent a few minutes ago.

What kind of rifle is that anyway? I know nothing about guns. An air rifle? For hunting animals, maybe?

She sees me looking. "I do biathlon these days. You know it? Cross-country skiing and shooting. We must hit five targets forty millimeters in diameter from fifty meters away." Her smile creeps back. "For two years now, I have been training in secret with my brothers. It was my focus, my raison d'être."

I understand her need for secrecy. After her horrific accident, the French press would have been all over her. Her pride was at stake. She didn't want the world to witness her struggle. I'd be the same.

"My back cannot survive no more impact. I am too old to be a snowboarder, anyway. But female biathletes peak when they are thirty-two."

And she's thirty-two, because she's a year younger than me.

Her smile widens. "I'm very accurate. I hope to make the French Olympic team."

I stare at her. It's an incredible recovery after such a life-altering injury, but I remember her focus and commitment as a half-pipe pro. If anyone could do it, she could.

"So what now?" Brent asks flatly from the corner of the room.

Odette studies our faces, as though she's wondering the same thing. Finally she seems to reach a decision. And from the way her lips press together, it's one she finds distasteful. She gestures to the door. "Out."

None of us move. She aims the rifle at my knee. My good knee. And just the thought of losing it is enough to make me scramble up. If I lose it, I'm completely stuck here.

Curtis sits unresponsive, almost catatonic. Brent drapes his arm around him and hauls him upright. Odette backs out into the corridor, edging away farther as we file out. She drags one foot slightly, I notice—her left one—the only sign so far of her injury.

She points toward the main entrance. "Walk."

I glance at Curtis and Brent. Should we try to tackle her? But it only takes one well-placed bullet, and how many shots could she get off in the time it would take us to reach her? As a biathlete, she must train to keep calm under pressure. The risk is too great.

Brent leads.

"Where's she taking us?" I whisper.

"No talking!" Odette snaps.

Through the glass panel in the door, everything is white. I try to catch Curtis's eye, but he's lost to the world, still processing what he did to Saskia, and I don't want to get him shot for my efforts. Anyway, we have a better chance of escaping from her out there than trapped in here, surely.

"Jackets off," Odette says.

It's a smart move. The colder we are, the more likely we are to be compliant. I slide my gloved hands out of my jacket sleeves and let it fall to the floor, hoping she doesn't tell me to take my goggles and gloves off, too.

Brent goes to pick up his snowboard boots.

"No," Odette says. "Out."

I swear inwardly—he's wearing his holey DCs. He pushes the door and a flurry of flakes blows in. I lower my goggles and step out after him. It's snowing heavily now. The wind is swirling the flakes around; the cloud has descended and it's a proper whiteout. I can't even see the cliffs. The rope barrier, half hidden by snowdrifts in places, is the only way you know they're there.

This could work in our favor. If she can't see us, she can't shoot us.

A pair of long, narrow skis and sticks lean against the outside wall. Odette reaches for them, without taking her eyes from us. We huddle together while she clicks her boots into the bindings. My teeth are chattering already. I shoot a look at Curtis and Brent. Should we run? But where? And how far would I get with my knee like this?

Curtis gazes into the whiteout. I need him to snap out of it. I grip his elbow but he doesn't react. Like me, he wears his goggles and gloves.

Poor Brent has neither. He pulls his hood up and sticks his hands into the pockets of his jeans. His black Burton hoodie stands out a mile against the white background, as does Curtis's purple fleece. In sea green, I'm no better off.

Odette points across the glacier. "Walk."

We set off in single file, Brent in front, shielding his face from the falling flakes with a hand, followed by me, then Curtis. I check around me for more traps as I limp—not that I would see them. We're sinking in up to our knees, so it's slow going. Pain spirals up my leg with every step.

I glance back at Odette. On skis there's no trace of her earlier stiffness. Her movements are smooth and fluid, as though the skis are an extension of her legs.

"Where are you taking us?" I call.

She just laughs. If she wants us dead, why doesn't she just shoot us?

Oh, God. I think I know the answer. If we're found with bullets in us, they might be able to trace them back to her, but if we're found in a crevasse, it looks like just another tragic accident.

I wrap my arms around my chest. The wind is cutting straight through my hoodie. I check over my shoulder again. Odette's keeping a careful distance. We should fight back, but the sight of that rifle terrifies me. She might not want to shoot us, but she will if she has to, and if her aim is as good as she says, she doesn't need to get close.

Disbelief builds as I walk onward. Every step is taking me closer to my grave. Why don't I try to fight back? Yet what can I do? Given a choice between being shot in the back if I run and freezing to death in that crevasse if I don't . . . They say that when you get cold enough, you don't feel the cold anymore. You feel warm again. And we'd be in there together.

The wind is a constant roar in our ears. She can't hear us now. Brent walks just ahead of me. I catch him by the sleeve. "She's leading us to the crevasse," I whisper.

Brent looks thoughtful for a moment, then he smiles a sad smile. And calls over his shoulder: "I could show you where Saskia is."

What's he playing at? The glacier moves at a rate of about a hundred meters a year—I know because I looked it up.

"Do you think I'm stupid?" Odette shouts. "It's been ten years. The crevasse won't be there anymore."

But I detect a grain of doubt.

"How do you know?" Brent shouts.

"What are you doing?" I whisper.

He ignores me and points up the slope. "It's up there."

"Shut up!" she shouts.

"Her final resting place," Brent says. "Don't you want to see it?"

Odette stops and considers. "Okay. Show me."

We change direction. We're heading up toward where we built our jump yesterday.

I still don't know what Brent's planning and it's making me very nervous.

Brent grips my hand. Lowers his voice. "I'm going to make a break for it. Lead her up there away from you. It's me she wants. I started this. You two have your boots on. Leg it back to the building and get your boards."

"No, Brent."

He squeezes my gloved fingers. "I'm fast. She won't see me."

Except he'll be running in the wrong direction up a crevasse-riddled glacier in skate shoes. And to get down, he'll have to get past her.

"Please don't do this," I say.

But he's looking up the slope, preparing to run.

I could go after him. But that would mean leaving Curtis.

"I'm giving you a chance, Mills. Don't waste it." Brent tugs his hand from mine.

And I let him.

CHAPTER 63

PRESENT DAY

I pretend to trip and throw myself to the snow. My groan isn't feigned.
My poor knee. I think I just tore it some more.

"Get up," Odette says sharply.

Over my shoulder I see her pointing the rifle at me. Brent's giving me a chance and I'm returning the favor. Giving him a few precious seconds' head start.

He'll need it.

"Now!" she shouts.

It's working. She hasn't noticed Brent's departure. I picture him running through the whiteout in long strides.

"I don't think I can," I say.

"I will shoot your knee."

I clutch my leg, willing him onward. "I can't walk anymore. It hurts." A couple more seconds; that's all I can give him.

"Hey!" She's realized Brent is gone.

I hold my breath as she makes her decision. Will she shoot us, then go after him?

"Don't move!" She slips her arms through the straps of her rifle and slings it onto her back. Looks like Brent guessed right. She wants him the most, so she doesn't want to risk his getting away. Or maybe it's simpler than that. She knows I won't get far with a blown knee, so she'll take Brent out first, then return for me and Curtis.

She grips one long ski stick in either hand and pushes off uphill, arms and legs working in tandem. Her rapid acceleration horrifies me. She has disappeared into the fog already. I feel sick. Brent won't stand a chance.

I try to close my ears to the sound of a rifle shot that will surely follow. Curtis stares blankly into the whiteout.

I hear Brent's final words. *Don't waste it.*

I grip Curtis's arm. "Curtis. Run."

No response. I shake him. "Curtis. I need you."

Slowly, his head turns. I see the effort it takes him to bring himself out of it.

"We need our boards," I say.

"Can you ride?" Curtis asks.

"I have to."

He takes my arm and we hurry down the slope. I clamp my lips shut, trying to blank out the pain. Any minute now I'm going to hear that rifle. I speed up my pace.

The dark shape of the Panorama building looms through the fog.

"Wait here," Curtis says. "I'll grab our boards."

He's back a few seconds later, with our boards and jackets. We pull our jackets on, but it's no use putting the boards on yet. We need to get across the flat to where the trail down begins. Curtis puts his arm around my waist, supporting me, and we run as best as we can through foot-deep powder along the cliff top.

My lungs strain for oxygen. "The crevasse," I gasp.

"We'll go round it."

And hope there aren't more.

I'm still waiting for a rifle shot. "I don't think she wants to shoot us."

"Why not?" Curtis says.

Snowflakes blow into my mouth every time I open it. "She'd rather get us . . . in the crevasse." I pant for breath. "So it looks like an accident."

"Faster," Curtis says.

The whiteout takes a gray tinge. I'm close to blacking out, but Curtis is taking half my weight and he's still running, so I keep running, too.

I don't know if I've ever pushed myself this hard. From memory, we've nearly made it across the flat.

A rifle shot rings out. And another. And another. *Brent.* My stomach wrenches; my legs nearly collapse beneath me.

Curtis's arm tightens around my back. "Keep running."

Tears spring from my eyes, pooling inside my goggles. *I can't stop caring, Milla.*

And he really did. Still. He just proved it.

And I actually thought you cared about me, too.

Why has it taken me until now to realize how much I *did* care? And he'll never know it now, because I never showed it. *I'm sorry, Brent. So, so sorry.*

I need to box these thoughts away and fight for survival, but I'm hiccupping and gasping out great sobs. All the times I hurt him. I hate myself for that. He didn't deserve it. And I didn't deserve him. He did what he did to Saskia because of me and spent the next ten years—his last ten years—suffering for it.

Maybe Odette missed. Or just wounded him.

Curtis points. "Look!"

A streak of black ahead—a piste marker. That's the slope down.

Reality hits. Odette could be here any minute. If she took out Brent, we're next. We don't stand a chance. What is a biathlete, really, but an elite hunter?

I'm slowing Curtis down. On his own, he has a chance of escaping.

"Go," I say. "Get your board on and go."

"I'm not leaving you," he says.

"My knee hurts too much. I need you to ride down and get help."

"No."

We don't have time to argue. "Remember what I said earlier?" I say desperately. "I say 'jump' and you jump?"

"Remember what *I* said earlier, about being ready to mix you with my life?"

"Curtis." I can't afford to cry any more.

"What about you? If I go, what will you do?"

"I'll hide." Is that the wind or is it the hiss of skis? I squeeze Curtis's fingers urgently. "Go. Please!"

He looks at me. And squeezes my fingers back. "I'll bring help."

As he disappears, I trip over something in the snow. The ice axe. I snatch it up and look around for somewhere to hide myself. There's only one option and it's something I hoped I would never do again. Clutching the axe, I jump into the largest snowdrift in sight and scrape snow over myself as best as I can.

I cover my legs and torso. The weight of it holds me down. My arms and head now. Panic flares inside me. I won't be able to breathe.

Come on, you can do this. You have to.

Oh God, I hear skis already. She's still stronger than me, physically and mentally, even after breaking her neck. Taking one last breath, I scrape snow over my face, then burrow my arms below the surface. Wet and cold, it sits on my cheeks. A terrible notion occurs to me. The snow might set in place around me.

Pinning me here forever.

Every instinct screams at me to get up, but through a chink in the snow, I see Odette approach. My heart races. I daren't breathe through my nose in case I suck it in and choke, so I draw in tiny sips of air through my lips.

She's looking around. I didn't have time to bury myself properly. Any second now, she's going to spot me.

There's a piercing whistle from somewhere down the slope. Odette lets out a shout and pulls the rifle off her back. Why did Curtis have to do that? I watch with horror as she aims the rifle.

She lowers it with what sounds like a curse. The whiteout. She can't see him. I imagine him racing down the long, steep slope back to the plateau. He's made it.

Odette pulls something from her backpack—a dark object about the size of a brick. What *is* that? She fiddles about with it and hurls it down the slope.

She covers her ears and a few seconds later, there's a boom. Silence. Then a loud *whooomp*. And a rumbling that gets louder and louder until it sounds like the whole mountain is crashing down around us. Through my shock I realize what it is. She couldn't see him, so she triggered an avalanche.

And judging from the sound of it, that whole slope just slid.

CHAPTER 64

PRESENT DAY

An avalanche is like a slow-moving wave of concrete. The force of it drives all the air from the snow, causing it to set solid as soon as it stops moving.

My gut twists as I imagine Curtis's body tossed over and over down the slope.

Don't panic. He knows what to do. He'll swim with it if he can, to stay near the surface. As it slows, he'll clear a breathing pocket around his head.

If he didn't lose consciousness in the slide.

He knows to keep calm and conserve his air supply. All he can do now is wait for rescue. He's wearing his transceiver; I'm wearing mine. Avalanche victims have a 90 percent chance of survival if they're found in the first fifteen minutes.

After half an hour, the chances drop to just 35 percent.

I have to get to him. But first I have to get past Odette.

She clearly thinks both of us are down there because she's still facing the other way, goggles raised, peering into the whiteout. Gripping the ice axe, I inch myself out of the snowdrift. Every minute counts.

My goggles have misted up. I jerk them to my forehead. Odette straps her rifle onto her back and clicks her left foot into her ski. She's going to race down and check we didn't escape the slide. I limp toward her, praying she doesn't hear me.

The irony of this. I spent years beating myself up because I thought I'd injured her terribly, only I hadn't, not exactly. But now I must. Where should I aim for? Her upper body is swathed in layers, so her leg seems a better option, her right one—the one she doesn't drag.

I creep forward, gloved fingers tightening on the wooden handle as I near her. She still hasn't seen me. I bring the axe back but my stomach squirms. I don't think I can do this. She clicks her other ski on.

Images appear before my eyes. Curtis, broken and buried under the snow. Brent, somewhere up there with bullets in him. Dale and Heather, together in the ice. As hard as I can, I hack the blade into Odette's right leg just above the knee. With a terrible shriek, she tips sideways. Now we're even.

"Curtis!" I shout.

Odette writhes on the snow, clutching her leg. I raise the axe again. Now that she's down, her skis hamper her. She flails at the bindings to get them off. I swing the axe at her thigh. I need to disable her so I can get to Curtis.

She rolls, dodging the blow, one ski off already. I swing again and catch her just above her hip. Judging from the sickening crunch, I hit bone. She screams.

Her other ski is off now. She reaches for her backpack. The rifle! I toss the axe aside and wrestle her for it.

Precious seconds tick away as we grapple. I have to get to Curtis. I prize the rifle from her gloved fingers and struggle to my feet with it. God, this thing is heavy.

Loud as I can, I shout: *"Curtis!"*

The sound rings out across the mountains. If he's down there, he'll hear it. My ears strain for a response but there isn't one. He's buried.

Odette struggles to her feet, white camouflage trousers soaked red, and dives to the snow nearby. The axe!

I don't have time to aim the rifle and I'm not even sure how to fire it—does it have a safety catch on?—so I fling it to one side and leap for the axe. Pain shoots through my knee. As Odette's hand closes around the wooden handle, I kick it away as hard as I can with my good leg. The axe flies through the air into the fog.

We freeze, rifle in one direction, ice axe in the other. She runs for the axe. Up close like this, it's a better weapon, but I'll never get there in time, so I go for the rifle and snatch it up. She's still groping about for the axe, the powder turning pink around her.

I aim the rifle. "Stop!"

Her head turns. She lost her goggles and hat in the tussle and her hair is coated with snow. Before I can react, she staggers empty-handed into the whiteout, back along the cliff top toward the Panorama building. I can't search for Curtis while she's on the loose. She must have other weapons stashed there—the missing kitchen knives at the very least, and quite possibly more rifles—so I chase after her.

The blood-streaked snow makes it easy enough to follow her trail. She's losing so much blood I'm amazed she can run, but Olympic hopefuls don't give up easily. The pain in my knee has reached a whole new level. Still, I was once an Olympic hopeful too, so I push it from my mind and limp faster.

The shape of the building looms. Odette's nearly at the door already. She'll run in for weapons and be out here in seconds hunting me again.

"Stop or I'll shoot!" I shout.

Given my complete lack of experience, my chances of hitting her at this range are minimal. And clearly she thinks so too, because she keeps running.

What can I possibly say to stop her?

Desperate, I shout: "She never loved you!" It's a dangerous tactic; it risks making her even angrier.

Odette stops in her tracks.

"She cheated on you."

She turns to face me. "You must have started it," she says coldly.

"I was taken in by her just like you were."

Odette doesn't answer but she comes slowly toward me.

"Know what she told me after our night together? That it was just a strategic move to upset you before the Brits."

"I don't believe you."

"It was her only chance of beating you."

"You're lying."

I pull off my glove. "She gave me this after our night together." I slide the silver-and-blue chain from my jacket pocket.

There's a flash of recognition in her eyes. Odette steps closer.

I back away, mindful of the cliff edge somewhere to my left. "Put your hands up!"

Slowly her hands raise. I keep the rifle trained on her as she approaches.

From five meters away, she stares at the bracelet. "She wouldn't do that. She loved me." But her voice shakes as though she already senses truth in my words.

"You loved her, and you still do. I can see that. But she was just using you like she used everyone else."

"No." The word lacks conviction.

"You did all this for her but she didn't deserve your loyalty."

"Shut up." She steps nearer still.

I don't trust her. I back up, straining into the whiteout for the red of the rope that marks the cliffs. "It's too late for the others. But at least let me try to save Curtis."

She glances all around, as though weighing her options. My finger tightens over the trigger. I can't tell what's going through her head. There's nowhere for her to run. But will she try to take me out with her?

I could shoot her in the leg. That would put her out of action long enough for me to search for Curtis. Only I don't trust my aim and I don't want to kill her. I could—

She glances sideways again. Too late I realize what she intends.

She takes a step toward the cliff. And another. She's going to jump!

"No!" I shout. It's way too high.

But she steps to the edge. And leaps.

The fog folds around her and she disappears.

Cautiously I move to the cliff edge and peer downward. I can't see the bottom but there's surely no way she'll have survived the fall.

Numb with shock, I limp back toward the piste marker. I can't process this right now. Curtis must have been under the ice for ten minutes already and I haven't even started looking for him yet. What if I'm too late?

By the time I reach the marker, my knee is about to give out, so I dump the rifle and slide down the slope on the seat of my pants. The piste is a lumpy mess of ice boulders. I pull my gloves off and reach into the neck of my hoodie, hands shaking so much I can hardly get my transceiver out. Hope I can figure out how to use this thing. I flick the switch on the side. *Search Mode.*

I hold the transceiver out. *Come on, find him.*

Nothing. The avalanche might have missed him. He might have ridden it out and escaped. But I've seen footage of avalanches in nature documentaries. The power, the acceleration. Far more likely Curtis is under there somewhere, buried out of range.

I stagger down the slope. *Where is he?* I've just lost Brent. I can't lose Curtis as well. The minutes tick away in my head. It must be more than half an hour already. I push aside the image of him frozen and still.

A flashing arrow appears on the screen, along with a number—45—and my heart lights up. Curtis is under there somewhere, forty-five meters away.

The fog is thicker here. I limp across the snow, tripping over lumps in my hurry to get to him. The numbers count down: 39 . . . 25 . . . This is taking far too long. At last the whole screen starts flashing. I've found him.

I fall to my knees to scrape at the snow with my bare hands but it's not budging. I claw myself upright and kick at it with my good leg. It's no use. The snow has set solid.

Curtis is directly beneath my feet.

But I can't get to him.

EPILOGUE

It's that time of year again.

The time the glacier gives up bodies.

The ice is thawing faster than usual in the recent heat wave, so they're predicting a higher-than-average yield. I've taken to checking online several times a day.

Now, of course, there are two particular bodies that I'm waiting for.

But just as a watched pot never boils, it seems a watched glacier never produces bodies. Not the ones I want, at any rate. So far this month we've had three climbers still roped together and what is thought to be the Austrian couple who went missing in 1999.

I cross my fingers and scroll down the screen. Nothing. No new bodies. The wait is killing me.

"Milla!"

Curtis's voice. From the bedroom.

"Just a minute!" I delete the search history. No need for Curtis to see what I've been looking at. There's something distinctly unromantic about knowing your girlfriend is checking for your sister's body.

Needing to know for sure that she's dead.

I don't know if Curtis ever checks for it. I guess his family would be told soon enough if she turned up. I shut the laptop down and head to the bedroom.

Curtis lies on his back with his arms folded behind his head, sheets in a tangle around his waist. Sunlight streams through the open window onto his bare chest. It's only seven but it's warm already. A breeze tugs at my hair, carrying with it the scent of cut grass and a distant clang of cowbells. I love Switzerland in August.

"Come here," Curtis says.

I remain in the doorway. "Is that an order?"

A slow smile spreads across his face. "Yeah, it's an order."

"What if I don't?"

"I might have to make you."

I approach the bed, intending to stay just out of reach, but he grabs my wrist with one large hand, draws back the sheets with his other hand, and hauls me down on top of him. The hard-packed muscles of his chest cushion the impact; his strong arms wrap around my back, pulling me tight. His body feels warm and solid beneath mine.

If he weren't so physically fit, he might not be here with me right now. His strength allowed him to last the long minutes under the snow until I limped back up the slope, found the blood-streaked ice axe, and dug down to him.

He wasn't breathing by the time I hauled him out. I performed CPR—lucky the gym made me do all those first-aid courses—and he started breathing again, but he was dangerously cold and he'd dislocated his shoulder in the slide.

My knee had almost had it but we somehow hobbled fifteen kilometers down the trail through the raging snowstorm. Beyond speech by that point, we simply clung to each other for balance and concentrated on putting one foot in front of the other. It took us six hours to reach the village. We were rushed to the hospital. Police spoke to us and took Odette's brothers into custody—for all the good that did. They denied all knowledge of their sister's vendetta and ended up losing only their jobs, not their liberty.

The next morning, the doctors released me with my leg strapped up, telling me I'd need knee surgery once I got home. Leaving Curtis in the hospital, I rode the lifts back up to the glacier with the Mountain Rescue and watched them winch Heather's and Dale's bodies from the crevasse.

As we returned to the Panorama building, the second team of rescuers skied down toward us, dragging a sledge between them. Until that point, I'd held out hope that Brent had somehow survived. That he'd dodged the shots or merely been wounded. That he'd been able to make his way back to the building and shelter there overnight. Then the mound on the sledge came into view. Still and silent. Covered over. And all hope died.

As for Odette, the snowstorm had dumped half a meter of fresh.

Which might or might not explain why her body was nowhere to be found.

An hour later, Curtis and I walk to the cable car, hand in hand.

When he asked me to move in with him in London after we left Le Rocher, so we could go through surgery and rehab together, I wasn't sure. I'm hard enough to live with as a failed ex-athlete; as an injured one I'd be a hundred times worse, and I sensed he'd struggle with being injured as much as I would. In the end, I figured if we could get through that . . .

Anyway, we got through it. Then he asked me to coach teenagers in his freestyle camps.

He puts a protective arm around me as the cable car swings into motion. The cabin is only a quarter full, far quieter than it would be in winter, a mix of pro skiers, snowboarders, and locals. I scan the faces to see if any of our kids are in here, but it's early still and they went out last night. I'm very into my snowboarding again and I may yet try another backflip.

We sail over stunted trees, wooden lift shacks, and stationary chair-lifts. The river is a gushing torrent of opaque blue-gray meltwater. I think of another river—a frozen one that flows too slowly for the eye to see. And the bodies that may or may not flow with it.

No. Don't think of that.

Soon we're above the tree line. Bright purple flowers scatter the Alpine tundra below.

"I love it here," I say.

"Me, too," Curtis says. "I used to ride here with my sister."

I force a smile. He hardly mentions her these days and I never know whether he thinks of her much or not.

A second cable car takes us to the summer ski area on the glacier. It's a full twenty degrees colder by the time we step out. I glance into the operator booth as we pass it and a scarily familiar set of blue eyes looks back at me. Goose bumps come up on my arms.

But it's only Curtis's reflection.

Stupid. I should be used to this by now because I see her or Odette at least once every day we're up here. It's the price I pay for having a guilty conscience.

Curtis didn't tell his mum what he learned about Saskia's final hours. How could he? Instead, after much debate, he handed her Saskia's lift pass, found (he claimed) by a Le Rocher local out hiking recently, as proof she was training up there on the day she disappeared. That her death, though untimely, was an accident from doing what she loved.

The lift pass, now neatly framed, looks out from the wall at his parents' place, amid a gallery of photos of her. A dozen sets of blue eyes watching us, every time we go around for dinner.

Curtis reaches for my hand as we walk across the ice to the snow park. He shakes his head at the state of the snow cover. "If we lose any more there'll be none left."

Glaciers across the Alps have suffered record retreats this year, thanks to global warming.

Coaching doesn't begin until ten a.m., but two of the girls are already at the snow park, warming up.

"They're keen," Curtis says.

I smile. "I know."

Coaching has given me a new purpose in life. Perhaps I can help others achieve what I couldn't achieve for myself. And these two girls—*my* girls—have everything going for them. They're young, they're fit, and they have that killer instinct, the will to win above all else.

A rush of nostalgia sweeps over me as I watch them. My competition days are over but theirs are just beginning.

Jodie hoists her foot onto the rope barrier to stretch her hamstrings. And Suzette . . . What *is* Suzette doing? She's crouching over her board, rubbing something onto the base. There's something furtive about the way she's doing it. She catches my eye and slips whatever it was back in her pocket. It wasn't snowboard wax, that's for sure.

And when she props the snowboard against the other one and joins Jodie at the rope, I realize something else.

That wasn't her snowboard.

When the coaching session finishes, I tell Curtis about it. "I'm guessing it was surfboard wax. Luckily it didn't seem to affect Jodie's board much. I mentioned it quietly to Jodie."

"What did she say?" Curtis says.

"She flushed and said she'd taped clear sticky tape down Suzette's edges yesterday."

He laughs. "Remind you of anyone?"

"I didn't know if I should say anything or if I should just leave them to it."

"Don't ask me." Curtis turns serious. "Sometimes I wonder if I did the wrong thing with you and Saskia. A few times I stopped you from fighting back and maybe I shouldn't have."

"Who knows," I say lightly. "We can't change the past."

"So which of them is Saskia and which is you?"

"I haven't decided. Possibly they're as bad as each other."

You're just as bad as her. I still remember the day he told me that. He doesn't realize how true it was.

All these years I've kept the secret. But when the ice eventually releases Saskia's body, will they perform an autopsy? I know I shouldn't have done it but I only intended to tire her out. To hamper her performance in the British Championships, like she hampered mine in the Le Rocher Open.

After all this time, will they still be able to detect the sleeping tablets I crushed into her coffee that final morning?

They were prescription-only tablets and the prescription was in my name. I try to convince myself they made no difference on top of all the other things that happened to her. But they were damn strong and I gave her four. If I hadn't drugged her, she might have been able to fight Heather off. Or regained consciousness faster. Heather thought the bag moved as they transported her to the glacier. Maybe she wasn't dead at that point but simply out cold from the pills. Or— *Stop.* I can't change the past.

Curtis is looking at the knife-edge ridge above. I squint into the sun and see two figures up there. A shocked sound bursts from my throat.

"What?" Curtis says.

I blink. It's not them. It's just a rock formation. Two spindly columns of rock that don't look the slightest bit human. He pulls me close. I stand in his arms, looking over the Swiss Alps toward France, thinking again of that frozen river. Wondering if somewhere in the glassy depths, Saskia and Odette have found each other. I hope they have.

Another thought surfaces. I try to quash it, as I always do when this particular thought occurs, but it just won't seem to stay down.

I've won.

ACKNOWLEDGMENTS

To my dad. You will never read this book, but you inspired it in so many ways. And to my mum, the strongest woman I know. You gave me a childhood of mountains. Thank you for everything.

To my incredible agent Kate Burke, for your fantastic editorial advice and story-doctoring, and expert judgment, including the handling of a ten-publisher auction. I'm so fortunate to have you as my agent. To Julian Friedmann, for his enthusiasm and expertise in selling the TV option. To James Pusey and Hana Murrell in foreign rights, for selling *Shiver* to so many different territories, and the rest of the team at Blake Friedmann.

To my two amazing editors, Jennifer Doyle at Headline UK and Margo Lipschultz at Putnam in the U.S., for your passion for this project, brilliant editorial assistance, meticulous attention to detail, and for being an absolute pleasure to work with. I'm extremely grateful to you both for investing so much time and effort in this book. Huge thanks also to the rest of the teams at Headline and Putnam, as well as Hachette Australia.

To Sue Cunningham, first reader of this and all my other projects, a fountain of fabulous ideas. And Gail Richards, grammar guru, synopsis queen. Brilliant sounding boards, moral supporters, and fantastic writers in your own right. I couldn't have done it without you.

To thriller writer Angela Clarke, who so generously gave up your time to mentor me during my previous project with your astute advice. And thriller writer Ann Gosslin, for your wise words and generous support. To my other writer friends: Julia Anderson, Paul Francis, Danielle Hastie, Jodie Mehrton, Linda Middleton, and all the writers I met through the Curtis Brown Creative online courses, including Shannon Cowan, Justin Podur, Stuart Blake, Adrian Higgins, Wiz Wharton, Merlin Ward, and Jenny Fan Raj. You taught me, encouraged me, and inspired me. Thank you.

To my boys, Lucas and Daniel: love you so much.

To all my friends, including Anita Phelan, who was like my own personal angel this past year; my bestest surf buddy, Celine Ruettgers; Amanda Townsend, for cheering me on all the way from Melbourne; Steve White, who carried out suspicious online searches for me; and all-around inspirational person Tammy Esten of Mint Snowboarding School. To Uncle Fred: sorry about all the swearing.

To Gold Coast city council and library staff, for a truly world-class library system. In an era when councils in parts of the world are closing libraries and slashing library budgets, I'd like to point out that as a low-income mum of two, if I hadn't had library access, this book would not exist.

Many thanks also to the Queensland Writers Centre, Brisbane and Byron Bay Writing Festivals, and the writers and publishing professionals whose workshops I've attended.

Martin and Scott: you were a massive part of my winters. Mika, Dave and Dave, and all the other snowboarders I met and rode with: thanks for the memories.

If any old snowboarder friends remember me from my winters, get in touch and let's organize a reunion <evil laugh>. No, seriously, in those pre-Facebook years I moved around a lot and lost touch with so many people. I'd really love to hear from you.

To the snowboarders, past and present, who have taken the sport to the incredible level it's at today, I'm in awe of your skills, physical and mental strength, and sheer balls. You are inspirational. To snowboarders everywhere: happy riding, stay safe. Treasure those memories.

And to my readers, wherever you are, thank you so much for taking a chance on a debut author and choosing this book. I hope you enjoyed it.